# The Wanderer's Children

**The Angelorum Twelve Chronicles:**

TRINITY STONES

The WANDERER'S CHILDREN


**Coming Soon:**

Prequel Novella HOPE'S PRELUDE

# The Wanderer's Children

The Angelorum Twelve Chronicles
Book 2

## L.G. O'CONNOR

Published 2014
Printed in the United States of America
ISBN: 978-0-9907381-0-7
Library of Congress Control Number: 2014915277

For information, address:
Collins-Young Publishing, LLC
1 Sentry Lane #6
Chester, NJ 07930



Cover Design: Derek Murphy, Creativindie

# Dedication

To my husband Leo, for all of his support.
To my writer whippets, Chloe and Nevada…and to all my readers who
enjoy the world of the Angelorum as much as I do.

Journey forth in peace and love.

# Acknowledgments

I want to say thank you to my tremendous team for all your love and support. Without you, the final book wouldn't have been what it is today. Thank you to my critique partner, Joan Sorensen; the "cross-stitch" beta reading crew (Marilyn Keyes, Pat Campbell, Lesley Aman, and Eileen Higgins); my new beta reader, Wendy Rossi, the New Providence Writers Group; my developmental muse, young adult author, Trisha Leaver. Without them, this book wouldn't have been nearly as good.

# Excerpt from the *Book Of Human Angels*—5 Enoch (Hidden) Translation: Essenes Aramaic papyrus text scribed second century BC

*"As it was so spoken, and then written, much time has passed since Michael bound the Watchers, led by Semyaza, to the confines of darkness. Wrath has been meted upon the Nephilim spawn. Their bodies and souls ripped from their being, leaving them shades of darkness to wander the corridors between Hell and Earth without peace."*

. . .

*"A new breed of Watcher has come, three hundred strong, to live among and as man to understand their strife and to empathize with their pain. Protected now by the children of Uriel, these Watchers will balance the Fallen who have been cast down from Heaven."*

. . .

*"The forces of darkness unite to battle for their freedom, to reach the key that will deliver them from Judgment Day and remain forever free. To acquire their promised reward, the forces of both darkness and light must abide by the laws of balance under the ever vigilant eyes of justice, or be forever vanquished by their enemy."*

. . .

*"It is with the birth of the First of Holy Twelve that the prophecy begins, it is with the battle that the prophecy ends."*

# Glossary Of Terms And Proper Nouns

(See **Endnotes** for full Character List, Angelorum, and Dark Ones Hierarchy)


**(the) Angelorum** (pr. n.)  All members of the protectorate, consisting of the three hundred descended angels that make up the next generation of Watchers, the Nephilim Guardianship, the human Messenger families, and the human Soul Seekers.

**(the) Angelorum Sanctuary** (pr. n.)  The central headquarters of the three hundred Angelorum Watchers and the Nephilim Guardianship located at an undisclosed underground location in the French countryside.

**(the) Angelorum Twelve** (pr. n.)  The twelve souls who will lead the Angelorum into the final battle against Lucifer, the Morning Star, and his fallen minions, the Dark Ones.

**(the) Angelorum Watchers** (pr. n.)  A group of three hundred angels who approached God after the Great War in Heaven and requested to be sent down to earth after Lucifer and his fallen minions to provide a protectorate to oversee the balance of good and evil as the next generation of Watchers. The request was granted provided the angels incarnated as humans. However, they were allowed to remain "awakened," which would allow them to always retain their original angelic identity, their memories of Heaven, and their past lives with each incarnation. They are physically marked by the lack of a vertical indentation above their lip (philtrum). Also known as the Sanctus Angelorum protectorate or *Defensores Contra Malum.*

**Calling** (n.)  Official request by the Angelorum for acceptance into the Angelorum. For a Soul Seeker within a Trinity, it's the time during which the Center Stone of the trinity is revealed and the full powers of the Soul Seeker are activated.

**Center Stone** (n.)  Physically, the Center Stone is held in the middle of each Trinity Stone, representing the soul in which the Trinity is tied and in which the mission is centered.

**Cloaking** (v.)  Nephilim power. Hiding behind the veil of invisibility. To hide someone under the veil requires physical contact. Those connected under the veil can see and hear one another but cannot be seen or heard by anyone outside the veil.

**Dark Ones** (pr. n.)  Angels who were cast out of Heaven with Lucifer (the Morning Star) after the Great War in Heaven. Their wings were torn from their bodies so they could never return.

***Defensores Contra Malum*** (pr. n.)  Another Latin name for the Sanctus Angelorum protectorate. Translates to the Protectors from Evil and contained in the hidden scripture, the *Book of Human Angels.*

**Demon** (n.)  Disembodied spirits of Nephilim spawned by Semyaza and the first Watchers. Used as Hunters for the Dark Ones. Show up as a black inky haze before manifesting into physical form of demonic satyr. Members of the Angelorum can feel the demon presence through the onset of a sudden migraine-like headache, and through the taste of tar on the tongue. When they die they turn to black ash.

**Divine Visitation** (n.)  An interlude between an angel of the Powers and a descended human angel of the Angelorum, resulting in the conception of a Nephilim child.

**Enoch** (pr. n.)  Appears in Genesis, the seventh of the pre-Deluge Patriarchs. Great-grandfather to Noah. Believed to have been taken from Earth to become the angel Metatron. The apocryphal Books of Enoch attributed to him. Semyaza and the angelic Watchers inhabited Earth during his lifetime, and he bore witness to their sins.

**Fallen** (pr. n.)  See Dark Ones.

**(the) Flow** (n.)  The electromagnetic field surrounding Earth used by the Angelorum for communication and healing energy.

**Guardian** (n.)  Nephilim warrior. May or may not be actively assigned to a current Trinity. As part of a Trinity, they have an oath to protect the members of their Trinity.

**(the) Guardianship** (pr. n.)  The Nephilim warriors who provide protection for the Angelorum. Guardians can be assigned to a Trinity to protect a Messenger and a Soul Seeker as they pursue their mission.

**Hunter** (n.)  Trackers working for the Dark Ones who hunt and destroy Soul Seekers and other Angelorum members. Can be either disembodied entities or physical human soulless.

**Irin** (pr. n.)  Angels assigned to watching the Watchers and recording human history on Earth. Also known as the Archivists. They are the librarians for the Flow.

***Libre Homo Angelorum*** (n.)  Translated from Latin as the *Book of Human Angels*. The hidden scripture not contained in the Bible that tells the story of the Angelorum Watchers.

**Messenger** (n.)  A human who has the ability to communicate directly to the Angelorum Watchers. Messengers have telepathic abilities that are awakened when they are Called to become part of a Trinity. They provide communication and guidance to the Trinity. Messenger traits are inherited through the bloodline of their fathers.

**Nephilim** (n.)  Being that is conceived by one of the Angelorum-descended angels in partnership with an angel of the Powers through divine visitation. Child is half human and half angel. Angelic characteristics include hidden wings and the ability to fly; telepathic communication with other Nephilim and their Trinity; ability to use the angelic prayers (an example would be the ability to hide behind a veil of invisibility when needed); and ability to use the angelic language (an example would be the ability to speak with other beings or former beings of Heaven). In addition, the Nephilim are born without the ability to procreate and can live for up to five hundred years. Much improved version from the evil Nephilim of Genesis who were created by Semyaza and the disobedient angelic Watchers.

**Nephilim class** (n.)  Every century of Nephilim has a class number. Once a Nephilim turns one hundred years old, they enter the One Hundred Class and with each subsequent century they enter the next class. The last class is the Four Hundred Class, when they turn four hundred years old, and their lifespan ends prior to turning five hundred years old.

**Powers** (pr. n.)  The 9th Order of Angels in Heaven. The great warrior angels considered the last defense of Heaven.

**The Prophecy** (n.)  The prediction that a final battle would occur between the Angelorum and the Dark Ones, led by twelve souls who have the power to overcome evil and banish the Fallen into the prison where they belong for the rest of eternity.

**Semyaza** (pr. n.)  Fallen angel of apocryphal Jewish and Christian tradition. Believed to be the leader of the angelic Watchers sent to Earth to watch over man.

**Sentinel** (n.)  One who keeps watch and identifies members of the Angelorum and the Fallen.

**Soul Seeker** (n.)  A human who is bound to the soul of another. When the time is right, the Seeker will be Called to partake in an event of the bound soul (Center Stone) which has significance in the balance of good vs. evil. The Seeker is the part of the Trinity, partnered with a Messenger and a Guardian, with the farthest link to the Angelorum Watchers for the protection of both parties. Seekers can have healing and/or other abilities.

**Soul Separator** (n.) The angelic sword used to cast out a demon that is in possession of a live human.

**Soulless** (n.) Human who relinquishes their soul as food for the Dark Ones. The aura of a soulless human is black and cloudy, the same as a demon. When killed they turn to black sand.

**Sphinx** (n.) Ice minions controlled by Emanelech. Creatures who stand guard at the entrance into the first circle of Hell. Conjured in the form of twins, Chaos and Destruction. They have the ability to block the Nephilim and Trinity telepathic communication. A force more powerful than Nephilim, yet few in number.

**Transporter** (n.) Suborder of the Powers, the 9th Order of Angels. Type of angel who transports souls to their final resting ground, be it Heaven or Hell. Another name for a Reaper.

**Trinity Pool** (n.) A pool of white sand containing the Trinity Stones which represent each Trinity assigned to a current or future event that could tip the balance of good vs. evil. The Trinity Pool is located in the inner sanctum of the Angelorum Sanctuary. The stones in the pool are alive and continually change as free will decisions are made by the individuals, which could impact the outcome of events. They pulse with colorful light and can speak to those who can hear them. They are the link between Heaven and Earth.

**Trinity Stone** (n.) A smooth triangular stones with rounded edges and sectioned into three parts—representing each member of the Trinity—which surround a Center Stone embedded in the middle—representing the soul in which the Soul Seeker is connected and who will be part of an event that will tip the balance of good vs. evil. As free will decisions are made that lock in destinies, secrets are revealed.

**Trinity** (n.) Three parties joined together by a Center Stone: a Soul Seeker, a Messenger, and a Guardian.

**Uriel** (pr. n) Archangel and leader of the Powers.

**Watchers** (pr. n.) Also known as Grigori. Fallen angels who broke their covenant with God by fornicating with human woman to create evil half-breed Nephilim and sharing the mysteries they were prohibited from teaching humans. Created Nephilim spawn who were destroyed in the Great Flood referenced in Genesis. The Archangel Michael has bound them for seventy generations in the valleys of Earth until Judgment Day.

# Prelude



*Los Angeles, California. County Hospital*

KATHY KING GAZED DOWN, her eyes filled with love at the newborn nursing at her breast. Her fingertips glided over the tiny arms poking out of the swaddling, drinking in the silkiness of his skin. Ten perfect fingers and ten perfect toes. Blond fuzz topped his head, and his eyes held the promise of the same blue as his father. She didn't think she was being biased; he was truly the most beautiful baby she'd ever laid eyes on. Big and pink, bypassing the tight squeeze of the birth canal, he'd entered the world wearing the healthy glow of a caesarian baby.

She smiled, placed a kiss on his tiny forehead, and deeply inhaled his sweet baby scent. *You had it pretty easy, little man. May you always be blessed with good fortune.*

A wave of fatigue reminded her that she had asked the nurse to return soon to take him back to the nursery. Until then, she wanted to savor every moment with her beautiful baby boy.

Sensing she and the baby were no longer alone, her eyes shifted up.

"Hi, Kathy," he said from the open doorway.

The air left her lungs. "Scott. What are you doing here?" she asked, breathless.

Pushing off of the jamb, he smiled sheepishly. "Not the greeting I hoped for, but one I can understand."

A mixture of apprehension and desire churned up into the center of her chest. Dressed in jeans and a T-shirt, his tawny-blond hair was tousled from wearing the motorcycle helmet he held in his hand. His arms were tanned and toned to Californian perfection like the fine rippled abs she knew lay hidden underneath his clothes. Although she hadn't seen him in almost eight months, he still made her heart flutter.

She let out a silent sigh. He was more handsome than anyone deserved to be. Not to mention way too intelligent to be hanging around Hollywood working as a bartender waiting for an acting career that would most likely never come.

He held her gaze with glowing blue eyes. "I'm sorry. I didn't mean to startle you. I stayed away… like you asked. Mind if I come in?"

"Of course not," she said, forcing some of the tension from her shoulders and waving him in. Done nursing, she readjusted her gown to fully cover herself.

Under different circumstances, she would've enjoyed the sense of comfort and the overwhelming attraction she usually felt when Scott was around. Instead, her nerves ignited. If she hadn't been lying in this hospital bed, she would've been dressed in her nurse's uniform and working on the cardiac floor. Worry etched into her brow. She hoped no one she knew saw them together. The last thing she needed was pesky questions about why a sexy, younger man—who wasn't her husband—was visiting her in the maternity ward.

Part of her still wondered how it had all happened. Ten months ago, when they'd struck up a friendship at the bar where he worked, she never envisioned herself ending up here. But stopping for a beer on Tuesday nights after her shift soon took on a life of its own, and it wasn't long before the desire burning in Scott's eyes matched hers. Then it happened. Only twice. Two nights filled with the most magical lovemaking of her life. No one had ever made her feel as beautiful or as desired, pleasing her in ways she never thought possible.

Funny, her Tuesday night drinking ritual had started when she'd suspected her husband was having an affair. Frequenting The Boca where Scott worked was her one act of passive defiance. The irony of her situation struck her many times over the past nine months.

Scott pointed at the door. "Okay to close this? To give us some privacy?"

"Go ahead," she said, cradling her newborn closer.

He slipped into the chair beside the bed and gazed with longing at the baby boy she held. Lifting his eyes to meet hers, he asked, "May I hold my son?"

Suppressing any residual apprehension, Kathy transferred her precious bundle into Scott's hands.

He positioned the baby tenderly in his arms and settled back into the chair. His features softened as he beamed at his son. "What's his name?"

"Brett," Kathy replied, her lips turning up into a smile. Her heart unexpectedly melted watching Scott. Then a pang of disappointment followed, echoing inside her. She wished her husband radiated the same kind of love when he held the baby.

Scott looked at her in earnest. "If I send you something, will you give it to him when he's old enough?"

She thought for a second and decided it was the least she could do. One of their amazing nights had given her Brett—her little gift from Heaven. "Yes, I promise," she said, and then cleared her throat and attempted to lighten the mood. "So how are things at The Boca?"

He gave her a small smile, his manner unassuming and genuine. "It's still standing. How are things with Richard?"

She nervously smoothed the thin covers over her lap. "Pretty good, thanks for asking." Scott's compassionate ear for her problems had initially gotten her into this situation. Her desire came later. But once she found out she was pregnant, she came to her senses and decided to make her marriage work for her twelve-year-old son, Colin, and for the baby Scott held in his arms.

A worried look passed over Scott's face. He glanced at the contented newborn tucked comfortably in his arms. "Richard doesn't suspect anything, does he?"

Kathy sighed and shook her head. "No." Her blonde hair and blue eyes were similar enough to Scott's. Richard wouldn't suspect a thing. She'd taken a chance by telling Scott about the pregnancy. Fortunately, given his situation, he had no desire to openly stake a claim. Other than her, he was the only one who about knew Brett's true paternity. For some unknown reason, she trusted Scott to keep their secret.

He blew out a breath, looking relieved. "That's good." He leaned down and kissed the baby's forehead. "I'd better be going. Thanks for letting me hold him. He'll grow up to be a good man with you as his mother, Kathy."

Her lips turned up in a half-smile, and a tear welled in her eye. "Thanks. I'm glad you think so."

He gave her one of his heart-stopping smiles. "It's true." Then as quickly as his smile blossomed, she watched it fade. "Just to set your mind at ease, I won't be bothering you again. I'm moving back East."

With one last look of longing, he handed their son back to her.

"Oh…" she said, trying to keep her relief from showing. "If you send me your address when you're settled, I can send some pictures," she offered, knowing her words sounded halfhearted. She couldn't help it; she was glad that he planned to put some distance between them.

"I'd like that. Take care." Leaning down, he kissed the top of her head and his T-shirt softly brushed her cheek. The scent of cotton and citrus filled her senses as he pulled away.

She watched him go, and knew in her heart that she'd never see him again.

Scott walked out of the hospital into the dry heat of the sunny June afternoon, and his heart convulsed with pain. He brushed the back of his hand over his eyes, and swore this would be the last time he'd create a child and leave it behind. Even though he'd done it in the name of the Angelorum and for the good of mankind, he had difficulty reconciling the emotional and intellectual sides of his mission.

He ground his teeth. Next time, he'd claim his child as his own.

Had he imagined the difficulty of this assignment when Constantina approached him five years ago, he would've declined. But at the time, to his twenty-something hormone-addled brain it had sounded simple… multiply and hide the bloodline to keep it safe.

"Not just anyone can take this on," she'd explained, "only someone from your immediate family."

He wasn't naïve; he'd looked in the mirror enough to know why Constantina had chosen him over his five brothers. His handsome face and charm were undeniable assets in the mission to get unsuspecting women into bed for the greater good. Certain aspects of his job he absolutely enjoyed. What single man in his twenties wouldn't? Beside that—a fair exchange is no robbery—he was highly trained in the art of sensual pleasures and the women he seduced were guaranteed a memorable evening.

Constantina had wisely advised him not to get too close; to keep his distance.

In hindsight, he never counted on his honor or paternal instinct kicking in. He couldn't stay away. He had to hold his children and tell them that he loved them… at least once. Maybe if that was all he did… but it wasn't. He would keep track of Brett just like the rest of his children.

*What the Angelorum don't know won't hurt them*, he thought with defiance.

Having sex with women he didn't love? He could live with that. Leaving his children behind? That's where he had difficulty…

He reached his Harley in the parking lot and hopped on. Kick-starting it with the heavy heel of his boot, the bike roared to life beneath him.

A small smile crept across his lips as he strapped on his helmet. *Too good to be a bartender, huh?* He'd plucked the thought from Kathy's mind. It pleased him that she glimpsed something more behind his packaging. Although, she'd probably be surprised to learn he'd completed his MBA in Finance at Stanford University just last month. But she'd never learn that… or his real name.

His smile faded, and with a deep sigh, he pulled out of the parking lot. His decision was made. The Angelorum would need to find someone else to take on the mantle of the Wanderer.

*I'm done*, he thought with a heavy heart and drove off.

A week later, Kathy pulled a small box out of the mailbox with no return address. The box contained a note that simply read, "For Brett," and a simple silver ring with Brett's name. She smiled and put it in her jewelry box for safekeeping. She would give it him when he was older, just as she'd promised.

# Chapter 1



*BRETT*

*Los Angeles. Beverly Wilshire Hotel. Saturday, May 11, 10:30 AM PT*

*WHAP!*

Brett King cracked open one eye and groaned. His skull threatened to split in half if he so much as blinked. Everything above his shoulders hurt down to his hair follicles. Silk sheets caressed his body on the monster-sized bed at the Beverly Wilshire. The good news: he was in a bed. The bad news: he didn't remember how he'd gotten there.

A hand came down a second time on his ass. *Whap!*

"You're welcome."

"What the hell?" Brett turned over to protect his backside, and spun his head in the direction of a familiar, pissed-off female voice.

Roxy sat Indian style next to him like an irate pixie, her arms crossed over her chest. One of his stylishly ripped T-shirts covered her petite body. Python scales inked a trail up one side of her collarbone, looped around her neck, and came back down the other side, disappearing into the T-shirt. Her kohl-rimmed blue eyes stared at him, the rest of her makeup long gone. Her short cap of black hair stuck up in angry spikes, and a small row of hoop earrings crawled up the curve of her left ear like a silver caterpillar. Roxy was a force to be reckoned with when he was

6

fully alert; he couldn't imagine what he was in for after being woken up from a drunken sleep.

"Why are you hitting me? And why are you in my bed wearing my clothes?" he croaked, his voice ragged. Thankfully, he didn't have to sing again for at least a week. The moment after he asked the question, he could feel the color drain from his face. Lifting the covers, he peeked down to see if he was still wearing his underwear.

Roxy rolled her eyes and shoved him. "Oh, for crissakes, King! Your virtue is safe with me. Even you couldn't tempt me to go straight. I'm wearing your fucking shirt, you moron, because you vomited all over my dress on our way up to the room last night."

No wonder his mouth tasted like an acidic jock strap. He stuck his head under the pillow and wrapped it down around his ears. "Stop yelling, Rox, or my head will explode."

She reached over and poked him. "So, I'll say it again. You're welcome."

Pain shot through his skull. He flipped the pillow off his head and looked at her with daggers in his eyes. "Okay, thank you. Now, tell me for what, and stop poking me. It hurts."

Arching a brow, she smirked. "You really don't remember, do you?"

"If I remembered, I wouldn't be asking," he mumbled, resting his cheek against the cool mattress, wishing for an ice pack to dull the pain in his head.

Leaning back on her elbows she straightened her bare legs, crossing them at the ankles. A look of wicked delight lit up her face. "Well, let me start by saying that you sure know how to end a tour with a bang."

Brett and his band King Metaljam had done their penultimate concert in Los Angeles the night before, capping off their nine-month tour. Technically, they still had one more date in New York to make up for a prior cancelation.

"Rox, if I'd ended the tour with a bang, I'd be waking up next to Rachel right now instead of my lesbian best friend." He'd known Roxy since their sophomore year at the University of Southern California, right before he dropped out and the band hit it big. Not only was she his best friend, she was also his publicist and doubled as his stylist.

"Ha! Like *that* was going to happen after you and Rachel traded drinks in the face last night. Truth is, she's a bitch, and you're better off without her." Roxy gave him a self-satisfied smile.

His face twisted into a scowl. "Thanks. Tell me what you really think." His heart sank for a moment as the memory slowly returned. His ten-month relationship with his model-actress girlfriend, Rachel, had shown signs of strain the closer the tour came to ending. He'd had high hopes when they'd first met, but as time passed, he was less sure which she loved more: him or his money and rock star status. He hungered to find someone with whom he could escape the plastic reality of the limelight when he wasn't working. Disappointment filled him when he realized Rachel would never be that person.

He'd already consumed five drinks too many by the time they'd gotten into an argument about taking a vacation when the tour ended. All he wanted to do was return home to San Francisco, relax, and enjoy some privacy. The conversation ended with him calling Rachel a gold digger, and her telling him to fuck off, punctuated by her flinging a drink in his face. Without thinking, he tossed the remainder of his drink back at her.

He groaned. "*Uhhh*. Is that all?"

Roxy smirked and pushed her finger into the sensitive skin of his cheek. "Not. Even. Remotely."

Pain jolted through his face, and he pounded the bed with his fist. "Ow! What the hell?"

"Lucky for you, I saved your pretty, surfer-boy face after Randy's first punch."

*Punch? What punch? Why would his bass player want to beat the crap out of him?* Brett knitted his brow. "Why did Randy hit me?" Then he added, "And don't call me 'surfer-boy.' You know I hate that." So he was blond and he surfed, so what? She liked to tease him that the only two things separating him from being a bad-ass rock star and a surfer was a pair of black leather pants and the fact that he didn't own a puka bead necklace.

Roxy circled her neck, cracked it, and then gave him a mischievous smile. "That would have to do with my saving you from the two harlots who planned to take you upstairs and bear your bastard children nine months from now."

He looked at her in pained disgust. "What?"

Tilting her head, she said, "Yup. It happened after the fight with Rachel."

*Shit, how much did I drink last night?* Ironically, he was the lead singer in a rock band and could have any woman he wanted—or two, or ten—but he abhorred one-night stands. Strangely enough, he preferred monogamy. Less complicated that way. He caught more than his fair share of abuse for that from the band, but he didn't care.

"So what does that have to do with Randy popping me in the face?"

She covered her mouth with her hand and chuckled. "One of them was his wife."

His gut clenched, and he suddenly felt sick. "Oh, fuck me." He buried his head back underneath the pillow. *That's it, no more alcohol until further notice.* How he could stray so far from his own sense of civilized behavior, he didn't know. It had been a long time since he'd felt like this much of a jackass.

"I'm afraid to ask, but anything else?" Peeking out from under his pillow cave, he braced himself for Roxy's reply.

She gave him a sour look. "Yeah, and you owe me big time for this one. I held your hair back while you worshipped the porcelain god."

"Ugh. Thanks, Rox."

"Now go take a shower—you stink. I'll check to see if you created any more PR disasters last night." She crawled off the bed and grabbed her phone.

"What would I do without you to prop up my ego?" Slowly, he sat up, the silk sheets slipping down around his waist. He caught a whiff of what she meant. She was right. He reeked.

Roxy scrolled through the e-mail and snorted. "You don't need me to prop up your ego when more women than you can count would willingly drop to their knees and blow you." She turned and wiggled her eyebrows at him. "Oh, and don't forget, number eight on this year's hottest bachelor countdown."

Brett rolled his eyes. How could he forget? Roxy reminded him every chance she got. She'd submitted him for consideration via a friend of hers at a well-known publication. The photo shoot had been painful. He'd spent hours, half-naked in nothing but leather pants, locked in poses under hot lights. The experience gave him a new respect for models.

Frowning at her, he grumbled. "Come on, Rox. You know me better than that. That's not what I'm about. I'd rather have something meaningful."

"Meaningful, huh?" She cocked a brow at him. "Then why did you check under the sheets when you thought maybe we'd slept together?"

He gave her a wounded look. "It could've happened. It's not like it hasn't before," he said defensively, leaning back against the headboard. He'd lost his virginity to Roxy back in college, and she'd seen him naked probably as many times as any of the woman he'd ever dated.

Her expression softened. She came over to him and put her arms around his neck. "We were nineteen, King. I hadn't come out yet." Leaning over, she kissed his forehead. "You're such a girl when it comes to women. It's one of the things I love about you. But I'm serious, go take a shower. You smell like ass." She pushed away from him.

"Fine. I can take a not-so-subtle hint." He swung his legs over the side of the bed, and shuffled off in the direction of the bathroom.

Roxy ran in ahead of him and snatched her black leather dress from where it hung on a hook next to one of the fluffy white robes and headed for the door.

"I'm heading back to my room. Be ready in forty minutes. I've scheduled an interview for you at noon."

# Chapter 2



***BRETT***

THE DOOR CLOSED WITH a *thunk* on her way out. Brett squeezed his eyes shut and whimpered, not only from the pain in his head but also at the thought of seeing anyone before tomorrow.

His hands shook as he gripped the sink firmly and hung his head as the marble floor chilled his feet. Time to survey the damage. He swept his gaze up into the mirror. *Fuck me.* The image staring back at him in the wall-length mirror was barely recognizable. His six-foot-tall frame was bent and quivering. Dark circles were etched underneath his blue eyes and made them appear sunken in his face. Matted tawny-blond hair touched his shoulders, framing his fine-boned face. Definitely not number eight bachelor countdown material. In fact, his injuries made his twenty-six look more along the lines of someone the age of the Crypt Keeper.

He turned his face to examine the colorful bruise on his left cheek.

The jury was in—his face officially looked like shit.

*If they could only see me now*, he thought.

At least he looked the same from the neck down. The mother-of-all-hangovers couldn't erase the hard, crisp lines of his muscles, thanks to his workout schedule and the occasional trip to a mixed martial arts studio when Roxy's brother, Skylar, flew in to join him on tour. He accepted Roxy's belief that his body meant more "box office" from female fans, so he long ago abandoned his modesty and spent a lot of time parading around on stage without a shirt, offering himself up as eye candy. Roxy's latest mission—convincing him to get more ink. He wasn't tatted up enough for her standards, another contributing factor to her "surfer-boy" insult.

So far, he'd won. He preferred his ink spare and private. His only visible tattoo cut across the tanned, hairless skin of his abs and showed above his underwear: an arched pair of feathered angel wings with the script initials of his motorcycle club, "AABC," in the center. The only other tat was lower and for private viewing only. Partially out of spite, he couldn't bring himself to get any more.

Assessment done. He took a deep breath. At this point, a shower could only help. That and the aspirin he had on the counter. Placing three in his palm, he popped them in a dry swallow. As drunk as he'd gotten the night before, privately, he lived a more conservative lifestyle than his profession allowed. Not many people knew he'd been a vegetarian since he was sixteen, or that other than alcohol, aspirin was the strongest drug he'd ever taken.

Slipping off his underwear, he staggered to the shower hoping, just maybe, he could ease himself back into full consciousness. Turning on the hot water, he stepped inside.

Brett thought about the interview and groaned. That was the last thing he wanted to do. One more date in New York to make up for the cancelation was all he had to get through.

He grimaced. No doubt, between Roxy and his agent, they would be on his ass as soon as the tour ended, trying to get him back into the studio. But shit, he was burned-out.

There was only one logical solution he could think of.

Thirty minutes later, Brett picked up his cell and dialed the band's head of private security.

"Frank, I need an assist. No eyes."

"Um… 'kay. Thought you weren't due to leave until this afternoon," he said.

"Change of plans."

Frank cleared his throat and asked gingerly, "Does Rachel need separate transport after last night?"

Brett cringed, forgetting that everyone but him knew what went down the night before. His shoulders tightened as a wave of shame and disappointment rolled through him.

"Who the hell knows. Yeah. I guess. If she turns up." He raked his hand through his damp hair and sighed, trying to dispel his agitation. *There goes ten* months of his love life that he'd never get back. It wasn't like the signs weren't there. Being on tour is hard enough on a relationship, but the last few months had turned into the "gimmes"—"gimme this, gimme that." While he rehearsed and prepared for shows, Rachel made ample use of his credit card. After the shows, she spent less and less time by his side, disappearing to God knows where. Then there was the sex and her recent loss of enthusiasm for it. At least she didn't have the key to anything. Maybe he'd give her a call once he cooled down. Or maybe not.

"'Kay. Be up in five to take your bags."

"Appreciate it, but hurry. I need to haul ass before Roxy finds out I'm leaving." Brett hung up and massaged his throbbing temples. He knew the drill. It would be at least another twelve hours before his hangover subsided.

He drew his hair back with an elastic band and then stuffed the things he wanted into a duffel bag and placed it with his guitar case next to the door. Roxy would take care of the rest if she didn't burn his shit out of spite for what he was about to do.

Wearing jeans, a T-shirt, and boots, he added his LA Dodgers cap and tucked his ponytail underneath. Not the best disguise, but at least it wouldn't draw attention. The hat would conceal his face enough for him to slip out of the hotel unnoticed.

Halfway through his shower he'd realized that he needed to disappear until the last concert date. Granted, this wouldn't be the first time he'd slipped away during the tour. The last time was two months ago when he'd reached a saturation point and snuck off for a long weekend.

He did one last sweep of the suite. The moment his feet hit the threshold of the sitting room, the skin on his arms pebbled and pain speared his skull down to his molars with the speed of a bullet train, dropping him to his knees into the plush carpet. He cradled his head in his hands and muffled a scream.

Brett's vision blurred, his breath coming in short pants. He squinted at his duffel across the room with despair. Channeling every drop of energy he had, he dragged himself over to the bag. His heart pounded and his hands shook as he riffled through the pocket where he kept his aspirin, wishing for something stronger.

*Fucking hell.* This made the fifth attack in as many weeks. He wanted to cry in relief as his fingers found the familiar plastic bottle. As he twisted off the cap, the pain disappeared.

Gone.

Like it had never been there… just like the other attacks. Brett collapsed back onto the carpet, quaking with residual tremors as he recovered.

Might be time to see a doctor, Brett thought. He'd make an appointment when the tour ended. Either way, Roxy couldn't find out. He shuddered. No one could.

Moments later, a soft knock sounded at the door. Brett pulled himself up and glanced through the peephole. Frank, a former linebacker for the NFL, filled the doorway through the fisheye lens. Brett cracked the door open and stepped aside to let him in. Frank's head almost touched the top of the doorframe. Wearing a short, dark military cut, he was the size of a human refrigerator.

Frank paused, giving Brett a once-over. "You okay?"

Brett nodded. "Been better. A little more hungover than usual."

Frank eyed him warily and then lunged for his stuff. "Car's downstairs out back. Where you going?"

"Home," Brett lied. He had no intention of returning to San Francisco, but best to avoid Frank getting all up in his business.

Frank raised a brow. "Uh-huh. You need to hang tight until the last gig in New York. You don't want me comin' after you this time."

Brett snorted. "Last I heard, it's still a fucking free country. I'll be there." Frank had ripped him a new one after his last little adventure.

Frank dropped his bags, turned on him, and pushed his face into Brett's. Eyes hot and hard, his breath traveled over Brett's cheek. As Brett took a step back, Frank's hammy hand shot out. Sausage-sized fingers sank into Brett's upper arm and pulled him into Frank's cement-hard chest. "Don't fuck with me, Brett. Once the tour's done, you get your life back. 'Til then, your ass is mine. No more disappearing acts. *Capiche*?"

Frank's bonus would be on the line if Brett disappeared a second time during the tour.

*Fuck it*, Brett thought, *I'll make him whole out of my own pocket.*

Brett glared at him and gritted his teeth. "I got it. Now let me go." As much as he wanted to pull a self-defense move out of his mixed martial arts arsenal, he needed to get out of the hotel before Roxy found him. At the end of the day, she scared him far more than Frank ever would.

Frank pulled back and his eyes lost some of their fire. "Good. But if I find out you left the golden state of California without my permission, we're going to go a couple rounds. Got me?"

Brett blew out a breath, and grabbed his guitar case. "Yeah."

Five minutes later, Brett sat comfortably in the back of small, nondescript Town Car with tinted windows. Now at a safe distance, he texted Roxy: HAD TO JET, SORRY ABOUT THE INTERVIEW. SEE YOU IN NYC. Then he turned off his phone to escape the tirade he knew would follow.

"Pacific Coast Highway to San Francisco, sir?" asked the driver.

"Nope. LAX."

# Chapter 3

***BRETT***

***United Airlines Flight. Saturday, May 11, 9:30*** PM ET

ALMOST TO HIS DESTINATION, Brett stared out the first class window and listened to his iPod with his LA Dodgers cap pulled down around his ears, trying to maintain a low profile.

Where he planned to go, he wouldn't have to fight off any fans.

He had an open invitation to stay at his Aunt Adela's place in Connecticut—his one safe haven—anytime. When he'd called earlier, he was disappointed to find out she was on business again in Paris, but that didn't stop her from calling ahead to have the house stocked with food in time for his arrival.

Her fifteen-acre estate was located ten minutes from town in a park-like setting. Private, but not remote. He smiled at the thought of the little red Mercedes SLK sitting in one of the three garages. Subtle—not—but no one would expect him to be there.

Another thought hit him, and the corners of his mouth turned up in a smile. Taking out his phone, he scrolled through his contacts until he found the name he was looking for...

Cara Collins.

*Methinks it's time to collect on that breakfast.*

Arching his brow, his smile widened as he remembered how attracted he'd been to her when they'd met in March at the outdoor café. Not just because she was pretty, but because she seemed to genuinely like him for himself. Of all the people in his life right now, he could count the ones he considered real friends on one hand.

Then he recalled that he'd skated over the truth about his identity, and his smile dampened. When she'd asked what he did for a living, he'd claimed to be a songwriter, not a well-known rock musician. Not a lie, but only the partial truth.

His smile faded altogether and his forehead wrinkled in concentration. If he told her now, would her eyes glaze over, turning her into just another female fan? Something in his gut told him he could trust her, that she wasn't that shallow. But what if he was wrong? Telling her might expose the only place he truly felt safe.

*Shit.* He put his phone back into his pocket. Yeah, he'd definitely have to think about this more carefully before he did anything stupid.

He relaxed back into the seat and thought about his home away from home. He'd spent summers there from the time he was ten years old until he went to college. All year long he looked forward to returning to the smell of the fresh baked bread and pies his Aunt Adela would make for him when he visited. His life in Connecticut enveloped him in tranquility and allowed him to pretend he'd had a normal childhood, as opposed to the reality of his life as a latchkey kid in urban Los Angeles.

His parents divorced before his first birthday, leaving his mother to raise him and his older brother, Colin, alone. There had been some hard years as his mom worked two nursing jobs to keep them in decent housing. His brother, almost fourteen when his parents split up, took it hard and quickly fell in with the wrong crowd. Colin left home at seventeen. At twenty-two, he was dead of a heroin overdose.

After his brother's death, his mother sent Brett to Connecticut every summer, ostensibly to get him away from the hot LA summers. But he knew the truth: his mother didn't want him hanging around LA while she worked day and night. She didn't want him to end up like Colin, and believed Brett was safer in "horse country." He had to admit, he liked the idea. Plus, his aunt and uncle couldn't have kids, so they enjoyed having him around.

The stewardess tapped Brett gently on the shoulder to get his attention, pulling him away from his reflections. "Sir, can you please put your seat up? We're about to land."

Startled, he looked up and unplugged the earpiece. "Sorry, what was that?"

"Please put your seat up. Thanks." She smiled, but didn't recognize him.

As the plane landed, Brett already felt better. Stress drained from his body and was replaced with a sense of freedom and anticipation. A twinge of something more than relief hit him. He couldn't put his finger on it, but he had the strange notion that he wouldn't be returning to the life he'd just left in LA.

# Chapter 4



*ACHANELECH*
**France. Versailles Gardens. Monday, May 13, 12:05 AM GMT+1**

"WHAT TIME IS IT, *Chérie*?" Achanelech asked, feeling his brow pinch in irritation. He waited with his consort, Emanelech, under the cover of darkness by the tree line near one of the many fountains in the geometric gardens of Versailles.

Humidity—the smell a mixture of acid rain and summer heat—hung in the silent night air and covered his skin in an unwanted layer of pungent moisture. Impatiently, he scanned the well-groomed periphery. The full moon shimmered off the surface of the nearest fountain, illuminating the now-deserted park.

Strolling through these gardens over the centuries had given him great pleasure. He had to tip his hat to that megalomaniac Louis XIV for building them. But they weren't here tonight for a pleasant stroll to admire the maniacally ordered shrubbery. They had business to conduct with their sworn enemy—a meeting that was long overdue.

*One did as one must*, he thought. Especially when trying to gain a tactical advantage in the war to survive.

"Five minutes later than the last time you asked," Emanelech snapped. "A few minutes after midnight. Our source will be here any minute."

Achanelech *tsked* at her and paced, making heavy use of his cane to support him. His bones creaked as he walked; the stiffness in his leg unbearable since his last tête-a-tête in Hell. The jeweled top of his walking stick dug into his palm. Attached to a concealed knife, it was a replacement for the one he'd lost back in April while attempting to dispatch that scientist, Dr. Kai Solomon.

He glanced at Emanelech, thinking he also should've worn a cloak to protect him from the cloying dampness. Then again, her reasons had nothing to do with the weather. She wore it to cover her still healing injuries from when they made payment for their botched assignment.

Their Master had been clear: capture Cara Collins, don't kill her. They'd failed in the first, and nearly succeeded in the second when Achanelech had wielded his knife at Dr. Solomon only to have Miss Collins dive in front of the blade.

Achanelech hadn't quite anticipated Cara's willingness to forfeit her life for the good doctor. A mistake he wouldn't make again…. Had Cara died, Achanelech would've single-handedly destroyed his chance and that of his Master, Lucifer, and all of his brethren for winning their prize and escaping Judgment Day. Not his intended or desired outcome by far, yet one for which he and Emanelech bore the full brunt of their Master's displeasure.

As for the cloak, Emanelech refused to be seen uncovered in public. The scarring on her arms and the deep slash over her right eyebrow continued to cause her angst. Nothing a few more meals of human souls couldn't heal.

They'd come a long way on their road to recovery over the last eight weeks, crawling back from charred lumps of demon flesh to their former selves and current human guises. Well almost. Even after two months he still had trouble sleeping on his back.

A figure dressed in a hooded cloak emerged from the darkness. The dark-colored garment swirled around the wearer and gave its movement the appearance of gliding across a smooth surface.

Crickets that had been silent seconds before began to chirp in symphony, and the surrounding forest came alive with the sounds of night creatures.

Lulled into safety by the presence of an angel, perhaps? He scowled, irritated that God's creatures insisted on hiding in his presence. As if they sensed a predator… or something worse.

"It's about time," Achanelech muttered under his breath, hoping to make this a quick and productive encounter. His priority was to return himself and Emanelech into Lucifer's good graces. As such he needed to gain something of value from tonight's meeting.

"What do you have for us?" Emanelech asked anxiously before he could even form words.

"News of the Twelve," said the gender-neutral voice from underneath the hood. Standing midway between a tall woman and a medium-sized man,

Achanelech couldn't surmise if the obscured figure was either male or female under the garment.

"Names? How many?" he asked. His pulse quickened. That would hold them over. Beside one possible suspect they'd been pursuing since childhood, Cara Collins was the only confirmed member of the Holy Twelve who would lead the battle on the side of their enemy.

"The 'possible' has been confirmed, and a new member revealed."

"That's all?" he groused, his hope short-lived. Three in total. The Angelorum was sure taking its time assembling its little army of twelve.

Emanelech stepped on his foot. Pain shot up from the claws at the end of his toes, and he let out a grunt. *Bitch. She'll pay for that later*, he thought.

"We appreciate your taking this chance to tell us," she gritted out, glaring at Achanelech with glowing eyes from under her hood. Her less-than-gentle reminder this was her contact, not his.

Her voice turned to a purr as she addressed the angel. "The new name?"

A gloved hand pulled an envelope from within the cloak and handed it to Emanelech.

"You'll find it in there. Burn it once you are done. One more thing, they're expected at the Sanctuary before month end." Without another word, the figure turned and glided away, disappearing back into the night. The insects and night creatures fell back into silence with the angel's departure.

Emanelech tore open the envelope.

Calling a flame to his forefinger, Achanelech crouched next to her to illuminate the paper.

He skipped past the name he already knew. A smile spread across his face when he saw the one he hadn't.

Chamuel, Son of Eae.

A plan rapidly unfurled in his mind. He cackled with glee. This might give them exactly what they needed to gain back Lucifer's favor… not to mention help even up the score with his angelic nemesis, Eae.

There was no mistaking the aura of love that surrounded the Nephilim male when Cara lay dying in his arms at the warehouse as Dr. Solomon attempted to save her life. If his feelings were returned by her, he'd make the perfect bait.

He set the paper and envelope on fire, watching the flame lick across the creamy paper leaving black ash in its wake. The delicate charred flakes broke off, spinning in pirouettes to the ground until nothing remained. A chortle rose from his throat as he rubbed his hands together to relieve them of residual ash.

"Acchie, you're thinking what I'm thinking, aren't you?" purred Emanelech.

Delight filled his demon heart. "*Oui, Chérie.* Cara Collins, once again, will be ours."

# Chapter 5

*CARA*

*New York City. Fifth Avenue Penthouse. Thursday, May 23, 9:25 AM ET*

"PICKLED DUCK EGGS, Cara, really?" The distaste in her mother's voice rattled her.

"Quail eggs, Mom, not duck eggs," she replied, tightening her grip around her cell phone and trying not to grind her teeth.

"Sweetie—duck, quail, pheasant—who cares? Can't we choose more *festive* appetizers for your cocktail hour? The wedding's on the Fourth of July. What's wrong with mini hot dogs?"

*Just kill me now*, Cara thought, wanting to slam her head against the back of the mahogany deck chair she was stretched out on. All she wanted was to enjoy her cup of coffee and a little therapeutic sunbathing on the terrace before starting her crazy day. Debating Simon's eclectic menu selections with her mother was so far down on her to-do list, not to mention worrying about the delicate taste buds of her father's culinary-challenged side of the family. She had far more important things to worry about… like staying out the clutches of the Dark Ones.

"Mom, he's French and a trained chef. What else can I tell you? Feel free to discuss this with Simon if you're unhappy with his choices," Cara said, pushing down her exasperation and calling her mother's bluff. Cara was convinced her parents would trade her for Simon in a heartbeat… well, not really, but they undeniably adored their new son-in-law-to-be. He could do no wrong in their eyes.

"Oh, honey. I can't do that," she said in a hushed whisper. "I don't want to offend him."

Cara sniffed. "Oh, but it's okay if I offend him?"

Her mother released a breath of surrender. "Then pickled quail eggs it is. Whatever you both want… your father and I just want you to be happy," she said. "Would Simon mind adding a few crowd-pleasers for our meat-and-potatoes relatives?"

Cara's lips tipped up in a smile. "That I can ask him."

"Are you still meeting the wedding planner later for the site review at the farmhouse?"

"Yes, around three," Cara said.

Her mother sighed. "I really wish I could go with you, honey. I'm so sorry my work schedule has been impossible. Speaking of, I have a meeting in a couple of minutes." A career woman through and through, Corrine Collins had worked Cara's entire life. Vice President of Human Resources at a large pharmaceutical company, her mom had always been her role model. Cara had followed in her footsteps quite nicely as an investment banker up until her grandmother's letter had changed her life a couple of months ago, along with the gift to heal people, and a mysterious $50 million inheritance that needed to remain secret.

"Don't worry, Mom. It's fine," Cara said. "I'll see you Sunday."

"See you then, honey. Love you."

"Love you too, Mom."

*Where was I?* Cara settled back into the cushions of the chaise lounge. From the terrace of her penthouse apartment, she could see Central Park over the tree line across the street. Tuning out the city sounds below, she tried to relax for a few more minutes in the unseasonably warm morning sunshine.

Silly her. She'd decided to plan a wedding on her break from saving herself and the rest of the free world.

Green eyes closed, her auburn hair cascaded over the back of the chair from the high ponytail on her head. Sun bathed her creamy Irish skin, covered by only a string-bikini, in warmth. Thanks to her new Nephilim DNA, she no longer feared skin cancer. And her skin now turned a light golden brown rather than the color of boiled shrimp dappled with freckles.

A loud yawn sounded beside her. Cara opened one eye and turned her head to the side.

Her Whippet, Chloe—the canine sun goddess—lay stretched out on her side on the lounge chair next to Cara. She reminded Cara of a paper cutout silhouette with her dark greyhound-like profile against the light-colored cushions. A white heart on the back of her neck and the white tip of her tail were the only interruptions in her dark brindle coloring. Next to Chloe's chair sat a dog bowl filled with water and a bottle of SPF 50 for her delicate pink underbelly. Looking at her dog, no one would ever suspect she was an Angelorum Sentinel who could see demons.

*All she's missing is a pair of sunglasses*, Cara thought, eyeing Chloe jealously and wishing she could be as carefree as her companion. But Chloe didn't have a to-do list a mile long to take care of before the day ended. All she had to do was stave off any demon attacks if one were to pop up.

Cara wanted to make every minute count before her eight-week hiatus ended in five days and her Trinity—she, Michael, and Simon—had to report back to the Angelorum Sanctuary next Wednesday. Her lips turned down in a frown. They weren't really a Trinity anymore now that Simon had been removed as her Trinity Guardian and his best friend, Isaac, had taken his place. Then again, the fact that Simon was named the Second of the Holy Twelve to her First was a more important position than being just a Guardian. Plus, she had a whole security team of Guardians now, not just one. A shudder traveled over her sun-warmed skin. The fact that she needed a security team in the first place still freaked her out. Not to mention her role in the future of humanity to lead the battle between good and evil.

Squeezing her eyes shut, she took a deep cleansing breath and let it out slowly. Five more days. She could pretend to be normal for five more days. Opening her eyes, she reached for her lukewarm cup of coffee and took a sip. *Blech!* She wrinkled her nose.

*Maybe it's a blessing in disguise*, she thought, and put the cup down. Coffee probably wasn't the wisest choice anyway. A restorative cup of herbal tea or a power smoothie would be better than a substance that would cause her to hang from the ceiling by her fingernails.

Simon had left at eight o'clock to meet Michael at his dojo in Brooklyn for a sparring match, but not before they'd had a little "sparring match" of their own. A wicked smile touched her lips followed by a rush of heat. Cara had a hunch new DNA was responsible; she'd been insatiable lately and Simon was only too happy to oblige.

Cara hadn't finished counting all the pluses and minuses of her altered state, but then again, only two months had passed since Kai had injected her with the Nephilim vaccine to save her life. She hadn't decided yet if she considered her increased "appetite" a blessing or a curse.

Cara shook her head. What a difference two months can make; too bad most of it she couldn't discuss without risking lives. Even now, other than Simon, no one knew about the inheritance; everyone still thought she had a lucrative house-sitting gig between the penthouse and the Connecticut farmhouse. Eventually, she would announce that she and Simon had purchased both properties, making life a whole lot easier. Straddling between friends and family who lived normal lives and those who engaged in the war between angels and demons was both challenging and exhausting.

At least she could talk about her engagement. Of course she couldn't mention Simon was 147 years old and sprouted angel's wings on occasion, but the fact they were living together was fair game. He'd moved into the penthouse with her, and over the course of the last couple of months they'd made it their home. Most of his clothes now occupied half of her walk-in closet, his favorite canvases adorned her walls, and his best pots and pans filled her kitchen cabinets.

Her cell phone rang again. Looking at the caller ID, her brow furrowed as she calculated the time in San Francisco. "Hi, Kai."

"Hey, Cara." He released a breath. "Listen, I can't make the flight later. Something's come up with Melanie."

Cara sat up when she heard the strain in his voice. "What's the matter?"

Kai let out a sigh. "Can I give you the CliffsNotes version now and the full scoop when I see you?"

"Sure, whatever you're comfortable with," she said, not wanting to push. Between their nine-year friendship and their soul connection, Cara could read every nuance of Kai's emotions, even over the phone. Out of respect for his privacy, she never pushed the boundaries of her enhanced ability to connect with him. Other than using it as a cosmic GPS, the rest had gone untested.

"It's not that… it's complicated. Bottom line, Melanie's asked to be checked into a psychiatric hospital," he said.

Kai's wife, Melanie, had been possessed by a demon for almost a year. As a result, she'd been drafted as an unknowing accomplice in the kidnappings of Kai and their four-year-old daughter, Sara. After Simon drove out the demon, they'd all expected her to make a full recovery.

"What?" Cara couldn't keep the alarm out of her voice.

"Listen, she's had a rough time since she came home from the clinic after the rescue. She's been hearing voices. I don't know how to help her." He paused. "I need some time to get this squared away before I drop Sara off in Virginia with my mom. All going according to plan, I should still be there in time to leave for the Sanctuary."

Kai had been asked to accompany her, Simon, and Michael on their trip back to the Angelorum Sanctuary. As typical, Constantina had provided few details, but Cara assumed it had something to do with finding the rest of the Twelve. Kai had also shown signs of possessing a Messenger bloodline when they'd rescued him and Sara from Achanelech. Cara had figured that out when she'd suddenly been able to speak with him telepathically—quite a surprise after their long history together.

Cara frowned and clutched the phone to her ear. "What did the Angelorum clinic say about this?"

"They admitted that they've done all they can and suggested specialized psychiatric help from here on out."

Cara, sensing Kai's despair, asked gently, "Do you need to stay behind? This sounds important."

Kai released a breath and Cara pictured him running his fingers through his conservatively cut blond hair. "No," he replied. "Besides, the doctors won't allow any family contact for the first two weeks after she's admitted. It's okay. I'd rather be with you guys than here going crazy by myself."

"All right," Cara said, relieved. She would rather keep an eye on him anyway. When it came to Kai, she tended to be overprotective. He'd accused her of being a mother hen more than once during their long friendship.

"How are you feeling? Any changes I need to know about before your next blood test?" he asked, his scientist hat securely back on.

She felt his mood lift with the change in topic, probably because it was something he could control. Then again, all her male friends seemed to thrive on control. She wondered what that said about her.

She groaned. "Stop. You're making me feel like a lab experiment."

"Well, you kind of are," he said matter-of-factly.

She debated what she should tell him, not wanting to add to his worry. "Well, there've been some things…"

"Like what?" She heard the curiosity in his voice.

"Call me crazy, but my skin is getting… smoother. The tiny laugh lines around my eyes I've had since I was twenty-one—gone. And my clothes are tighter."

"You sure that's not Simon's cooking?" he said with a chuckle. There was no denying Simon's prowess in the kitchen matched his prowess in the bedroom.

She rolled her eyes even though he couldn't see her. "Very funny. He's a brilliant chef, but I'm not getting fat, Knucklehead. I'm getting… muscular. For the first time in my life, I have a six-pack, and I'm not talking about the Sam Adams in my refrigerator."

"Really? Lucky Simon," he teased. That's it, she was *so* not telling him about the increase in her sexual appetite.

"Come on, Kai. I'm serious. I'm getting taller, too. I've been putting pencil marks on the door jamb like a five-year-old. If the marks are right, I'm two inches taller than I used to be. Could I really be growing?"

Kai sighed. "It's possible. Have you had any pain? Growth spurts are normally accompanied by muscular and bone pain."

She released a breath, rolled her shoulders, and debated how much to reveal to Kai given the heavy load already on his mind. "Yeah. Last night was the worst, enough to keep me awake." Understatement. At one point, she could've sworn she was being ripped in two.

Kai paused. She could almost hear his mind working on the other side of the phone. "Huh. I'll have you scheduled for an appointment with the Nephilim physiology department when we go to the Sanctuary next week. We'll take more blood and do some additional tests," he said.

"Okay, thanks. Check in on Sunday and let me know how things are going and when you think you'll be here. Good luck, Kai. Let me know if you need anything."

"Will do." He hung up.

Cara decided to leave out the part about the wicked mood swings—a definite minus on her running list of DNA-related changes. Like PMS on steroids, they gripped her instantly and ignited like a flash fire.

Fragments from the night they'd rescued Kai and Sara were trickling back into her consciousness. She still didn't remember being stabbed during the rescue though.

Cara picked up her now-cold cup of coffee and gave it one last look before putting it back down. She took some more cleansing breaths and mentally reviewed her laundry list of tasks for the day. She had to pick up her engagement ring from the jewelers, meet Sienna for lunch in the Garment District to preview her wedding and bridesmaid dress designs, and pop up to the farmhouse in Connecticut to meet the wedding planner. At least she didn't need to rush over to Simon's loft and prepare the guest quarters for Kai. And Michael and Simon had let her off the hook today for weapons training with the promise she'd be there bright and early tomorrow morning... Well, maybe not that early. She found herself needing more sleep lately and theorized that it must have something to do with the growth spurts.

On second thought, maybe not so bad of a day planned after all.

But the madness would start again tomorrow when two of her bridesmaids, her closest girlfriends from college, arrived for the weekend—Jessa from California, and Irene from Washington, D.C. The three of them hadn't been together in almost three years. Cara thought it might be fun, in lieu of a shower, to have some quality girl time before the jam-packed weekend of her nuptials next month.

Cara nervously fingered the diamond she wore around her throat. Deep inside, she knew the wedding would be her last hurrah. She sensed darkness on its way even though Constantina assured her that they had a half-decent shot of making their wedding date without incident.

Chloe jumped off the lounge to stretch and take a drink of water from her bowl. Without missing a beat, she hopped back up and lay down on her other side.

Cara shook her head and chuckled. "I think you and your Aunt Sienna were separated at birth." Chloe loved the sun as much as Cara's best friend. Speaking of Sienna, Cara glanced at her watch. She needed to get started on her errands if she had any intention of getting to Nicolas Alda's design studio by noon, and avoid Sienna's wrath for being late.

# Chapter 6



*IRENE*
*Fort Meade, Maryland. Thursday, May 23, 9:45 AM ET*

"MISS HICKEY, we understand that you still have a close personal relationship with Miss Collins," said the disembodied voice of one of the NSA agents in the darkened conference room. "We need your help. Your country needs your help."

Irene Hickey had received their phone call yesterday at the State Department where she worked as a linguist for the Foreign Service, specializing in Semitic languages including Hebrew, Arabic, and Aramaic.

*Is he serious?* she thought as she sat in the bowels of the National Security Agency, wondering why she was there…until the full-screen image of her former Georgetown roommate and close friend, Cara Collins, was projected onto the ninety-inch LCD monitor in front of her. Thank God the room was dark. She hoped they hadn't heard her gasp when Cara's image popped up on the screen.

As if to prove their point, the screen changed to a photograph Irene had posted on Facebook from Cara's visit last spring. They were standing in front of the Capitol building, both wearing large smiles with their arms draped casually around each other's shoulders. The Japanese tourist had snapped a frame-worthy picture. Five feet two and ninety-eight pounds soaking wet, Irene was the smaller of the two. Even though they were the same age, Irene looked like Cara's kid sister with her short, red hair and a fashionable pair of black, cat's-eye-shaped glasses framing her green eyes.

"Why are you showing me Cara's picture? Has she done something?" Irene asked, not happy that they'd hacked into her Facebook account. Her privacy settings were set as tight as they could go, and these guys were definitely not on her Friend list.

"We're not saying she's done anything. We want you to listen and watch a satellite feed we picked up on the first of April at a warehouse thirty miles south of San Francisco."

A green-tinted night vision scene played, showing a dark warehouse complex and a parking lot. A moment later, the chatter started.

Irene froze. After a full five minutes, she leaned back in her chair, baffled. Although the language had some familiar elements, she'd never heard it before. She picked up hints of the Semitic languages, but different. Her first instinct was that she was hearing a proto-language, a language from which others had evolved.

"I've never heard that language before," she finally said into the darkness. The sound intrigued her, reminding her of her studies in the divine languages used for religious purposes. Most were no longer spoken today. "How did you get this?"

"We tapped into their wireless radio system. The exchange captured our interest for two reasons. One, we were already monitoring the warehouse for suspicion of terrorist activity by an individual known as Le Feu; and two, because we haven't found a single linguist yet who knows what language they're speaking."

One of the agents fast-forwarded. The next scene showed a large crowd of men arriving on motorcycles. They parked next to some black SUVs then disappeared into the darkness while the strange chatter continued in the background.

"This is about thirty minutes later." The scene jumped ahead.

The bikers reappeared and settled on their motorcycles, waiting with a few others who milled around. A small child was among them sitting on the lap of a handsome black man with long braids. The picture focused in on the little girl's face.

*Oh. My. God.* Irene thought with immediate recognition.

"The child is the daughter of Dr. Kai Solomon," said one of the agents.

Irene knew Kai well—he was a mutual friend of hers and Cara's. He'd been a senior at Georgetown when she and Cara had been freshman. Cara and Kai had a long history, starting with their relationship during Cara's freshman year.

More people appeared from the darkness. The satellite zoomed in on Kai as he entered the light. His daughter, Sara, ran toward him. Leaning down, he scooped her up into a tight embrace.

Another man emerged, carrying someone in his arms.

The satellite camera moved in, revealing an unconscious Cara.

This time, Irene couldn't hide her sharp inhale.

"A large blond man carried your friend, Cara Collins, out of the warehouse. He is, as of now, unidentified. A ghost. We have nothing on him."

The camera moved to another face. "The next person in the frame is Michael Swift Jr. He owns a martial arts studio in Brooklyn, NY. He and the blond man have been seen frequently with Miss Collins over the last several months. On the rest of this group, we have absolutely nothing. They're all ghosts, every last one of them."

*How could this be?* Irene wondered, her heart pounding against her ribcage. "You think Cara is a terrorist?"

"We don't know, Miss Hickey. Why don't we show you the last minute of the footage and you can decide for yourself."

Irene watched the screen. The SUVs and bikes took off as the warehouse behind them blew up in a massive ball of fire. When the scene ended, the lights came up, illuminating the room.

Irene swallowed, feeling faint. "I know Cara. She's not a terrorist."

"We understand you were asked to be in her wedding party?"

Irene's temper flared. "What'd you do? Tap my phone?"

"I don't think I really need to answer that, do I?"

Of course they had and of course they didn't. *Bastards*, she thought, and eyed the two agents warily. "What exactly do you want from me?"

"We know you plan on spending the weekend in New York with Miss Collins," said the shorter one with big ears named Caswell.

It was true. Irene was scheduled to leave after work tomorrow for New York on the Acela from Union Station to stay for the weekend with Cara and their friend from Georgetown, Jessamine.

"And?" she prodded.

"We want you to observe. Find out what you can about the blond man, anything about the language you heard, and what your friend's connection is to the others," he said.

"Is that all?" she deadpanned. *Great, they want me to spy*, she thought with distaste. "Can't you just listen in on her or something? Why do you need me?"

They looked at her, straight-faced. "That would be a violation of her privacy," said Ellerton, the taller one who wore glasses.

Irene glared at them. "Like that's ever stopped you before?"

One of the agents let out a breath. "Let's just say we've tried. Our attempts at external monitoring have failed. This needs to be an inside job. At the moment, what we have is circumstantial. She was unconscious when we spotted her, so she didn't necessarily have any direct involvement in the bombing. She could've been rescued, for all we know. Right now, we can't prove anything. Not to point out the obvious, but we couldn't understand what was being said, so nothing we have is directly incriminating."

Now she understood; they didn't have *bupkis* without her. Arms crossed in front of her, she asked, "Remind me again why I should do this?"

The agents gave her small, disingenuous smiles. Ellerton answered, "I would think that at your age, you still have aspirations within the State Department. We know that your father would like to get another foreign post before he retires. Scandal can always crop up and destroy anyone's hope of receiving a well-earned position… or pension."

Irene's face reddened to match the color of her hair. "Are you actually blackmailing me?"

"Blackmail is such an ugly word. We don't subscribe to such measures. But, your country would appreciate it if you shared anything you learned that could be of value."

Irene frowned. The bastards weren't giving her a choice. Not that she really expected them to, given they'd dragged her over here in the first place.

"Fine," she spat. "But don't expect me to happy about it." She'd investigate all right and prove Cara was innocent, not a terrorist.

Ellerton handed her a large manila envelope. "Inside is a cell phone and any other instructions she might need. We're programmed into the first three speed dial settings. One is the hotline for this investigation, and the other two are our cell numbers."

A third agent with a nice haircut entered the room. "Miss Hickey, Agent Pembrooke will take you down to the lab and familiarize you with the contents of the envelope. But given your former occupation with the CIA, there's not much you shouldn't already be familiar with," Ellerton said, staring over the rim of his glasses.

Irene glared at them and stood to leave.

"Miss Hickey, we'll be watching you," he said with an unfriendly smile.

"I wouldn't expect anything less for our tax dollars." She gave them a tight smile. What she really wanted to give them was the bird, but that would be unprofessional.

Nothing left to say, she followed Agent Pembrooke out, swearing under her breath—*Bastards.*

# Chapter 7

*MICHAEL*
*Brooklyn, New York. Rising Sun Dojo. Thursday, May 23, 10:00* AM ET

"YAHHH!"

Michael's arm shot up to block Simon's bare size fifteen foot coming straight for his face, and countered with a low kick to Simon's thigh, knocking him off balance. Simon hit the gray cushioned mat with a loud *thunk*. Michael suppressed a satisfied smile. In less than five seconds, Simon was back on his feet.

*"That the best you can do, Messenger?"* he asked telepathically, and smirked.

*"I'm not the one whose butt just kissed the mat,"* Michael said silently and glared, trying to catch his breath. Michael held a defensive stance as his blond-ponytailed Nephilim sparring partner circled him on the mat in the sparsely decorated main studio. The scent of mild disinfectant, mixed with rubber flooring and overexertion, circulated through the air. Painted white, the room had a floor-to-ceiling mirror covering the front wall, while neat rows of pads and headgear of varying sizes dotted the back wall. None of which they used. They sparred unprotected, just the way Michael liked it.

Wearing just the bottoms of their *gi*, Michael's smooth, hairless chest glistened with sweat despite the air conditioning while Simon appeared unaffected. Unlike humans, Nephilim didn't perspire or react to temperature changes.

Bouncing on the balls of his feet, Michael stared into his opponent's eyes, a striking blue only a shade or two lighter than his own. Six feet seven with powerful sculpted muscle wrapped around his V-shaped torso, Simon's shadow could swallow Michael whole. Not that Michael was small by any means at six feet and one eighty-five. Quite the opposite. Up until he opened the dojo a year ago, his body had been his livelihood as a male model. Without a doubt, Michael could match Simon ripple for hairless ripple, but Simon had one advantage beyond his size that Michael didn't. Simon wasn't 100 percent human, which was the only reason his chest wasn't dripping with sweat like Michael's. Same for its baby-bottom smoothness. Michael had only his father to blame in the bald chest department—though he'd resisted blaming him for anything while he was alive. Dying, that was the only thing he blamed him for now…

Simon returned his scrutiny and circled with the assurance of a panther. Intimidating for sure, Michael knew beneath the red tattoo of the Guardianship crest on Simon's smooth pectoral beat the heart of a true warrior and a loyal friend.

Michael brushed his hand over his own red tattoo. The Swift family crest combined with his given name made up his Mark as a Trinity Messenger.

He was in his element here. On the mat he was free. A place he could let down his perfect façade, push aside his insecurities, and be judged solely on his skill. A place he could escape the feelings of loss from his father's death. A place he'd hidden from his past since he was eight years old.

Earning his first black belt at the tender age of nine, by eighteen, Michael had won several national championships. Now, at twenty-six, he'd mastered all of the striking martial arts and achieved his dream of teaching what he loved.

He continued to eye Simon, reading his body language for clues. If he didn't stay on his game, Simon would kick his ass.

No reason to rush. He didn't open until eleven on Thursday mornings.

Usually Michael looked forward to their morning sessions with Simon. Today, not so much. His foul mood had dogged him since he'd woken up, throwing off his concentration and making him sloppy.

This time, Michael anticipated Simon's blow, moving back in time for it to miss its mark and to throw a blow of his own. Simon grabbed his arm and in a heartbeat, Michael was on his back, staring up into Simon's grinning face.

Anger welled up inside of Michael. To hell with his exhaustion; his rotten mood urged him on. He took Simon's proffered hand, shifted his weight, and arched his back. Jumping back onto his feet, he did a back aerial somersault and landed in an offensive position. Surprise registered on Simon's face right before Michael struck him with a flying butterfly kick, knocking Simon flat on his back with a hard *thump*.

This time, Michael was the one offering his hand. He reached down to Simon, using verbal speech to break the silence. "I could use a breather. You want some water?"

"Not before I do this," Simon said, and again, Michael was on his back staring up into Simon's self-satisfied face.

Michael pounded his fist on the mat. "No wings! You're a sore loser." It was the only rule they'd both agreed to. Simon couldn't use his wings and the power they contained during a match. And then there was the one rule Michael covertly added: he wouldn't use his natural born ability to read minds to anticipate Simon's moves. A secret Michael intended to keep. As close as he was to Simon and Cara, they didn't know the extent of his true talents, which went well beyond the ability to use their telepathic channel.

Simon raised his eyebrows. "I'm not the sore loser here." He pulled Michael to his feet.

"But you cheated!" Michael, incensed, glared at Simon as he paced. *What's wrong with me?* He wasn't often in such a vile mood. Usually, not much bothered him. He swiped his hand through his dark tousled hair. Was it because he'd be seeing Sienna in the next couple of days and forced to finally confront his cowardice?

Simon gave him a sideways glance. "Michael, is everything all right? You usually don't mind if I end with an enhanced move when you know you've already won. What's the matter?"

Michael grabbed a towel and wiped the sweat from his face and chest.

Simon stared at him with laser focus, undeterred. "I can feel when something's wrong. You can tell me. I'll keep your confidence."

Michael knew Simon's intent wasn't to pry but to protect him and Cara. Even though Simon was no longer officially assigned to their Trinity, he still shared their strong psychic connection which kept their collective emotions tied together… sometimes too closely. Michael understood being part of the Angelorum required flexibility when it came to his privacy, but it made him uncomfortable. There were some things he'd never be willing to share.

He grabbed two bottles of water from the portable fridge next to the two large glass cases on the wall outside the sparring area. One case contained Michael's personal trophies alongside the team trophy Michael's dojo had won six months ago. The other case held training weapons and remained locked at all times.

He handed a bottle to Simon, then opened his own and nearly drained it in one long swallow.

"Well?" Simon was like a dog with a bone when his mind was set.

Michael gave up, and let out a long breath. "It's Sienna." Even her name passing through his lips rattled something inside of him.

A slow smile replaced the look of surprise on Simon's face. "Cara and I suspected that something had changed between you both while we were in San Francisco. What about her?"

They sat down on the long bench at the edge of the sparring area and Michael looked at his hands. Other than the couple of conversations he'd had with Cara when they'd first met, he hadn't shared anything about his personal life with anyone in a very long time. It felt safer to keep it all inside, but Simon meant well and might have some insight to offer.

Because right now, he couldn't stand himself.

His jaw tensed. "I kissed her," he said tightly without looking up.

Simon let out a deep chuckle. "She's very beautiful. That must have been enjoyable," he said softly. "Did this happen recently?"

Michael shook his head. "No, after dinner before we rescued Kai. Right before you called me into the kitchen. And yes, it was more than enjoyable." So enjoyable, in fact, that he could have easily lost control and taken her right then and there.

"You haven't seen her since?"

Shaking his head again, Michael replied, "Not since the night I dropped her off after we got back from San Francisco." *Coward*, he thought, hating his weakness.

Simon's brow pinched. "That was almost two months ago. Why have you been avoiding her?"

He swept his hand over his face and blurted, "I'm afraid she's going to want something I can't give her." The partial truth seemed better than admitting his desire for her terrified him.

Understanding seeped into Simon's blue eyes. "You won't find out if you don't speak to her."

Michael leaned forward, resting his arms on his thighs and wringing his hands. "You're right. I feel like a jerk, and I'm not 'that guy.'"

Large fingers grasped his shoulder and applied gentle pressure. Simon's voice was kind. "I know you're not. Make sure you let her know that, too. Be honest with her, and see where things take you. Learn from my mistakes. Being dishonest can hurt you both." Simon referred to his deception with Cara, hiding his true identity as her Trinity Guardian while he dated her and they fell in love. It nearly cost him their relationship and one hundred years of imprisonment. Ultimately, he got off easy by only losing his position as their Trinity Guardian and suspension from the Guardianship. Michael witnessed the pain they'd both experienced firsthand; it was palpable.

Simon's hand fell away.

"Well, I can't avoid her for much longer unless I skip your party on Saturday night." He massaged his temples with his fingers. "She was upset that night, and I just wanted to make her feel better." He remembered pushing back the black, silky curtain of hair to reveal the tears in her sky-blue eyes, and how his heart had softened. And how she'd skirted his considerable defenses.

"Is that all?"

Michael let out a deep sigh and looked over at him. "It would be so much easier if that was all it was and if she wasn't Cara's best friend."

Michael had met Sienna when Cara had asked them both to accompany her for a long weekend to the Connecticut farmhouse, the same trip that turned into a cross country adventure to rescue Kai. From the moment they'd met, he and Sienna were like two caged tigers, swiping at each other every chance they'd gotten. Sienna elicited primal reactions from him that were way out of character for someone who prided himself on good manners and as a sensei. Michael followed the code of humility, respect, compassion, patience, and calmness both in and out of the dojo. At times, he took it almost to the extreme, making his reaction to Sienna even more puzzling. Then it all changed the moment she needed him... really needed him. Like someone had flipped a switch in his brain. All that borderline hatred turned into a fiery passion Michael had never felt before. And it scared the living daylights out of him. He'd promised Sienna they would talk afterward. Instead, he ran, and he was still running. And then there were those damn dreams...

"Speaking of confrontations," said Michael, changing the subject, "how are you handling Kai coming to town and staying at your place?"

Simon groaned. "Good deflection, Messenger."

Michael lips quirked up in a small smile. "Sorry, I didn't mean to hit a nerve." He knew Simon's history and how he'd punished himself after losing both his first love, Calliope, and the Soul Seeker in his last Trinity, Mina. Over one hundred years had passed before Simon put himself back in the Trinity rotation and became their Guardian. During Kai's rescue, Simon had watched Cara almost die, again helpless to save his Soul Seeker. Michael knew Simon's masculine pride had taken a hit when Kai saved her, doing what he couldn't. Another man whom Cara had loved and who'd loved her.

"I'll always be grateful to Kai. But I guess we both have some demons to face, no pun intended." Simon looked at him and sighed. Michael saw fresh pain there. "You've been avoiding Sienna, and I've been avoiding thoughts of San Francisco."

Michael made an exception and let his shield slip for a moment. Simon's private thoughts flooded his consciousness.

*"Kai saved her when I couldn't... Would she still have chosen me if Kai hadn't been married? He would've been able to give her a child."*

The last part took Michael by surprise, unaware this could be a real issue in a Human-Nephilim relationship. Even with her altered DNA, Cara might still have the ability to bear children. Simon, on the other hand, as a natural-born Nephilim, lacked the ability to procreate—a condition of the Angelorum's pact with God.

Michael reached out and touched Simon's shoulder to reassure him. "Hang in there. She and Kai have a long history, but you're the only man she loves." Michael didn't need to read Cara's thoughts to know who'd captured her heart.

Simon nodded. "Thanks."

"No problem. By the way, did Constantina tell you anything about our trip next week?"

Simon snorted. "What do you think? Even though she birthed me in another life, it doesn't give me any special privileges. One thing you can trust is that she has her reasons and they'll be good ones. All I know is when and where to be for our flight to the Sanctuary. If it makes you feel any better, I find it equally maddening."

Michael shrugged. "Thanks. It was worth a try."

Simon gave him a pointed look and grasped his shoulder. "If I knew I'd tell you. Just because Cara and I are together, doesn't mean we keep things from you."

Guilt hit Michael in the chest. As honest as Simon and Cara were with him, he couldn't see a way to completely return the favor.

"Besides, we may have bigger issues," Simon said. The bench creaked and shifted as Simon stood.

"What do you mean?"

"I've spent hours researching everything I can find on the prophecy short of having the *Book of Human Angels* at my disposal. I'm not buying the obvious. There's something more at stake here for the Dark Ones. I'm hoping to make some headway when we go back next week."

"What do you mean by 'the obvious'?" Michael asked.

Simon's forehead bunched in concentration, his hand resting on his chin as he paced silently back and forth on the mat. "Even if we consider the addition of genetically engineered Nephilim for the Dark Ones, I don't see this playing out as pure hand-to-hand like the confrontation in San Francisco. The battle will be far more epic. That'll mean some options I'm not seeing yet."

"*Hmm.* What does Isaac say?" A sense of uneasiness traveled through Michael. His feelings were similar to Cara's; neither of them savored where this could lead.

Simon shook his head. "Haven't told him. I need him to focus on Cara's safety until we get to France. The two latest recruits started this week which makes five Guardians—in addition to Isaac—to assist until we leave on Wednesday." Isaac had taken Simon's place as their official Trinity Guardian, but the Angelorum agreed Cara needed more protection and they couldn't lose Isaac as the leader of the Tri-State team. At this point, Isaac's role was ceremonial at best. Michael knew

Cara was less than pleased with the selection, and that Simon's best friend, Isaac, didn't rank high on Cara's list of favorite people.

"What about Cara? Does she know?"

Simon shook his head. "No. The time between now and next Wednesday means everything to her. She needs to focus on the wedding and to spend time with her friends. I won't burden her unless I have to… which leads me to my second concern. It's been way too quiet in New York. Even the Nephilim rogue hasn't been making as many sporadic guest appearances. Something's brewing. I can sense it. I'm not sure how much longer we'll be safe here. We're like sitting ducks."

"You and Cara?"

Simon gaze hardened. "All of us."

"I don't like the sound of that." Michael said, his shoulders tensing. He'd worked his butt off to get where he was, and it would take nothing short of death to keep him away from New York. Turns out, Cara wasn't the only one who needed to stay unburdened between now and next Wednesday.

"We'll assess the situation once we're at the Sanctuary, but we may need to remain there for a while." Simon stopped pacing, and crossed his arms over his smooth, broad chest.

"What about your wedding? Didn't Constantina say we still had some time?" Michael asked.

Simon frowned. "She did, but she thinks too much is shifting in the Trinity Stones to be completely sure. We could be knee-deep in the apocalypse by the Fourth of July."

"That's a depressing thought," Michael mumbled and scrubbed his hand down his face. The discussion put him right back in the middle of his black mood. Facing Sienna and the apocalypse. *Brilliant.* If it came down to a choice, *I'll take the apocalypse*, he thought.

Simon shrugged. "It is what it is."

Michael glanced at the wall clock. "Why don't we get some weapons and finish up? If we don't get going we'll be swarmed by my eleven o'clock senior citizen self-defense class." His two full-time instructors, Deva and Rodney, weren't due in until eleven-thirty, so it was all him until then. "Hit the showers by ten-thirty, cool?" Maybe some hot water and steam would reset his attitude.

"Sounds good. By the way, I'm prepared to work through whatever comes our way over the next five days and keep Cara happy. That said, I need to be in SoHo by eleven-fifteen. I'm meeting with the caterer about the menu for Saturday night's party and to pick up the alcohol for the bar."

"You're not cooking?"

Simon's mouth turned down in disappointment. "Not this time."

Michael smiled and thought that Cara didn't know how lucky she was…

He selected a set of knives from his locked case, and they headed back to the center of the mat to finish their workout.

Simon's words resonated in his head. The Fourth of July was around the corner… that didn't leave them much time.

# Chapter 8

*CARA*

*New York City. Thursday, May 23, 11:25 AM ET*

CARA HURRIEDLY CLIMBED the subway stairs outside of Rockefeller Center not far from her first stop—the Diamond District on Forty-Seventh Street—and melted in with the other pedestrians on the sidewalk. The familiar energy of her unseen Nephilim security team dogged her every step from a respectable distance. A necessary precaution in her life these days.

A quick glance at her watch made it the third time in ten minutes. 11:27 AM. *Crap.* She needed to pick up her pace if she expected to be on time for her meeting with Sienna at noon. Running late set Cara's teeth on edge, especially when it wasn't her fault.

Her morning had gone horribly wrong from the moment she had tried to get dressed in more than a string bikini and a big fluffy bath robe. She must've grown overnight. It took over an hour to find something—*anything*—that fit. Good-bye, size six! Only last month, she'd said good-bye to size four. Thank God for knit tops containing spandex and peasant skirts with drawstring waists. Even her bra was on its last hook. Her feet? They no longer fit into her dainty size seven shoes. As of this morning, they appeared to be a whole size larger. Fortunately, she'd found a pair of flat, open sandals to squeeze into.

In a panic, Cara called Gretchen, her new personal shopper at Saks whom she'd stumbled on last month after the first growth spurt. She'd wisely kept Gretchen's number in case she needed her again. Good call—and problem solved. A new batch of clothes, underthings, and shoes would be delivered by dinner. Too bad she couldn't have gotten them earlier.

A quick examination in the mirror after her phone call with Kai confirmed her theory. Although the same face with its dewy complexion, full lips, and sage green eyes—minus a few laugh lines—still stared back at her, everything from her neck down looked... different. Her curves were still in all the right places, only a proportionally larger version, and she was packing on muscle like Linda Hamilton in *Terminator 2*. Her arms, legs, back, and abs had taken on a crisp and rippled definition... noticeably more than yesterday. Even the notch on the doorjamb had leaped a full inch overnight.

At first, she'd attributed the initial changes after the rescue to exercise and her training, but this level of muscle development was next to impossible without steroids and intense weight lifting.

Dread had settled in the pit of her stomach with this morning's discovery. There was no way she'd be able to hide it from her mother's eagle eye on Sunday. Not to mention, she expected an unflattering comment to come her way later from Sienna regarding her less-than-fashionable outfit. Better than going naked, she supposed.

Cara made haste getting to the jeweler to pick up her engagement ring. Passed from Constantina to Simon, it was a vintage 1920s beauty—a two-carat cushion-cut diamond set in platinum and surrounded by sapphires. She'd barely had the ring for a week when one of the stones was lost during their post-Tribunal vacation in Monaco. The replacement stone had taken two agonizing months to make. At least now she'd be able to produce evidence of her engagement for her friends and family

She ducked into a tiny lobby and rang the bell. The door latch released. Pushing past the heavy metal security door, she ascended the dark, narrow stairs into the small shop.

The jeweler's eyes lit up. "Cara, so good to see you," he said with a thick Swiss-German accent. In his early sixties, Wilfred Hancock had a slight build, a head of steel gray hair, and a kind demeanor. A personal friend of Constantina's and a member of an old and trusted Messenger family, he came highly recommended.

She leaned in for a European-style kiss, one on each cheek. "Hello, Wilfred. I'm excited to see my ring."

"You'll be very pleased, indeed. The stone is a perfect match. Wait here and I'll get it for you, *Liebling*," he said and disappeared behind the velvet curtain.

Tapping her fingers on the top of the glass case, Cara glanced around the room. The shop looked deceptively small without any exterior windows. Expertly lit and finely appointed, the showroom contained only six waist-high cases circling the perimeter of the floor. Cara knew from her last visit that there was a walk-in vault and a private viewing room in the back.

She moved her palm and stared down into the dazzling case while she waited. Her ring was beautiful, but this jewelry was in another league. Dripping with diamonds and other precious stones, some of the chunky, jewel-encrusted bracelets appeared so heavy her wrist ached just looking at them. Given the value of Wilfred's inventory, Cara wondered why he didn't choose to be in the International Gem Tower with its state-of-the-art security.

Wilfred returned through the velvet curtain, carrying a small pouch.

"Cara," he said and extracted the ring. "Give me your finger, *Liebling.*"

She held out her hand, and he slipped the ring on her finger up to her knuckle… where it wedged with no chance of making it any farther.

A look of alarm passed over Cara's face before she gave herself a mental kick. *Duh! My feet have grown so my hands must've, too.*

Wilfred's eyebrows drew together, reminding Cara of a bushy gray caterpillar. He pulled her hand toward him for a closer examination. "What happened? Has this ring ever fit? Do you want me to size it for you?"

Cara politely twisted away. "I've been retaining water. I forgot to take my pills this morning. It'll be okay." She removed her necklace and strung the 18k white gold chain through the ring, refastening it around her neck. The ring hung next to the single solitaire, her personal talisman, already on the chain.

Wilfred looked distressed. "What are you doing putting that beautiful ring on your necklace?"

She pasted on a smile. "It's so I won't lose it. By tonight, I'll be able to put it on without a problem." She reached into her purse. "How much do I owe you?"

He waved her off. "Constantina has taken care of the bill. Are you sure you don't want me to size the ring for you?"

Another quick glance at her watch confirmed she needed to leave. "No, really, I'll be back if we need to get it sized," she said kindly.

He narrowed his eyes. "You won't take it anywhere else?"

Cara gave him a look of wide-eyed innocence. "Never!"

"All right, then," he conceded. "Give Simon my well wishes."

Her lips turned up in a smile. "I will. Have a wonderful day, Wilfred." She turned on her heel and left as fast as she could.

Eighteen minutes and counting. If she walked really fast, she could make it to the Garment District by twelve.

At one minute to twelve, Cara caught her breath and walked into the building where Nicolas Alda had his office and design studio. The building looked like all the other nondescript buildings in midtown between Thirty-Fourth and Forty-Second on Sixth Avenue.

She headed straight for the receptionist. "I'm here to see Sienna Sargent."

The willowy receptionist gave her a bored look. "Ms. Collins?"

Cara cocked her head and smiled. "Yes."

Willowy dialed Sienna. "Um-hum, she's here. I'll send her up." She hung up and pointed. "Elevators are to the right, eighth floor."

Cara had never visited Sienna at work. Her office was on the executive floor, one floor above the design studio. The elevator doors opened to reveal Sienna waiting for her, holding a sketch pad. Sienna was one of those women who stopped traffic—even on a bad day. She was conservatively dressed today—for Sienna—in an above-the-knee black pencil shirt, a white fitted blouse with the top two buttons open, exposing a large silver necklace, and a towering pair of Christian Louboutin heels that put her somewhere in the neighborhood of six feet tall.

Cara stepped out into the hallway as Sienna stood, mouth agape. Her long jet-black hair hung straight and full to her mid-back, and her sky-blue eyes sized up Cara over a pair of black-framed glasses that were more for show than necessity.

*Here it comes…* Cara thought.

"What'd you do?" Sienna asked snidely. "Knock over a Goodwill store on your way here?"

*And there it is—the comment.*

"Thanks. Nothing like saying exactly what's on your mind," Cara said, shaking her head. She loved Sienna, but the woman lacked filters of any kind. They'd been best friends since they were sixteen years old, growing up in Summit, New Jersey. Over the years, their friendship had required a lot of tolerance and acceptance, but the rewards had far exceeded the friction.

"Just sayin'," Sienna said, holding up her sketch pad in surrender.

Cara shoulders slumped. "Nothing in my closet fits. The vaccine Kai gave me is causing all sorts of funky things to happen." Cara knew Sienna didn't understand exactly what the vaccine had done—only that it had saved Cara's life.

Sienna sighed and rubbed her forehead. "Don't worry, Carissima, I'll get you fixed up. At least as far as a wedding dress is concerned," she said, using Cara's nickname like she always did when she wanted Cara to feel better.

Cara followed Sienna back to her office and sat down at her conference table. Lunch had already been ordered in—a salad and a bottle of water.

Sienna reached for a calculator and a measuring tape, and then pulled the interior curtains closed in her office and lowered the external shades, transforming it into a dressing room. A small dais that she used for her models stood in the corner.

"Okay, bag lady, take off your clothes down to your underwear so I can assess the damage and make some calculations," she said.

"I thought we were going to look at more designs?"

"Uh, yeah. We will. But, I need to see what I'm dealing with first."

With a heavy sigh, Cara removed her clothes until all that was left were her bra and panties.

Sienna's eyes went wide and nearly dropped her measuring tape. "Shit, what have you been doing? Pumping iron with Simon? You have biceps and a fucking six-pack for shit's sake!"

Today was the first time in almost a month that she'd seen Sienna in person. Between Cara's training schedule and Sienna's preparation for the winter collection, they'd been limited to connecting over the phone or through text. Sienna's reaction didn't surprise her, but she didn't enjoy it, either.

Cara rolled her eyes. "Way to make me feel like a freak. What'd you think? I was getting fat?"

Sienna shrugged. "Well, yeah. Sorry, I didn't mean to make you feel freakish. Actually, you look great—very Xena, Warrior Princess," she said, gesticulating with her hands.

"Thanks," Cara said with a sardonic smile. It wasn't often she could fluster Sienna.

Sienna put the measuring tape around her neck and flipped through a small notebook. "Let me get your last set of measurements. Maybe I can extrapolate how big you'll be if you continue to grow from now until the wedding. I'll make three dresses: one in your size today, one with a growth projection, and one in between. That way, we should be pretty safe and only need minor alterations."

Cara had to admit it sounded like a good plan. "Okay."

"Go stand on the dais."

Cara obeyed and turned to face Sienna. Her eagle eye honed in on Cara's neck. "Is that your engagement ring on your necklace?"

Cara glared down at her.

"Oh, never mind." Sienna snorted and then pulled the tape from around her neck. She went to work, measuring Cara from top to bottom, jotting notes along the way.

"So, how's the Winter Collection going?" Cara asked while Sienna worked.

"I'm up to my eyeballs in parkas and mukluks. You're a welcome escape, trust me."

"Do I sense an Eskimo theme?" Cara asked, amused.

Sienna scowled. "Nico was inspired by his vacation in Alaska, and here I am producing a collection of igloo-chic for next winter."

"How's everything going for Fall Fashion Week?"

"Ugh. More hell to bear."

Cara frowned. "Senny, are you sure this is okay? I feel bad taking you away from your work to make all these dresses."

Sienna stopped what she was doing, stood up, and planted her hands on her hips. "Are you nuts? You're my best friend, I'm your maid of honor, and I'm a designer. Who else do you think I would let make these dresses? Not to mention, we'll get them at wholesale."

Cara threw her hands up. "All good points. My bad."

A few minutes later, Sienna glanced over her notebook. "I have what I need. I think we can still go with the original design, but I have some other ideas that could work."

"I'll defer to you, my fashion maven."

Cara put her clothes back on and sat at the conference table, eager to eat her salad as Sienna walked back to her desk.

Sienna's eyes sparkled as she held up a large manila envelope, wearing a conspiratorial smile. "Before we look at the dresses, want to see what I got my hands on?" There was no mistaking the spring in her step as she rejoined Cara at the conference table.

Cara put down her fork and gave her a sideways smile. "You look like a cat who just ate a canary. What've you got?"

Sienna wiggled her eyebrows at Cara. "Better if I show you." She slipped a bunch of contact sheets and a couple 9" x 12" photos out of the envelope and slid them across the table. The images were all variations of the same man. The hard, sculpted muscles of his hairless chest and abs glistened on his near-naked body as he modeled a wardrobe consisting of various pairs of scant white cotton underwear. Very little was left to the imagination. His face was shown either in profile, staring into the distance, or giving the camera a penetrating stare with intense royal-blue eyes under the now-familiar mahogany brows. His pictures dripped with a smoldering sex appeal that sent a rush of heat right to her core, leaving her breathless. Cara's primal reaction rocked her.

Cara gasped. "Michael!" She fanned herself with a napkin while looking at her near-naked Messenger. "Is this the Calvin Klein underwear campaign?"

"The one and only," Sienna said smugly.

Cara stared wide-eyed. "How'd you get these?"

Sienna *humphed* at her. "Child's play. I called in a favor from a friend of mine at Calvin Klein. The campaign is almost five years old, so it took him some time to get his hands on the file."

Cara shook her head and smiled. "Our little Michael."

Sure, Michael was one of the best-looking men she'd ever seen, but it wasn't until the day in Connecticut when Sienna had outed him as a former Calvin Klein underwear model that Cara had learned about his former career.

Back then, Sienna and Michael had been like oil and water, needling each other every chance they'd gotten. So it wasn't a complete surprise when Sienna pounced on Michael's embarrassment and called his manhood into question. Cara had never seen Michael that mad or mortified before or after that day. Warm, kind, and always in control, Michael typically had the most impeccable manners of anyone in the room—next to Simon.

"I don't know if I'd call him ours. Yours, maybe. And, he's definitely not so little," Sienna said, placing her finger directly on his crotch in one of the 9" x 12"s.

Cara sized her up. "Come on, Senny, admit it. I saw you two together before we left San Francisco. You really like him, don't you?" By the time they'd all returned from San Francisco, things had changed between Michael and Sienna for the better, or so Cara had assumed. But Sienna wasn't talking.

Sienna turned red, opened her salad, and picked up her fork.

Cara frowned at her. "Come on. Why won't you tell me what happened? It's so unlike you to keep this to yourself—for so long!"

Sienna just shrugged.

"Senny, *pleeeeeaaaaasssse* tell me," Cara begged.

Sienna let out a breath. "He kissed me," she muttered and put a forkful of salad in her mouth.

Cara's eyes widened. "What! Really? I can't believe you've been holding out on me!" Maybe she'd been right about them after all…

Giving her a dirty look, Sienna said, "That's why I didn't tell you. I didn't want you to make a big deal out of it."

Catching the undercurrent, Cara decided to tread carefully and asked softly, "Did this happen in San Francisco?"

Sienna nodded.

*Uh-oh.* "Have you spoken to him since?"

Sienna shook her head, and Cara could see her friend's eyes glisten.

Cara's heart deflated. "I'm sorry, sweetie. What can I do to help?"

Sienna brushed an escaping tear from her eye. "Nothing, I'm fine. He just promised we would talk about it, but there hasn't been any opportunity since then. Like I said, it's no big deal."

"Senny, if it wasn't a big deal, it wouldn't have made you cry," Cara said gently. "You'll see him at the party Saturday night. You should talk to him then…"

*Damn.* Cara hated when crap like this happened. Sienna and Michael were two of her closest friends, and having friction between them was not good for any of them. In her heart, she believed they would make a fabulous couple. Granted, she knew Michael was not in the market for a girlfriend and, truth be told, Sienna was still recovering from her breakup with her boyfriend, Mark, whom she'd dated for four years.

Rather than giving Sienna the engagement she had hoped for, Mark broke up with her to get engaged to someone else. Cara had never liked him. On the surface, he'd treated Sienna well enough, but Cara always suspected he'd cheated on her behind her back. For all Sienna's bravado and tough exterior, she was really a marshmallow inside and deserved much better than what she'd been given.

Sienna nodded. "I know." She gave Cara a wan smile. "I guess I do like him… a little."

Cara gazed into Sienna's eyes. "I love you both, but he's an idiot if he can't see what's right in front of him."

Sienna shrugged and her mouth tugged up into a half-smile. "It was a good kiss…"

Cara touched Sienna's arm. "How about you show me some dresses? We'll worry about Michael later."

Sienna nodded and picked up her sketch pad. They looked at designs while they finished their lunch. Sienna had come up with six incredible designs, three for the wedding dress and three for the bridesmaid dresses. Cara liked them all.

Cara pointed to one in particular for herself. "If I have to choose, I like the one that covers my shoulders. Anything you can do to conceal my new Amazonian proportions from my family would be greatly appreciated."

There was a brief knock at the door before it swung open. A colorful man in his mid-30s sashayed in through the doorway.

"Sienna, *mia cara*—" he said in a thick Italian accent, but stopped when he noticed Sienna wasn't alone. "Please forgive me. I didn't know you were in a meeting."

Sienna stood and smiled. "Nico, this is my friend and our client, Cara Collins."

Cara stood and extended her hand. "I'm very happy to meet you."

Nico beamed at her, taking her hand and kissing the top, rather than shaking it. "Cara is a lovely name. *En Italiano*, it means 'dear.' I'm so sorry to interrupt, but we are having a *piccolo problema* downstairs," he said, holding his thumb and forefinger about an inch apart.

"I'll be there in five minutes?" Sienna stated more than asked.

"Yes, of course, mia cara."

Nico turned to leave when he spotted the pictures of Michael still spread out on the conference table. He picked up the nearest photo. "Who is this juicy morsel?" he asked with a salacious look in his eye. "Is he one of our models?"

"He's a friend of ours," Sienna said tightly, carefully removing the picture from Nico's hand and gathering the rest to put back inside the manila envelope. Cara recognized the territorial tone of her voice.

Nico threw up his arms. "I meant no harm," he said and then narrowed his eyes. "Ah, he is your boyfriend, no?"

A blush spread along Sienna's cheeks. "He's not my boyfriend, just a friend. A *straight* friend," she emphasized, raking him with a glare.

"Okay, okay. I'll see you in five minutes, yes?"

"Yes."

Nico left with the same flourish he'd entered the room with, closing the door behind him.

Sienna sat with her head in her hands.

"Senny, I should go. But I want to make sure you're all right first," Cara said, concerned.

"Yeah. I'll be fine." Sienna sighed. "You're right. I need to talk to Michael this weekend. I need to know if there's anything there."

Cara got up and wrapped her arms around Sienna's fragile shoulders. "Everything will work out exactly as it's supposed to," she said. Using her gift to soothe emotions, she pushed a loving energy into Sienna.

"Thanks, I feel better already," Sienna said with a puzzled look on her face. Then she squinted. "You did that thing again, like you did in Connecticut, didn't you?"

"I have no idea what you're talking about." Cara said innocently and shrugged. "What time are you coming to the penthouse on Saturday morning? I want to text the girls."

The "girls" were all her bridesmaids: Jessa, Irene, and Cara's sisters Emma, Courtney, and Camille. They were scheduled to meet to review the designs and to have their measurements taken followed by lunch and a spa afternoon.

"Can we say eleven? That should give us the time we need to get everything done before we leave for the spa." Sienna opened the door to her office. "I'll walk you out. I need to get downstairs before Nico has a meltdown."

When they arrived at the elevator, Cara turned and gave Sienna another hug. "See you on Saturday morning, and I'll say a little prayer that Michael, aka 'the juicy morsel,'" she said air-quoting with her fingers, "snaps to his senses."

Sienna chuckled. "Speaking of Michael, tell him he needs to help you pick out some new clothes," she said, giving her hand a squeeze.

"Ha! He's been too busy. I had to replace him." Since their one big trip to Barney's in March, Michael hadn't found time for another excursion.

Cara left Sienna's building and headed uptown to pick up Chloe and her SUV for her drive to Connecticut. Luckily, she wouldn't see Michael until tomorrow. She'd have trouble keeping a straight face after seeing those campaign pictures. Sienna was right: he looked well endowed. She hoped he wouldn't let it go to waste, and would use it for good…

"Like making Sienna scream with pleasure," she mumbled, before she realized that she'd spoken out loud.

# Chapter 9

*KAI*
*San Francisco. Thursday, May 23, 12:00 NOON PT*

KAI JERKED AWAKE, the leather desk chair groaning underneath him. He sat up and yawned. Bleary-eyed, he passed a hand over his face, and then glanced at his watch. Noon. He released a brief sigh of relief; he still had some time to gather himself together.

Cara's file lay open on his desk. He'd spent some time reviewing it after they'd hung up and he'd discovered Melanie sleeping peacefully upstairs. Rather than waking her, he'd pushed her admission at Sequoia Park Hospital, an Angelorum-affiliated facility, to two o'clock.

The night before had been hell. Neither of them had gotten much sleep. Melanie spent most of the night, shrieking and crying about the voices in her head as he'd held and comforted her. Thankfully, he had the foresight to send Sara and her Guardian Ishmael next door to stay the night, anticipating where the situation could lead.

Too bad his impromptu nap did little to ease the dull ache behind his eyebrows.

The leather chair squeaked as he leaned back and shut his eyes. Competing emotions played tug-o'-war inside of him as he tried to figure out how he should feel and what he should do. He loved her, and it killed him to dump her—even temporarily—into some institution. He rubbed his temples, trying to wake up and dispel his stress.

Looking back, he could see the exact moment when the shit had quietly hit the fan. The downward spiral had started when he'd discovered the secret project he'd been working on for Forrester Research Labs wasn't what it appeared. It had taken him almost twelve months to put all the pieces together and take action. Hours after finding the missing piece, he and Sara had been kidnapped. *Nothing's been the same since.*

An earsplitting scream tore through the air.

*Melanie.* Kai's eyelids shot open. His heart pounding, he bolted from his chair.

Ten strong fingers bit into his shoulders from behind as he passed over the threshold into the hallway. *"Wait!"* Luke said through their telepathic link. *"Let me go first."*

The scream ended, followed by silence.

Kai's skin erupted in gooseflesh.

Blade drawn, Kai's Guardian stepped around him and raced for the stairs. Kai followed behind the hulking black-clothed figure. His lungs constricted with fear, taking the carpeted stairs two at a time.

Luke stopped outside of the open bedroom door and held up his hand.

*"Wait here,"* he said telepathically then cloaked and promptly disappeared. Luke's deep voice sounded from inside, "Kai!"

Kai raced through the doorway to find Luke crouched over a motionless Melanie, the blade no longer in his hand. Fresh from a shower and still wearing her white robe, Melanie lay crumpled on the rug outside the bathroom door, her blue eyes wide with fright and her lips moving in silent conversation.

"Melanie!" Kai dropped to his knees next to them and brushed back a wet piece of blonde hair from her face. "Baby, can you hear me?"

She stared through him with vacant eyes, her lips moving.

Desperation crept into his voice. "Mel, sweetie, can you hear me?" He clenched his fist in frustration, overcome with helplessness. He glanced at Luke crouched next to him. "Have any ideas?"

Luke's dark eyes held empathy. He shook his head and let out a heavy sigh. "I wish I did, my friend."

Kai scrubbed his hand over his face and took a deep breath.

"Do you want me to carry her over to your bed?" Luke asked softly as he stood up.

Shaking his head, Kai gave him a weak smile. "Thanks. I'll take her." He appreciated the offer, but if he allowed Luke to do that for him, it would snap something inside of him. He'd feel like an even worse husband than he already did.

Guilt chewed at his gut daily since he'd found out about Melanie's demon possession and her unknowing hand in his kidnapping. Logically, he knew it wasn't her fault. She had no knowledge of what had happened while she was possessed. Yet, he couldn't help feeling betrayed. He and Sara could've been killed. He hated himself for feeling this way… for blaming her.

Kai scooped Melanie's petite frame up into his arms and carried her to the bed. He laid her down and secured her robe more tightly around her, not knowing what else to do.

"Step back!" Luke shoved him roughly away from the bed. "Do you hear that?"

"Hear what?" Hairs bristled on the backs of Kai's arms.

"Listen," Luke hissed, snapping the hilt of one of the blades from his belt. It blazed to life in his hand.

Kai listened while his eyes darted around the room trying to locate the source of the sound. Low murmurs at the threshold of Kai's hearing. Whispers and overlapping voices, quiet, building into sharp static. Demonic whispers.

A chill rippled down his spine and a familiar dull throbbing started at the base of his skull.

Melanie sprang up from the bed, only the whites of her eyes visible. Her hair rose around her head, free-floating. Her mouth moved and demonic sounds filled the air.

*Holy hell.* Kai's eye widened in horror, and he froze in back of Luke. "Help her!"

"I can't use this blade, it'll kill her," he said. "Stay back!" Luke seized her by the neck and spun her into his chest. She went limp and quiet in his arms. The hellish whispers continued around them.

His head jerked around to look at Kai.

"Shit, she's marked. Look." Luke gave him a hard stare, his jaw tense. The skin on the back of her neck pulsed, and the shape of rune—a sigil—rose in angry red lines. "Go to Ishmael next door, stay with him and Sara."

"But—"

"Go, now! They're going to use her as a portal. Now go!"

The pain in Kai's head intensified as a black, inky haze rose out of the sigil on the back of Melanie's neck, forming a dark cloud.

Kai was no match for a demon; only Nephilim, like Luke, could handle the weapons necessary to destroy them.

He looked between Melanie and Luke and his heart squeezed. How could he leave her?

Luke glared at Kai. "I've got this, go to Sara. Run!"

Black demon haze filled the room.

Grasping the sides of his head, Kai did the only thing he could do… he ran to find his daughter.

52

# Chapter 10

*CARA*
*Greenwich, Connecticut. Thursday, May 23, 3:00 PM ET*

AS CARA LEFT THE HIGHWAY, she lowered the back window for her canine companion to hang her head out. Chloe sniffed the air eagerly, her eyes partially closed and her ears pinned back in the sharp breeze.

Ten minutes later, Cara spotted her landmark—the sign with the three house numbers. She slowed and turned the Land Rover onto the private lane which led to her farmhouse on the left. Another estate lay straight ahead with a third off to the right.

As she drove up, the majestic gray shingled house with the wraparound porch came into view from behind the trees. Over twenty varieties of summer perennials were in full bloom surrounding the huge flagpole in the center of the circular drive, providing a colorful welcome.

*This really is the perfect venue for an outdoor wedding,* Cara thought with a smile.

She pulled into the circle and parked. Checking her watch, she had over an hour before the wedding planner arrived for the site walk-through. During the drive, Cara had received a text from her, apologizing profusely for the last-minute change to their appointment.

Glad for the extra time, Cara grabbed Chloe's leash from the passenger seat and stepped out into the warm sunshine. With a quick tug, she opened the back door and Chloe leaped out, heading to the nearest patch of grass.

Her business complete, Chloe raised her ears and twisted in a fast circle before returning to Cara's side when Cara uttered the magic word: "Walk?"

No sooner was the lead clipped to Chloe's collar than she was off, tugging Cara down the driveway to the private road. Her ears were snug against her head so they touched as she broke into a brisk trot. Rather than stopping to sniff and meander like she usually did, Chloe led Cara with purpose toward the property up the lane.

"Come on, Chloe. Slow down, will ya?" Cara frowned with her arm extended straight out in front of her. Passing a honeysuckle bush so quickly it was almost a blur, the sweet smell wafted after her. Only a couple of months ago, the fragrance would've set off a chain reaction of uncontrolled sneezes and watery tear ducts. Not anymore, thanks to her new Nephilim DNA. After a lifetime of allergies to almost every floral variety she could now breathe their heady scents with pleasure.

The top of the large colonial estate with Roman columns loomed closer over the eight-foot-high stone wall. Though well maintained, it sat unoccupied, judging by the lack of energy present the few times they'd come to Connecticut.

Not today.

Music filled the air and grew louder as they approached the usually vacant house. A male voice and guitar sounds could be heard from the other side of the stone barrier. The appealing melodic tenor brought a smile to Cara's lips.

As they drew near, Cara's curiosity peaked and she decided to covertly investigate. Before she'd had a chance, Chloe surged forward, jerking the leash from Cara's hand.

Stunned, Cara watched Chloe tear away at greyhound speed with the lead dragging behind her, disappearing through the open black-iron gate.

*Freaking great.* "Chloe! Come!"

Nothing.

So much for obedience training.

The music stopped.

*Shit!* Cara sprinted after her, gravel crunching under her sandals as she rounded the corner.

In the distance, Chloe stood on the stairs with her tail swinging frantically. A guy wearing jeans, a black T-shirt, and boots sat perched on the top step of the porch, petting her vigorously. His tawny blond hair fell down around his face, obscuring it from view. A guitar lay next to him. There was something familiar…

He looked up and tucked his hair behind his ears. A dimple punctuated the wide smile that broke out on his face. "Hey, don't you ladies owe me breakfast?"

It took only a moment for her to recognize him and for a curl of his energy to reach her. *Brett!* Cara's heart quickened. The last time she'd seen him, he'd been wearing a baseball cap with his hair hidden underneath. But there was no mistaking that show-stopping smile.

Reflexively, she smiled back. Several times since their chance encounter back in March, she'd wondered if he would ever take her up on her offer.

Brett stood up from the stairs. With a slow, sexy swagger, he headed in her direction, Chloe leading the way. He was even more attractive than she'd remembered, with high cheekbones and a chiseled jawline in a face that rivaled Michael's. Even though she was spoken for, there was something about Brett that elevated her heart rate.

He caught her gaze as he came closer. Those eyes. *Gah!* A sexy, bright blue. Absolutely panty-melting in an unassuming, "I'm not doing this on purpose, I just have nice eyes" sort of way.

The pull of Brett's energy was even stronger now than when she'd first met him, sucking at her in a way that made her lower half clench and warm. For the second time today, her body betrayed her for a man who wasn't her fiancé.

Cara wanted to hang her head in shame. Instead, her feet unconsciously carried her toward him. Before she knew what'd happened, he'd swept her into the firm muscles of his chest. Faintly familiar, his touch crackled over her skin, making her momentarily forget the world outside of his arms.

His breath warmed her hair. "It's so good to see you. I planned to call you and collect on that breakfast." His words rang true and sweet on her tongue. Had he been lying, she would've tasted bitterness. A newly awakened ability, tasting truth and emotions added a new dimension to her everyday communication.

He leaned back, wearing a puzzled look. "Hey, you seem taller for some reason."

Cara swallowed, thinking fast. It was true. Even though Brett was slightly over six feet tall, they were closer to eye level with Cara's extra couple of inches. Unable to come up with a plausible explanation, she looked at him innocently and shrugged, still in his arms.

His lips turned back up in a smile. "My imagination, I guess."

A blush colored her cheeks. The clean, fresh smell of his soap, or maybe it was his shampoo, drifted her way. She resisted sinking her nose into the warm skin of his neck and inhaling.

*Oh, please God. Enough.* She gently pushed her way out of his embrace. Being that close to him was too intoxicating. If she didn't create some distance between them, her knees would give out.

As delicious as Brett was, Simon was the only one with the key to her heart, making this even more unnerving.

*Yikes! What the heck is wrong with me?*

"It's really good to see you, too," she said sheepishly and pointed to his guitar lying on the porch. "Are you working on a song? I heard you singing from the road."

A look of worry momentarily passed over his face. "Yeah, did you like it?"

She nodded vigorously.

He tipped his head, motioning her toward the porch. "Can you stay for a few minutes? I'll play you the whole song."

"I'd love to," she said, having time to spare before the caterer arrived. Brett had told her he was a songwriter when they'd met, but based on the small bits she'd heard from the street, he could really sing.

She glanced around the wooded property as she followed him back to the columned porch. In addition to sharing the private lane leading to individual driveways, all three estates had once shared one huge wooded parcel of land that had been subdivided sometime during the nineteenth century. "Wow, this is gorgeous. Is it your aunt's place?"

"Yeah. She's traveling on business in Europe." He sat on the porch and rested his boots on the steps. Reaching for his acoustic guitar, he maneuvered it into a comfortable position on his lap.

"What about your uncle?" Cara sat down beside him.

"He passed away a while ago. He was a lot older than my aunt."

"Oh," she said softly, feeling slightly awkward, and then cleared her throat. "I guess we're neighbors. My house is on the right as you head back out."

"So that's why you're in the neighborhood," he said. "I wondered who'd bought the Haskins place."

She blushed. "I, um, acquired it right before we met." Before digging herself into a hole, she said, "Anyway, I'd hoped that you'd eventually take me up on my breakfast offer. I just didn't realize it would be this soon. You seem fond of this place."

He looked down at his guitar. "You could say that. I've been coming here every summer since I was ten years old. My aunt and I are pretty close. She and my uncle couldn't have kids, so I was like the child she always wanted… at least that's what she used to tell me." His cheeks turned pink as he spoke while his fingers found the strings and played a quiet melody.

A smile touched Cara's lips as she imagined him as a young boy. She sensed an underlying vulnerability that warmed her heart.

Glancing up, he caught her gaze. "Can I play you that song?"

"Absolutely." She wrapped her skirt around her legs and gave him her full attention. Chloe trotted past and leaped up onto the cushioned wicker sofa at the far end of the porch.

"I just finished writing this one," he said and played the song she'd heard.

His fingers moved expertly over the guitar strings, delivering a rock ballad accompanied by a flawless tenor voice singing a song of love, loss, and finding a way home. His evocative sound kept Cara enthralled, and the expressive look on his face as he sang had her magnetized. The corded muscles in his arms worked as he played. He had beautiful hands with long, graceful fingers. On his right hand he wore a silver ring, but no other jewelry.

When the song ended, he glanced her way. "What'd you think?" he asked, and then tensed as if bracing for potential criticism.

Cara shook her head, her mouth open, speechless.

"That bad?" he teased.

"Brett, that was amazing! With a capital *A*. You're really good. You should be in front of a crowd. Have you ever considered one of those shows like *The Voice* or *American Idol*?"

He shrugged, giving her a sheepish look. "Not really."

"Well, you should," she said emphatically. "I mean it."

Shifting next to her, he smiled wryly. "You really think so?"

Far from a musical expert, she could still judge talent when she heard it. "Um… yeah."

"Thanks," he said, his cheeks turning pink again.

"So, who do you consider your largest musical influences?" she asked.

His fingers picked away on the guitar, and he gave her a mischievous look. "How about I play some of my influences, and you guess the song and the artist?"

Cara's face lit up. "I'd like that."

"They may stretch you a bit. I tend to like the classics," he teased.

She rolled her eyes. "Oh, please. I grew up on classic rock and grunge thanks to my dad." It was the newer stuff that presented a problem for her. Bumping his arm with her shoulder, she said, "Play me some songs." Like an old friend, she was just as comfortable with him now as she was the day they'd met in the café.

His laugh was full and rich. "You got it." He played a tune, choosing the final chorus to tear into, hitting all the high notes flawlessly.

Cara, feeling like she was on a game show, shouted out, " 'Stairway to Heaven,' Led Zeppelin! Impressive. Not many people can give Plant and Page a run for their money."

He smiled and teased, "Oh, you liked that? I love a girl who can appreciate Led Zeppelin." Then without missing a note, he moved on to the next tune and peeled out a surprising selection.

Cara stared, incredulous. " 'Suspicious Minds,' Elvis Presley? You weren't kidding when you said you liked the classics." She'd only gotten that one because her grandmother was an Elvis fan.

He gave her a thumbs-up and rapidly moved to the next tune. "'Evenflow,' Pearl Jam!" Cara said.

As Brett moved to the fourth tune, a chill passed over Cara, her senses suddenly on high alert. Gazing in the direction of the woods, she was no longer paying attention to Brett.

Chloe jumped off the sofa and raced past them, her hackles raised. A vicious bark rose from her throat, echoing through the surrounding trees. Her eyes turned to blue lasers as they scanned the property, her bark reaching an ear-piercing crescendo.

Cara froze. The hairs prickled on the back of her neck and her skin turned ice cold. The last time this happened…

Pain slammed into her head with the force of a bulldozer. Brett dropped his guitar next to her. She looked through squinted eyes to see him clutching the sides of his head, too. Fighting it, she grabbed Brett's hand. "Run!"

A look containing a mixture of confusion, fear, and pain passed through his eyes as she pulled him roughly to his feet, her Nephilim strength taking over. As Chloe guarded the front of the house, Cara's hand locked onto Brett's and she hauled him in the opposite direction.

Chloe's powers as a Sentinel would keep the demon at bay until it transformed from the black, inky haze into the ten-foot, satyr-like monster with red scales—if no one destroyed it first.

Cara sent a silent, telepathic scream to her Guardian team and Simon as she and Brett raced deeper into the woods behind his aunt's house. She maintained her iron grip on Brett as they ran, not slowing down as tree branches scratched and jabbed at her exposed arms while she protected her face with her free hand. Chloe's barking grew more distant behind them.

A single thought drove her—*keep Brett safe.*

She could feel the pounding of his heart in his fingers, his panic coloring his energy as he followed alongside her.

Suddenly, Brett's hand was ripped from hers and he was gone. Before she had time to react, a second Guardian scooped her up from behind, knocking the wind out of her and lifting her off the ground in one swift movement. Both of the Guardians were cloaked, so neither the Guardians nor their passengers could be seen. Angels flying through suburban Connecticut wasn't something the Angelorum wanted featured on the evening news.

The pain disappeared and Chloe stopped barking, signaling the demon had been taken care of by one of the Nephilim back at the house.

Her back securely tucked into his chest inside a strong embrace, she recognized Isaac's energy behind her as they flew above the trees. "What the *hell,*

Isaac?" She asked, winding herself up into a nasty snit while her heart bucked like a bronco. The wind whipped up under her skirt as they flew.

She and Isaac had started out on the wrong foot when they'd met during Kai's rescue. Since Isaac was Simon's best man—and now her official Trinity Guardian—she needed to bury the hatchet… eventually. But she was still pissed that he blamed her for Simon's near fall from grace. Like it was her fault he'd lied to her. But in her heart of hearts, she suspected his iciness had more to do with the fact that Simon's first love, Calliope, had been his sister.

Isaac's voice was calm. "If that's your way of asking about the demon, it wasn't sent for you. It was hunting Brett."

She'd been about to rip him for falling down on protecting her, but instantly deflated when she heard his reply, frowning so deeply her eyebrows almost touched. She must have heard him wrong. "Why would a demon…" The answer came to her as she asked the question. "Brett's Angelorum?"

"Messenger blood, but he hasn't been Called yet. He doesn't know. He's been protected since he was a child. That is, when he's not sneaking off to hide here in Connecticut."

"What do you mean, sneaking off to hide?"

Isaac hesitated. "Sorry. I shouldn't even have told you that much."

"Shouldn't have told me that much? Why does everything have to be such a damn secret? A heads-up would've been nice," she snapped.

For a split second, Cara had the urge to bite the arm closest to her mouth. Instead, she released an exasperated sigh, and the memories of the hellish week she'd found out she was a Soul Seeker came crashing down on her. She couldn't help but feel sorry for Brett.

Isaac circled overhead rather than landing. "Why are you circling?" she asked, still annoyed.

"I figured you might need a moment, and I wanted to give Constantina time to arrive."

"Constantina's here? Why?" Cara asked anxiously. Every time Constantina left the Sanctuary, she put herself in danger. Her energy practically threw up red flares for the Dark Ones. Was Brett also one of her charges? Cara's rapid speculation gave her a brain cramp.

"I'm sure you'll find out. I'll take you down now."

Cara watched as they descended through the treetops, the ground coming up to meet them. Being a Guardian's passenger was more like being on an amusement park ride than experiencing the sweet sensation of flying people have in their dreams. Lucky for her, she didn't get nauseated riding roller coasters.

When they landed and uncloaked, Brett looked shaken and green under his tanned skin. He sat on the top stair leading to the porch. Two towering, dark-haired Guardians flanked him, wearing the traditional uniform—black pants, T-shirt, and duster. Chloe sat in Brett's lap, licking him gently on the arm to soothe him.

Brett's eyes bulged when he spotted Cara, fear written on his face. "Are you okay?"

Her lips tipped up into a wan smile. "I think I should be asking you that question. This is just another day at the office for me," she said, hoping she didn't sound too sarcastic.

Cara nodded at the Guardians standing on either side of Brett. "Noah. Zeke."

Noah gave her a smile and a small salute while Zeke sauntered over to give her a hug. A rakish smile crossed his baby face.

"Good to see you, doll," he said, picking her up and lifting her feet off the ground. She had gotten to know Zeke during the rescue. Simon and Isaac had practically raised him as a young Nephil. Unlike Isaac, with his ice-blue stare, Zeke didn't make Cara feel like a villain. A young Guardian by Nephilim standards at sixty-three, he had an irreverence that Cara found refreshing. She was quite fond of him. His warm, brown eyes were always filled with a touch of mischief.

"Put me down, Zeke." She chuckled.

He squeezed her tighter. "Gotta get my hugs in before Si gets here. Don't want him to fly into a jealous rage over me touchin' his girl," he teased.

"Funny," she said with a smile as her feet touched the ground. "Is it safe for me to take Brett for a walk?"

Isaac ran his fingers through his blond brush cut and looked up from his phone. "Simon says to behave and yes, you have ten minutes."

His words made her bristle. *Behave? What?* Then she remembered. Simon had observed her first meeting with Brett and their "almost kiss," sparking a little unhealthy jealousy.

She cocked a brow at Isaac and smiled wickedly. "If Simon wants to tell me to behave, he can tell me himself. But if he knows what's good for him, he won't."

He snorted and shook his head, muttering something she couldn't hear.

*Ugh. Nephilim men.* For all their modern ways, Simon and Isaac hadn't completely outgrown their Victorian roots.

She beckoned Brett with her outstretched hand; he nodded and put Chloe down. Walking over to her, he willingly placed his hand in hers while his haunted stare searched her eyes for answers.

Lacing her fingers through his, she squeezed. "It'll be okay. Trust me?" she whispered.

Without a word, he licked his dry lips and nodded again.

She pushed soothing energy through her palm and he relaxed under her touch, closing his eyes for a moment. She turned toward the woods and led him along beside her. "We'll be back," she yelled over her shoulder.

"Zeke will patrol until Simon arrives. Call him if you need him." Isaac's calm response came from behind them.

When they were out of earshot, Brett started to speak. "Cara—"

Cara pulled him to a stop, giving him a look of empathy. "You must have lots of questions."

His hand was sweaty in hers, the haunted look still in his eyes. For some reason, she felt fiercely protective of him. She wanted to take care of him like Michael had taken care of her. She beat back the odd desire to run her fingertips over his naked skin, chalking them up to the Nephilim hormones running recklessly through her body.

Brett swallowed and dropped her hand. Agitated, he ran his fingers through his tawny-blond hair, and pointed back in the direction they came. "What the hell was that back there?"

She gave him a half-smile. "Which part? The demon we were running from or the Guardians who swept us up and flew off with us?"

He paled at her question. *Hmm…* maybe she needed some sensitivity training.

Brett stepped back, fear suddenly filling his eyes. "What are you?"

His words stung like a slap in the face. "A woman, last I checked," she said, hurt. Not a lie, yet not the whole truth.

His shoulders slumped and his face went slack. He looked at the ground. "I'm sorry. What about me then? Why was that thing after us?"

She touched his shoulder. He didn't back away this time, but rather held her gaze, searching.

She replied with the best answer she could think of. "You're special. That's all I know."

The naked vulnerability in his eyes tugged at her heart. "What does that mean?"

She wished she could tell him but it wasn't her place. Besides that, all she had right now were her suspicions. Now she knew how Michael must've felt the night they met. Having been in Brett's shoes recently, she knew he'd need someone, and she was determined not to let him go through this alone. Her role suddenly shifted from pupil to teacher.

"Soon. I promise. But now we should head back. There's someone you need to meet." As she said the words, she realized they were the same words Michael had spoken to her after she'd almost been killed by a demon, before her Calling. At least Brett had fared better than she had—his attack had been prevented. "Don't be afraid. I won't let anything bad happen to you."

"Thanks… I think," he said, still a little shaken.

As they walked back, he asked, "Who's Simon?"

Brett's question rocked her back to reality, reminding her why she'd come to Connecticut this afternoon. *Shit, the wedding planner.* Cara looked at her watch. She would have to call and beg forgiveness when they got back.

A pang of guilt rippled through her as she sensed Brett's underlying interest, and she suddenly wondered if she'd somehow misrepresented herself—besides her body's traitorous physical reaction. She took a deep breath and said, "He's my fiancé."

"You're getting married?" he said, looking slightly offended. She tasted his shock more strongly than she had anticipated.

Fingering the engagement ring on the chain around her neck, she gave him a sheepish look. "Yes. My wedding is in five weeks."

He caught her forearm and stopped her, his touch electric on her skin. "Shit. Were you engaged when we met?" His tone held more than curiosity; it held deep disappointment. He must have felt the same pull she'd experienced; the question was why?

She shook her head and started walking as he followed next to her. "No, it happened fast. It's amazing the difference a couple of months can make sometimes."

He raised his eyebrow at her. "I'll say."

Her cheeks reddened at the implied meaning of his words.

Brett reached out and gently grabbed her shoulder, stopping her at the edge of the woods. "What's happening? I feel like I just stepped into the damn *Twilight Zone.*"

She let out a deep sigh, knowing nothing she could say would be adequate. "I know. I was where you are now only a short time ago. Would you feel better if I promised it will all make sense very soon?"

He rolled his head back in frustration and rubbed his eyes. "Not really."

Cara smiled and offered her hand. At least he didn't seem so afraid any more.

"Come on," she said, leading him back to the porch as Simon's Escalade pulled into the driveway.

# Chapter 11

*BRETT*
*Greenwich, Connecticut. Thursday, May 23, 4:30 PM ET*

A BLACK ESCALADE PULLED into his aunt's driveway and parked. As Brett clutched Cara's hand, he hoped he wasn't cutting off her circulation. Then again, she had one of the tightest grips he'd ever felt.

He couldn't even begin to understand everything he'd experienced in the last hour. The phrase *angels and demons* played in a continuous loop inside his head. At least now he understood the source of his headaches. This last one had been skull crushing. But demons? He would've taken it better if he'd been told he had a fucking brain tumor.

And why hadn't he been attacked before?

Not to mention that he'd almost barfed when that angel guy Noah had jerked him off the ground and flown him back to the house. The fact that he'd actually flown? He wasn't ready to go there yet. As Cara came back with the other guy, he could have sworn he saw a pair of gigantic white wings fold up and disappear behind the guy the split second after they landed and became visible.

Then there were his feelings. True, he'd been attracted to Cara the moment he'd met her in March, but when he saw her again on the driveway... Holy crap, the vision of her hit him like a sledgehammer. He wanted her in his life. Badly. It didn't make any sense. The feeling wasn't just sexual but rather a heartfelt yearning.

His heart had deflated the moment he'd found out about her engagement, like she'd been stolen out from under him. Maybe if he'd taken a chance and gone to breakfast with her and her friends that next morning, it could've made a difference. None of this made any sense. But, there was one thing. He felt safe with her, and his gut told him he could trust her.

But nothing could substitute for the stiff drink he really needed right now.

All four doors of the SUV opened simultaneously, and four people emerged—one from each door. He assumed the driver, a giant blond dude with a ponytail, must be Simon. A small, delicate, blonde woman stepped from the front passenger side, wearing a simple blue sleeveless dress with sandals, her hair twisted into an elegant bun on her head.

Brett's heart jerked and his eyebrows knitted in confusion upon the appearance of the last two passengers. He instantly recognized the two Hispanic men, their skin the color of warm caramel. One man was his friend and the leader of the Avenging Angel's Biker Club—Angel Benitez—followed by Paco, his second-in-command.

*What the hell?*

Cara squeezed his hand and then released it. Simon, dressed in the same black uniform sans his duster, made a beeline for Cara. His blue eyes fixed with worry as he drew near.

"Lemme guess, fiancé?" Brett mumbled to her under his breath as Simon approached.

"Yup," she mumbled back without moving her lips.

Simon swept her up into his arms, her feet no longer touching the ground, just like Zeke had done except with a tad more passion.

"You took one hundred years off my life when you sent that distress call," Brett overheard him say.

Brett watched out of the corner of his eye as Simon gripped her in a hug and buried his face in her hair. Slowly releasing his grip, she slid down along the front of his body until her feet touched the ground. He lowered his lips to hers and kissed her deeply, cupping the back of her head in his large hand. His other hand pressed into her lower back, drawing her closer.

A surge of jealousy coursed through Brett.

"Yo! Get a room, you two," yelled Angel from behind. "Time to focus on little brother over here before he has a hormone meltdown."

Brett's face turned beet red. *Hormone meltdown?*

Simon released his hand from Cara's back and raised his middle finger to Angel.

"Have some respect for your mother, *muchacho*," Angel snipped.

Brett's eyes found the small, blonde woman, who looked at him kindly. Brett noticed something slightly off about her face, yet nothing that detracted from her beauty. But, she sure didn't look old enough to be Simon's mother.

"Simon, dear one. Why don't we retire to the porch to speak with Brett and Cara? There will be time later to express your relief over Cara's safety." Brett watched as Simon stiffened. He released Cara, his gaze shifting to Brett for a split second, long enough for Brett to read Simon's message: "Back the fuck off of Cara."

Angel, wearing black leather biker's clothes and a wide smile, strolled over to Brett. Paco followed. "Amigo," he said and embraced Brett in a man hug, "you're still a skinny kid. When are you going to put some meat on those bones?"

Brett had been dealing with Angel's sense of humor on the subject of his vegetarian lifestyle since he was a teenager. Angel could never understand how anyone could just live on "beans and lettuce," as he put it. That said, Angel always thought of creative ways to slip the word *meat* into the course of their conversations, hoping Brett would see the error of his ways.

"*¿Por qué estás aquí?* What are you guys doing here? How do you know these people?" Brett asked in Spanish, unable to contain his questions any longer.

"Patience, *m'ijo*," Angel said as he rested his hand on Brett's shoulder.

Cara looked over at Brett, her expression encouraging. "Come."

Her hand disappeared inside Simon's as he led her up the stairs onto the porch. Brett trailed behind with Angel and Paco.

The petite, blonde woman stood waiting for him at the top of the stairs, while the others filed around her and took seats at the end of the porch where Chloe had already settled on top of a cushioned ottoman.

"Brett King, Son of the Wanderer, I'm Constantina—Angelorum High Council member and mentor to Cara," she said, her arms outstretched and a warm smile on her lips. Brett only understood half of what Constantina said.

On autopilot, Brett placed his hands in hers and a warm wave of energy rolled over him, engulfing him in calm serenity. He found himself staring into her warm, ocean-blue eyes.

"I don't understand. You said, 'Son of the Wanderer.' Why?"

Constantina smiled. "There are things you don't yet know about yourself. Things that you believed were true, but are not. What I'll share with you now is that you're very special, and your gifts go beyond your musical talent."

Her words both disturbed and comforted Brett, but he knew she spoke the truth. He could somehow taste it.

"We've known about you for some time, Brett King. Come, let's sit down and talk with the others. We'll tell you what we must now, and then you'll come and visit us to learn the rest." She led him over to where the others were seated.

Brett sat and all eyes turned to him as he held his breath. He felt like he had just jumped the rails of reality. He wasn't afraid, but he still wanted that drink he'd thought of earlier.

Angel Benitez leaned forward in his seat. "Brett, we go way back, no?" Angel had watched out for him since he was a ten-year-old, when his brother Colin died, and was the only one of the rough crowd his brother ran with who was worth knowing. When Brett turned sixteen, Angel taught Brett to ride, and he'd been a member of Angel's motorcycle club ever since.

Brett nodded his head, wondering where Angel was going with his question.

"Trust me when I say you're like a little brother to me. But now there are truths that must be shared."

Sweat formed on Brett's brow as his anxiety rose. "Like what?"

Angel rested his forearms on his knees, engaging him with his dark-brown eyes. "I'm not who you think I am, amigo. I never knew your brother, Colin... I knew your father."

Brett's head snapped back. *His father?* His parents had divorced before his first birthday. His dad moved to Seattle with his company, leaving them behind. Very soon afterward, he remarried. Other than the occasional birthday or Christmas card, he never saw or heard from him. The last time Brett saw his dad, he was nine years old. It was a visit made during a business trip. They went to McDonalds for a hamburger and fries. Good, old, classic junk food for when you can't think of anything better to do with your kid.

Angel shook his head and said softly. "Not that one."

Brett's heartbeat ramped up a few notches. "What do you mean?"

Angel eyed Brett's hand. "That ring you wear? It's a gift from your real father."

Brett looked down at his hand and the silver ring with his name. His mother had given it to him on his sixteenth birthday. Bile rose in his throat. "My mother...?"

"She's your mother. No surprises there."

Anger flared inside of him. "That's not what I meant. She cheated on my father? Is that why he left?"

"No, Brett, that's not why he left. Your father was the one who cheated on her with the woman he later married. Your mother only spent a couple of nights with your real father, and you were the outcome. Richard King doesn't know that you aren't his child."

A chill took hold of Brett. He trembled, unable to stop his body from shaking. Constantina touched his arm, and he flinched. He stared at the mostly unfamiliar faces around him. Overcome with claustrophobia, he jumped to his feet, ready to bolt.

*Who are these people? Who am I? Is my entire life a lie?*

Before he could even blink, Angel stood at his side. "Let's go for a walk, amigo. This is a lot to take in."

A snide laugh rose from Brett's throat, and a tear of frustration sprang to his eye. "I need a drink. This is just too much." He walked over to the stairs and sat down as Angel followed.

"Paco, get me two cold ones from the fridge," Angel yelled over to his second-in-command. In less than a minute, Paco walked up to them with two frosty longneck Buds in his hand.

Brett took his and drank half of it without taking a breath. Wiping his mouth with the back of his hand, he said, "Vodka would've been better." Actually, a dark hole to crawl into would've topped even that.

Angel led Brett back toward the woods.

Brett finished the bottle and tossed it with all his strength deep into the trees. Angel handed him the other bottle.

"You don't want it?" Brett asked as he took the bottle.

"Little Bro, I think you need it more than I do," Angel replied.

Brett guzzled down the beer and threw the bottle in the direction of the first. Then he planted his feet on the ground in a defensive posture and threw his arms in the air. "Okay, now that we are away from the rest of them, *what the fuck*!" His voice echoed through the woods, setting off a flutter of wings above him from the surrounding trees as birds sought a quieter place to perch. His emotions were a swirling tornado inside of him making him feel like he'd been stripped naked and sucked off in front of an audience.

Angel rubbed his hand across his brow and released a deep breath like he was thinking. Finally, he looked at Brett, his eyes dark and his mouth a hard line, wearing a don't-screw-with-me-and-listen look. "The first thing I'll tell you: your real father was a good man and he loved you more than that worthless shit-bag your mother married."

Brett's face went slack. "*Was* a good man?"

"Yes, was. He's dead." Angel's words hit Brett like a punch in the stomach. In a span of few minutes, he had found—and lost—his real father.

Swallowing his frustration Brett asked, "Who was he?"

"We called him the Wanderer, since his job was to reproduce and to hide his bloodline."

Brett's brow wrinkled in confusion. "Huh?"

Angel's dark eyes softened. "Brett, there are many forces in the world that you've never seen before. Some are here to destroy humanity and others are here to save it. Today, you've witnessed a small taste of both sides. And you, my friend, have very valuable blood running through your veins. One of the reasons me and mine have been protecting you since you were a child is because you're one of the Wanderer's children…"

"There're more of us?" Brett asked, his head snapping back.

Angel nodded. "Yes, more; older and younger, but you're the first to know."

*Holy shit.* He had half-brothers or sisters.

Brett's mind raced with questions. "Why am I the first to know?"

Angel shrugged. "Sometimes that's how destiny works, m'ijo."

"What does my mother know?"

"Only that you've been in danger since your tenth birthday. She's been helping us protect you, but she knows nothing else that could put her in danger."

Gazing at Angel, Brett's eyes hardened. "What are you?"

Angel gave him a crooked smile. "I guess you could say I'm your guardian angel."

Brett smirked, his arms crossed in front of him. "Let me guess, you have wings."

Angel huffed and scrubbed his hand down his face. "You're such a little shit sometimes, you know that?" he said, slipping off his leather jacket and throwing it at him. Brett caught it with a look of surprise.

Without a word, white wings rapidly emerged behind Angel's shoulders and unfurled. Snow white with high arching ridges and feathers, the wings blazed brightly behind him. He shook them once before fanning and extending them to their maximum wingspan, a good ten feet tall by eighteen feet wide.

Angel glowed from within as he gazed at Brett. "Satisfied, m'ijo?"

Brett stood transfixed, clutching Angel's jacket with an unhinged jaw.

"Close your mouth before you attract flies," said Angel with a smirk.

Brett squinted from Angel's brilliance. "Um… can I touch them?" he whispered.

Angel nodded and maneuvered a wing toward Brett's outstretched hand until the underside glided across his fingertips. Brett couldn't help the girly gasp that flew out through his lips. The feathers were soft and silky, similar to, yet different from, the wings of a bird. Awestruck, his eyes traveled over Angel's wings. They appeared as powerful as they were beautiful.

He reached out along the wing closest to him to touch the thick, curved edge.

"Careful of the larger edge's feathers; they're sharp enough to slice you up," Angel warned.

Brett swallowed and jerked his hand back. Beautiful, and dangerous.

"Enough touchy-feely?" Angel asked.

Brett nodded, speechless. Angel snatched his jacket out of Brett's hands as his wings folded and disappeared behind him.

"I hope you paid attention in Sunday school, m'ijo. It's real. Welcome to the battle between good and evil. You've just entered the game."

# Chapter 12

*CARA*
*Thursday, May 23, 5:45 PM ET*

CARA DROVE AS BRETT stared out the passenger side window of the Land Rover, lost in thought. She glanced into the rearview mirror. On the backseat, her trusty Sentinel lay curled and asleep in the dog bed wedged next to Brett's duffel bag and guitar case.

After apologizing profusely to the wedding planner and rescheduling their appointment for Monday, Cara convinced the others, while Brett and Angel took their walk, to let her take Brett back to the city. Simon hadn't been happy about her request, but had conceded anyway, knowing her mind was set. Constantina had wholeheartedly agreed with Cara.

Their plan was for Brett, Paco, and Angel to bunk at Simon's Greene Street loft in SoHo, a safe house that would hide their presence and get Brett out of Connecticut. Constantina would stay the night with Simon and Cara at the penthouse and then return to the Sanctuary where she expected to see them later next week. Brett, if he accepted his Calling, would accompany them.

"You okay?" Cara asked gently, venturing toward contact. They'd been on the road ten minutes and Brett still hadn't uttered a word since he'd returned looking shell-shocked from his talk with Angel. He'd walked past them without a glance and into the house to pack his things.

Looking at his hands, he released a breath and shifted his eyes over to her. "Sorry. I'm not great company right now."

Cara could feel confusion and anxiety consuming him. She took a deep breath and tried to figure out what she could actually tell him. Then, focusing on the road ahead, she decided she would just tell her story… or at least some of it.

"Ten days before I met you in March, my entire life changed. I received a letter from my grandmother who had been dead for twenty-three years. I found out I had a gift, and because of that gift, I'd be able to help people I loved when the time came. But I was given a choice—I could accept my Calling, or I could walk away. You'll have the same choice. No one will force you."

"This happened before we met?" he asked, his apprehension turning to curiosity.

"Part of it did." She smiled and took advantage of the opening. "Before I met you, I decided to accept my Calling when it came. Ironically, the same morning we had breakfast, I was officially Called. Less than two hours later, I was on a plane to San Francisco with my Trinity to rescue my friend Kai—"

"What's a Trinity?" he asked.

"Sorry," she said, forgetting how much knowledge she actually took for granted now. She went for the simple explanation. "It's a team of three people assigned to someone, called a Center Stone, who will play a part in an event that could tip the scales between good and evil. Trinities work on behalf of the Angelorum. In my case, we had to rescue my friend Kai to stop a vaccine from getting into the wrong hands." Cara shook her head. "Sorry, that must sound strange." It did even to her ears.

Out of the corner of her eye, she saw him shrug. "No weirder than anything else I've learned today."

She glanced over and gave him a shy smile. "As I was saying, right after I met you, I was on my way to San Francisco to find my Center Stone, Kai. That's where I met Angel. You could say he and his motorcycle club rode to our rescue."

"Huh." He paused a moment. "That was the last week of March, wasn't it?"

Cara cocked her head and glanced at him, picking up on the abrupt shift in his emotions. "Yes…"

"You didn't happen to stay in a house in the Marina District, did you?" his lips slowly turning up into a crooked smile.

She narrowed her eyes and looked back at the windshield. "Why?"

He laughed. Out of the corner of her eye, she caught him twist in the seat and lean against the passenger door. "I'm just trying to figure out if you slept in my bed."

"What? That was your house?" She loved the house they stayed in during the rescue, with its modern, open floor plan and roof deck overlooking the Golden Gate Bridge.

"Yeah, I rent it out sometimes when I travel. Angel called me and told me he had friends coming into town and arranged a one-week rental with my management company." Then he sniffed. "He was the last person I expected to see today."

Cara's mind worked overtime, her brows knitting together in a frown. "Wait a second. Constantina told us the house belonged to a rock star who was on tour with his band."

When she turned her head, Brett stared at her with one eyebrow raised. Extending his right hand, he took hers off the steering wheel and shook it. "Brett King, lead singer of King Metaljam, nice to meet you."

She cringed, and said, "*You're* the rock star?" The pieces of the puzzle snapped into place. Now she was sure of it. Meeting Brett hadn't been a coincidence. And another thing, he was more important than just a Trinity Messenger. He had to be one of the Twelve. She'd ask Constantina later to confirm her suspicion.

"Yeah. That would be me," he said, amused.

She couldn't hide the look of embarrassment she wore. "Sorry about that *American Idol* comment."

He chuckled and looked at her warmly, his dimple reappearing as he relaxed a little more. "No, it was cute. I'm sorry I didn't tell you. I liked knowing you enjoy my company for me and not because of who I am."

Cara sensed a yearning behind his words that warmed her heart. "Well, to embarrass myself even further, I still don't recognize you. But my opinion stands; I think you're incredibly talented. Hopefully, you don't think I'm a musical misfit."

His pushed his hair back behind his ear and leaned closer. "How could I ever think a girl who loves Zep and the classics is a misfit? Never happen. But while we're baring our souls here, I should tell you the reason I'm in town. My last tour date is Saturday night at the Beacon Theatre. Angel's paranoid about my safety, and just confessed to purchasing the entire front row of seats. Want to come?"

Cara eyebrows lifted. "That couldn't have been easy this late."

Brett snorted and cradled the back of his head in his hands. "It would've been impossible. No, he went to my manager before the tour started and bought out the first row in all the venues before the tickets went on sale. I wondered why I kept seeing familiar faces. So, you want to come?"

Her smile was tinged with disappointment. "I wish I could. Two of my friends are coming from out of town and staying over the weekend. I don't think I could leave them."

"Bring them. I have more than twenty seats to fill."

"Serious?"

"Dead," he said with a smirk. "Uh… maybe that was a bad word choice. Yup, I'm serious."

Cara loosened her grip on the steering wheel and brightened. "Okay, that sounds great. We have a party celebrating Memorial Day weekend planned on the roof at Simon's loft. We can start it a little later. Sounds like the makings of a fun night." If she could ignore the obvious—the potential for more demon attacks—it really did sound like a lot of fun.

Cara's smile faded. "Brett, I meant what I said earlier. I'm here for you… no matter what. I remember how I felt when this happened to me, and I don't know what I would've done without my friend Michael."

For all his lighthearted bravado, she'd struck a chord. Brett looked at her with raw emotion that touched her. "Cara, I…" The sentence died in his mouth as he looked down, his energy swirling wildly. "It's been a long time since I made a friend who… didn't wanted to be there just to touch the fame. That's why I didn't come clean when we first met."

She took his hand and squeezed it gently. "Brett, I don't care what you do for a living. You're funny, you're nice, and I would be proud to be your friend under any circumstances. Period. End of story."

A shy smile tugged at the corner of his mouth. "Thanks, that means a lot. Too bad your fiancé wants to kick my ass." He squeezed her hand back and released it.

She laughed to release the tension inside her. "This *so* isn't a laughing matter, but sometimes, if I didn't laugh, I'd cry."

Brett's ass wasn't the only one in jeopardy. If Simon knew the thoughts she'd had today about Michael and Brett, he'd quickly add her to his ass-kicking list. She needed to get to the bottom of her hormonal dilemma *tout suite*, but the thought of discussing it with Kai filled her with dread.

"What did you mean in the woods when you said I was 'special'? Angel said something about the blood running through my veins," he asked. Even though he looked relaxed, she pushed more energy through her hand to ensure he stayed that way. His emotions kept bouncing around like a ping pong ball, making her dizzy.

"Brett, you have Messenger blood. The ability to be a Messenger is passed down through the males in families. I'm guessing the Wanderer must've come from a bloodline that's very important to the Angelorum, which means you probably have some special gifts. But since you haven't been officially Called yet, chances are those gifts are still dormant."

She glanced at him from the corner of her eye.

"What kind of gifts?" Brett asked, chewing his bottom lip nervously.

"It can be different for everyone, but mostly it consists of telepathic communication and a direct link to the Angelorum. Michael can fill you in when you meet him."

Brett suddenly grasped her shoulder, his jaw tightening. "Did you know anything about me before we met? Did you know any of this?" The sour cherry flavor of his emotions hit her tongue with a vengeance. There was hurt... and betrayal in the subtext of his words.

Her eyes widened. "No, I swear. The first I heard you had anything to do with us was after Isaac snagged me off the ground as we ran from the demon. He told me it was you, not me the demon was after, and that you were under our watch. That's how the Angelorum works; they don't tell us anything in advance. Otherwise, it could interfere with free will." His hand dropped from her shoulder.

"Free will? What do you mean?"

"Yeah. That's one of the rules. The Angelorum can't interfere with a person's free will or get directly involved in human affairs. That's why the Trinities exist. Sorry, I'm probably getting way ahead of myself." Cara gave him a sheepish look.

"Who's the Angelorum exactly?" he asked, not letting her off the hook so easily.

She released a deep breath. "I think Constantina should be the one to answer that question, but since I know how crazy that kind of answer used to make me, I'll tell you this. You, me, and everyone you met today—our job is to help keep the balance of good and evil in the world tilted toward good."

The last thing Brett needed was for her to reveal she suspected he could be one of the Twelve. She had a feeling Brett was already dangerously close to reaching the limit of what he could digest in one sitting. Plus, she didn't want him to sense her own doubts and fears over her future role as part of the Twelve. If she could wish it away, she would. Instead, she carried a hard pit of fear in her stomach that she constantly tried to ignore.

She saw him roll his eyes in her peripheral vision. "So, we're like some kind of superheroes or something? Next thing you're going to tell me is vampires and werewolves are real, huh?"

"Uh, no. Sorry to disappoint, but we're only human. And as far as I know, vampires and werewolves are still limited to the pages of fiction novels and movies."

"If that were true, what's the deal with the giant white wings Angel sprouted out of his back?"

Cara arched a brow. Angel must have played show-and-tell in the woods. So she opted for the direct answer. "The Guardians are the only enhanced humans among us. They're Nephilim, half man, half angel, and make up what we call the Guardianship. They protect us from demons, which can only be killed with their weaponry."

"Angel is a Guardian, then? And those guys who rescued us this afternoon?"

"Yes, all of them—Angel, Paco, and Simon."

Brett raised his eyebrows. "Simon? Does that make you—"

"A Guardian? No. Simon is the former Guardian of my Trinity—long story for another time—and I'm a Soul Seeker. My gift is the ability to heal people—among other things." Granted, she was no longer one hundred percent human herself, but enough is enough for one day.

"Are they immortal? Guardians? Because now that I think of it, Angel hasn't aged a day since I met him when I was a kid," Brett said.

Cara smiled at him warmly. "Your head must be spinning. I know mine was. To answer your question, no, Guardians aren't immortal, but they live about five hundred years. Simon is almost one hundred and fifty years old. Angel and Paco are much older, over four hundred. Nephilim generally don't age like we do after the age of twenty-one. The oldest they ever look is about forty."

She heard Brett gulp next to her. "Really? What about Messengers?"

"Sorry, bud. You'll age like everyone else."

"Bummer."

*Be careful what you wish for*, Cara thought with chagrin as they entered Manhattan.

# Chapter 13

*CARA*

*New York City. Greene Street Loft. Thursday, May 23, 8:00 PM ET*

A KNOCK SOUNDED FROM the stairwell door next to the elevator. Chloe raced over, wagging her tail and circling with excitement.

"I'll get it," Cara volunteered, leaving Simon to prepare dinner while Constantina and Paco kept him company in the kitchen over a drink.

Only one person ever felt compelled to use the stairs versus taking the elevator that opened directly into Simon's fifth-floor loft.

*"Hey Cara, it's me, Michael,"* Cara heard in her head.

*"Like I had to guess. Remind me again why you won't take the elevator like a normal person?"* Cara pulled the door open.

Michael's royal-blue eyes sparkled at her under his dark brows. "Because it takes too long, and I don't mind the exercise like some people I know," he said aloud, his voice rich and full, before leaning in and giving her a kiss on the cheek followed by a teasing jab to the ribs.

"Hey!" Cara chuckled and batted his hand away. "I exercise more than enough and see no reason to snub the elevator." God knows she'd run enough today, and in sandals, no less!

"Uh-huh." He arched his brow, unconvinced. "So, I heard I missed all the fun today."

Chloe nosed his leg and demanded her own hello. "Hey, girl," he said, bending down to give her a quick scratch behind the ears. Satisfied, Chloe returned to the kitchen and the source of all food.

Cara sniffed. "Excitement, yes. Fun? Um… no."

"Have Isaac and Angel arrived yet?" Michael glanced over her shoulder toward the crowd in the kitchen.

"Nope, but they should be here soon. Why?" she asked, closing the door behind him.

"I have some news from the Angelorum."

"Sounds ominous."

He shrugged, frowning. "Let's have dinner first. No use spoiling Simon's meal."

As always, Michael looked the right combination of stylishly casual and mouthwatering. Perfectly tousled near-black hair and a heart-shaped face punctuated by high cheekbones and a sexy cleft chin gave him a face that was equal parts masculine and beautiful. A white button-down with the sleeves rolled up revealed the corded muscles of his forearms and the Patek Philippe watch he'd inherited from his father. A flattering pair of dark Armani slacks and leather loafers minus socks completed the outfit.

The images Sienna had shown her from the Calvin Klein campaign came flooding back. Blushing, she shoved them aside and thought of the demon attack. Sometimes, she swore Michael could read her mind. Telepathic communication was one thing but true mind-reading was another. The last thing she wanted was for him to catch her visualizing him in his underwear. Or to reveal Sienna's secret stash of photos.

Michael narrowed his eyes at her. "What?"

*A good offense is always the best defense,* she thought, and gave him a sweet smile. "I saw our mutual friend today."

His energy spiked the moment she mentioned Sienna. "How is she?" he asked, raking his hand through his hair and avoiding her eyes.

*Busted,* she thought as he tried to move by. Grabbing his arm, she stepped in front of him to block his way. "You know I don't like to meddle, but aren't you both a little overdue for a chat?" Or as Zeke had said the night of the rescue, for "twenty minutes in a dark closet"?

He let out a sigh without meeting her gaze. "I know, and we will. I'll talk to her Saturday at the party. I promise."

Cara gently touched his shoulder. "Michael, relax and give each other a chance."

This time she connected with his royal-blues. He nodded and gave her a bland smile. A wisp of lemony fear wafted toward her. But rather than ask, she held her tongue. Michael deserved his privacy. Sometimes her newfound perception was as much of a burden as it was a gift.

When it came to Sienna, his responses baffled her. Nothing and no one unwound him as much as Sienna did. Then again, knowing Sienna like she did, this time his fear might not be misplaced.

"What are you both whispering about out there?" asked Simon from the kitchen as he cracked open another bottle of Chianti.

"Nothing. We're coming," Cara said, letting go of Michael and heading back to the state-of-the-art kitchen. Simon had spent a fortune on the renovation long before they'd met, making it larger with sleek European cabinets, dark granite, and stainless, professional grade appliances. The hood vented up, disappearing into the fourteen-foot-high, black painted ceiling. The effect cleverly forced the eye to focus lower.

Constantina sat ladylike on one of the barstools sipping wine while Paco leaned on the island having a beer. Strong and silent with molten brown eyes, he tipped his chin thoughtfully as they approached.

Paco was under strict orders to keep watch over Brett until Angel arrived with Isaac. Last thing they needed was Brett slipping away again. Paco, Angel's second-in-command, was a member of the Avenging Angel's Biker Club, a front for a retired, and somewhat rebellious, group of Four Hundred–Class Guardians—with the exception of Brett who was a charge under their protection. For her and Brett, that last part had been today's news flash. According to Paco, Angel had been in charge of secretly guarding Brett since the age of ten. The AABC took on special cases for the Angelorum at their discretion, and as one of the Wanderer's children, Brett seemed to qualify.

The delicious smell of tomato sauce and fresh baked bread mixed with the scent of the sweet sausage as Simon sautéed it in the skillet. Chloe sat next to him in her "good dog" pose with one paw daintily held up, hoping for a second piece of meat as she licked her chops from the first.

"Smells incredible, Simon," Michael said as he glided up to Constantina and gave her a double-cheek kiss followed by a solid handshake for Paco. "Good to see you again." They'd met during the San Francisco rescue.

Greetings dispensed, Michael glanced around. "Where's our new friend?"

"He's in the guest room," Cara said. "Simon filled you in?"

"Yup. Lead the way," he said with a sweep of his hand, all traces of his angst over Sienna gone.

Acoustic guitar music grew louder as they walked through the living room, past Simon's painting studio, and down a narrow hallway toward the guest room in the back.

"Michael," Cara reached for his arm, and gently pulled him to a stop. She looked into the eyes of her Messenger, the pillar of her Trinity, appreciating the warmth and strength she always found there. "I want to thank you… for those early days with me. Now I understand what you went through. I feel it with Brett." During these last few months, Michael had been her protector, teacher, and occasional shoulder to cry on. Now she considered him a close friend.

His lips turned up, and he kissed her forehead. "You made it easy."

Sharp and enhanced by her heightened sense of the smell, the woodsy scent of his cologne embraced her. A lump rose in her throat when she tasted the loneliness wrapped inside his words. The spicy taste of cinnamon he sometimes gave off reminded her that as close as they were, there were some painful secrets Michael kept deeply hidden.

Cara knocked softly on the door.

The music stopped. "It's open."

She twisted the knob and walked in.

Clean and sparse with only a bed and a dresser, the small white room had exposed brick on the exterior wall, and one of Simon's large oil landscapes over the bed. Propped up with a mound of pillows behind his back, Brett sat on the double bed, cradling his guitar on his lap. He seemed relaxed now… like before the demon attack.

"Brett, I'd like to introduce you to Michael, my Trinity Messenger."

Setting aside his guitar, Brett got up to greet them. "Hey, man. Brett King, nice to meet you," he said, offering a handshake and a smile.

"Michael Swift. Nice to meet you, too. I'm a big fan."

*Am I the only one who doesn't recognize him?* Cara wondered.

"Cara told me we probably have a few things in common," Brett said.

Michael nodded. "I'm sure we do. I'm happy to answer as many questions as I can."

"Good. Cara filled me in a little already."

An easy and immediate rapport unfolded between them, flooding Cara's senses with harmonious vibrations.

Constantina poked her head inside the door and politely interrupted. "Dear ones, may I take Cara away from you both for a minute?"

The guys nodded, and Cara excused herself to join Constantina in the hall.

"Cara and I will be on the roof deck," Constantina said as they passed through the kitchen where Simon stood dumping the pasta from the pot into a strainer in the sink. The sausage had been transferred to the sauce and a row of glasses filled with wine stood breathing on the island. Dinner looked almost ready. Paco sipped his beer, offering silent companionship to Simon as he finished up.

"Don't go too far. Dinner will be ready in about five minutes," said Simon, casting a serious glance in their direction before checking the bread in the oven.

"Fear not, my dear. We shan't be long."

Cara tried to hide a smile at the subtle reprimand hidden in Constantina's tone. Her "my dear" was the equivalent of Cara's mother giving her a stern "Cara Catherine Collins."

Constantina led Cara up the stairs and out into the roof garden, one of Cara's favorite spaces. Set up to be private, three sides of the deck were surrounded by a high decorative wood fence while the fourth overlooked the street below and featured a view of the setting sun. A lavish container garden filled with plants, herbs, and fruit trees lined the walls beside the fence while a pergola stood over the raised dining area at the center of the deck. There was a bar at the far end, and lounge chairs circled the perimeter. The perfect party space for this weekend's Memorial Day blast—their last hurrah before duty called.

The fading light brought with it a cool breeze. Cara shivered as they settled into two lounge chairs next to some fig trees. The scent of an early blooming gardenia bush filled the air with sweet perfume.

Cara drew the fragrance into her lungs, welcoming a few minutes alone with Constantina. Thousands of questions had been swimming around in her head ever since Isaac had announced her arrival.

"I can feel your distress over my visit," Constantina said, taking Cara's hands in hers. A gentle wave of cleansing energy rolled over Cara, enveloping her in comfort and clearing her head of worry. Cara gazed at Constantina's Grace Kelly beauty, her eyes no longer bothered by the missing philtrum—vertical indentation—above Constantina's top lip. The mark, placed by the angel Layela during the soul's descent, erases memories of any past lives. Missing the distinguishing mark signified Constantina was "awakened," and retained her memories of all her earthly lives, as well as her angelic existence in Heaven.

"I'm guessing Brett must be pretty important for you to be here. Can I ask you something?"

"Of course."

"You knew I'd meet Brett in Connecticut on the day of my Calling, didn't you? There are no coincidences, right?" Cara asked with a tilt of her head.

Constantina smiled and let go of her hands. "I think you already know the answer to both of those questions."

Encouraged, Cara leaped right in. "He's one of the Twelve, isn't he? And the Wanderer is the connection…"

Folding her delicate hands on her lap, Constantina replied, "Yes, the Wanderer and his children are of importance to us."

"So, Brett is one of the Twelve?" Cara leaned forward, barely able to contain her excitement.

"Again, you already know the answer. But I caution you, those revelations aren't without peril or risk for those involved. They must be allowed to unfold as intended."

"But there's something I don't understand," Cara said.

"What's that, dear one?"

"If Angel has been watching over Brett since he was a child, why wasn't he the First, or even the Second? Why were Simon and I revealed before him?"

Constantina pressed her lips together and nodded before answering. "It's all based on the laws of probability and the sequence of free will decisions reflected in the Trinity Stones."

"How so?" Cara considered herself smarter than average yet struggled to understand some of the more subtle intricacies of the Angelorum.

"*Hmm*," Constantina clasped her chin in thought. A moment later, her eyes lit up. "I know. Have you ever watched that game show on television, the one where they spin the wheel for profit and solve puzzles?"

Cara chuckled, surprised that Constantina even watched TV. "You mean *Wheel of Fortune* with Pat Sajak?"

"Yes! That's the one." Constantina clapped her small hands excitedly. "Think of the Trinity Stones as puzzles you're trying to solve, and each letter as a free will decision. At the beginning, you choose a group of letters to start your puzzle. Sometimes many of the letters you choose are part of the puzzle. Once they light up and are turned over, you can guess the word or phrase right away with almost absolute certainty. Other times, your guesses may be off. The letters may not reveal one obvious answer, but rather many possible answers. It's only when all the letters are turned over that you can see the final answer."

"Uh-huh…" Cara said slowly.

"It's the same with the Trinity Stones. Your place as the First was revealed on the day of your birth—all your letters were showing. Your puzzle solved. Whereas with Simon, only a few letters were visible. Although recognized as one possible member of the Twelve, many of the decisions that drove his final choosing were made only recently. There was an equally high probability that his decisions could have cast him out of the Twelve. Finally, as for Brett, many of the letters predicting his place had already been revealed when he showed up as a child. But it was his decision to leave his tour a second time and come back to Connecticut that sealed his fate, making him the Third of the Twelve."

"Wow," was all Cara could think to say. "What about the others?"

"They remain, as of now… possibilities. Some much closer than others."

Cara shook her head to clear it. What she would give to buy a few vowels right now. "Speaking of Brett, how can I help him? This won't be easy for him."

"Just do what you're already doing."

*Hmm*, she thought. That could get her into trouble if she didn't get a handle on her body chemistry. Then a thought struck her. "Is that why you called us to the Sanctuary next week? Is it about the Twelve?"

"Partially." Constantina gently rested her hand on Cara's shoulder. "More so because the Dark Ones are planning their next move, and we need to prepare."

Cara's whole body tensed. "I thought we had until after the wedding."

"According to the Trinity Stones, that's probably still true, but preparation takes time and we have much to do before our next skirmish."

*Probably?* Cara had a lot riding on a "probably." In the scheme of things, a wedding wouldn't make much of a difference in her commitment to Simon—they were already mated per the High Council—but it gave her an excuse to avoid the inevitable. She wondered if she'd ever be prepared. As much as she tried, feelings of doubt and unworthiness continued to gnaw at her. Not to mention the constant knot of fear that ate at her middle. At least she hadn't had any major panic attacks since the rescue. Thank God for small mercies.

Constantina captured her gaze, reading her emotions. "Worry not. You're but one. There's a reason why twelve will be selected. Together, your collective strength will drive your success. Doubt and fear are tools of the Dark Ones. Never yield to them."

"I understand." Cara hadn't realized how much she missed Constantina's day-to-day mentorship and support. Their discussions lately centered on the human side of their relationship and the upcoming nuptials to her son. That would change next week when she visited the Sanctuary. Constantina planned to begin the next phase of Cara's training.

Cara hesitated. "May I ask you something else?"

"Of course."

Swallowing, Cara prayed that Constantina would apply her usual sense of pragmatism without judging her. "Something has been happening to me lately… It may have to do with the vaccine."

"Oh?"

Fingering the ring on her necklace, she told Constantina about the painful growth spurts and her increased appetites for food, sleep, and sex. "Another thing. I've been physically reacting to men… other than Simon."

Constantina cocked her head. "Brett, perhaps?"

Cara's mouth went dry, and she nodded.

"Who else?"

Frowning, Cara told Constantina what happened when Sienna had shown her Michael's Calvin Klein campaign pictures. "I'm not even interested in Michael that way."

Wearing a wide grin, Constantina said, "Ah! It sounds like you're experiencing something similar to Nephilim adolescence. It's not uncommon when a Nephilim reaches fifteen or sixteen years of age to undergo such things."

Panic washed over Cara. "Please tell me I don't have to go through puberty again."

"Not in the way that you think. It's the final transition into Nephilim adulthood, and lasts no more than four years."

"Four years?" Cara's eyes widened as she dug her fingers into the cushioned arms of the lounge chair. "I feel like a nymphomaniac, and if I keep growing…"

Constantina broke into sweet lyrical laughter and patted her hand. "Dear one, relax. I said similar, not the same. Your DNA was taken from adult Nephilim. Your body is most likely adjusting as it sees fit. In any case, modern medicine can help to regulate your overabundance of urges and the pain caused by the growth spurts. I can't imagine that you'll grow much more, dear one."

*"Dinner's ready,"* Simon's voice echoed in her head.

"We've been summoned by the chef." Feeling only slightly relieved, Cara pouted and moved to get up.

Constantina's small hand grasped her wrist. "Simon can wait. I must explain something important to you regarding the Twelve."

Cara sat back down, her gaze connecting with Constantina's.

Shifting closer to Cara, she said, "The Trinity Stones of the Twelve are magnetically drawn together for a reason. They're surrounded by powerful emotions. Sometimes those feelings and emotions will manifest when you physically meet one of the others." She paused and gave Cara a contemplative look. "I think your reaction to Brett is a combination of both his relationship to the Twelve and an underlying attraction that could've existed anyway. If you weren't betrothed to Simon, I believe you may have pursued a relationship with Brett. And him with you. But too many choices have already been made. Brett is now meant for another."

"Good to know." Cara blushed, embarrassed at Constantina's accurate diagnosis of the situation. It's true. Had Cara not met Simon, Brett would've been an attractive option.

"One last thought… at times love will be the Twelve's greatest strength, and at others, their greatest weakness."

# Chapter 14



*CARA*

CARA AND CONSTANTINA RETURNED downstairs to find Isaac, Angel, Paco, and Simon clustered in a tight ball over the kitchen island and engaged in a silent yet serious discussion.

Michael and Brett rounded the corner from the living room.

Simon looked up as they all entered. "Come take a plate. The food is on the stove. Meet at the dining room table," he said, and then turned his attention back to the telepathic conversation among the Guardians.

Cara walked by the muscled horde and took a plate.

*"Are you going to fill us in on what you're talking about?"* she asked Simon through the private Trinity channel they shared with Michael. Isaac had reluctantly allowed Simon to maintain his access to their original Trinity frequency while establishing a second as their new Trinity Guardian for himself, Michael, and Cara. Rank as one of the Twelve obviously gave Simon some privileges.

"Yes, my love."

*"I have news, too. We'll need to compare notes,"* Michael chimed in.

Cara ladled penne onto her plate and topped it with meat sauce. Using the tongs, she dropped some Caesar salad next to her pasta and grabbed a slice of the freshly baked Italian bread. On her way to the table, she picked up a glass of Chianti.

She sat next to the head of the table where Simon would sit. Michael sat down beside her while everyone else trickled in.

Once everyone was seated, Simon lifted his wine glass to Constantina. "Welcome, our esteemed High Council member."

She dipped her head in acknowledgment.

Simon shifted his gaze to the opposite end of the table. "Welcome, our West Coast brothers, Angel and Paco." Then he eyed Brett. "Brett King, charge of the Angelorum, welcome to the bounty of our table and into the protection of the Tri-State Guardianship."

Brett regarded Simon politely and tipped his glass. Cara noticed Brett's buttered penne and made a mental note to ask him later if he ate meat.

Angel raised his glass higher. "Thank you for this fine meal and for your hospitality to me and mine." He turned to Isaac. "We owe you, Brother, for your team's service."

Cara joined in as glasses clinked up and down the table before everyone took a sip to seal the toast. Congenial on the surface, tension rode through the atmosphere in an underlying current, crackling over Cara's skin.

"Please enjoy the meal before we discuss business," Simon said, picking up his fork.

The moment the sweet sausage hit Cara's tongue, her hunger ignited. She had her plate wiped clean before anyone else was more than halfway done. Embarrassment over her Nephilim-fueled appetite didn't stop her from returning to the kitchen for seconds, though midway through devouring another pile of pasta Angel cleared his throat and pushed his own plate aside. "Your permission to start, Chamuel? Unless you'd like me to wait for the señorita to finish…"

"No. Start," Cara managed to choke out mid-chew, her hand covering her mouth.

"Yes, Benedictine, why don't you and Isaac start," said Simon using Angel's former Guardian name, returning his sign of respect. Since Simon's suspension, he was no longer required to use his Guardian name, Chamuel, so he'd been exclusively using his civilian identity, Simon Young—the name under which Cara had fallen in love with him.

Cara glanced around the table as she ate. Tense jaws and shoulders abounded. The one exception was Constantina, who radiated her usual sense of calm and serenity.

Angel's dark eyes were somber as he clasped his hands in front of him on the table and looked at Constantina. "Eae," he said using her angelic name due to their long history, "Isaac and I convinced the Guardianship to cough up some intel after you left Connecticut. We're not sure what it all means yet, but I hope we can figure it out together."

"Do go on," she answered evenly, folding her napkin.

Angel took a deep breath. "First, we've located Le Feu. He's been spotted in and around Paris, but he's not staying there. Looks like he's taken up residence at his château not far from Versailles. The last time he lived there was back in the mid-1800s."

Le Feu and his entourage had disappeared without a trace two months ago during Kai's rescue.

Constantina's expression transformed from serene to guarded, her eyes narrowing. "I'm aware. What else?"

"The demon sent for Brett was Achanelech's but it wasn't sent on his behalf."

Brett swallowed, the color behind his tan fading a bit as he listened silently to Angel's debrief.

"Oh? On whose behalf was it sent?" Constantina asked.

"Seems it was on loan to his badass cohort, Amon," Angel said, naming one of the thirteen Lieutenants serving the Morning Star. "Amon has been going by the name Escher Grant and living part-time in California for the last couple of decades, keeping a low profile. These assholes seem to like wine country."

"Probably has more to do with the proximity to Hell's North American portal," chimed in Isaac, stern faced.

*Didn't he ever crack a smile?* Cara wondered.

Constantina's expression soured. "We need to find the connection to Brett. I must say, I expected Le Feu to be responsible." An old nemesis of Constantina's and one of Lucifer's Lieutenants, Le Feu was the name assumed by Achanelech, the Demon King of Fire. He'd been their only active enemy up until now.

Angel shrugged. "So did we. We'll find out."

"Any news from Luke?" Constantina asked, referring to Kai's Guardian.

Shaking his head, Angel snorted and leaned back in his chair. "He's been busy. At least now we know how the demons keep getting into their house. Kai and Luke found a portal sigil on the back of Melanie Solomon's neck, right before a gang of demons poured out of her."

Cara froze as she mopped the last of the sauce from her plate with a piece of bread. "What happened to Melanie?"

He waved his hand at her. "Don't worry, señorita. Everyone's safe. Luke took care of business, and Señora Solomon is in Sequoia Park Hospital."

Relief flooded through Cara, but why hadn't Kai let her know about the demon attacks? She made a mental note to text him after dinner.

Angel's brow tightened as he turned his attention back to Constantina and stayed silent.

Constantina eyed him suspiciously. "What are you holding back, Benedictine?"

His eyes turned from liquid brown to hard black coals. "Before I answer that Eae, I need to understand what you know." Angel and Constantina shared the longest history of any two people sitting around the table, well over four hundred years across Constantina's many human incarnations. And Cara had been around Angel enough to know that there was no such phrase as "where angels fear to tread" in his vocabulary. He would go toe-to-toe with anyone, even Constantina.

Constantina shifted in her seat and stared him down. "What are you implying?"

All eyes turned to her. Simon frowned but remained quiet while Michael held his breath.

Angel's eyes bore into Constantina. "Eae, I know you wouldn't knowingly play games with us. But you aren't in the habit of sharing everything you know, either. I think the time has come to share what you know."

"Benedictine—"

He pounded his fist on the table. "Don't say it! I respect you as much as my own mother, but forgive me when I say—screw noninterference and free will." He pointed around the table. "Look at these faces. Do you want to get us all killed? We might as well declare defeat right now and hand over humanity to the Dark Ones wrapped in a big bow."

Cara's mouth dropped open. *"Michael, Simon, what the hell is going on?"*

*"Heck if I know…"* replied Michael.

*"Not sure, love,"* said Simon. Cara cast a glance at him and noticed a muscle jump in his jaw.

Constantina gathered her petite frame and rose from her seat, glaring at Angel. "Benedictine, what is it that you know that leads you to believe I'm placing those I love in jeopardy?" Angry energy flowed off of her in a current that pricked uncomfortably at Cara's skin.

Angel dropped his voice. "The Wanderer's children… who else knew about them?"

*Where's this going?* Cara wondered, suspecting yet another layer of secrets.

Constantina's eyes hardened and her voice held a strict warning. "Let us gather them first, Benedictine. There's a reason for the order of things. Do not force revelations upon those who are not yet ready to handle them. Otherwise, it will be you who kills us all."

"Have it your way. But don't expect me to walk like a lamb to slaughter," he said, crossing his arms over his chest.

"I've always respected your opinion, Benedictine, even when it meant breaking the rules. My expectations of you are unimportant. It's your expectations of yourself that you should be questioning. But I do ask that you trust me."

Angel tensed at her words, his teeth grinding behind his twitching cheek. "Don't make this about me."

"Your grief makes this about you. It fuels your impulsiveness and your exile."

Rage mixed with pain behind Angel's eyes. "I'm going to forget you said that."

"Enough!" barked Simon, slamming his fist on the table. "This is counterproductive. Benedictine, what are you getting at?"

Angel's lips tightened in an angry, thin line. "Eae, do you want to tell him or should I?"

Calm slipped back over Constantina's expression and she remained standing, her back rigid. "Angel wants me to admit that I believe there's a traitor on the High Council."

Cara gasped. *"Could that be possible?"*

Neither Michael nor Simon replied to her telepathic question.

"Well, do you? Believe it?" Angel asked.

"Why is it that you do?"

Angel narrowed his eyes at Constantina. "Because you know as well as I do that the Wanderer was murdered."

Cara's gaze fixed on Brett as the color drained from his face.

# Chapter 15



*CARA*

**New York City. Fifth Avenue Penthouse. Thursday, May 23, 10:45** PM ET

"SIMON, would you mind pouring us all a nightcap?" Cara asked, extricating the key from the lock and following Simon, Constantina, and a trotting Chloe into the penthouse. After single-handedly consuming a full bottle of wine over dinner, it wasn't like she really needed another drink. Then again, another drop of alcohol might help to dull the ferocious ache in her bones—an indication that she might wake up taller again tomorrow.

Her plan was to detain Constantina long enough to untangle their messy evening, and get some answers before they all headed off to bed.

The dinner conversation had ended abruptly with Angel's unceremonious revelation about Brett's father's murder and Constantina's subsequent departure from the table. In Cara's opinion, Angel had fully earned the Alexander Pope moniker for *fool* after tonight's fiasco by doing exactly what she'd expected—"rushing in where angels fear to tread." Michael's news about increasing security due to an uptick in Dark One activity—yada yada yada—paled in comparison to the bombshells Angel had dropped.

With a nod, Simon headed for the bar in the living room, while Constantina unclipped the lead from Chloe's collar and then followed Cara to the seating area.

No sooner had Constantina sat in the love seat across from Cara than Chloe hopped up beside her and nestled into a ball, resting her head on Constantina's lap. Chloe stuck to Constantina like a magnet to a refrigerator, making Cara feel like leftovers.

The little traitor.

Constantina let out a heavy sigh as Simon returned with three glasses of tawny port. "My apologies for the disastrous dinner discussion," she said, accepting a glass. "I'm sure you both have questions."

*Understatement*, Cara thought, and took a sip from her glass. Her eyes opened wider as the layered taste hit her tongue. Simon had pulled out the good stuff they'd been saving; it was from their bottle of thirty-year-aged port.

"Yes, many." Simon placed his glass on the coffee table and sank back into the couch next to Cara, a frown etched deep across his forehead. "Can we start with the possible breach in the Council? Followed by the murder, and then what Benedictine did to put such a chip on his shoulder and throw him into exile however many years ago?"

Constantina gave them a wan smile and petted Chloe. "That may be a tall order. Benedictine's story is… complex. I'll tell you what I'm able, but I daresay, finding some of those answers will be part of our collective journey."

"More is better than less right now. Anything you can share will be appreciated," Simon said, leaning forward and resting his elbows on his thighs.

With a nod, Constantina said, "I've long suspected a possible breach within the Council— since before Cara's birth. But there's been no way to prove it short of catching the person. If my assumption is correct, then it certainly explains how the Dark Ones found out about Cara and now Brett. The question we need to be asking is, 'Why?'"

"What's your theory?" Simon asked.

"None of my theories make sense," Constantina replied with a frown. "Until they do, I will journey forth with caution in mind."

A light bulb popped on in Cara's head. "Can we access the historical records in the Flow like the Tribunal did with me and Simon? To see if any of the Council members interacted with the Dark Ones?" Like a cosmic digital recorder, the Flow recorded and stored every moment of human history on Earth. Cara would never forget their Tribunal hearing when all the intimate times she and Simon had spent together were plucked from the Flow and projected in all of their three-dimensional glory for the Council to witness.

Constantina shook her head. "I'm afraid not, dear one. Access to the Flow's archives is restricted to Council members. Requests are usually made by committee, though can sometimes be individually entertained. Not to mention, the Council has special privileges around their own recorded activities. In the same way diplomatic immunity protects ambassadors in the United States, we are protected by the Irin, our archivists, from one another."

"Oh," Cara said, deflated. "So one of you could murder someone and get away with it?"

Constantina's hand froze mid-stroke on top of Chloe. "Cara, whether or not an act of willful murder can be revealed doesn't change the fact that the act has occurred. Something such as murder will be engrained on the soul and can never be hidden from God. Ultimately, we are all held accountable for our actions—seen or unseen. From there, we have only two choices. We may either choose redemption or to fall."

"Sobering thought," Cara said and took another sip of port.

"That means the Council Member in question is at least forty-five years old in this incarnation. Said another way, at least eighteen when Cara was born," Simon said, resting his chin on his clasped hands.

"Dear one, I believe that may be too limiting. Besides, almost all members of the Council are presently over that age with only a couple of exceptions," Constantina said. "I'm afraid that doesn't narrow down our suspects."

Simon's expression turned from concern to contemplation. "Maybe we should do a little digging."

"No. You cannot," Constantina snapped.

"Why?" Cara asked in unison with Simon.

"A Council Member's activities recorded in the Flow may be protected by the Irin, but as you've already learned, yours are not. Because I sit here with you, this discussion is protected and cannot be viewed. Were you to have this discussion without me, it would be discoverable. Understand? I cannot stress this enough. We cannot let the traitor gain advantage by making ourselves vulnerable through discoverability."

Cara gasped. "Does that mean the traitor could be watching our every move?"

"Not unless the traitor wants to be caught," Constantina said. "If anything, I suspect they have been gleaning their information using more conventional means. That doesn't mean when the time is right, they won't make a move when it could hurt us most."

"I'm not following," Simon said.

Constantina folded her hands and released a patient breath. "All requests attached to anyone suspected now or in the future to be part of the prophecy have been flagged and appear as part of a daily report issued by the Irin to all Council Members. We'd know who requested recordings and the reason provided. Just because a Council Member's personal activities cannot be revealed via the Flow, it doesn't protect their requests to view the recordings of others. That said, I don't believe they would make such a request until the battle is upon us. On the other hand, the Council may have legitimate reasons to review those recordings, and in doing so, accidentally stumble across damning information. So do be wise in your disclosures."

"Wow. I suddenly feel like I'm living in a Communist state. Big Brother and all that," said Cara, gesticulating with her hands.

"You shouldn't feel that way. Most of the daily goings-on won't do much to help or hinder our enemies. But being aware of the rules around our observance can only work to our advantage. I believe I was able to convince Benedictine of this before we left this evening."

Cara thought of something else. "What about the Dark Ones? Can we see them in the Flow?"

"Lucifer and his Thirteen Lieutenants carry the same exemption as the High Council… to keep it balanced. We cannot access their past in the Flow, but we can view possible links to our future in the Trinity Stones… if the stones are willing to reveal them. And as I'm painfully aware, the future places the heavy burden of nondisclosure on me as a member of the High Council."

It struck Cara that certain rules seemed almost civilized. Not something she expected in a battle between good and evil. Then again, the Dark Ones weren't the ones who had set the rules.

"Sometimes I don't understand why you can see the future if you can't do anything about it," Cara said, more to herself than to Constantina.

"It is a test and a testament to Semyaza and the first generation of Watchers who came before us. Just as we wear the mantle of humanity to empathize with your plight, we must face temptation and maintain God's trust."

Cara's discussion with Constantina next to the Trinity Pool came rushing back. Angels, like humans, were created with free will, giving them the ability to fall and join the Dark Ones. Sounds like one of them might be on their way…

"What about the Wanderer? Who knew about him?" Simon asked with sudden impatience.

"That's the thing, my dear, only Angel and I knew the identity of the Wanderer. No one else. Not even Angelis, our High Council leader."

"Was he murdered?"

Constantina's distress suddenly matched Simon's. "My dear, that's mere supposition right now.

"What about Brett?" Simon asked. "He's the next to be revealed as one of the Twelve, isn't he?"

"In truth, he's already been revealed. Cara and I have already conferred on the matter. But even though I've shared that with you both, you must keep that knowledge to yourselves. Brett's not ready to learn it. Frankly, there are far more important questions that you should begin to ask as we gather the Twelve. The biggest is, 'Why Cara?' or more specifically, 'What secret is hidden inside of her soul?' That answer will be the key to all the others."

*Why me, indeed,* thought Cara with a sinking feeling of dread.

# Chapter 16

*CARA*

CONSTANTINA ROSE FROM THE SOFA, delicately stifling a yawn with the back of her hand. "Worry not, dear ones. We'll discuss the rest of the implications when we're all together next week. In the meantime, enjoy your leisure time," she'd said then turned to Cara. "Be a friend to Brett."

The thought of remaining close to Brett made Cara blush, but also ignited a fierce desire to protect him.

Simon retrieved Constantina's suitcase from inside the front door and followed her down the hall with Chloe in tow.

"Would you like to join me for another port, love?" Simon asked when he returned, snatching up their glasses on his way to the bar.

"Guess so," she mumbled. The ache in her limbs had reached a steady throb, but that didn't stop her awakening libido.

She leaned back and stared at Simon as he poured their drinks, memorizing every nuance. A smile crept onto her lips; she never grew tired of looking at him and feeling her heart swell. He'd changed out of his uniform into washed-out blue jeans and a black T-shirt to cook in. His dark golden hair was pulled back in a leather tie, allowing her gaze to dance over the angles and curves of his profile, catching only the side glimpse of his crystal blue eyes before resting on his luscious lips and the unexpected scowl she found there.

Frowning, she immediately put any thoughts of seduction on hold.

He carried over the port and sat down next to her, placing the glasses on the coffee table.

Pressing her lips to the base of his warm neck, she gave him a little kiss. "What are you thinking about?"

A contented rumble rose from his throat, and his hand brushed over her hair before he gently pushed away to meet her eyes.

"Just thinking about what Constantina shared with us," he said softly. "I've never seen her so worried."

"I have to think a traitor is a pretty big deal, especially now," she said, tucking her legs beneath her.

"I don't like how this is unfolding," Simon distractedly replied, brushing imaginary lint from his jeans.

Cara narrowed her eyes, sensing something else. "What's really bothering you?" One of the things she loved about Simon was he always told her what was on his mind if she asked.

He avoided her gaze, and asked quietly, "Can I ask you something?"

Her stomach unexpectedly tightened. "Of course."

This time he met her gaze. "Do you still love Kai?"

On reflex, Cara's face pinched in confusion and her skin tingled with discomfort. "Whoa! What? Where's this coming from?"

He swallowed. "If Kai hadn't saved you…"

A wave of fear rolled off of him, and hit her squarely in the chest. She understood. Taking his hand, she brushed his knuckles with her lips. "You're afraid of losing me. Please don't be," she whispered, holding his hand to her cheek. "Everything happened as it was supposed to…"

Anguish blazed behind his eyes. He pulled his hand away and stood up to pace. "I watched… Kai wouldn't give up. There was love and desperation in his eyes as he did CPR. He couldn't lose you any more than I could." His eyes turned glassy, and he growled. "I couldn't save you…"

*But Kai could*, she completed his thought. This time she completely understood. In his mind he'd failed her as he'd failed Calliope, his first love, and Mina, his first Soul Seeker, unable to save them from death.

Her heart squeezed in her chest and she stood, pulling his large frame into her arms. She rested her head against the hard ridges of his chest. His heart beat against her cheek through the soft fabric. "Why is all this coming up now? Is it because we're seeing Kai in a few days?"

Simon wrapped his arms around her, surrounding her in his warmth. He rested his chin on the top of her head. "Probably. It's forcing me to remember. I still dream that you've left me. The pain was unbearable when I'd thought I'd lost you, first because of my deception and then to death." His breath warmed her hair as he spoke.

They'd never spoken about the events in San Francisco. Cara assumed Simon had gotten over them. Apparently she was wrong. Circling her arms around his waist, she clasped her hands together in the small of his back and pressed him closer until she could feel every peak and valley of his torso. The familiar citrusy scent of him comforted her.

"I'll never leave you, Simon. I promise," she said. Flattening her hands on his back, she pushed a loving blast of energy into him.

The tightness drained from his shoulders and his body relaxed against her. "Thank you for easing my mind," he said softly.

She smiled, loving his purity of spirit and beautiful soul.

"I love Kai. Just not in the same way. That chapter of our lives is closed, but his soul is as connected to mine as yours. I'm in love with you, and only you." She kissed the back of his hand. "If I hadn't jumped in front of Kai, at least one of us would be dead right now."

"Fair point. I'm grateful to Kai and forever in his debt," he said, clearing his throat. "I'm sorry. I've never felt emotions like the ones I have for you."

"I understand," she said.

His energy shifted, the heaviness cleansed and swept away. He sat down and pulled her into his lap. "I've been meaning to ask you, why is your engagement ring on a chain around your neck?"

She reached up to finger the ring on the chain for what felt like the hundredth time that day and took a deep breath. "The ring doesn't fit anymore."

"What do you mean?" Simon frowned.

"I'm growing…"

"Have you spoken to Kai?" he asked, his brow etched with concern.

She nodded and wrapped her arm around his neck. "Yes, this morning. We'll do more tests next week. Constantina thinks I might be going through something like Nephilim adolescence."

"*Hmm*, that's possible. I've noticed that you're getting more muscular, but it's hard for me to notice changes since I see you every day."

She sighed. "If it wasn't for my clothes and shoes, I'm not sure I would've noticed, either. Sienna's making the wedding dress in three sizes, just in case." Cara pulled her hands away and wrung them in her lap. "I've noticed some other changes, too…"

"Oh?"

"I've never been so hungry before. I'm tempted to eat everything that's not nailed down. It's crazy. And then there's my hormones… I'm surprised I haven't worn you out with all the sex we've been having."

She thought better of adding any comments about all the sex her body seemed to want with anyone male, regardless of how she felt about it.

He buried his face into the soft skin of her neck and nipped. "I'm enjoying that part," he said in a deep, sexy growl, hugging her close.

His lips sent a tingle across her scalp and she giggled. "Lucky for me. Now, if I could just stop growing."

"You have a long way to go to catch up to me," he said, his lips turning up in a wry smile.

She laughed and dropped her arm, poking him in the ribs. "I hope that's not meant to make me feel better. No way I want to be six feet seven and built like a linebacker."

He looked slightly offended. "Is that supposed to be a compliment?"

"Yes, if I'm talking about you—not if I'm talking about me. How big do Nephilim women get, anyway?"

"Not as large as males, but females could be as tall as six feet two."

"Oh, great," Cara crossed her arms over her chest and sulked.

Simon gave her a squeeze and kissed the side of her head. "I doubt that will be the case with you, my love. Don't panic until we know more. Let's wait and see what happens, and then we'll get your ring sized."

"Stop being so pragmatic; it's not helping."

"I'll love you even if you grow to be as tall as I am," he said, chuckling at the thought.

*Having fun at my expense—we'll see about that,* she thought and gave him a wicked smile. "Well, you won't be laughing if I'm the one carrying you to bed."

His laughter gave way to a slack jaw before he stood and swept his arm under her legs in one deft movement, his blue eyes darkening with desire. "Let's hope that day never comes. Why don't we forget the port? I'm feeling the need to express my relief from this afternoon."

*Brilliant idea.* She threw her arms around his neck as a rush of heat hit her core, anticipating his naked body next to hers in T-minus sixty seconds.

"Lead on, Sexy Nephil," she said, happy for those extra hormones as he carried her toward their bedroom.

No man could ever take his place.

# Chapter 17



*BRETT*

*New York City. Greene Street Loft. Thursday, May 23, 12:00 MIDNIGHT ET*

BRETT SAT ON THE BED in the guest room listening to a steady stream of high-pitched expletives pour out of his cell phone.

"Calm down. Rox. Rox. Roxy!" Brett yelled, holding his cell at arm's length to prevent a busted eardrum. He'd had a hunch it would be a mistake turning his phone back on.

"Where were you? You blow off an interview with *Rolling*-fucking-*Stone* magazine! What the fuck's the matter with you?" she screamed.

How could he even answer that? "It's a long story," he replied in a weary voice. He'd forgotten about the 7:00 PM photo shoot and interview, along with all of his other commitments for the night. They all seemed much less important than everything else that had been unloaded on him today.

"Whoever you have your cock buried in, she'd better damn well be worth it!"

Brett pulled the phone from his ear and eyeballed it with disgust. "I'm hard to offend, but you just fucking managed it, Rox. I think you know me well enough that, one, if that was the case, I wouldn't have answered the fucking phone! And two, as my best friend and publicist, you'd damn well know who I was sleeping with! And three... fuck you!" Brett's face flamed by the time he finished his tirade.

There was only one woman he wanted to "bury his cock in," and she was taken, thank you very much.

Roxy let out a deep controlled breath. "You let everyone down tonight, King. But you're right. I do know you better than most. It's not like you to no-show on me twice in two weeks. So what the fuck happened tonight?"

Brett ran his hand across his face and swore to himself. "Someone tried to kill me."

"What? And you didn't call me? Are you okay? We need to get—"

"I'm fine, but I've been in freakin' lockdown all day. Angel and Paco are with me and they're playing bodyguard for the foreseeable future," he said, cutting off her rapid-fire line of questioning.

"But Frank, the Beacon—"

"Frank's already in the loop. I've hired a private security company, and they'll have the concert covered inside and out. Angel bought out the entire first row. Everyone will be either a friend or with the security team." Brett decided not to mention his date with Frank in the cage at Skylar's MMA studio when he got home to make up for his little disappearing act, or the twenty-five thousand dollar bonus he'd be paying him out of his own account.

"Shit," she said quietly.

"Rox, you've got to keep this out of the tabloids at all cost. I'm not kidding. And don't tell the band. I'm the only target."

"Got it. Will you be at the rehearsal tomorrow?"

"Yeah. Don't worry. I'll be there." There's no way the guys would play his three new tunes on Saturday night without it.

She blew out another stunned breath. "Okay. Let me know if you need anything else."

"I will, and sorry about the interview. My head's been somewhere else."

"I can't believe I'm saying this, but I understand. Next time, call me and… stay safe, King."

Brett turned his phone back off and tossed it into his duffel bag. Sighing, he looked around and noticed the artwork for the first time. He eyed it with appreciation. He was glad he'd called dibs on the bedroom behind Simon's studio, letting Paco take the guest room next to the master bedroom where Angel would sleep until Saturday night. Since Simon and Cara planned to stay at the loft after the party, he wanted to create as much physical space between him and them as possible. The last thing he needed was to overhear any vigorous lovemaking.

*What a fucking day.* When he'd seen Chloe bolt through the gate that afternoon, his heart had soared. He'd known Cara couldn't be far behind. Those few minutes they'd spent together before all hell broke loose had been great. He would've given anything just to have a few more of those minutes, enjoying her company in blissful ignorance rather than having his reality ripped right out from under him.

His brain was still on overdrive trying to figure out all the shit that had gone down today.

Constantina invited him to come with Cara and the others next week to a place she called the Sanctuary. According to her, what he'd learn there could change the current course of his life. He'd reserve judgment on that one. At least Michael had filled him in on some of the basics of what it would mean to be a Messenger once he went through the ceremony… if he went through the ceremony. Despite the insanity of it all, he wanted to learn more… about himself and his real father. What the hell. He had the time. He'd planned on taking a month off anyway after the concert. It wasn't like he had anything to lose. In all honesty, he hadn't felt this alive offstage for the last couple of years. Although, he could do without the near-death encounters, and a potential battle of biblical proportion.

Not to mention, he needed to get over this crazy attraction to Cara. The feel of her in his arms even for a few seconds this afternoon—wow. She made him feel safe and… wicked desirable. If only she weren't engaged…

He stared at the ceiling not tired in the least. Screw this. He hauled himself off the bed to do a "Louis and Clark" around the apartment.

Wandering into Simon's art studio, he snapped on the overhead light. Canvases of all sizes lined the walls in various stages of completion, some barely started, and some fully framed ready to be hung. Covered by a drape cloth, a large canvas rested on an easel positioned in front of an antique, one-armed daybed.

Brett peeled away the edge of the cloth, revealing a woman's arms poised over her head, languishing in a comfortable repose. A quick jerk and the cloth fluttered off the painting to the floor, unveiling a naked Cara lying in a seductive pose, her eyes filled with passion and promise for the painter.

Brett's heart rate spiked. This was the landscape he craved to have waiting for him in bed at night…

Like watching a train wreck, he couldn't look away. He studied the canvas, knowing this was as close as he'd ever get to seeing Cara naked. His breath caught, his eyes traveling over the painting, drinking her in. Breasts, full and beautiful with perfectly pink nipples, a waist curved in to narrow hips and a flat stomach. Lower, a perfectly manicured thatch of hair the color of autumn leaves led the way to what he could only imagine was a slice of heaven. Hands down, she was magnificent… and someone else's.

*The lucky bastard*, he thought. Too bad his timing was for shit. Fuck it; no use pining over another man's woman. He draped the cloth back over the canvas and snapped off the light.

With a heavy sigh, he made a beeline for the wine tower in the kitchen to grab a bottle of red, a glass, and a corkscrew before heading back to his room.

His intention was to drink enough to pass out and not dream about Cara lying naked in front of him.

# Chapter 18



*MICHAEL*
*Brooklyn, New York. Friday, May 24, 8:30* AM ET

MICHAEL DRAPES HIS ARM around Sienna, consoling her in the small recording studio inside the San Francisco safe house. He's taken her over to a small love seat, the only piece of furniture among the microphones and musical equipment. She feels so good, fragile, and warm, fitting against his chest like she belongs there. Instinctively, he tightens his arm around her delicate shoulders.

He brushes a piece of her silken black hair behind her ear, and tips up her chin to see if her tears are gone. He can't bear to see her cry. Her tears sidestep his defenses, resounding with the broken pieces of himself that he keeps securely hidden.

She lifts her gaze. Her sky-blue eyes, surrounded by wet spiky lashes, lock on his. His eyes drift down to her rosy lips, only inches from his. A single breath hangs in the air between them. Before he can think, he leans in and kisses her. At first, his lips melt softly into hers, and then, overtaken by an uncontrollable passion that has been building since they first met, he increases the pressure. His tongue parts her lips, hungrily deepening the kiss. Desire flares inside him like a flash fire, coursing through his veins with white-hot heat.

"Michael..." she moans, responding without hesitation. Michael draws her closer. Reaching down along the slender curve of her back, he presses her into the hard muscles of his chest. His breath comes in ragged pants as his desire suddenly overwhelms his senses, unleashing a primal urge inside him.

Without warning, every internal alarm sounds, freezing him in place. His inner voice screams that he isn't worthy—that he's damaged goods.

She cups his cheek, and her eyes graze his lips before licking her own. "I want you, Michael." Her free hand caresses the hollow of his spine above his backside, sending chills over his skin. His fingers clutch her silky hair with longing, releasing the scent of jasmine. More than anything, he wants to believe her.

*Coward*, he chides himself. *She'd never want you if she knew the truth.* The scent of cinnamon fills his senses, nearly crippling him with shame. He fights back hard with every fiber of his being.

*No, she's different*, another part of his brain counters. *It won't matter to her, you'll see. Prove you're worth something.*

"Are you sure?" he whispers and holds his breath.

Her fiery gaze locks on his and she kisses his lower lip. Nuzzling her cheek next to his, she whispers back. "More than you know."

Her warm breath on his ear sends a shiver down his spine, and the dam breaks inside him, flooding him with the courage to push down his debilitating doubt. His muscles relax. If this is what she wants, he was hers for the taking.

"I want you, too," he confesses, his voice deep and gravelly. Gently, he pushes her back onto the sofa and leans over her.

Her eyes are welcoming and filled with anticipation. Here like this—beautiful, desirable, and vulnerable—there isn't a man in his right mind who wouldn't fall all over her. He'll show her what she does to him and how much he wants her. He'll give her enough pleasure to erase her fears. Enough pleasure to keep her from looking too deeply inside of him.

No more thinking. He lifts the clingy, low-cut shirt over her head and tosses it to the floor. His breath hitches as he looks at her with yearning. He's denied himself for too long.

Reaching around, his fingers find the clasp on her bra and unhook it, releasing her firm breasts—perfect handfuls.

"You're so beautiful," he says quietly, glancing up to see the shy smile on her lips.

Her tanned nipples stand erect and waiting, calling for him to taste them. They should be savored, he thinks.

Glancing over at his wine, he dips his fingers into the glass. Dripping with a fine Sancerre, he reaches down and rolls the taut peaks between his wet fingers.

She closes her eyes and arches her back, moaning with pleasure. His groin fills and tightens.

He leans in and hungrily licks and sucks the wine from her breasts, kneading them with his fingers and passing his thumbs over the hard tips as his hands and mouth work in tandem. Her delicate skin tastes sweet on his tongue underneath the cool sharp taste of the wine.

She lets out a small cry and threads her fingers into his hair.

"I need to see the rest of you," he breathes. Leaning back, he pushes up her skirt and, in one fluid movement, removes her thong. His gaze slowly travels up her long, shapely legs before settling in between them.

"*Mmm.*" A sound of approval rises from his throat at the intoxicating sight of her. She is almost fully bare. He hasn't seen a woman with a Brazilian since he modeled. From this vantage point, he has a clear view to her delicious folds, wet and glistening, as they call out to him like a siren's song.

His erection swells to capacity, screaming for release from inside his jeans and threatening to exit through his waistband. He reaches down to his belt, but she's already there, unbuckling it with astounding speed.

Before he can react, she takes him firmly in her grasp, and her mouth engulfs him in warm bliss. His breath comes in panting gasps as his nerve endings nearly explode with need.

"No. Not yet." He moans low in his throat. Gathering every shred of control he has, Michael carefully extracts himself from her grip.

She shoves his clothes to his ankles. Stepping out of his pants, he kicks them aside and quickly removes his shirt.

A mixture of vulnerability and lust flashes in Sienna's eyes. "Take me, Michael, right now."

He's only too happy to comply. But he wants to taste her before he buries himself into her wet heat. Gently, he pushes her back onto the sofa.

Returning to his wine glass, he takes half a sip and dives down onto her, mixing the crisp wine with her wetness and drinking it. He revels in the silky softness of her inner thighs against his cheeks and her musky sweetness on his tongue as he explores her cleft and soft, sexy folds.

Her head drops back, and a curtain of black hair shimmers behind her. She cries out and grasps his shoulders. "Please, Michael, don't make me wait!"

The husky voice that rises from his throat surprises him. "I won't."

He shifts off the sofa and rises to stand, settling between her thighs. As she lies open to him, he wraps her legs around his hips and pulls her onto his swollen shaft. His body quivers the moment he enters her warmth. Wet and tight around him, he eases into her to ensure he doesn't hurt her before sinking himself in deep. The feeling blows his mind, turning him into a mass of pure sensation and forcing his eyes to clamp shut. His jaw goes slack and he releases a guttural sound of pleasure he doesn't recognize.

Afraid to come too quickly, Michael controls his thrusts, memorizing every silky contour. Sienna tightens her legs around his hips and coaxes him in faster. Picking up speed at her urging, his toes curl into the rug to keep him upright as his knees weaken with each satisfying stroke.

Head thrown back, a low growl escapes from his throat as the exquisite pressure of release mounts inside of him with each rock of his hips. His fingers firmly grasp her thighs, his forearms flexing with each inward thrust. He can't imagine Heaven feeling better than this. And right now, there's no place on earth he'd rather be than buried inside Sienna. He glances back down, meeting her heavy-lidded gaze as she watches him wearing a look of pleasure.

"I won't break. Don't hold back," she breathes. Her words almost snap his control.

Time to bring her home.

Still joined, he sinks back onto the sofa and positions her beneath him. Caressing her face with his fingertips, he traces a trail over her cheekbone and down over her soft, parted lips. Her beauty both stirs and inspires him. He presses his mouth to hers, their tongues meeting in a sensuous dance for a deep, penetrating kiss.

Breathless, he breaks away and grits his teeth, willing himself to hang on to seek out the spot he knows will drive her wild. Changing his angle with a small rotation of his hips, he hits home and smiles when she screams and her body pulses around him.

Something exhilarating and unfamiliar shifts inside of him.

Unable to hold back any longer, he slides his hands to her waist and increases his pace, surrendering to the moment. Thrusting fast and deep, his stomach muscles bunch with each stroke as her wet heat surrounds him in a tight handshake, setting his nerve endings ablaze in ecstasy. One last thrust and his thick shaft kicks wildly inside her as he explodes.

"Sienna!" he screams, not caring if the whole world hears him. His body shudders with pleasure for what feels like an eternity. Spent, he collapses down next to her, breathing hard.

Wearing a satisfied smile, she meets his eyes. "That was"—she gasps, trying to catch her breath—"amazing."

"You inspire me," he whispers back, his chest heaving. But that was only half true. More than inspire him, Sienna strips away his inhibitions and allows him to fully express himself without a care or worry. How she does that, he doesn't know, but he'll take it.

Closing his eyes, his lips find hers, needing to taste another kiss. Then he recognizes the unfamiliar feeling coursing through him... a feeling he hasn't experienced in more years than he wants to count.

Happiness.

The buzzing alarm clock shattered Michael's bliss-filled dream. He woke up covered in a thin layer of sweat with an unrelenting hard-on. Deep disappointment hit him in the chest—like it always did—after he dreamt of Sienna. What he'd do to make something like that real…

"Ugh," he mumbled, kicking off the wet, sticky sheets. He hoisted himself out of bed and padded naked down the hall toward the bathroom in search of a cold shower.

This made the sixth dream with Sienna in the San Francisco recording studio since their kiss eight weeks ago. The dreams usually ended at the moment of climax. This one he got to linger in the afterglow.

Too bad the hottest sex he'd ever had was while he was unconscious. Sienna may have provided a hot fantasy, but they were far from dating, much less having mind-blowing sex.

Michael grabbed a fresh towel from the hall closet, his dark brows drawn together in thought. He wished that he could actually let himself go like that in real life—without a care or hesitation. Or a condom.

What he'd told Simon was true: he was afraid to go there with her, or anyone for that matter. He wasn't ready to lay himself bare… he may never be. But he couldn't deny that he had enjoyed their kiss, which is all that ever happened. The dreams were another story. They took him to a place they could've gone had he not backed away. He wished… on second thought, better not to wish for something he may never be able to have.

Damn dreams. Because of them, the mere thought of her made him rock hard. He'd never experienced such a visceral reaction to a woman like he did with Sienna, conscious or unconscious. His super intelligent strategy? Avoiding her like a case of typhoid rather than dealing with it like an adult.

*What a jerk*, he thought with a shake of his head.

He turned the water to cold and jumped in, letting it chill his skin and kill his hard-on. Once his dick shrunk to half its normal size, he flipped the water over to hot.

He wasn't exactly sure what his problem was, per se, when it came to relationships. Well, maybe he did. He just didn't like admitting it. As long as nothing was expected of him—like with Cara—he was fine. Over the last couple of months, they had developed a very close friendship, which he'd welcomed. It was nice—refreshing even—and he didn't have to worry. She'd never fall in love with him or ask him for more than he could give. No use denying it— whenever a relationship headed toward commitment, he bolted. Not for lack of caring or an inability to love, but out of terror—overcome with his irrational fears that his secret would be exposed.

Michael drew in a breath and fought back the revolting smell of cinnamon that rose up to torment him. Squeezing his eyes shut, he willed away the shameful reminder. Would his past ever release him?

Anger gripped his gut. This never happened with the ones he didn't care about, the ones he dated under his "friends with benefits" policy. They knew the ground rules. Just sex. No commitments. No strings. For him, that meant no nightmares, no reminders of his past, just safe companionship.

Funny, he hadn't called any of his "friends" since he'd met Sienna.

Michael paused as he ran the soap over his chest.

Then again, it wasn't like he'd never had a relationship before. He'd had two. The first was with Deva, his high school girlfriend, now a friend and loyal employee. And a second with a girl named Cathy when he'd attended Yale. Both had ended with him hitting the self-destruct button.

He'd learned his lesson, sticking to nice girls who let him call the shots and ending things before he could fully risk getting found out.

He rubbed shampoo onto his hair, lathering it up. He'd been doing just fine until he'd met Sienna. Even with all the picking, prodding, and provoking she'd done during their trip to Connecticut back in March, he'd held his own until that morning on the porch… when she'd exposed his secret about his former modeling career and the Calvin Klein campaign to Cara.

It wasn't so much what she'd found, but how she'd used it against him, making him feel violated and ashamed of an accomplishment he'd been so proud of. And then when she'd called him "pretty boy," he'd almost snapped.

He sighed deeply, rinsed the shampoo out of his hair, and slapped on some conditioner.

As much as he wanted to avoid the mess he'd made with Sienna, the fact that she was Cara's best friend meant chances were good they'd continue to cross paths.

He blew out a breath. It was about time he manned-up and confronted her. He'd keep his promise to Cara and talk to Sienna at the party tomorrow night. Honestly, the thought of doing battle with a demon caused him less anxiety.

Turning off the water, Michael leaned over to grab the towel he'd placed on the rack. Glancing down, he frowned at his naked, well-endowed body. If he could only be sure he wouldn't be sporting wood the moment he saw her, he'd be just fine.

**_SIENNA_**

"Michael!" Sienna screamed, waking herself in the middle of a powerful orgasm.

_Why can't I have sex like that when I'm actually awake?_ she thought panting, and collapsed back against the pillow, deflated.

Ever since the kiss they shared in San Francisco, dreams of Michael provided nights of sweet torture. By her count, this was the sixth dream of them back in the recording studio. Too bad waking up meant dealing with reality and her hurt feelings.

Rather than keeping his promise to address what had happened, Michael had managed to sidestep any real conversation for their remaining time in San Francisco. Even so, something had changed between them after their encounter. A new respect and awareness, affection even, crackled between them. At least from her perspective. He'd barely left her side while Cara was unconscious in the hospital.

That's what made it so annoying. They had reached a truce, yet he'd treated her like a leper… for two solid months.

The corners of her mouth dropped into a pout. Why do men promise things that will make you happy and then take them away? Everyone was happy, why not her? Didn't she deserve to be happy?

She couldn't bear telling Cara about the dreams when they'd had lunch. If Cara hadn't pressed her, she wouldn't even have told her about the kiss. How could she admit that she'd been having wet dreams that had surpassed anything she'd ever experienced in real life, with a man who'd been avoiding her for months?

Let's just say, her lips were sealed. Well… at least one set of them.

Sienna closed her eyes and thought of the dream. Her heart skipped a beat and a rush of heat filled her lower body as she remembered Michael, moving himself deep inside of her and touching parts of her she'd never known existed.

The most shocking part wasn't the sex, but that Michael had given himself over to her so completely. In real life Michael was a little… um… uptight. Or more accurately, he had a major stick up his ass. But underneath his tenderness that night, she'd sensed a strong passion trying to break the surface. Would having sex with him in real life be as good as in her dreams?

Hell if she knew. The only thing she could be sure of was that she'd be seeing him tomorrow night at Cara and Simon's party.

She'd make sure she looked extra hot and bring her best game. Even if he didn't speak to her the entire evening, he sure would know that she was there.

# Chapter 19



*ACHANELECH*

*France. Château du Feu. Friday, May 24, 2:00 PM GMT +1*

"WHAT CAN I DO FOR YOU, Master?" Achanelech warily eyed his visitor from across his desk.

Luc Morningstar smiled pleasantly at him from his chair. One leg crossed over his knee, he clutched a jeweled staff planted vertically next to him. Achanelech gave Luc's staff a brief glance, but he had more pressing matters to worry about than the smoldering hole it would leave behind in the antique Aubusson rug covering the library floor.

Quite the handsome Devil, Luc was finely dressed in a Savile Row suit with his sleek, black hair pulled back into a ponytail. He had a handsome face worthy of female attention… until you looked into his eyes. Appearing black, they blazed a deep red more often than not.

He hadn't seen Lucifer *topside* parading in human form lately, and wondered about the nature of his visit. After he'd phoned in the names of the Twelve garnered from their source, he'd expected some peace and quiet while plotting his next move.

"Can't an old friend drop in for a visit?" Luc asked with a brilliant, white smile.

How Achanelech wished that were true. Old, yes. Friend, no. Suppressing a shudder, fiery discomfort crackled over his skin with the memory of their last encounter in April. Lucifer hadn't been wearing the attractive guise of Luc then; rather, he'd been in demon form with full scales and red skin—the creature of nightmares.

The meeting had been far from social. He had the healing scars to prove it.

"Don't think me rude to assume that this is more than a casual visit," Achanelech replied, unable to stop the involuntary twitch of his eyelid. "Have you an assignment for me and Em?"

A tendril of dread coiled around him. He wanted nothing more than to be left alone to continue his convalescence with Emanelech while his plan to capture Cara Collins came to fruition.

"Nothing like that," Luc said, his eyes flashing red. "I want you to host... a party."

"What kind of party?" he asked slowly, immediately suspicious. When Luc held a party, Achanelech wasn't typically invited.

"More like a business meeting really," he said. "I think the time has come to formulate our execution plan."

Achanelech's stomach dropped. "Why me?"

A hiss escaped Luc as he shot out of his chair and lunged across the deck, his hand clasping Achanelech by the throat. "Because you're the idiot who forced our hand with the Angelorum," he said, breaking into Hellspeak.

Achanelech felt the force of Luc's grip nearly crush his windpipe as he choked for air. Stars danced in front of his bulging eyes as he fought for breath.

"Any more stupid questions?" Luc asked calmly, his head tilted to the side.

Tearing at Luc's hand, Achanelech gasped a nearly inaudible "No."

"Good." Luc replied and released him. Achanelech fell back into his seat with a thump, while Luc returned to his relaxed position across the desk.

Achanelech picked up a pen in his unsteady hand. "When would you like to have it?"

"Soon."

*So much for peace and quiet,* Achanelech thought with a painful swallow. "Do you have a guest list that I can reference?" he rasped.

"All of them. Invite them all for a little strategy meeting."

Achanelech paled. "You want a Convocation?" Not just any strategy meeting. Lucifer wanted him to host all of Lucifer's Thirteen Lieutenants—a thankless endeavor at minimum. After the last Convocation held four hundred years ago in Rome, the hosting Lieutenant spent a decade recovering. Then there was the cost and potential unwanted attention. The capture of food alone would require full-time help, and there were only so many bodies that could be hidden in and around Paris in this day and age without raising suspicion.

That's if they didn't destroy each other first.

With that much pride and envy under the same roof—not to mention a heavy representation of the other deadly sins—anything could happen.

Luc glared at him. "Exactly."

"Yes, Master." Lowering his head, he jotted down some notes.

*Em's going to have a herd of Holsteins when she hears this*, he thought, using the latest phrase Em had taught him in an effort to modernize his vernacular. She hadn't felt up to guests, and having Lucifer's Thirteen in their midst would be nothing short of harrowing. He didn't know which he feared more—Em's wrath or the Convocation. But his refusal would only spell his demise.

Luc leaned his staff up against the desk and tented his fingers. "Anything new from our source?"

"Nothing since the names and their estimated arrival," Achanelech said.

*Cling-clang-clong.* The door chime echoed off the high plaster ceilings of the château. A shudder rolled through him. "I'm not expecting anyone," he muttered, not meaning to speak aloud. None of his invited guests used the front door.

Flashing a smile and checking his watch, Luc picked up his staff and tapped it into the rug eliciting a *hiss* followed by the smell of burning wool. "I am… and they're right on time."

A few moments later, Achanelech's personal butler entered escorting the unexpected guests. Achanelech bit back a gasp behind an impassive face as he watched Escher Grant, the only one of the Thirteen with whom he maintained a mutually beneficial unholy alliance, walk into the room. More shocking, standing by his side was Achanelech's pet Nephil. No longer wearing white slave garments, his Nephil stood tall and proud, draped from head to toe in black leather—a sharp contrast with his light coloring.

"Escher! So good of you to come when called," Luc sneered, popping up out of his chair.

As impeccably dressed as Luc in custom tailoring, Escher could easily blend into a crowd of London bankers. With short dark hair, piercing green eyes, and a British accent, females dropped at his feet. But that only suited him if they were willing to play in his sadistic dungeon.

Escher bowed at the waist and gave a brief tip of his head. "But of course," he replied in a pinched upper-class accent.

Luc swept his hand to the chairs in front of the desk. "Sit. We have a few things to discuss."

Achanelech tracked his Nephil as it trailed behind Escher. "My pet has behaved well under your care?"

Escher gave him a tight smile. "Very. As a matter of fact, while we've been waiting for more information from your source, Samuel has been gathering an inordinate amount of intelligence on our enemy."

"Samuel?" Achanelech asked, confused. "Who's Samuel?"

Escher snorted. "Acchie, you really are a wanker, you know that?" He pointed at the hulking Halfling standing with his eyes averted behind him. "Your Nephil, you idiot. You've had him for a hundred and fifty years, and you still don't know his bloody name? Or is it that you just choose not to use it?"

Heat rose in Achanelech's fingers until they snapped and sizzled. He pointed at Escher and threw a bolt of white fire. "Show some respect under my roof. Since when have you developed a love of lesser creatures?"

Escher's palm shot up to block the attack, the heat turning to mist. "You'll have to do better than that, old boy. And I've never supported cruelty to animals," he said with a glint in his eye and a knowing smile. He winked. "You know I have a penchant for blonds." Achanelech cringed at the thought, knowing more than he wanted to about Escher's penchants.

"Children, stop arguing," Luc snapped. "We have more important things to discuss." His eyes bore into Achanelech. "Like how you've managed to attract even more attention to our revenue sources in the United States."

Achanelech's mouth went dry, his forked tongue sticking to the back of his bottom teeth. His tongue was the only thing beside his clawed toes that he couldn't seem to wrestle into human form. "What do you mean?" he squeaked.

"Congratulations. You managed to alert the NSA and put yourself at the top of their terrorist watch list."

"How did I do that?" Achanelech blurted.

"The warehouse in Menlo Park. It was compromised," Luc glared.

*More like blown to High Hell*, he thought. "But-but-but," he sputtered. "I haven't been there in months! How do we know that it's true?"

"I ate the soul of one of their agents, you imbecile!" Luc slammed his hand on the desk, his eyes blazing red. "So, not only must we hide our activities from the Angelorum, now we need to elude the NSA. The last thing I need is human intervention in demonic matters. I should kill you now, but the pleasure would be too short-lived," he spat and waved his hand at Escher. "That's why I asked Escher here. He will take over your North American operations in addition to the research projects he's already managing for you."

Achanelech's jaw dropped. "Wait, but—"

His internal calculator rang up the monumental losses this could mean from his personal coffers, and the resulting debt he would incur to Luc. He'd be bankrupt in no time.

"No *buts*. I need you out of the limelight, and somewhere like here where you can't do any more damage. What better than making you my personal events coordinator?" he said with an evil red shine in his eyes.

A million other things came to Achanelech's mind. Despair wrapped like a noose around his neck.

"Escher, give us an update before I do something rash." Luc ground his staff on the floor and glowered at Achanelech. More burnt wool and an accompanying sizzle.

Escher clasped his hands together and sat back in his chair. A smug smile spreads across his face. "I think I'll have Samuel give it."

Achanelech narrowed his eyes, trying not to react to Escher's goading.

Samuel looked up, his crystal-blue eyes hard and uncompromising.

*My, how my Nephil abomination has changed over these last two months*, he thought. Escher must've been telling the truth and taken him on as a lover, given his elevated rank and fine clothes. Escher was nothing if not equal opportunity when it came to choosing his playmates.

Samuel glanced at Luc. "At your request, Master, we launched a surprise attack on the rock star just to shake things up and throw them off track of our true intent." The Nephil's deep melodic voice grated on Achanelech's nerves to the point that he hungered for violence.

He continued, "As expected, the attack was thwarted by the Guardianship." A euphemistic way of saying one of his demon minions was used as a throwaway on a fake attack. Achanelech's anger rose, his hands clenching into fists under his desk. At least now he knew why they'd borrowed some of his demons.

"What about the Collins girl? What of her transformation?" Luc asked with an impatient wave of his hand.

"Nothing unusual yet," said Samuel. "No invisibility, no appearance of wings, nothing obvious that points to her being anything but human at this point."

"Then we're no closer to battle," Luc said. His eyes bore into Achanelech. "Are you sure that the scientist used the Nephilim vaccine to save her?"

*Of course he wasn't sure!* The vaccine had failed to turn Achanelech's three test subjects; why would it turn the girl? Regardless, he gave the only answer he knew he could get away with, "*Yessss*," he hissed.

"Doesn't matter," Escher piped up. "One of our other labs should have a vaccine version ready for mass production within a week. She'll transform into a Nephilim one way or another."

"Excellent. Better if it's on my schedule than theirs," Luc said, and stood up. "Before I go, you," he said, pointing to the Nephil with his staff, "go back and keep watch over the girl until we're ready to take her. She's the only one that matters right now. And throw a few more red herrings at them to keep them chasing their tails." Then he turned to Escher. "You—get rid of the bloody NSA, and get me my Nephilim army."

Finally, with a parting glance at Achanelech, Luc said, "I'll have my secretary send you the list of what I want for the Convocation. And one last thing: don't screw up this time or your last visit will feel like a trip to the spa."

Achanelech gulped and watched the trio head for the door with a pit of dread in his stomach. He needed to rethink his plan to capture Cara Collins, and fast. If Luc managed to seize her before she'd made it to France his chance to regain his position would be lost.

Some days, it just didn't pay to get out of bed. Even for a demon.

# Chapter 20



*CARA*

*New York City. Fifth Avenue Penthouse. Friday, May 24, 9:30* AM ET

CARA STOOD IN HER walk-in closet, admiring the new additions to her wardrobe. At least today she had some decent clothes to wear. Gretchen had come through for her with a fantastic selection of designer merchandise in the next three sizes. Her bag lady fashion statement from yesterday was already boxed and ready for donation to Goodwill.

She flipped through the hangers and chose a simple, short-sleeved Calvin Klein top and a pair of True Religion jeans, and then pulled out a new pair of Manolo Blahnik low-heeled sandals from her shoe rack.

Clothed in her new designer togs, she did a slow spin in front of the mirror and let out a sigh of relief. Everything fit perfectly. Too bad the clothes did nothing to hide the dark circles under her eyes.

Cara yawned, still exhausted and recovering from Simon's "expressing" his relief over her safety after the demon incident—twice. Moments into their postcoital snuggle, Cara was asleep wrapped in Simon's arms. They'd gone traditional—no blanket of wings last night, only the covers on the bed. Even Cara's growing pains hadn't kept her awake. Other than reciprocating Simon's soft kiss, she'd barely woken when he'd left this morning.

But Simon's expression of relief wasn't all that had kept her from having a good night's sleep. The voice from her Calling had invaded her dreams again last night. The words in the angelic language still echoed in her head—the ones whispered to her during her confrontation with Le Feu, giving her the strength to taunt him.

Last night, the moment she'd heard the words, the memories that hung at the fringes of her consciousness came rushing back in one giant burst. Details from that night filled the gaps in her memory: the knife as it pierced her side; her relief at blocking it from killing Kai; her short-lived death that followed… In the end, it hadn't changed much. But the haunting words continued to niggle at her. She just wished she understood what they meant. Another puzzle to solve later.

This morning definitely warranted a caffeine boost stronger than anything she had in the kitchen. *Starbucks Triple Espresso, here I come,* she thought.

At least today would be less hectic than yesterday. Even Chloe was taken care of: Simon had dropped her off at doggie daycare on his way to take Constantina to the airport before meeting Michael.

Wandering into the bathroom, she brushed her hair up and corralled it into a ponytail.

Topping her list today was checking in on Brett. After lunch she'd drop by his rehearsal at the Beacon under the guise of picking up the concert tickets and all-access passes. A lot had been dumped on him yesterday, and she wanted to make sure he was okay without making a big deal out of it.

She feathered on some blush and smiled at her reflection. *Plenty of time to get back before Jessa and Irene arrived for dinner.*

Grabbing her backpack, she stuffed in her workout clothes, cell phone, wallet, and keys and then zipped it up. She was ready to go. With her change in lifestyle, she'd long since abandoned handbags during the day, reserving them for more formal occasions.

Cara left the penthouse and wove her way through the maze under the building, exiting several buildings away—an added security feature of her living arrangement.

The day promised to be sunny and warm, not a drop of rain in the forecast. Her spirit lightened with the perfect morning weather despite her serious need for caffeine. With a spring in her step, she headed straight for Starbucks, conveniently located on Eighty-Seventh Street on the way to the subway.

Blending into the crowd, Cara lost herself in the flow of bodies. Cars and trucks lumbered past her, trailing clouds of exhaust while she competed for sidewalk space with pedestrians in work clothes and nannies pushing strollers. As Cara passed a bakery, the aroma of freshly baked goods wafted out in greeting. Her Nephilim hunger flared. The two bananas she'd wolfed down on her way out obviously weren't enough. Maybe she'd treat herself to a slice of cake with her cup of coffee… and an egg sandwich. Her stomach grumbled. Make that two egg sandwiches.

After missing yesterday's workout, Cara looked forward to her session with Michael and Simon. Over the past two months, she'd come a long way, able to hold her own in a fight—with or without a weapon.

A *pling* sounded from inside her backpack. Reaching inside, she pulled out her cell to see a text from Kai: MELANIE IS SAFE. WORKING ON CLOSING THE PORTAL FOR GOOD. EXPECT TO ARRIVE SUN OR MON.

His message filled Cara with relief. She hoped Kai was more at ease now than when she'd spoken to him briefly after dinner last night. His distress had been palpable. She didn't know which was worse—his guilt or his fear.

Cara's head snapped up from the small screen at the sound of tires screeching and burnt rubber filling the air, followed by the hard thump of flesh meeting the metal of a car hood.

Fifteen yards away, a man lay bleeding next to a mangled bicycle in front of a taxi. Cara stuffed her phone in her backpack and ran, pushing her way through the crowd forming around him.

A foreign man in his early twenties lay on the ground at her feet; a courier based on his shirt's logo and the scattered packages surrounding him.

Cara quickly surveyed the damage. His torso and head were covered in blood, and his right leg lay at an odd angle. His panicked eyes caught hers as he slipped into shock and his energy ebbed.

In a split-second decision, Cara dropped to her knees beside him. She'd try to heal him, or at least keep him alive until an ambulance arrived.

The taxi driver stood nearby, holding his head in his hands and screaming in a language she didn't understand. Someone from the crowd tried to calm him while five or six concerned faces looked on.

One woman kindly asked her, "Is there anything I can do to help?" Whoever said New Yorkers were uncaring must have been standing on another street corner.

"Call 911," Cara directed before launching into her silent opening prayer, calling the Flow down to her. She felt the familiar sensation as it crashed down through the crown of her head, traveling around her heart and radiating out of her hands.

She said an extra prayer to cover the light show that would accompany her healing, but there was nothing she could do about the pulse of energy that would fly across people's skin in a sharp breeze.

Her hands hovered over the injured man. As her skills had advanced, she'd found that she no longer needed full contact to transfer the healing energy. It offered her a less invasive option for strangers.

The bright, white light threw out a ring of power ten feet in diameter, pushing the crowd back and enveloping Cara and the man inside.

"Close your eyes," she whispered. As if in a trance, he complied.

Cara cycled energy through him and watched his injuries heal. The gashes on the man's chest closed and his leg straightened, mending correctly as if never broken. The scrapes on his face and chest disappeared, leaving behind a look of serenity on his face.

And then it got quiet… too quiet. With a start, Cara noticed the world stood frozen outside her ring of power.

"You really shouldn't have done that," said a calm voice behind her.

Cara gasped and looked over her shoulder. A young man dressed in a bright, white tunic and pants walked up and stood next to her. Well, not exactly a man on account of the white, high-arching wings folded behind him.

Cara rose.

His eyes, an intense purple, were the first thing she noticed. Not a color she'd ever seen in nature, and one she'd not soon forget. His gaze locked on hers. His dark hair and medium build made him handsome enough, but his eyes… they were beautiful and hypnotic. She shook her head to break away from their pull.

"Who are you?" Cara asked, stepping back.

He stared, expressionless. "I'm Jonas, but I don't think that's relevant. Has no one explained the rules?"

Cara felt a chill traverse her spine. "What rules?"

"The rules of noninterference," he said, his voice taking on a patronizing tone as if speaking to a naughty school girl.

"What are you talking about?" Cara asked, knitting her brows in confusion. A quick glance confirmed the world outside her power ring was still frozen in eerie silence.

*Did Jonas do that?* It sure as heck wasn't something she could do.

Clasping his hands together in front of him and rocking back on his heels, he cleared his throat signaling a lecture was forthcoming. "Your power is a gift to use in the battle against our common enemy. You're prohibited from changing a human's destiny outside of the Fight. You mustn't interfere with free will."

Cara frowned, continuing to bristle at his tone. "How is saving someone's life interfering with their free will? Did this guy purposely ride his bike in front of the taxi? Did he ask for this? Are you telling me I'm not allowed to help people?" She planted her hands on her hips. "*Who* did you say you were again?"

This time he smiled, breathing life into his otherwise expressionless visage. "I like your spunk. I can't answer your question on the man's intent, but what I can tell you is that *I* was supposed to be here. A better question for you to ask would be: *what* am I?"

That one took her by surprise. She tipped her chin at his wings. "You're not Nephilim?"

"Most certainly not," he said, looking mildly offended.

"Okay, I'll bite. What are you?"

Keeping his hands clasped in front of him, he moved a step closer. In response, Cara moved a step back.

"I'm a Transporter. You might be more familiar with the term *reaper* but it has such a negative connotation, don't you think?"

Cara cocked her eyebrow. "You're kidding, right? Where's your black cape and scythe?"

He glowered at her, his eyes taking on a darker shade of purple. "My point exactly. Although I collect the souls of the dying and transport them to their final destination, I also deliver the souls of the newly born. It's a two-way transportation system, you know."

Not what she expected, but now suspecting why he was here.

"Sorry, I'm the last person who should be casting stones," she said, backing down. She glanced down at the man on the ground. He seemed to be in much better shape. "So, did I save his life?" she asked, and turned back to Jonas.

"That you did," he replied, his face again expressionless, apparently over her quip about the cape.

She sighed. "And he was supposed to die?"

His features softened. "That he was."

Cara carefully avoided looking directly into his hypnotic purple eyes. Something about them made her nervous. "I changed his destiny?"

"Yes."

Cara huffed in frustration, crossing her arms over her chest. "How could I just let someone die?" The answer was that she couldn't. Another item to add to her list of questions for Constantina. Then it struck her. "Wait, who's our common enemy?"

With an unexpected and kind smile, he answered, "We're not so very different, Cara Collins, but merely separated by the skin of humanity. We both serve the same God and share a spark of the divine."

Hearing her name pass through Jonas's lips was jarring. At least she knew why he hadn't asked. He'd already known.

"How do you know me?" she asked.

"We all know you," he said, and then spoke the angelic words she'd heard in her dreams.

"Hold on! What does that mean—what you just said?"

His face dropped back into an emotionless mask. Cara found his lack of expression unnerving.

"It mean's God's Sacred Healer… among other things," he replied cryptically.

A ripple of energy passed over Cara's skin.

Jonas's head snapped right then left as he looked around with sudden agitation. "I must go. I cannot hold time still any longer."

"Will I see you again?" Cara asked, not nearly finished with her list of questions.

His eyebrows lifted in answer. "You owe me a soul," he said and disappeared.

Sound assaulted Cara's ears with a *whoosh* as time resumed and her ring of power evaporated. An ambulance wailed in the distance and people gasped in awe as they looked down at the man, transformed, but still unconscious.

Before Cara could process Jonas's parting shot, she was pulled backward off her feet and pressed securely into a large muscular body behind her then propelled forward and carried like a football toward the end zone.

"Miss Collins, sorry to manhandle you, but Chamuel would kill me if anything were to happen to you," said an accented female voice behind her.

One of her new Guardians was a woman? Even so, she felt like a man.

"We're cloaked?" Cara asked, feeling like chattel but thankful she wasn't being hauled away in a fireman's carry, butt to the sky.

"Of course," the Guardian replied.

*Great.* She'd just disappeared in front of a crowd of people. At least no one could hear them speak behind the veil of invisibility. *So much for feeling normal today*, Cara thought.

"May I suggest a cab from here to the dojo?" the female voice asked as she swiftly carried her through the pedestrians on the sidewalk.

"That's not going to be easy strapped to your chest like an invisible, oversized doll," Cara's tone was less friendly than she meant it to be. "Sorry, I'm just a little shaken up. What's your name?"

"Chamuel gave us strict instructions to remain unseen. I doubt he would be pleased if I told you my name," she stated.

"I'm sorry, but that's just dumb." Cara snapped. "I'll take care of Chamuel. What's your name?"

The Guardian hesitated, finally answering, "Valeria."

"That's a beautiful name," Cara said.

"That is very kind of you to say," Valeria replied, followed by a tiny burst of caramel on Cara's tongue indicating her pleasure at the compliment.

They stopped a few blocks away, and Valeria set her down, keeping one hand on her shoulder. The moment Valeria released her, Cara would be outside of the veil and Valeria would remain invisible.

Cara had never met a female Nephil, given their rarity—only one in twelve births. She wanted to see one.

"I sensed two of you. Is my other Guardian here, too?" Cara asked to distract her already knowing the answer. In one deft movement, she clutched Valeria's hand and turned around before the other woman could react. They both gasped as Cara stared up into the face of a beautiful woman sporting Amazonian proportions with high cheekbones and bright blue eyes, her hair held in a high, dark ponytail. Cara stood frozen staring with wide eyes, taking in her Guardian.

Her uniform was standard-issue black like the males', but rather than a T-shirt and cargos, she wore tight-fitting pants and a matching tank. The only thing that was the same was the weapons belt around her waist. Valeria must have left her duster home. Small breasted and standing over six feet tall, Cara could picture her as one of Sienna's models sashaying down the catwalk during Fashion Week... until she looked at her arms. They were solid, carved muscle. Valeria looked like she could bench press a Volkswagon. Cara couldn't help but wonder if she was staring at her future self.

"You shouldn't have done that," Valeria said with a panicked look in her eye. "Chamuel will be angry that you've seen me."

Cara closed her slack jaw. "I won't tell him. I promise."

Tension drained from Valeria's bunched shoulders. "To answer your question: yes. She's been traveling with us. But I can't tell you her name. I'm sorry."

*Two women! What the hell?!* She wondered how Isaac and Simon had pulled that off with so few women in the Guardianship. They must've been transferred in from other units.

A thought struck her and raised her ire. Didn't Simon trust other men to guard her? Didn't he trust her? No wonder he wouldn't tell her their names! Did he really think she wouldn't find out?

"I understand. But you have to report this incident to him, correct?"

"Yes, I'm afraid so," she replied.

"Which was what exactly? A demon?"

Valeria cleared her throat and shifted in her steel-toed boots. "No. Something worse... death. I felt death. I'm not sure... It's only happened to me a few times in the last one hundred years." She shook her head, and looked away. "I'm sorry. I don't mean to scare you with my old Ukrainian superstitions."

Since Jonas had appeared flaunting "wing" within her ring of power, chances were high he couldn't be seen by anyone but her. "Thou shalt not expose feather in public" was most likely as staunchly upheld as the noninterference rule he had berated her for. Still, she asked, "You didn't happen to see anyone else standing nearby dressed in white, did you?"

Valeria paled, her eyes once again reflecting fear. "Oh no, did I miss something?"

*Not really*, she thought. Theoretically, Jonas was in fact an angel of death. But she would keep that nugget to herself until she had time talk it over with Michael and Simon. Cara pushed calming energy into Valeria. "No. It's not important," Cara said gently. "Everything's fine."

She heard Valeria exhale slowly. "Okay, you can let go of my hand now. We'll follow the taxi."

Cara released her and reappeared near the street corner. No one seemed to notice she hadn't been there a second before. She stepped out into the street to hail a cab to Brooklyn when it occurred to her: *Shit.* She'd never gotten her Starbucks.

# Chapter 21

*CARA*

***Brooklyn, New York. Rising Sun Dojo. Friday, May 24, 11:00 AM ET***

CARA WALKED INTO THE DOJO forty minutes late balancing three cups of coffee, her backpack, and a bag filled with four egg sandwiches. Two for her and only one for each of the guys since they'd already had breakfast.

When she'd sent a text to Simon and Michael earlier, she'd let them know there had been a bit of an incident and she'd explain when she arrived. No doubt, Valeria had already reached Simon.

No sooner had she opened the front door than Michael grabbed the food and Simon sweep her up into his arms. Michael looked on as he deposited breakfast onto a nearby table, wearing a look of concern.

"Are you all right?" Simon whispered into her hair, holding her in a Nephilim death grip inside his arms, her feet dangling above the ground, his fear buzzing over her.

"I'm fine," she squeaked, "You're suffocating me." Startled, he promptly loosened his grip, allowing her lungs to fill with air and her feet to touch the ground.

She gave him a quick kiss on the lips. "I was never in danger. Honestly. I'll fill you both in. But let me change first, so we can get started afterward, okay?"

They only had until one o'clock before Michael's first class, and she wanted to get in at least a sixty-minute session. Simon released her and she picked up her backpack, which had fallen to the floor when he'd pulled her into his embrace.

Simon nodded without speaking, his fear ratcheting down a few notches.

"I received the strangest vision." Michael's voice was tense. "So, I'm eager to hear your story." The subtext in his statement was clear. Michael's personal control didn't usually extend to patience on investigating important information, so she was proud of him for keeping "radio silence" instead of grilling her using their telepathic link. It gave her some time to mull over her encounter with Jonas and try to make some sense of it.

Cara turned and grabbed Michael's hand, giving it a gentle squeeze. "Thanks for not bombarding me on the way over."

He squeezed her hand back and smiled.

"I'll meet you both in the weapons area in five minutes." She pointed to the food. "Don't let that get cold. Just leave me two."

She headed to the locker room to put on her *gi*, and then met them back in the center of the floor with her breakfast.

"Before I tell my story, maybe Michael should share his vision," Cara suggested, easing herself down onto the mat and tucking into the bag.

Simon and Michael sank to the floor to join her.

Michael took a deep breath. "I saw you run to the accident and call down your ring of power. Then you dropped off the grid for a full five minutes. You came back on when the Guardian grabbed you and pulled you away from the scene." There was no mistaking his distress or the taste of his guilt.

Setting aside her sandwich, she grabbed his wrist and gave him a reassuring smile. "I'm fine, Michael. You can't be in two places at once. That's why I have a whole team of Guardians, remember?" Michael's job as her Messenger wasn't to protect her, but to provide a conduit of information between their Trinity and the Angelorum. Just because he could kick ass didn't mean he was required to save hers.

After draining her coffee cup to wash down her egg and cheese on a roll times two, she recounted her story of how she had saved the bicycle messenger and her encounter with Jonas—most of it.

Simon's eyes went wide at the mention of his name. "You met Jonas?"

"You know him?" Cara asked, relieved and eager to learn more.

"I know of him," he replied with trepidation.

Michael looked puzzled. "Not me. Never heard of the Transporters other than the common myths. It wasn't part of my Angelorum training."

Simon shook his head. "It wouldn't be. It's Advanced Angelology and required only for Guardians. The Transporters are a suborder of angels. Unless you're about to die, you shouldn't see them. Jonas is their leader."

A tingling sensation traveled down Cara's spine. "So… why did I see him? He wasn't there for me; he was there for the courier."

"And he was inside your ring of power?"

"Yup," she confirmed.

Simon furrowed his brow. "And time stopped?"

Cara shrugged. "Apparently. Except for me and Jonas. And possibly Michael, since he tracked me in elapsed time through our psychic link."

Michael's brows furrowed in thought while Simon spoke slowly. "Yes, that part makes sense. The Transporters can only be seen by those individuals who have the sight to see the spirits of the dead. Jonas's revealing himself is what I find puzzling."

A tingle spread across Cara's scalp. "Do you think that I have the ability to see dead people?"

"If you did, you would've known by now. I believe it could be a combination of things."

"Like what?" Michael asked.

Simon let out a deep breath, his blue eyes flecked with worry. "He wanted to meet her, beyond admonishing her. There's no other reason for the leader of the Transporters to work a common assignment. But he had to wait for the right opportunity, so he could manipulate time using her ring of power. The question is why? What does either of them have to gain from this exchange?"

"I think I've gained something. He repeated the words to me that I've been hearing in my dreams," Cara said.

The furrow between Simon's eyebrows grew deeper. "You've been hearing voices in your dreams? You never told me that."

Cara winced, finding it hard to miss the hurt in his voice. True, she hadn't told him. She hadn't told anyone. "Sorry," she said, giving him an apologetic look. "I've been having dream fragments of the night we rescued Kai. Little bits have come back slowly, but this morning they flooded back all at once."

Then it clicked. "Wait! I have seen someone who died," she blurted, evoking curious stares from Simon and Michael.

"When was this?" Simon asked.

"I remembered this morning that I died for those few minutes while Kai performed CPR. I saw my grandma Hannah at the gates of Heaven. Does that count?"

Simon's lips parted and Michael blinked before they exchanged a quizzical look. "Could be," Simon said. "What are the words you've been hearing?"

"I don't know how to say them. They were spoken in the angelic language," Cara said, her shoulders slumping. Identifying the language wasn't a problem for her ear, but speaking it was another skill entirely.

Michael piped up. "If you think of the dream, can you hear the words in your head?"

"Yeah, but I just can't make those sounds with my throat."

Michael gave her a Cheshire Cat grin then looked at Simon whose mouth formed a slow smile. "You thinking what I'm thinking?"

"You bet."

Cara looked at them like she'd been left out of a joke. "What?"

"Hold hands," Michael said, and then it hit her. *Duh.* They could link their gifts via the Trinity. Michael and Simon could speak the angelic language even though she couldn't. Her hands disappeared inside theirs.

"Just remember the dream the way you would speak to us telepathically," Michael said.

She remembered the words from the dream, and then for good measure pulled up a snippet of Jonas repeating them before dropping their hands.

Michael and Simon sat pale faced with their mouths agape when she finished. Simon mumbled something in the angelic language then did something she'd never seen him do—he made the sign of the cross over himself.

Michael's eyes shifted from Simon to Cara.

Her mouth went dry, their reactions sending a shiver over her skin. "You're both scaring me. Jonas said it meant God's Sacred Healer," she said, panicked.

"That's not all it means," Simon whispered while Michael just looked ill.

Cara swallowed to wet her parched throat. "Tell me."

Simon took her hand in his, locking his gaze on her. "It means, God's Sacred Healer, Mother of Souls, and Killer of the Morning Star. It means..." he paused and cleared his throat. "The last part means two things: you're the warrior prophesied to kill the Morning Star, and in turn, the Morning Star is the only one who can kill you."

"But—"

Simon held up a finger to signal for her to let him continue. "I'm sure that Le Feu wasn't too pleased when you jumped in front of the knife to save Kai. Although he technically didn't disobey the Morning Star's order not to kill you, but if you had died... I can't believe it would have gone well for him. It also explains why there haven't been any attacks on you since San Francisco. It means they'll focus on the rest of the Twelve, since you're off limits."

Good and bad news. Fear coalesced in Cara's stomach, hardening into a tight ball. "The first time I remember hearing those words was during my confrontation with Le Feu at the warehouse. They were whispered by the voice from my Calling,"

Cara said. "I guess that's why I wasn't afraid." *And that must be why Brett was attacked,* she thought. "But, wait. Does this mean I can't be killed at all or it's just the Dark Ones who aren't permitted to kill me?"

Simon's eyes darkened. "Not sure. The prophecy's unclear but my guess is the latter—you can still be killed, just not by them. As a Nephil, your powers to heal are greatly increased, but you can still be killed."

It didn't make Cara feel any better. She couldn't imagine anything worse than Lucifer himself coming after her. Unlike Simon, her Nephilim DNA hadn't erased her ability to feel temperature. The chill of the air conditioning raised the hairs on her arms and she shuddered. "I don't understand what this all means," she whispered.

Simon started to speak, but Michael put his hand on Simon's arm to stop him. "The prophecy says that in the final battle, an avenging angel will engage the Morning Star and ultimately defeat him. The assumption has always been that the angel would be the Archangel Michael with Uriel and his order backing him. Almost like a rematch. Since the Archangel Michael cast him out during the Fall he was the logical assumption."

Cara eyes grew wide and her body felt limp. During her training with Constantina she'd learned all about the Great Fall, Michael, and Uriel's role within the Angelorum. Uriel, in addition to leading the 9th Order of Angels, the Powers, was the angelic sponsor of the entire Angelorum protectorate. His order of angels provided the last defense against attack in Heaven, so they were the perfect choice to father the warrior Nephilim who made up the Guardianship.

Simon took Cara's hand. "If you're the avenging angel then one point is clear. If any of the Dark Ones cause your death they forfeit the battle. The same is true of our side. No one but the avenging angel can engage the Morning Star." The civilized rules of engagement strike again.

"I'm only human with a little Nephilim DNA thrown in for good measure. I don't even have wings." Cara's shoulders slumped, her voice reflecting a flash of despair.

Simon gathered her up in his strong arms. "We'll consult with Constantina and figure this all out. Don't worry, love. The road ahead is still long, and there is much to learn. I'd never let you go into battle alone."

Michael placed his hand on her shoulder and squeezed. "Neither would I."

Conviction blazed in their eyes with a loving energy. It touched her heart.

"Thank you." She smiled. "I love you both. Enough self-pity," she said, and wriggled out of Simon's grasp. "We have some work to do. Let's do a cleansing prayer and start our session. We'll have time to think on this later," she said, refusing to let this surreal revelation paralyze her.

*Bloody hell. What else I am going to have to deal with?*

They joined hands, and Cara did her thing, channeling the power down and bathing them in a bright, cleansing light that left them calm and invigorated.

"I'll get the knives," Simon volunteered, heading over to the weapons cabinet.

Her mind flashed back to Valeria, and riding atop a sudden surge of PMS-like moodiness, she remembered she had a bone to pick with Simon. "I have a question for you, *darling*."

His shoulders stiffened and he tried for nonchalance. "Yes?"

"How come I have a female Guardian?" Cara asked with a tight smile, batting her eyelashes for emphasis. Not wanting to rat out Valeria, she didn't let on that she knew that both of her Guardians were female.

Michael looked at Simon and chuckled. "You didn't."

Simon glared at Michael and then glanced back at Cara. "I thought it more appropriate."

Raising her eyebrow, she placed her hands on her hips. "Oh, really. Why's that? By the way, I don't remember Isaac having a female on his team. Where did he get her?"

She'd struck a nerve.

"Can we not talk about this here?" Simon asked, lowering his voice and meeting her gaze.

"I can leave for a few minutes," Michael offered, pointing toward the door.

"No. Stay. It's Trinity business." Needling Simon hadn't explicitly been in her plans, but his power play irked her. His age and Victorian sensibilities sometimes lent him to male-dominated decision making. She tilted her head. "You didn't answer my question. Why?"

Simon glared at her, pursing his lips. "Because I don't feel comfortable having other men watch over you. There, I said it."

"Is it because you don't trust me?" she asked. Self-admittedly, given her traitorous hormones, it might not be unwarranted.

He looked at her like she'd slapped him. "What? No. Of course not."

"You sure?"

His expression softened and he grabbed her in his muscled arms. "Cara," he said, leaning down and placing his head against her forehead. "I love you and trust you. Selfishly, this is all about my comfort. I'm sorry."

She sighed and put her arms around his neck. "Fine. I forgive you for being a big lug." Her lips met his in a make-up kiss.

Michael cleared his throat. "Can we get started, or do you two want to take this into the locker room?"

She blushed and released Simon. "Sorry, Michael. I don't know how you put up with us sometimes."

He gave her a wry smile. "It's because I have the patience of a saint."

"My apologies, Michael. I have again made an ill-advised male decision that has caused discord with the woman I love."

Michael sniffed. "What would I do without you to show me what *not* to do in a relationship?"

"Gentlemen, enough banter." Cara stepped away. "Let's get to work. Who's sparring with me first?"

"Simon and I will show you the routine that we worked on earlier, and then it's you and me, cupcake," said Michael, winking at her. Sounded like a somewhat safer option than facing the Morning Star.

Cara smirked. "Thanks. I've always wanted to be reduced to a pastry."

It wasn't until later that Cara remembered she had forgotten to tell them she owed Jonas a soul… she hoped he hadn't meant it literally.

# Chapter 22

*CARA*

*New York City. Beacon Theatre. Friday, May 24, 1:30 PM ET*

"IT'S HOT AS FUCK UP HERE!" Brett yelled through the wireless microphone. "Can you turn off half the lights?"

The stage lights dimmed.

Cara closed the door behind her and walked deeper into the darkened theater. Brett had arranged to have an all-access pass waiting for her at the box office so she could go backstage freely. She worked her way up to the front of the theater where Paco was seated and joined him with a quiet "hello."

A few minutes later, a Goth-looking woman with short spiky hair sat down in their row next to the aisle.

On stage, Brett stood shirtless in front of the band, his smooth, muscled arms and torso glistening with a film of perspiration. The top section of his hair was gathered into a ponytail, leaving the rest to touch his shoulders; the effect magnified his high cheekbones and intensified the look of annoyance in his eyes.

*Gah!* Even annoyed, he fit the bill for any girl's rock star fantasy.

Cara smiled. Peeking out above the waistband of his low-cut jeans was the top half of a large tattoo—a pair of angel wings flanking four script letters in the center. She recognized the markings from Angel's motorcycle jacket; it was the logo for the Avenging Angel's Biker Club. Glad Brett wasn't opposed to ink.

Chances were good he'd be adding more in the form of a red Messenger tattoo over his heart during his visit to the Angelorum next week.

Brett touched his ear and pointed to the guys sitting in the wings next to some equipment lit by tiny lights. "Back off the drums and turn up the string bass. It's got the counter melody on this one." Then he reached for the acoustic guitar on one of the three guitar stands and turned to the band. "Let's try it from the top in G." Positioning himself on a stool in the middle of the stage, he started to play, bathing the theater in sound. Brett strummed the strings of his guitar, joined by the bass and keyboard players. He played the opening verse, his tenor voice full of soul.

*I look at you, lying next to me*
*And I think I don't know you at all*
*But it's not only you, it's me, I don't recognize who I am any more*
*I need to go, and you need to find what you're looking for*
*I'm not the man you think I am*
*I'm no longer the man I want to be*

*Rescue me,*
*I need someone to rescue me*
*Take me home, and rescue me*
*I need you to rescue me*

*I'm lost, I was so lost*
*I didn't know how to be found*
*And then I saw your face*
*And it was you who I wanted to rescue me*
*Then I knew who I was supposed to be*
*Someone I want to be*

*Rescue me,*
*I need someone to rescue me*
*Take me home, and rescue me*
*I need you to rescue me*

*It's you, you're the only that can rescue me*
*Make love and rescue me*

The song ended to silence as they paused before starting the next one. Cara stood up and clapped.

Brett shielded his eyes and scanned the darkness. His face lit up when he spotted her. "Hey, Cara," he said and turned to the band. "Give me ten?"

He put the guitar back on the stand and removed his wireless mic, leaving it on the stool. Picking up a towel, he wiped his face and chest before leaping off the stage.

She broke into a smile and made her way toward the aisle to meet him. The Goth woman at the end of the row stood and moved into the aisle between them. Petite with intense blue eyes, she gave Cara an appraising look.

"Hey, Rox. I want to introduce you to Cara," he said as he reached them. He leaned in from a distance and gave Cara a kiss on the cheek. "Sorry, I wouldn't get too close if I were you, I'm melting."

Roxy's eyebrows shot up. "Let me guess, new squeeze?"

Brett hesitated and gave Cara an apologetic, dimpled smile, then clamped his hand on Roxy's shoulder and pressed—hard. "Nope. Friend. Cara, this is Roxy. My publicist, style guru, and bigmouthed best friend."

Roxy twisted away from his grasp and shot him a nasty look before extending her hand to Cara. "Good to meet you."

Cara shook it. "Brett hired my fiancé's security firm. I'm his liaison."

"Huh. How long have you two known each other?" she asked with a shrewd look in her eye.

"Enough, Rox. Cara, don't answer that or you may see yourself on TMZ tonight," Brett said, maneuvering Roxy out of their path.

"King, stop manhandling me," Roxy snapped.

He gently grabbed Cara's arm and said to Roxy in a hushed whisper, "She saved my life, Rox. That's all you need to know. And that stays out of the rags like we discussed."

"Fine," Roxy said begrudgingly, and then glanced at Cara. "Nice to meet you. Thanks for… you know… keeping my boy safe."

Cara nodded, warmed by Roxy's genuine concern.

Brett led Cara away toward the side stairs under the ornate golden archway. He opened the heavy door and she followed him into the hallway next to the stage away from prying eyes.

"Sorry about that. Roxy and I go way back. She tends to be over protective," Brett said.

Cara chuckled. Kind of like her with Kai. "I like her. Doesn't mince words, does she."

"You have no idea." He smirked and shook his head.

"She cares. It's nice." Cara shrugged. "That said, you were great up there! I can't wait to hear more."

He blushed and gave her a disarming smile. "Yeah? You're my new favorite fan," he said, his eyes finding hers. He stepped closer. His look turned to longing, and he pushed a stray piece of hair back behind her ear. Catching himself, his smile faltered and his hand dropped away. "Sorry."

The chemistry between them flared, going way beyond her wanting to protect him.

*God help me*, she thought. Unable to stop herself, she grabbed his hand and held it firmly. "Don't apologize, okay?"

He entwined his fingers in hers and squeezed, his eyes filled with want. His body was coiled, ready to take her into his arms if she'd only say the word.

Her heart beat wildly. The look in his eyes ignited something within her. She recognized him on some level, a familiarity distinguishing him from the near stranger he was to her. Giving herself a mental shake, she found her way back to rational thought.

"Sorry, but I know you feel it, too," he whispered, tugging her closer. "Roxy may be overprotective, but she's also perceptive." His gaze captured hers, refusing to let go.

His words were like a stake through her heart. Her reckless reaction tore at her insides. Only when they were alone did his pull on her grow this strong. Swallowing hard, her voice came out as a soft whisper.

"Brett… I do feel it. But it's not what you think. I love Simon. He was meant for me, and there's someone else meant for you. Trust me. I never want you to think I don't care. But all we're destined to be is friends. Can we make that work?" she pled.

He nodded. His hand still in hers, he pulled her into him and hugged her tight to his body.

Startled, she gasped and then relaxed in his arms. She felt comfortable there. Leaning her head into his neck, she inhaled. She could smell the underlying sweetness of his skin, musky from his performance. His scent filled her nostrils, sparking a deep physical desire for him.

He leaned his face against her hair. "I can make that work," he whispered. "I feel like if I'd done something different when we met…"

Cara shook her head. "No. By then it was already too late. Whatever's driving this pull between us, it's not because you and I are destined to be together. I can't be the one who makes love to you," she said softly, referencing the lyrics of his song.

He chuckled and slowly let her out of his embrace. "A guy can fantasize, can't he?"

She gave him a crooked smile. "I'll pretend I didn't hear that."

He stepped away, locking his arms across his chest. "Simon's a lucky guy, Cara. Seriously."

A blush filled her cheeks, accompanying the love for Simon burning in her heart. "Thanks." The tension eased and the tantalizing pull receded, releasing her. "How are you today? After yesterday…"

His smile slipped away. "Better. Still freaked out, but better."

"Think of me as your personal 911, okay? I know how screwed up this can get."

He bent in and pressed a kiss to her cheek. "Thanks, I appreciate that. I've got to get back on stage. I'll walk you to your seat. You gonna stay for a while?"

"Yup, at least for the next hour," she said, her cheek tingling where his lips had touched her. He hit the release bar and she walked through the door ahead of him.

Barely through the doorway, he pulled her to a gentle stop. "I feel better now that we've talked. It's all good. Really. I'm cool."

He dropped her off with Paco and hopped back on stage. Roxy was nowhere in sight.

Cara eased back into her seat as the band started their next song.

Mission accomplished. A pang of relief hit her to be off of Brett's romance radar. She hoped, now, that she could get back to discovering exactly how he fit in as one of the Twelve.

A few minutes later, Roxy slipped into the seat next to her. Leaning over, she whispered in Cara's ear. "He's one of the good ones. Don't hurt him. Got me?"

Cara whispered back, staring at Brett as he sang. "I wouldn't dream of it. Better yet, I promise to protect him with my life."

These were the only words she'd spoken to Roxy that were one hundred percent true.

# Chapter 23

*IRENE*
*Amtrak Acela, Washington–New York. Friday, May 24, 6:30 PM ET*

IRENE STARED OUT THE WINDOW of the Acela as it blazed a blurry trail to Manhattan. Her meeting with Creep and Creepier at the NSA had taken a toll on her mood. Bile rose in her throat at the thought of being forced to spy on one of her closest friends. She could picture it now; what should've been a joyous reunion and a great weekend would turn into a series of rummaging through personal effects, eavesdropping, and covert cell phone calls with the mother ship.

As the daughter of a diplomat, she had made her father proud with her career in government. Somehow, though, she didn't think this is what he'd had in mind. Especially after her false start with the CIA. What a disaster. Had he not emptied his basket of chits bailing her out after it all went pear-shaped, she might've been tempted to call him. For now, better to let him think everything was copacetic, and that she was safely ensconced in the State Department.

If it wasn't for the fact the NSA dangled his career over her head, she would've told them to take a hike. One thing she'd learned in the CIA was that two could play at this game. Rather than look for evidence to prove the NSA was right, she intended to prove that Cara was innocent. Maybe this was a blessing in disguise. Who better than she to exonerate Cara? If she did this right, she could protect her father's career and extricate Cara from this potential mess.

She eyed her purse. The instrument of her betrayal sat inside of it next to her cell phone. Yesterday's care package had also included state-of-the-art bugs and tracking devices, which she packed in her suitcase. Caswell had already bugged her, requesting that she text him as soon as she reached Cara's.

According to the train schedule, she'd arrive in Penn Station at seven-thirty. Originally, she didn't find it odd when Cara explained that she'd secured a new job working for her fiancé's private security firm and that their penthouse had a private underground entrance. Although Irene was on Cara's side, her CIA training instinctively kicked in. Filtering Cara's story through a lens of suspicion, Irene wondered if there was another reason for the heightened security.

*God help them all if there was,* she thought, taking a deep breath. No two ways about it, this weekend would be difficult.

On the upside, she looked forward to meeting Simon, the man who'd captured Cara's heart and broken Kai's iron hold over it. Cara had wallowed in unrequited love for Kai for almost a decade. Irene owed Simon a big fat kiss for saving Cara from herself.

Irene was dying to get a peek at him since Cara had yet to share a picture. Rumor had it he was amazing in the kitchen. For that alone Irene would have considered marrying him. According to Cara, tonight was intended to be a low-key affair with Simon making dinner at the penthouse in honor of her and Jessa's visit.

Another bright spot in this whole mess would be seeing Jessamine, who'd returned home to California after graduation and now owned a spa in Marin County. Irene hadn't seen Jessa in almost three years. She gleefully wondered if Jessa would have any psychic tidbits to share this time around.

Jessa reserved readings for only her closest friends, but most of her visions came unprompted. A psychic in a long line of psychics, Jessa was truly gifted, and her predictions were unerringly accurate—albeit cryptic. What Irene really wanted to know was if her dateless existence would be changing anytime soon. Fortunately, Jessa wasn't under any suspicion based on the information she'd been provided.

Then again… Jessa did live close enough to both San Francisco and where that warehouse had been located.

*Damn.* Irene shook her head to clear it, and removed her CIA hat. *This is ridiculous.* Her friends were innocent and that's what she would focus on. Guilt washed over her as she thought about the rest of the events: the spa day tomorrow with all the girls, the party at Simon's SoHo loft, the brunch with Cara's parents. The last thing she ever wanted to do was hurt the people she loved. This situation required her to walk a very fine line between protection and betrayal.

She sighed. Wine. She'd need wine, and lots of it, to get her through this weekend.

The driver let Irene off in the underground parking garage. Her stomach clenched into a ball of nerves as the elevator whisked her up to the penthouse. The doors opened to a large, opulent foyer with a marble floor, crystal chandelier, and dark wood paneling. Very Upper East Side. With only two apartments on the top floor, it wasn't difficult to find Cara's place.

Irene rang the bell.

Moments later, Cara flung open the door and threw her arms around Irene, hugging her in an iron embrace.

*Boy is she strong!* Irene thought.

"Eye! I'm so glad you're here."

Irene smiled at the nickname Cara and Jessa had given her. Cara's bouncy, auburn hair smelled like honeysuckle, filling Irene's senses. "I love your shampoo. It smells fantastic."

Cara had always been Irene's source for recommending the best beauty products. Ironic, since Jessa was the one who owned a spa. Jessa's mom, a well-known rock musician, died unexpectedly five years ago, right after graduation, leaving Jessa a healthy inheritance—enough to pursue her dream of opening her own business.

"I think you might be crushing me." Irene's ribs ached.

Cara blushed and released her. "Oops, sorry about that. I'm glad you like the shampoo. I have some in your guest bathroom."

Irene grabbed a soft lock of Cara's hair and gave it a quick sniff. "I thought you were allergic to flowers."

"Long story," Cara said with a small shake of her head.

"Hey, save some of those hugs for me." Jessa's voice came from behind Cara.

"Jessa!" Irene gushed as Cara stepped aside to reveal their willowy friend with the long, strawberry-blonde corkscrew curls. Jessa always reminded Irene of one of Raphael's angels with her pale skin, wide, hazel eyes, and those magnificent curls. Irene had envied those curls since college. Her own short cap of red hair grew out limp and boring, a good reason to keep the Pixie cut she sported. "Come here and give me a squeeze, girlfriend!"

She clutched Jessa's thin frame and gave her a peck on the cheek. "You look great. I hate you." Seeing them both, Irene realized how much she had missed their girl time.

Jessa chuckled. "I'm flattered… I think."

"When did you get here?"

"Couldn't have been more than twenty minutes ago."

Chloe started to whine at Irene's feet, her patience exhausted on waiting her turn for a greeting. "Hello, honey," said Irene, kneeling down, kissing the dog on top of her narrow head, and submitting to a couple of face licks.

Cara grabbed Irene's suitcase and closed the door behind them. "Come on in. Simon's in the kitchen making us a fabulous dinner."

Irene drew in a breath as she looked around the interior foyer with the large center table and three-foot-high floral arrangement. Her steps echoed on the marble floor. Straight ahead was a large living room area and hallways to either side led to other sections of the apartment.

"Wow, this place is gorgeous, Cara."

Cara smiled. "Thanks. Let's drop your suitcase off in the guest room." She led Irene deeper into the apartment and down past the other bedrooms. Jessa followed.

"This place looks like it belongs in *Architectural Digest*. I'm jealous."

"That makes two of us, and not just because of the apartment," Jessa said with a mischievous grin. Lowering her voice, she whispered into Irene's ear. "Wait until you see Simon."

"I heard that." Cara chuckled. "And don't be jealous. This place is great, but it comes with its own set of problems."

*I'd be willing to take on a stopped up toilet or two,* Irene thought, glancing at the museum-quality oil paintings that lined the hallway.

"Do you think you'll stay at Simon's security company long-term, or are you still looking for another finance job?" Irene asked. Cara had been laid off from her investment banking job in March, and within weeks, she had found Simon, gotten engaged, and uncharacteristically changed careers. Irene couldn't help but think that working with your future husband might be a dicey arrangement.

Cara shrugged. "I might. But after killing myself for five years at Cabot, I'm happy to have time to sort things out before I make another permanent move. For now, I'm happy working for Simon. Money isn't a problem, so why not?"

Irene added that to her list of things to be jealous over. Having a government job would never allow her the same flexibility.

Cara opened the door down the hall across from the master bedroom and led them into a nice-sized guest room with a private bath. The French décor was feminine and fresh, painted in mocha with a queen-size bed with oatmeal-colored linens. Landscape paintings graced the walls, and a blue slipper chair next to the bed offered a nice place to read.

Setting down Irene's suitcase next to the closet, Cara pointed to the bathroom. "There are fresh towels and every hair care product you can think of in the shower.

Freshen up if you like, and then meet us in the kitchen." Her face took on a dreamy look. "I can't wait for you to meet my honey."

"Me, too. I owe him one for saving you from your despair over Kai." Irene smirked. Having a ringside seat to the "Cara and Kai Show" after he was married had been painful. *Thank God that spell's broken*, she thought.

Jessa high-fived Irene. "Hallelujah, sister!"

Cara scowled. "Thanks. Sienna would join you in celebration if she were here."

"How is Sienna?" Irene asked, brightening. Although Sienna hadn't attended Georgetown with them, she'd come down often enough, and they'd kept in touch on and off ever since. Irene enjoyed Sienna's irreverence. Like a sister-in-arms, together they balanced the more conservative Cara and Jessa.

Cara released a breath. "She's good, but having some romantic challenges of her own."

Irene's eye lit up. "Oh, do tell!"

"I really shouldn't be sharing—"

"Oh, nonsense. Spill." Irene waved her hand and sank down onto the edge of the bed.

"I agree." Jessa plopped down next her, looking just as eager to hear the gossip. "It doesn't have anything to do with her ex-boyfriend, Mark, does it?"

Cara's shook her head and sat on the blue slipper chair. "No, thankfully." Taking a deep breath, she said, "She and my friend Michael, who you'll meet this weekend, are perfect for each other. Only they don't know it yet. I'm hoping they can hook up at the party tomorrow night and work it out."

"*Umm*, sounds intriguing," said Irene with a wide grin. "Anything we can do to help?"

"Yeah. Don't tell her I told you—or she'll kill me. And pray a little," Cara said, getting up. "We better get to the kitchen before Simon thinks we've gone AWOL."

Irene's cell phone rang in her purse and she went rigid.

"Why don't you get that, and then meet us in the kitchen whenever you're ready? It's down the hallway past the foyer," Cara said with a fleeting look of confusion like she'd picked up on something.

"Sounds like a plan. Be there in a couple of minutes," Irene said, pasting on a smile.

As the door clicked shut behind Cara and Jessa, Irene pounced on her purse and answered her phone. "What?" she snapped.

"Miss Hickey, have you arrived?" She recognized Caswell's grating voice.

"I just got here for Pete's sake. I don't have anything to report yet." The joy she'd been feeling trickled out of her.

"I realize that. Please activate one of the tracking devices, so that we know where you are," he said and hung up.

Irene sat on the edge of the bed, paralyzed. In a fit of defiance, she shut the phone off, placed it back in her purse, and headed to the kitchen. Forget them. She planned on having a good time tonight. She could play superspy tomorrow.

On her way, she took a mini-tour, poking her nose into the other rooms along the hallway. The place was incredibly huge and gorgeous, a far cry from her teeny-tiny one bedroom apartment in Capitol Hill.

*I'd give my eyeteeth for a fraction of this space*, she thought enviously.

Voices grew louder as she approached the kitchen from the long, narrow corridor. A rich, masculine voice joined Cara's and Jessa's. Irene spotted some white cabinetry through the open doorway. From what she could see, the kitchen was just as magnificent as the rest of the place.

A timer sounded from inside. "Stand back, ladies. The hors d'oeuvres are ready."

"I guess I'm just in time," said Irene, rounding the corner into the kitchen. The sight of the massive, ponytailed blond man wearing an apron froze her in place. Her knees buckled, and the air flew from her lungs in a sharp gasp.

*Holy Mackerel!* Simon was the guy from the surveillance tape.

Alarm filled Cara's eyes and she came running over with Jessa. "Eye, are you all right?" She grabbed Irene's arm to help steady her.

"I suddenly felt faint. I must be hungrier than I thought." Truth always makes the best lie. She'd learned that in the CIA.

Simon pulled out a glass and filled it with orange juice before joining them. "Here, drink this. It will help if it's your blood sugar."

Taking the glass, she stared up into his kind, concerned eyes and tried not to melt. He was breathtaking with the body of a god. His finely chiseled face was beautiful yet masculine with blue eyes so bright they blazed. Her gut screamed that the NSA's terrorist angle was bunk. His only crime, from what Irene could fathom, was probably stopping traffic and causing five-car pileups. One look at him and she'd happily plow her car into the back of another.

Her eyes stayed glued on him. She smiled and tried not gape. "You must be Simon. I'm Irene." She offered him her other hand.

He returned her smile, and her hand disappeared inside of his. "Simon Young."

"Cara, I agree with Jessa. He's worth being jealous over." She continued to stare.

His laugh was rich and deep. "Why, thank you. I'm glad you approve of Cara's choice."

She sighed. "Any more where you came from?"

Cara cocked her eyebrow. "Actually…"

Simon gave Cara a cautionary smile. "Sweetheart, we're still trying to smooth over the situation from the last time you played Cupid."

"Um, I think Constantina had a little more to do with Michael and Sienna than she's willing to admit. Don't you?" Cara challenged with a lifted brow.

"Perhaps," he said, mildly amused, and pointed to the tray of cooling hors d'oeuvres. "Ladies, may I interest you in some appetizers before they get cold? Dinner will be ready shortly."

She, Cara, and Jessa each took a stool around the kitchen island.

He transferred the hot canapés onto serving trays and put them out, and then opened a nice bottle of chilled Chablis. He poured them each a glass to enjoy while he completed dinner.

"These are fantastic," Irene said, popping a second one into her mouth and washing it down with the remainder of her orange juice.

Cara raised her glass. "Thanks so much for coming, guys. I've missed you and I'm so glad to see you both."

"Here, here," said Jessa, touching her glass to Irene's and Cara's.

Was it Irene's imagination or was there a touch of sadness surrounding both of her friends? As far as she was concerned, she was the only one here who had any right to be glum.

Irene frowned. "Hey, you two look like you're going to burst into tears any second. Stop it and drink up." She picked up her wine glass and downed the contents. "Wow! Fantastic Chablis."

Simon raised his eyebrow at her and smiled. "I'm not sure it will help your cause to drink so quickly." Lifting the bottle, he refilled her glass. "How about taking this one more slowly?"

"Aye, aye, Captain," she said and saluted. "So, what's for dinner? I hear you're an amazing chef."

Simon blushed as he worked. "You're too kind. Tonight, I'm making a favorite of Cara's. Chateaubriand with herbed potatoes and roasted vegetables paired with a nice French Cabernet. For dessert, chocolate soufflé."

Irene's mouth watered. "Sounds delicious."

"I'm one lucky girl." Cara winked at Simon.

He winked back at her. "I'm the lucky one."

"You guys are too cute," Irene said, wearing a grin.

"So, Jessa," Cara asked, "how's everything working out with Serenity?"

Jessa's face came alive. "Good, really good. We're growing, and finally, there's a nice cash flow."

"Well, I'd be interested to know how you think tomorrow's spa services stack up against your offerings," Cara said.

Jessa's eyes brightened. "I'll let you know. I'm always on the hunt for new ideas. I'm really looking forward to it." She turned to Irene. "How's Washington?"

Irene sniffed. "Political."

"And you wonder why I chose to go into finance." Cara chuckled.

"You always were the smart one." Irene raised her glass to Cara. "If it wasn't for my dad, I think I would've gone civilian. But the government really is a good place to work as a linguist." *Most days.*

Cara waved her hands in a fast flutter. "Oh, I almost forgot! I have a surprise for you guys. I hope you don't mind, but I rearranged some of our plans for tomorrow night."

"What? You've come to your senses and want a bachelorette party at Chippendales?" Irene asked, nursing a seed of hope.

Cara threw a sexy smile at Simon. "Who needs Chippendales when I have Simon?"

"Me," Irene whined. "Sorry, Simon. I see her point, but I'm not above looking."

Simon cleared his throat, an unmistakable flush across his cheeks. "Um, why don't I leave you ladies alone for a few minutes?" Holding up the timer, he walked toward the doorway. "I'll be back when this rings."

Cara winked at him before he disappeared through the doorway with Chloe. "Anyway, as I was saying… I have front row seats at the Beacon Theatre tomorrow night for King Metaljam."

Jessa fell back in her stool and her lips parted in surprise. "How the heck did you manage that?" Then she clasped Cara's shoulder. "Wait! I can't believe you've actually heard of King Metaljam!" Cara was self-admittedly musically challenged when it came to anything current. Stuck in the '90s, she'd never made it past Grunge.

Cara smirked at Jessa. "Thanks." Then she broke into a wide grin. "Brett King is my new BFF."

"What? How's that possible?" Jessa stared at Cara, dumbstruck.

"She leads a charmed life, or haven't you noticed?" Irene sighed.

"I met him at a café back in March, and now he's a client of our security company." Cara shrugged. "True, I didn't recognize him when we first met, but we've been hanging out lately. He's staying at Simon's loft until Wednesday."

Jessa shook her head, doe-eyed. "Irene's right. You do lead a charmed life."

Cara frowned. "Hardly. It only looks that way from the outside."

The buzzer rang in the living room and Simon returned to take their dinner out of the oven. "Ladies, the dining room table is set for you. Why don't you go settle in, and I'll serve you dinner there," he said, setting the Chateaubriand down on the stove top.

"What service," Irene said and hopped off the barstool.

"Are you joining us, Simon?" Jessa asked.

He reached into the cabinet and pulled out some plates. "No, I have some work to catch up on. And I wouldn't dream of imposing on your 'girl time,' as Cara puts it."

"Are you sure?" Cara asked.

He nodded. "Enjoy yourselves."

They left Simon as he prepared their plates. Entering the dining room, Irene let out a low whistle. Simon had set the table and lit candles for them, their glasses already filled with red wine. His thoughtfulness spoke volumes to her not only about himself, but of his feelings for Cara. This guy was a keeper. Her list of those she needed to prove innocent just increased by one.

They huddled at one end of the table that easily could have sat a small army.

"Tell us everything. How did you meet Simon again?" Irene pulled her chair up and clasped her hands together, eager to learn more.

Before Cara could reply, Simon returned, this time carrying three plates. He served them one by one. The presentation of the meal rivaled that of a high-end restaurant.

Irene spread her linen napkin on her lap after Simon departed. "Well? Don't make me beg. Give us all the gory details."

Cara sighed, resting her elbows on the table wearing a gooey "I'm in love" look. "I tripped and fell into his arms at a restaurant downtown."

"That crap really happens?" Irene asked, picking up her knife.

"Charmed life," mumbled Jessa, stabbing a potato with her fork and popping it into her mouth.

"Enough about me. What about you guys? Any new men?" Cara asked with interest.

Irene turned to Jessa. "Did she just deflect?"

Jessa arched a perfectly shaped brow. "She sure did, Irene."

Cara rolled her eyes. "Come on," she whined. "I want to hear about you guys."

"No men for me," said Irene.

"Me neither. Okay, that's us. Now back to you." Jessa grinned wickedly.

Tag-teaming, she and Jessa spent the better part of an hour weaseling details from Cara about Simon, the wedding, why her engagement ring hung from her neck instead of being on her finger, her family, and everything else they could discover about Cara's charmed life. By the end, Irene contemplated changing her career to private security, if for nothing else than to meet a man as hot as Simon.

Their dinner consumed and the soufflés still in the oven, Irene remembered Cara's hostess gift in her suitcase. Cara and Jessa chattered on as Irene excused herself and headed back to the guest room.

As she walked down the hallway, a beam of light from the master bedroom cut a swath in front of her. Her ears picked up the timbre of Simon's voice, the sound distorted through the wall. The carpet muffled her steps as she approached.

On her way past, he spoke again. This time, she caught the snippet of speech clearly. Her breath caught in her throat, and she stopped dead. It was the same language she'd heard on the surveillance footage, solidifying his connection to the suspected terrorists and the unknown language.

Holding her breath, she peered in through the partially open door.

Simon sat on the bed, his large, hulking frame hunched over, talking to Chloe. Her little Whippet head was cocked with one ear up, listening.

*Heaven help me, he's having a conversation with a dog in the proto-language!*

Taking a deep breath, she let it out slowly and cracked the door open wider.

Startled, Simon raised his head and Chloe's other ear shot up. They both fixed her with a wide-eyed stare but recovered quickly. Chloe jumped off the bed and trotted past her in the direction of the dining room as Simon rose to his feet.

Irene shifted uncomfortably. "Sorry to interrupt. Can I ask you a question?"

"Sure. Come in," he said, and motioned her inside. "How can I help?"

Entering the room, she followed Simon to the sitting area.

Irene lowered herself onto one of the two chairs and rubbed her damp palms together. "That language you were speaking, what is it?"

He flashed a controlled smile. "Cara tells me you're a linguist. I guess we have something in common. I have a degree in ancient languages. Chloe happens to be a gracious audience; she's fascinated by the sound." Simon crossed his legs and rested his clasped hands on his knees. The chair looked small under his huge frame.

Irene measured his words. Cara hadn't mentioned his education. "Yes, but it sounds like a proto-language somehow associated with the divine languages according to my studies." She'd done some research since her visit to the NSA, and was sure that's what she had heard on the security footage.

A slow smile crept back onto Simon's lips, his blue eyes dazzling her. She could have sworn his eyes got brighter the moment she mentioned her studies. "You have a very good ear," he said with a nod. "Its origin reaches back before Aramaic."

She regarded him suspiciously, narrowing her green eyes. "How is it that you learned to speak it? I can honestly say it would be almost impossible to learn, not to mention rare. There are no complete lexicons available anywhere in the world from what I know, only fragments."

He shrugged. "Not so. You'd be surprised what's hidden in the Vatican," he said, and winked. "And not impossible. That's the precise reason why I chose it.

My entire security team is versed in it. Using it eliminates the worry of electronic eavesdropping."

Irene's breath caught in her throat. Maybe he already knew about the footage and the NSA. A sharp intelligence peered at her through crystal blue eyes. Working in Washington, she recognized power when she saw it. Behind his polished and kind demeanor lurked the kind of power wrought from a backbone of pure, male steel. He could easily run a large company or lead troops into battle. But a terrorist? Her gut still said no. Regardless, she needed to tread cautiously.

"Huh." She couldn't dispute his logic, although it seemed highly improbable. "Where did you go to school?"

"France," he said, rising. "I need to check on the soufflés. Do you have any other questions?" For the first time all night, she caught the slightest hint of a French accent when he spoke.

*Besides asking if you have any brothers?* She stood. "Sorry for being so nosy, it's just such a thrill to meet someone who's skilled in linguistics. I'd love to learn more about your 'in' at the Vatican."

He smiled without answering. Placing his fingertips on the small of her back, he led her into the hallway. Her nerve endings lit up like a Christmas tree. *He really* is *all that, and a bag of chips*, she thought. If she were Cara, she'd never get out of bed.

Irene crossed the hall to her guest room while he headed in the opposite direction toward the kitchen. She opened her bedroom door and went to her suitcase. Rummaging through her things, she pulled out Cara's gift—French Country dishtowels from Provence. Cara had raved about her vacation with Simon in Monaco back in April, so Irene thought they were an ideal choice.

On her way back toward the door, she spotted her purse and gave it a sour stare. Why prolong the inevitable? She jerked it off the chair and fished out the NSA-provided cell phone, turned it back on, and hit the speed dial for Caswell.

"Are you in danger?" he asked flatly when he answered.

"No. Why would you think that?" she said, her face pinched in annoyance.

"I asked you three hours ago to turn on the tracking device."

"Fine," she said. Taking one out of her purse the size of a dime, she flipped it on and threw it back inside. "So, you want my report or not?" She decided to use the NSA to do some research for her under the guise of cooperation. They wouldn't suspect she'd be using the information to do just the opposite—prove Cara's and Simon's innocence.

"Yes, if it's not too much trouble," he replied dryly.

"Save the sarcasm," she snapped. "The blond man in the surveillance footage is Cara's fiancé, Simon Young. He runs a private security firm, and he lives with her on the Upper East Side. They're due to fly to France on Wednesday for business.

Cara mentioned something about an office in Paris. That's it." She omitted her discovery that he spoke the language on the surveillance footage. She'd hold that for later. Or never.

"Thank you, Miss Hickey. I'll be in touch," he said and disconnected.

Her stomach twisted into a knot. She hoped she wasn't making a mistake. That her gamble would pay off. She liked Simon, and the thought of hurting either him or Cara left a lump in her throat.

Her heart was in the right place, but then again, wasn't the road to Hell paved with good intentions?

# Chapter 24

*CARA*

*New York City. Fifth Avenue Penthouse. Saturday, May 25, 12:45 AM ET*

GIDDY AND EXHAUSTED, Cara dangled her arm over Jessa's thin, bird-like shoulder, while Irene did the same from the other side. They belted out the last chorus of "New York, New York" while attempting to walk three abreast down the hallway toward the bedrooms. It was a tight squeeze even without the Rockettes-like kicks in time with the music. That last bottle of wine had probably been a mistake. Come morning, Cara would know for sure by the size of her headache.

Without warning, Jessa jerked to a dead stop and her eyes went blank. Cara and Irene stumbled backward almost taking them down in a three-girl, multi-limb jumble before they regained their footing. The blank look on Jessa's face was all too familiar. Cara had seen it many times in their four years during college.

Irene eyed her and whispered, "Welcome back, Jessa the Walking Fortune Cookie." As weird as Jessa's episodes were, Cara and Irene were used to her slipping into a trance and bestowing pearls of wisdom to whomever was close by. Jessa found them distressing because she couldn't remember them. Generally, she accepted her unique abilities as a part of her life—despite being friend-limiting. Not everyone felt comfortable around someone with her kind of gift. During their years at Georgetown, she and Irene were Jessa's only close friends.

Cara understood now more than ever the discomfort of being different.

Jessa turned to Irene with unseeing eyes. "Trust the man you love to help you."

Irene looked at Cara and shielded her mouth with her hand. "Obviously, she must know something that I don't," she whispered.

Turning to Cara, Jessa stared through her. "When the hour is darkest, you will come into your own."

A chill traversed Cara's spine. In her experience, Jessa's fortunes always held meaning, and Cara already expected darkness. A sense of dread washed over her before she filed the fortune away for later.

Jessa's sweet singing voice resumed abruptly in mid-chorus for about ten seconds... until she glanced at Cara's and Irene's stunned faces. "What?"

"Um, you know... fortune cookie time," Irene said.

Jessa reddened, and her hand flew up to cover her mouth. "Oh, God. I didn't say anything horrifying, did I?"

"No, but I hope he's gorgeous—whoever he is," replied Irene.

"Who?" Jessa asked.

"The man I love who I'm supposed to trust. But knowing my luck, you could've been talking about my father."

"Gosh, I'm sorry, Irene." Turning to Cara, Jessa's eyes filled with worry. "Did I say anything scary to you, Cara?"

Cara smiled and yawned. "No, just cryptic." She gave Jessa a hug.

A strip of light at the bottom of her door indicated Simon was still awake. "This is me," Cara said, reaching for the door knob. "'Night, ladies. Prepare for a big day tomorrow."

Simon glanced up from his book, a leather-bound first edition of Charles Dickens's *A Tale of Two Cities*. "Did you girls have fun?" he asked. His dark-blond hair hung down around his shoulders as he sat comfortably reading on the bed wrapped in a downy white robe.

Cara had been shocked and amazed when she'd discovered the collection of rare books in the penthouse library. Recently, Simon had decided to reread all of Dickens's works and was methodically plodding his way through that section of the bookshelf.

"Probably too much," she said with a pained expression, walking past him and into their bathroom. She reached for her toothbrush next to Simon's and smiled, noticing the bristles on his were still wet. The simple things pleased her, making her feel like a normal woman in love with a normal man. In these brief moments, she could escape the weight of her destiny, even if only for a second.

After brushing her teeth, Cara changed into one of Simon's T-shirts, tossed her underwear into the hamper, and slipped on a robe matching Simon's.

Still awash in an alcoholic buzz, Cara crawled onto the bed and nestled in next to him. He curled his muscled arm protectively around her in a column of warmth and continued to read.

"Thank you for making us such a fabulous dinner," she said, staring up at his strong, chiseled jawline.

He kissed the tip of her nose. "Anything for you, my love."

A yawn escaped her as she snuggled her head onto his chest. "I had a great time. But I'll admit, Irene and Jessa's interrogation wore me out." Cara thought back over the night's conversations, and wondered if she'd let too many details slip in the half-truths she told. "I'm not sure if I should've mentioned the trip next week, even though I stuck with our cover story about the office in Paris."

He released a deep sigh. "You weren't the only one interrogated. Irene caught me speaking with Chloe in the angelic language."

Cara raised her chin and stared up at him; the fluffiness of his robe was soft against her cheek. "A real conversation? *With my dog?*"

His lips turned up in a smile. "Of course. And not just a dog; she's a Sentinel."

"Silly me," she said, rolling her eyes. "And you were going to mention this to me, when?"

He shrugged. "I assumed you knew."

Cara huffed. "Assume nothing. I feel like I've been wearing an eye patch with both hands tied behind my back ever since I got involved with the Angelorum. It's annoying."

Simon kissed the top of her head in appeasement. "I won't make the mistake again. But Chloe is the least of your concerns. Irene astutely identified the angelic language as a proto-language related to the divine languages. I managed to avoid revealing which one."

"A what?"

He put his book down on the nightstand and hugged her closer. "A proto-language. A language from which others are derived. Quick history lesson?"

She groaned into his chest. "All right."

He chuckled and squeezed her. "I'll keep it short. I promise. The Angelic language is really the language God used to address Adam and Eve in the Garden before their Fall from Paradise. It's the universal language of all God's creatures, including angels. Adam and Eve lost their ability to speak it when they fell from grace. Enoch, a liaison to Semyaza and the first Watchers, was the only man among men who could innately speak it after their fall.

"Adam created a proto-Hebrew language after he left Paradise based on his memories. It was considered the universal language until the confusion of languages at the Tower of Babel. Proto-Semitic languages grew from there and provide the base of what's now considered the divine languages. Agrippa created something in the sixteenth century which he touted as the divine language of angels, but the true lexicons only exists in the Book of Human Angels. I've convinced Irene my lexicon was gained through hidden texts in the Vatican." Simon snickered. "In reality, they'd do anything short of kill to get their hands on it."

*I should've paid more attention in church*, Cara thought, feeling inadequate as a lapsed Catholic. "Should we be worried about Irene?"

His brows bunched as he gave it some thought. "Yes and no. Outside of the Angelorum and the Dark Ones, the language hasn't existed since Genesis. My main concern is having her draw unwanted attention to us. But frankly, she'd be hard pressed to prove exactly what she heard."

Cara weighed his words. "Even if she knew about us, I don't think she would ever betray us. Problem is, she doesn't, and the girl has a dogged sense of curiosity. Is there anything I can do?" The thought of her two worlds colliding made Cara half-crazy.

"Let me think on it," he replied.

"So, what did you speak with Chloe about?" she asked, not really expecting an answer. Her fingers danced close to his heart, tracing the design of the red Guardian tattoo under his robe. She loved the feel of Simon under her fingertips, smooth and silky. Other than eyebrows, eyelashes, and the hair on their head, Nephilim had no body hair. One of the myriad changes affecting her lately: the hair on her legs and under her arms had stopped growing.

He rubbed her back, the warmth and movement of his large hand soothing her. "She's asked for us to breed her when she goes into heat. She wants to have a litter of puppies, believing more Sentinels will be required shortly. Oh yes, and she finds blue brindle or pure fawn males the most attractive, but says as long as he's companionable and can sire her pups, she'll be satisfied."

Cara's jaw hinged open. "Seriously?"

When Chloe was offered to her as a puppy four years ago, the owner gave her a hefty discount on the condition that she not be fixed so that she could be bred for one litter. Since the owner was a friend of Cara's mother, Cara had agreed. Funny, her mother lost touch with the woman shortly afterward. In hindsight, Cara smelled another Angelorum set-up.

"Yes, seriously," he said with a smug look.

"And she told you this… how?"

"Mostly telepathically with a couple of barks thrown in for emphasis," he said, his eyes holding a shine.

Cara shook her head and chuckled. "Okay, that's weird, but Jessa takes the cake for weird tonight." *Weird* was Cara's new normal. So why not a conversation with Chloe and a fortune from her psychic friend? On a scale of one to ten, they only ranked about a three.

"Oh? Does she want puppies, too?" he asked with a smirk.

She snorted. "For the record, that was an awful joke. No, she had one of her psychic episodes in the hallway."

"Psychic episodes?"

"She went all trance-like and gave a fortune cookie's worth of info to me and Irene. She's had these episodes and random visions her whole life. It's a bit jarring when she slips into her trances, but worse for her. She doesn't remember them." A shudder passed through Cara as she recalled Jessa's words.

Simon, wearing a sudden look of concern, squeezed her tight. "What did she say to you?"

Cara hesitated briefly, uncomfortable with the idea of repeating it aloud, and then sighed and threw it out there. " 'When the hour is darkest, you will come into your own.' I'm not sure what it means. I never am when she spews her fortune tidbits. But they always seem to mean something later when you least expect it."

"Well, it doesn't sound like a bad message," he said, relaxing his hold.

Cara buried herself further into his embrace. "It doesn't necessarily sound like a good one either," she mumbled, wearing a pout. "I'm terrified every time I think about where this is headed. What makes me so special? Why do I have a better chance of saving the world than someone else?" The pit of fear she carried in her gut clenched tighter while dread tightened its grip around her windpipe.

He tucked her head under his chin. "My love, you're the first genetically engineered Nephil, and that alone makes you special. More than that, you're the woman I love." He rested his cheek on her head.

His words warmed her, wishing they were enough but knowing they weren't. "So far, it's just Brett, you, and I who've been chosen as part of the Twelve. I'm interested in what he brings to the table besides a fan base of screaming women."

"Look at me," he said softly, giving her a little squeeze. She craned her head to meet his gaze. "Don't be fooled. Be prepared for this to come together quickly. The other nine may be closer than you think."

She eyed him warily. "Do you know something you're not telling me?"

He shook his head. "No, but I have experience and instinct. I think we should turn to the *whys*. As much as this appears random, it's not. One thing I know with certainty, your soul didn't choose this randomly. At some point, we need to find out who you are."

"What do you mean *who* I am?" Her scalp tingled as she remembered Constantina's question from the other night, "Why Cara?"

He locked his eyes on hers and ran his large hand over her hair. "Cara Collins is who you are now, but your soul is eternal. Cara is not who you always were. Think of Eae. Constantina in this life, but her true essence is Eae, the Angel Who Thwarts Demons."

The tingling along Cara's scalp grew stronger. "Are you saying I'm an angel?"

"That depends on whether you were a resident of Heaven as a human soul or if you were in the employ of our Creator. I don't know the answer. My knowledge of our relationship in Heaven is as limited as yours—to the vision in the Meadow the night we made love for the first time."

Cara thought back to the vision and to placing a pearl-sized piece of her soul within Simon on his last day in Heaven before this life. How he'd become her soul mate had stayed with her while the rest of the vision had faded almost immediately after they'd made love. A feeling of unease told her there was something she needed to remember…

Her hand played over the hard muscled landscape hiding underneath his robe. "You know what I find so ironic? Irene and Jessa's misplaced jealousy, when all the while I envy them their blissful ignorance."

He pulled his head back to look at her. "If you had chosen ignorance, we might never have met in this lifetime."

"If that's the trade-off then I'd choose you every time," she said, staring into his eyes, overwhelmed by the abundance of love she had for him. She was more than ready to leave this discussion behind and to move onto something more… fulfilling.

"I'm glad to hear that." He leaned down and pressed his warm, firm lips to hers. His touch on her skin always managed to send a delightful pulse of electricity through her.

Breaking the kiss, she smiled at him wickedly. "Irene wanted to know if you ever cook for me in just an apron."

"She did, did she? *Hmm.* Maybe I should try that some time," he said with a soft growl, pulling her on top of him. Giggling, Cara sat up and straddled his lap.

His eyes darkened with desire. "I can tell when you're ready for me. You smell like wildflowers."

"I do?" she said, wrinkling her nose.

"You do," he said, his hands reaching inside her robe and settling on her hips. "When your Nephilim senses fully develop, you should be able to smell my desire for you, too." As if on cue, he hardened beneath her, filling the space between his stomach and the fabric of his robe between her legs.

She closed her eyes and inhaled deeply. A smile formed on her face. "I sense a pleasant muskiness. Could that be you?"

A low growl escaped his throat. He sat up and worked to liberate her shoulders from her robe. "It's most definitely me." She slipped it the rest of the way off and threw it onto the floor.

Before he could tackle the borrowed T-shirt she wore, she returned the favor and separated his robe, revealing his naked body. Her eyes honed in on his oversized arousal as it stood ready and waiting against his chiseled abs.

"It most definitely is," she said, licking her lips and taking him in her hands. Her hormones surged through her with a jolt, overwhelming her with the need to take him, to possess him. "I'm driving. Lie back and enjoy," she said, planting her hand in the center of his chest and gently pushing him back so his shoulders rested against the headboard.

He stared at her with amusement. "I'm all yours."

High on the list of things she loved about Simon was his sense of confidence and security. His giving spirit, tenderness, and ability to occasionally relinquish his power in bed made him a true partner while his advanced skills in Sensual Pleasures made him a masterful lover. A winning combination in her book.

Staring down at him, she wondered how she'd gotten so lucky. With his open robe gathered down at his sides, he was spread out like a delectable smorgasbord of sculpted muscle and male desire in front of her. And she was more than ready to have her fill.

She reached for him, eagerly taking him into her mouth. His head arched back and he moaned the moment her tongue rolled back the smooth foreskin covering his finely shaped head. His size didn't give her the option of swallowing him whole. Instead, it required a coordinated dance between her mouth, tongue, and hands. Over the last couple of months, she'd perfected her game.

Her hands traveled over his shaft and down to cup and massage his smooth, hairless sack as her mouth worked its magic on his tip. The sweet taste of his skin mixed with the pleasant muskiness, shattering her senses and touching something instinctive within her. Her body flushed and the heat between her legs intensified.

Under her touch, his groin throbbed, and a loud groan vibrated from deep in his throat as his fingers gripped the covers on the bed. The sound of his pleasure sent another rush of heat to her core.

She released him from her grasp before taking him over the brink and crawled up to kneel over his midsection. Slipping the oversized T-shirt up and over her head, she tossed it to the floor revealing her own sculpted, naked body, flushed and ready.

"You're magnificent," he whispered. His lips parted as he watched her. Recapturing him, warm and hard against her palm, she positioned him at her opening and guided him in. Releasing a sigh, she enveloped him in a luscious, wet welcome, taking him in up to the hilt.

His hands clasped her hips, and he moaned, his eyes rolling back and then closing. Filling her with his length and girth, the velvet friction of his thrusts touched her in all the right places. When she'd first seen Simon naked the night of their engagement, she'd been intimidated by his size. But he'd turned out to be custom made for her, giving her pleasure she'd never imagined.

He rose to face her, drawing her into a kiss with a passion and intensity that shot right through her. She wrapped her arms around his neck, twisting her fingers in his long hair. Setting the pace, deliberate and sensuously slow, his movements activated every nerve ending she had, sucking them into the spiral of ecstasy building inside of her.

"I love you," he whispered between kisses, his eyelids half-closed and his arms securely encircling her waist as he rocked her in his lap.

"Right back at you," she said softly and picked up the pace. He rotated his hips, pulling her rapidly past the point of no return. Her breathing came in fits as the first wave of her orgasm swept over her. Throwing her head back, she let out a near quiet cry of pleasure and went boneless in his arms, her limbs no longer able to support her.

As she pulsed around him, he took over. Pushing her backward, he positioned himself on top, her legs wrapped around his waist. His lips covered hers in an urgent kiss as he pumped fast and hard. His body tensed, and in one large, seismic release, Simon tucked his head next to hers and roared into the bed covers.

As he throbbed inside of her, the aftershocks set off a second, sharper wave that carried her away once again. Balling her hand into a fist, she covered her mouth to suppress the sounds of her next release. The floral muskiness of their combined scent was unmistakable now, surrounding them in a cloud of fulfillment. She felt his ragged breath next to her ear as her body milked him in the aftermath.

"*Mmm.* I hope I didn't wake your friends," he said in a hoarse whisper.

Running her fingers through his hair, she said through panting breaths, "That goes for both of us. Good effort, though."

Still joined, he positioned her so they lay on their sides face-to-face.

"I can't move." He chuckled deeply. Their heads were at the foot of the bed. He struggled out of his robe to bare his back while holding her firm. Releasing his wings from behind his shoulder blades, they rapidly unfurled to their full glory. Gently, he rolled onto his back with her on top of him, maneuvering a wing to either side. He stretched and curled them overhead until they touched, creating a snow-white cocoon of velvet softness against their skin.

She sighed, contentment engulfing her. Eventually, she would slip down to sleep next to him. But for now, she would cover him with her body and be his blanket. The feel of him tucked up inside her made her tingle. She enjoyed the fullness and warmth. It was like a satisfying dessert after a hearty meal.

"Good night, my love," he breathed as he hugged her to his body inside their feathered sanctuary.

Cara yawned. Her body spent, she mumbled something unintelligible and dropped off to sleep.

# Chapter 25



*IRENE*

*New York City. Fifth Avenue Penthouse. Saturday, May 25, 3:30 AM ET*

IRENE'S EYES FLEW OPEN in the darkness at the sound of an old-fashioned telephone ringtone emanating from inside her purse. The red LCD digits on the alarm clock glowed 3:30 AM.

*Are they frigging kidding me?* Irene recognized the ring. It pulsed in time with the pinpoints of pain echoing through her skull from all the wine.

Grasping for the strap of her purse, she tumbled out of bed and onto the carpet slamming her head into the chair. Fully awake and angry as a rhino with a hemorrhoid, she answered the phone. "What?" she barked. "This better be good."

"Did you turn on your tracking device? We're not getting a signal," Ellerton said.

"Yes! Hours ago. Wait a second." She turned on the light and rummaged through her purse until she found it. Inspecting the little bastard, she determined it had been activated. "It's on. I'll turn on another one, if it'll make you happy." She depressed the near-microscopic button on another dime-sized device. "Done. Can I go back to sleep now?"

"Miss Hickey, we checked out your report on your friend's fiancé. Simon Young isn't his real identity."

"What's that supposed to mean?" Irene asked, her mouth going dry.

"The paper trail for Simon Young starts and ends with a New York Driver's License. The address belongs to some uptown law firm in Manhattan with branches all over the world. We've checked every system at our disposal and come up with nothing. There's no one listed under his name around his age or with his description in any of the fifty states."

"How was he able to get a license without any other identification?" Irene asked with a frown. "In DC, short of handing over your firstborn at the DMV, you have to prove your identity six ways from Sunday with at least two other government-issued documents."

"It means he has friends in high places… somewhere. Le Feu has ties overseas, so he could even be a foreign operative for all we know," suggested Ellerton.

"He said he went to school in France and he has an accent," she offered two more interesting, yet nonincriminating tidbits. As much as Irene tried to picture Simon engaged in terrorism, she just couldn't make it feel right.

"Okay, we'll check out that angle. Keep digging. We need more."

She narrowed her eyes at the phone. "Your wish is my command." *Douchbag.*

"In the meantime, Miss Hickey, congratulations. You'll be taking an all-expenses-paid trip to Paris next week courtesy of the NSA. Your tickets are waiting at your apartment in Capitol Hill. Make sure all those bugs and trackers are planted before you leave on Sunday."

Irene's jaw dropped. "You're sending me *where*?" Granted, it wasn't like he'd said Afghanistan, but really?

"It's the City of Love, Miss Hickey. How could you even remotely be disappointed?" he said flatly.

"But—"

Ellerton cut her off. "We'll be in touch if we don't hear from you first." The line went dead.

Irene stewed while her head nearly throbbed off her shoulders. Sleep was no longer an option. Taking a deep breath, she put on her robe and gathered two of the miniature state-of-the-art gadgets they'd given her. Wrapping them in a tissue, she stuffed the small bundle in the pocket of her robe.

*Damn them!* she thought, running a hand through her short hair.

On her mini-tour earlier, she'd found a library with a desk at the end of the hall. It seemed like a good place to start. If anyone caught her poking around, she could always say she couldn't sleep and was looking for a book to read.

Padding quietly in the darkness down the carpeted hallway, she reached the door of the library. She turned the knob slowly and eased the door open without a sound. Reaching inside, she swept her hand awkwardly along the wall, fumbling for the lights. As soon as she found a rectangular protrusion, she closed the door behind her and hit the switch.

The room lit up to reveal a massive collection of books lining the cherry bookcases on the surrounding walls. A large keyhole desk sat at the far end behind a seating arrangement in the center of the room—a brown leather Chesterfield sofa faced two wingback chairs with a low table in between. The room oozed English Manor House, reminding her of *Downton Abbey*.

Irene started with the desk. A slender laptop and a cell phone sat on top. When she touched the keyboard, the screen sprang to life—waiting for a password. Even in the CIA, her hacking skills had been nonexistent. Luckily, she'd had a tracker made specifically for snugging up next to the battery. Flipping the unit over, she removed the battery cover and placed the near-flat, half-inch square from the tissue in her pocket inside the casing.

Placing the computer back as it was, she moved on to the desk drawers, but not before she'd removed another small electronic bug and stuck it on the inside wall of the desk.

Perfect to catch any conversation…

Next, she tried the drawers. All were locked except for one. It slid open easily. She didn't have a clue what she was looking for, but maybe she'd get lucky and find a lexicon of the proto-language stolen from the Vatican. *Not.*

Irene sat down in front of the computer, sliding the chair underneath the heavy mahogany desk as she prepared to riffle through the contents. The drawer was jammed full of files. She thumbed through the hanging folders, finding nothing more than old household receipts from Cara's apartment downtown and work files from her former job at Cabot.

Disappointed, Irene closed the drawer and surveyed the rest of the room. She rolled the chair back, catching a stray power cord and jerking to a stop at the precise moment she rose. Her knee slammed into a low-hanging metal drawer on the underside of the desk.

"Shit," she said through gritted teeth, rubbing her stinging skin. *Weird.* The front of the desk was solid wood. A hidden drawer? Placing her palms up under the desk, she felt the cold metal against her hands. She pushed up and then slid the drawer forward. A five-inch unseen lip appeared and separated from its seams.

Inside the drawer, a manila file folder lay inside among some pens and pencils. No lettering, only a red triangular insignia surrounded by a pair of wings and crossed swords was visible on the folder. The center of the insignia held an inverted triangle with some unidentified markings and the shape of a jewel at the center.

Irene opened the file. A printed report lay inside.

```
CONFIDENTIAL
Guardianship Trinity Report
Subject: Collins Trinity
```

March 22nd: Rogue Nephil first detected during initial surveillance of Cara Collins. Rogue assisted Sentinel escape. No engagement. No energy footprint detected by the Guardianship. Verified worldwide.

March 23rd: Rogue Nephil detected post-demon attack on Cara Collins at Perry Street, West Village, NYC location. Suspected of arranging demon attack. No engagement.

March 30th: Rogue Nephil detected outside The Standard Grill. Meatpacking District, NYC. Lured by Chamuel, Son of Eae, to Pier 54. Engagement. Fight ensued while cloaked. Rogue escaped.

April 15th: Rogue Nephil detected in lower Manhattan. No engagement.

May 1st: Nephil detected at Collins's Connecticut farmhouse. No engagement.

May 20th: Rogue Nephil detected outside of Rising Sun Dojo in Brooklyn. This is the sixth encounter. Engagement has not occurred unless initiated. Guardianship hasn't been able to detect the identity or explain the presence of the rogue. Unlikely this Nephil is associated with the Angelorum, although alternative explanation unavailable. Potential association may exist with Nephilim genetics project. Rogue suspected of working for Le Feu. Cara Collins remains unaware of the rogue and doesn't seem to be in any immediate danger.

Irene stared at the report wavering in her trembling hands, her heart slamming underneath her breast. Cara's name in the association with the words *demon, Nephil, rogue,* and *danger* shook her to her core.

*What the heck was a Trinity? And what the heck was the Guardianship?* She wondered. Somehow this didn't sound like a communication from a normal company, or even a government agency, unless your name was Mulder and your job was investigating the X-Files. But Irene was certain of three things: Le Feu owned the warehouse that blew up in the surveillance footage. Simon Young didn't exist. And Le Feu and Simon were both French.

Placing the file back as she found it, Irene shut the drawer slowly. Her eyes scanned the bookshelves, impressed by the age and the titles of the books she found. Rather than returning to her room to retrieve her phone, she methodically inspected all four walls before she found a shelf containing what she was looking for: a full set of encyclopedias. Hard to believe this is what they used before Google.

She raced over. Taking out the volume containing the letter *N*, she flipped the pages until she found *Nephil/Nephilim*. Pacing with the heavy volume rested on her forearm, she rapidly scanned the section. As she'd suspected: Nephilim appeared in Genesis as the children produced between the Watchers— the "Sons of God,"—led by the angel Semyaza, and human women, the "Daughters of Men." She read through all the biblical references. But she didn't need an encyclopedia to tell her that *Angelorum* was the Latin word for *angels*.

Bleary-eyed, Irene sat and stared at the heavy volume in her hands. The proto-language Simon spoke earlier reminded her of the divine languages. What if that's exactly what it was? A divine language.

*Holy Cannoli.* She swept her hand over her face.

Simon Young doesn't exist not because he's a terrorist, but because Simon Young is a Nephil.

Could Simon Young be the Nephilim rogue? Could Cara be in danger from something other than the NSA?

*Oh my God…* Irene's heart went into free fall. What if Cara *is* sleeping with the enemy?

# Chapter 26



*ACHANELECH*
**France. Château du Feu. Saturday, May 25, 11:30 *AM GMT +1***

"I CAN'T POSSIBLY BE READY to host the Convocation next week!" Emanelech said, waving her tablet as she paced a rut across the antique Aubusson in her high heels. A tight black dress covered her scarred arms and clung to her curves, restricting her gait without slowing her down. Her long, black ponytail swished from side-to-side, reminding Achanelech of a fine horse.

She was so very pleasing to the eyes. Now, if he could only get her to shut up...

Achanelech passed a hand down his face, half-listening as she droned on. The sigil on the back of his neck throbbed, adding to his displeasure. His demon children wanted to come out and feed. "Not now," he snapped in Hellspeak.

Emanelech ground to a halt and glared at him, the nasty scar over her right ice-blue eye blazing a jagged red. "What? Are you listening to me?"

"*Mais oui, Chérie.*" Achanelech snapped. "Of course I'm listening. I've been listening to you rant for the last hour, but I'm no closer to understanding what it is you want from me," he said, throwing his hands up.

"Some help!"

"Can you be more specific?" he growled.

She clicked her tongue and passed her finger over her tablet. "First, a check. We need an entertainment planner. I'm thinking of Heinrich. He's prepared to fly in tomorrow, as soon as he gets a deposit—"

"How much?" Achanelech spat, anything for some quiet. He braced himself for the figure. It wouldn't be the first time he'd written a deposit for that overpriced party planner.

"Five hundred thousand."

His eyes shot wide and he grabbed the edge of the desk in a death grip. "Five hun… are you *insane*? He wants a million dollars for the event?"

She blinked. "The deposit is only for a third. A million and a half."

"*Chérie*, we can't afford it," he said with a shake of his head.

"He's expensive for a reason, Acchie," she purred, sidling up to his desk and pushing out her breasts.

No amount of her eyelash batting would seduce him into that sum of money.

He sighed. "Em, you'll need to find someone less expensive. Tithes to Luc have left our coffers low. We can't borrow for this. It will be seen as a sign of weakness."

Her mouth dropped into a pout. "But Acchie, if we screw this up, Luc will lock us in Hell and throw away the key. Look at this list." She shook her tablet at him. "The food and entertainment capture and disposal alone will require a small army. Then there's the upgrade to the playrooms and holding areas in the dungeon, redecorating the convocation meeting room, the sleeping quarters, the wine cellar, the servants—"

Achanelech rolled his eyes and pulled his checkbook from the drawer hidden under his desk. "Five hundred for the whole affair. If Heinrich can't do it for that, find someone else."

"But he's the only one with a fully bonded Dark One staff," she whined and stamped her high-heeled foot.

*Infernal woman.*

"Six hundred," he said, grabbing a pen. "Use your vast powers of compulsion and persuasion to have him see our point of view." He wrote it in Emanelech's name so that she could parse it out as necessary and handed her the check.

Her eyes lit up and she tucked it into her bra, and then she leaned in for a kiss. "Thanks, Hot Lips."

*She'll be my destruction*, he thought, wanting to roll his eyes.

"Anything *else* you need, *Chérie*?" he asked as she pulled away.

She wiggled her eyebrows at him, clutching the tablet to her chest. "Meet me in the dungeon later?"

A reluctant smile touched his lips. "Anything else?"

"May I borrow a couple of your demons? I want to hunt for some attractive entertainment before Heinrich arrives," she said, no longer showing signs of distress.

He eyed her warily. "How do you know he'll accept our offer?"

She looked at him with a coquettish glint in her eye, and flashed a smug smile. "He agreed to five hundred for the whole affair."

*Bitch.* "You lied to me," he said through gritted teeth as steam gathered at the top of his head.

"*Tsk-tsk.* No, my love, I manipulated you. There's a difference. If I'd quoted you a lesser amount, you would've given me less than what I needed. I'm doing this for us, Acchie. To save our hides." She blew him an icy kiss and smiled.

The kiss transformed into a small snow cloud, hovering over his head for a second before turning into tiny snowflakes and snowing on the top of his head. His hair hissed as fire met ice.

By Lucifer, he abhorred when she was right.

"Fine," he said. "But before I release my children and send you on your shopping expedition, what of our plan to capture Cara Collins?"

She smiled wide. "If Escher and his team fail in her capture, our backup plan is in place. She and Eae's Nephil spawn arrive at the Sanctuary on Wednesday. Plenty of time to set our trap before the Convocation begins."

His mood lightened. He chortled, rubbing his hands together with glee. Targeting another one of Eae's children filled him with such delight. Someday she'd pay for destroying his twin demon soul; the one who'd shared his throne of fire.

He'd waited almost six hundred years to exact his revenge, taking only small payments from her along the way. But the one he truly wanted was still hiding in this realm, he was almost sure of it. The one who'd done the actual deed with her consent. The one responsible for his battle injury and the V-shaped scar upon his face.

Like him, she had a twin soul.

Eae and Leo.

Together they were the Angels Who Thwart Demons.

With the battle looming, surely he'll make his appearance soon. Achanelech was counting on it.

"Acchie? I'm waiting," she said with an icy glare.

He blew out a breath and rose from his desk. "Stand back. Don't overfeed them while you're out." Otherwise, they'd be useless when he needed them next.

He summoned forth his demons in their native tongue. Leaning his head forward, the sigil pulsed and rose on the back of his neck, opening the gate and freeing his children.

A black haze filled the room.

"Come, pets. We've got work to do. I promise a nice lunch," Emanelech said in a sing-song voice. She glided from the room with the dark energy of his children obediently following behind her.

# Chapter 27

*MICHAEL*
*Brooklyn, New York. Rising Sun Dojo. Saturday, May 25, 4:30 PM ET*

MICHAEL STOOD FRESHLY SHOWERED after finishing his Pee-Wee class for five-year-olds, followed by an advanced weapons training class. He couldn't decide which class had been more difficult: the little tykes or the bruisers with a death wish. Typically, he had the patience of a saint, but his irrational anxiety over seeing Sienna later tonight had shredded his peace of mind.

The sound of Rodney, one of Michael's full-time instructors, and his class of ten-year-olds practicing katas echoed through the walls and into the dojo's staff locker room.

A towel wrapped around his hips, Michael gazed into the mirror over the double sink and ran a brush through his damp hair. Contrary to what Cara and Simon believed, he didn't spend a lot of time on it.

Glancing at his wrist, he checked the time. He had an hour before his meeting with the Guardians at Simon's loft.

The locker room door swung open, and Deva walked in dressed in her *gi*, her light brown hair gathered in a ponytail.

"Did you leave me any hot water?" she asked, giving him an appraising look and tossing her duffel on the floor next to the long teak bench in the center of the room.

He let out a breath. "You could've knocked, you know."

She winked and grinned. "It's not like I don't remember what's under that towel."

He scowled at her. "Come on, Dee. I don't need to be reminded how far back we go. I'm still your boss."

She threw her hands up, wearing a look of wide-eyed innocence. "Yes, Sensei. I'm just saying."

He'd met Deva in ninth grade English class at Dalton, the private New York City high school they'd both attended. Dee had loved competitive martial arts as much as he had. It hadn't taken long for them to become inseparable, spending all their free time studying, sparring, and gaming. Wherever one was, the other wasn't far behind. Everything was fine until they lost their virginity together at the start of their senior year.

They'd slept together every chance they could for a month… until she'd spoken in jest the same two words Sienna said on the porch. *Pretty Boy*. The first dream came that night. The terrifying, cinnamon-infused dream waking him to his own screams and leaving him saddled with a deep sense of shame. The memories of his black day, buried since he was a child, resurfaced with a vengeance and threatened to break free.

To this day, she'd never understood why he'd ended their physical relationship. His lie still mocked him like nails scraping a chalkboard. "I don't think I feel the same way you do." The truth was that his feelings terrified him.

His lie had also ended their friendship. A hole of loneliness filled with guilt was left in its place.

Then, eighteen months ago, Michael had run into Deva at a nightclub in Manhattan. Recently divorced from her college sweetheart, Deva had moved back to Brooklyn to lick her wounds and regroup. Agreeing to start fresh, they renewed their friendship. But a little over a year ago, he'd spent a night with her. They hadn't spoken about it since. When he opened the dojo a few months after that, he offered her a job as long as she agreed to his strict nonfraternization policy—namely, with him.

But even now, he could feel the heat in her gaze.

He turned to her and leaned against the counter. "I'm sorry, Dee. I'm just in a rotten mood. Can I ask a favor?"

"Sure."

"Give me five minutes? I just want to finish up." He said nicely and tried not to feel like a jerk.

Disappointment filled her eyes, but she did her best to hide it. "No problem. Can I leave my stuff here?"

He nodded. "Sure. Thanks… I mean it."

She closed the door behind her, and a pang of guilt hit him. He valued their friendship, but right now what he needed was to be alone. Relieved she was gone, he let his mind drift again to seeing Sienna later and his stomach clenched in a tight knot.

*Coward*, he chided at the mirror and hung his head. When people looked at him they saw someone bright, well-mannered, and kind. A façade he worked so hard to project. He hungered to be someone respectable and admirable like his father; a true role model who embodied all of the traits and values Michael aspired to have. Someone who valued family above all else. A loving husband and father…

Pain clenched his heart as he thought of his dad. Not one day had passed since his father's death that he didn't miss him. As much as he loved his mom, his relationship with his dad had been special. They'd been closer than most, in touch almost daily. Whether it was lunch, a run in the park, just a call, they'd been in constant contact. His father was the only person who knew about his gifts, helping him to harness and control them. With the exception of his dark secret, his father had known everything about him. His loss left him empty and alone. The best thing he could do now was honor him. If he could be even half the man his father was, he'd be happy.

Although apprehensive to confront Sienna, his dreams of her gave him a sliver of hope. Even hot sex unencumbered by his haunting fears would be enough.

*Why can't I be normal?* he wondered with a heavy heart. He had no answer.

He slipped into his clothes. As he picked up his gym bag, a wisp of fine energy flew past his face, encircling him and raising the hairs on his arms. A stream of melodic whispers followed, echoing inside his head as they called to him from the Flow.

News from the Angelorum.

He eyed the door, walked over, and locked it. Something he should have done when he'd come in. Taking a deep breath he closed his eyes and projected his thoughts upward into the Flow, connecting with the electromagnetic stream that surrounded Earth and the communications network embedded within it. Like a fingerprint, the molecules of Michael's body vibrated at a set rate, connecting him with his personal frequency.

*"Messenger Swift,"* the voice greeted him telepathically in the Angelic language. *"Be warned. Danger lies close to your Trinity. As the Twelve are gathered, so are those who will oppose them. Many are preparing to join power, a movement that has not happened in centuries. Be ever vigilant."*

The wisp of power disappeared, the message over. Michael opened his eyes and let out a breath, feeling invigorated. "Would have been nice to know when," he muttered.

Michael slipped on his shoes, and slung his laundry bag filled with dirty *gis* over his shoulder.

On his way to the subway, Michael stopped at the Chinese Laundromat around the corner. He collected his pink ticket and stepped outside.

Before Michael could react, his body was slammed backward, hard, against a massive male chest. A strong arm locked him in place with ease, and a pair of thick fingers rested on a nerve in his neck. "Don't move Messenger, or I'll drop you like a sack of potatoes. I mean no harm, just listen," the man said from behind him, the heat of his breath warm on Michael's ear.

Michael froze in confusion, feeling his friend's energy pressing against his back. It didn't make sense. Something was off. *Simon?*

A couple walked past holding hands, oblivious to Michael's plight, confirming he was hidden behind a veil.

Michael's pulse accelerated. *The rogue…*

"Who are you?" Michael gritted out, the Nephil's thick arm, uncomfortably heavy across his chest, was swathed in black leather.

"Not important."

*We'll see about that.* Michael dropped his telepathic shields and plunged into the Nephil's head. He slammed into a mental shield and bounced off.

*That's never happened before*, he thought with surprise as a shockwave of pain ricocheted inside his skull.

"Stay out of my head, Telepath," he snarled, putting pressure on Michael's neck. Without warning, Michael's legs buckled, going numb beneath him. The Nephil's arm pinned Michael in place, preventing his fall.

Michael snarled with frustration, unable to move his lower body. His pounding heart sent a surge of adrenaline through him with no effect. Michael fought to wrestle his arms free.

The Nephil's arm tightened around him. "Relax and be still. It's only temporary. Consider it a compliment. I'm trying to help you, but I don't need a shattered instep, kneecap, or anything worse for my trouble," he said calmly.

Michael struggled to get his breath back under control, tamping down his feelings of helplessness. "Fine. Why have you been following Chamuel?" he asked using Simon's Guardian name.

The Nephil hesitated. "Again, not important."

*Bingo*, Michael thought. *He is the rogue.* "What do you want?"

"To warn you," the rogue said. His voice held a combination of weariness and frustration but no malice. The tone was deep and rich. Close, but not an exact match to Simon's. If only Michael could catch a glimpse of his face…

"About what?"

"East will meet West in preparation."

"In preparation for what?" Michael gasped, suddenly starved for oxygen. "You're crushing me." The Nephil's embrace was like being wrapped inside a boa constrictor.

The rogue loosened his grip over Michael's chest, allowing his lungs to refill with air. "The Convocation. The dark powers are gathering with the intent to unite in preparation for battle against the Twelve. All the better if they can take care of some business in advance."

Michael's blood ran cold.

"When and where will the Convocation be held?"

"France. It will start within the next ten days…"

"How do you know all this?"

"Again, not important. Just be grateful I'm sharing what I know," he growled.

"Why are you telling me this?"

Silence, and then, ". . . I don't know."

*What the… ?* Michael wondered. Was it a trap of some kind? "How much time do we have before company arrives in New York?"

"They're already here. Prepare yourselves." His breath tickled Michael's ear again. "I apologize."

"For what?" Michael asked right before everything went black.

He awoke sitting propped up against a building in the alley behind the Laundromat with an ache in his neck. The bastard had dropped him anyway.

Wiggling his toes, he exhaled a sigh of relief. Feeling had returned to his legs. Michael pulled himself up and looked at his watch. He'd been out for only a few minutes. Brushing the dirt from his pants, he didn't bother to check for his wallet. He knew it was still there. If robbery had been the rogue's intent, his father's Patek Philippe—a watch Cara teased him cost him as much as a BMW—would've been gone.

*Why does he want to help us?* Michael wondered. One thing was for certain, he seemed to have better information than the Angelorum. Of the two messages, Michael had learned the most from the Nephil.

Michael continued on to the subway and made a silent call. *"Simon?"*

*"What's up?"*

*"I just met your rogue. Call in the reinforcements. One more thing…"*

*"What's that?"*

*"I've figured out why you're the only one he's following…"*

# Chapter 28

*MICHAEL*
*New York City. Greene Street Loft. Saturday, May 25, 5:45 PM ET*

MICHAEL FOUND THE EMERGENCY door propped open with a six-pack when he reached the fifth floor landing outside the loft. The corner of his mouth pulled up in a smile and he walked in.

It sounded like the party had already started.

Michael passed by the kitchen island—covered in alcoholic beverages and supplies for later—into the living room where the five hulking figures filled the leather sectional and the two matching chairs, sampling the night's beverage selection. Out of uniform, they looked like a social gathering of MMA fighters or NFL linebackers. The giant flat screen on the wall flashed with motion from a soccer game playing on mute.

Simon and Angel drew the chairs, while Isaac and two of his Tri-State Guardians, Zeke and Noah—the youngsters of the group—sat on the sectional, voraciously eating out of a bowl of chips on the coffee table between swigs of beer. Unlike most of the older Guardians, Zeke and Noah both had tribal ink wrapped around their biceps, poking out of their tight T-shirt sleeves. For some reason, they always seemed hungrier than the older guys.

Simon looked up as he entered and the room fell silent. "Take a seat, Michael."

Resting his elbows on his knees, Angel eyed Michael warily with his dark gaze. "We're eager to hear your news, amigo."

Isaac gave him a level stare. "I'm especially interested in what you discovered. The rogue has eluded us for months."

Michael joined Isaac and the Tri-State guys on the padded leather, and traded a nod with Zeke and Noah. Michael still hadn't gotten used to Isaac taking over for Simon as their Trinity Guardian. Suspended or not, Simon still mostly ran the show.

"I'm almost positive this rogue isn't a Guardian," Michael said, shaking his head.

"We suspected that. Can you give us a physical description?" Isaac asked, running his fingers along the top of his blond brush cut.

Michael shook his head. "No, he grabbed me from behind." He hesitated as he chose his next words. "And I have a theory why he's only shadowed Simon."

Isaac's ice-blue stare hardened. "Why's that?"

"He's got the same energy footprint. He feels exactly like him."

Several sharp intakes of breath sounded from around him, signaling his assumption was likely correct. Sharing the same energy, like sharing a fingerprint, was almost impossible.

Simon folded his arms across his chest. "How's that even possible? He's never felt familiar to me."

Zeke rolled his eyes and popped the top on his next beer. "Come on Si, don't be a dope. When was the last time you could feel your own energy? The answer is you can't; only everyone else's."

"Show some respect," snapped Isaac, shifting in his seat and looking like he wanted to dole out a head smack before he turned back to the team. "What does that leave us with? A double? A mimic? What?"

"Not sure, but it'll make him easier to find. We follow Simon or anyone we think is him and then flush him out," said Angel.

Isaac nodded over his tented hands. "Yup, could work. I'll update the alert." He glanced back at Michael. "So what else did you find out?"

Michael decided to keep out the part about being incapacitated and then knocked out. The anxious energy of the Guardians pulled at him.

"Here it is, for whatever it's worth: We need to prepare. We have company. They're already here from the West Coast. Between now and the time we leave for the Sanctuary, we may be attacked," Michael said.

Angel made a sour face and shifted forward in his chair. "Fuck. Le Feu in Paris leaves Escher Grant and his band of merry minions," he said, naming Lucifer's two West Coast lieutenants.

Michael glanced at Angel. "He said they'll try to attack before the battle. They've already targeted Brett, so they probably know Simon is one of the Twelve by now. At least Cara is off limits."

"Why's that?" Angel frowned.

Michael opened his mouth to speak, but Simon cleared his throat and sent out a silent message. *"Let me tell them."* Michael nodded in deference and stayed quiet.

Simon recounted the story Cara had told them the day before about her encounter with Jonas, the words he'd spoken to her, and the implied meaning of her role in the prophecy. When Simon finished, a murmur traveled around the room accompanied with looks of concern.

"I've got twenty Guardians on hand this evening to cover the Beacon; half of them are already there to watch over Brett as he preps for tonight's show," Isaac said, drumming his fingers on his thigh. "Simon and Cara will be covered. In the meantime, I'll make some calls and we'll start monitoring for movement around the city."

"We've got Frank working undercover as King Metaljam's head of security. He's ready with his people," Angel added.

Simon cocked an eyebrow at Angel. "His people are all Guardians?"

"Nope. Some are human. They think Brett's got a stalker and that an attempt has been made on his life." Angel slouched back in his chair with a cock-eyed grin. "Brett told Roxy the same. She thinks it's her job to keep it out of the tabloids."

"Sounds like we're covered then," Simon said, looking satisfied.

A surge of concern hit Michael when he realized Sienna was with Cara. Although Cara might be off limits, danger could still be close while she and her friends pampered themselves uptown. The sudden thought of anything happening to Sienna… He turned to Simon. "Do we need any extra security on Cara and the girls today?"

Simon leaned over and clasped his shoulder, giving him a knowing look. "The daytime team is inside the spa. And after your call, Isaac deployed two more Guardians to monitor them from outside."

"Good." Michael let out the breath he'd been holding.

Angel fixed them all with a hard stare. "Don't be too sure, li'l bro, that Simon and Cara are the only ones we need to worry about just because they've been named as part of the Twelve already. I know how this works, and any of you could be part of the nine still hidden inside of the Trinity Stones. Just 'cause we haven't been told yet doesn't make it less true. Chances are the Council already knows who'll be next. They just aren't sharing. If they know, we have to assume the Dark Ones might know, too."

Simon nodded. "I'm in agreement. I told Cara the same thing."

"How would they know?" Michael asked, feeling as if he'd missed something.

Angel sniffed. "As I said the other night, Constantina knows more than she's telling. She won't say it out loud, but we both know there could be a traitor on the Council."

Simon shot him a look and shook his head.

"All right, all right..." he said, scowling. "Discoverability, I get it." His statement was met with cryptic stares.

Simon's eyes shifted skyward. "Without a Council member present, anything we share becomes a discoverable moment within the Flow. Constantina spoke to me and Cara about it after dinner the other night," Simon said.

Two months into his assignment as Cara's Messenger and Michael still had a lot to learn. He leaned back in his chair and tried to release some of the tension in his shoulders. "Good to know. In the meantime, the reason for the company has to do with a Convocation the Dark Ones plan to have in France. They're paying us a visit on their way."

"Maybe that's why *Le Feu* resurfaced in Paris," Isaac said, clasping his chin.

"That's not all. The Angelorum contacted me right before my visit from the rogue. They both delivered the same message, more or less. Bottom line: the Dark Ones are gathering in preparation for the battle."

Angel clasped his hands together behind his head and smirked. "A Convocation, huh? It'd be the first time in over four hundred years the bastards showed up in the same place at the same time. They hate each other's guts. Can barely hold their shit together in the same room." He let out a low chortle. "Should be fun."

"Experience speaking?" Michael asked. Angel and Paco, as Four Hundred–Class Guardians, were the oldest Nephilim in their crew.

"You know it. Paco and I were young guns then, thirty years old during their last party. They held it in Rome, close to what's now Vatican City. The Pope would've shit his pants if he'd known." He chuckled as he reminisced. "Sneaky bastards hid it behind an outbreak of Bubonic Plague to cover the deaths."

Eyes lit up with interest around the room.

Simon waved his hand at Angel. "Be my guest."

"A lot was going on in Rome at the time. Made it easy for the Dark Ones to go unnoticed. Happened right before Galileo was imprisoned during the Roman Inquisition for coming out with his theory that the Sun was at the center of the solar system." Angel added with a mischievous smile. "Nice guy, by the way. Pissed off the Jesuits; that alone made him worthy of my respect."

Simon cleared his throat and gave him an impatient glare. "Do we know why they held the Convocation?"

"Keep on *sus calzones*." Angel said, waving him off. "They met to vote on a replacement for one of the Thirteen who'd come to... an untimely demise."

Simon's brows shot up. "What happened to him?"

Angel shook his head, giving him a pained look. "That, my friend, is a question for your Constantina. All I will say is that even the Angelorum is not error-free. And some mistakes are yet to be fully rectified."

*Sobering*, Michael thought.

"What does that mean?" Isaac asked gruffly with the full weight of his icy stare.

Angel's stare met his head-on. "Not everything is mine to tell. But I can tell you this. Alone, the thirteen lieutenants wreak their own pockets of havoc; but together, they're a force to be reckoned with." He glanced at Michael. "But just like us, they have a code. If they violate it, they forfeit the battle."

"It seems like they're calling all the shots," Michael said.

"That's the thing. The coin flip has been with them for longer than any of us have been alive. Le Feu threw down the gauntlet when he went after Kai and Cara. Bottom line, they're confident they can win or they wouldn't have done it. Now our job is to figure out their plan."

"And then how to defeat them," Simon added.

# Chapter 29

*BRETT*

*New York City. Beacon Theatre. Saturday, May 25, 8:45 PM ET*

BRETT PACED NEXT TO ROXY as they hung out with the rest of the band backstage, preparing to go on. Roxy tapped her foot and her entire body bobbed with energy. Despite her anxious tapping, her short, black hair—jelled into hard spikes—didn't budge. Between the hair, black leather dress, and heels, she looked her usual rock 'n' roll badass.

Nervous energy filled the room as Brett and the band mentally prepared. Clamping her hand on his shoulder, Roxy pulled him close enough so her lips almost touched his ear. "How are you holding up?"

He shrugged and gave her a crooked smile. "It's all good."

How could it not be? Frank stood looming in the wings. The front row was packed with Cara, her friends, and a full line-up of Guardianship muscle. No chances would be taken with his safety tonight. Angel and Isaac had pulled together enough firepower to stop a herd of demons. And it didn't end there. Paco, at Angel's request, would be pasted to his side for the foreseeable future starting with accompanying him to the Sanctuary on Wednesday. Brett was glad for the show of support, but he had trouble getting used to his biker buddies shadowing every piss he took.

Roxy didn't look convinced, crossing her arms over her chest. "I'll take your word on it... for now."

"What about your end?" he asked, throwing a glance at his band members who were all in the middle of doing their own prep.

"So far, so good. Not a hint of anything on the wires." She followed his gaze to the others, and said in a heated whisper, "They don't know a thing. Do the police have any idea who's after you?"

He hated lying and couldn't meet her eyes. "Nah, not yet. And I can't talk about it even if I did. Strict orders from the security team."

"I get it." She huffed and turned away. He didn't have time to worry about what could happen off-stage. Angel and his crew could more than handle anything that came their way. Right now, he needed to focus on controlling what happened on stage and giving a kick-ass performance.

They were scheduled to go on at nine o'clock and finish at eleven. After the show he'd shower then jump into the waiting Escalade that would whisk him downtown to the after-party at Simon's. He'd be skipping the backstage hangout and fan mayhem this time around. No big loss as far as he was concerned.

Brett paced, limbering up his muscles and thinking through his plan to dedicate one of his new songs to Cara without raising Simon's wrath. He agonized over which one to pick. Even in the short time he'd known her, she'd been great. Fuck it. More than great... the best. The fact that she was spoken for still stuck in his craw. But better her shutting that irrational shit down before he got himself into serious trouble.

Maybe he'd dedicate the song he played for her on the steps of his aunt's house. She seemed to like that one, and it didn't have any overt sexual overtones. Last thing he wanted was to offend Cara or get an ass kicking from his very gracious host.

He moved on to breathing exercises and scales to warm up his voice. His head cleared and vocal chords ready, he headed for the wings with the others and listened to the closing song from their warm-up band, Sonic Thunder.

Brett reviewed the playlist and costume changes in his head. He'd lost his argument with Roxy earlier and had to go commando under the leather pants.

"You don't want your underwear showing above your waistband, King," she'd insisted, hands planted on her small hips. He grudgingly agreed. Next time, he wouldn't be surprised if she asked him to go bare-assed naked.

Sonic Thunder took their final bow and then filed back behind the curtain, giving him and the band high fives as they passed by.

After the roadies set the stage for King Metaljam, Roxy strode out front to do the honors and announce them.

"New York City! How's everyone doing tonight?" she asked. The crowd responded with a round of wild applause and whistles.

"They were good, weren't they?" Another round of thunderous applause filtered back in response.

"Without further ado, put your hands together for King Metaljam!"

The crowd went wild.

Brett's heart raced like it always did when he was about to go on stage. The rest of the band had already filed out under the cover of darkness as Roxy spoke and opened with notes of their first song from their number one hit, "St. Petersburg." He turned on his combo in-ear monitor and wireless microphone, snapping the battery pack to the back of his leather pants. Then he sauntered onto the stage. The bright lights hit the top of his head and warmed his hair as he started with the first chorus. The audience spotted him. Excitement-filled screams and whistles greeted his arrival, his pulse quickening with the rush. This song only required vocals, making it the perfect choice to start. He eyed his guitars, tuned and lined up just right of center stage.

He belted out the familiar tune, the theater alive with music. The energy of the fans electrified him into action as he moved around the stage. There was no greater high for him than this—being in his element and hosting a party fueled by his music. Bright lights limited his view but not as much as usual. The lighting engineers had cut the lights in half at his request, leaving just enough to see the faces in the first few rows. He liked nothing more than picking out a female fan in the crowd and singing to her.

He moved with a practiced ease across the stage, his hands free to do whatever moved him. Starting with a favorite tune always drove up the energy in the room. After the first song ended, he grabbed one of his guitars and pealed into a second favorite. He did his best not to focus on the first row after he caught Cara's eye and winked.

In no time, he was ready for his first costume change, exiting the stage while the band played an instrumental riff to cover for him. On his return, he dragged the stool to center stage and picked up his acoustic guitar.

Speaking through the wireless mic, he said, "I'd like to dedicate this next song to a good friend of mine. She was so impressed that she suggested I try out for *American Idol*."

A roar of laughter came from the audience.

"In all fairness, she didn't know who I was at the time. This one's for Cara." He found Cara glaring up at him from the front row and smiled.

"Please don't kill me later. This one's called 'The Price of Fame,'" he said into the mic, and then launched into the song he'd just written. He'd let the crowd be the judge if it was any good or not.

Deafening applause descended after the last note, letting him know he had a potential winner.

Picking away at his guitar as a transition between songs, he said to the crowd, "I just finished a few new tunes that I'd like to try out on you guys. Cool?"

Encouraging shouts, screams, and whistles filled the air.

"But first… I need someone to sing to," he said, and gave one of his disarming dimpled smiles. The women in the audience went nuts, making his smile even wider.

"*Hmm…*" he said into the microphone as he scanned the first row, looking for Cara's wedding party.

*Maybe one of those ladies wouldn't mind a little attention?* he thought devilishly, not bothering to look for anyone but Cara up until now. His eyes flitted across the faces and came to rest on a woman he'd never seen before. The sight of her knocked the air from his lungs. Was she even part of Cara's party? Her hair was long with light-colored curls surrounding the wholesome face of an angel.

*Holy shit, who's that?* he wondered, and unconsciously licked his lips.

"I see someone," he said, wiggling his eyebrows at the crowd. He put down his guitar and walked over to the edge of the stage. Bending down in front of her, he held out his hand, beckoning her with a smile and a raised eyebrow.

She looked at him with her lips parted and her eyes wide like a deer caught in headlights. Slowly, she shook her head no.

*No? Really?* he thought with disbelief.

Digging deep into his well of charm he put on his best puppy dog eyes and mouthed, "Please?"

Her look of shock gave way to a smirk as she extended her hand to meet his. Paco lifted her over the barrier and onto the stage. A strange excitement gripped Brett as he led her to the stool and sat her down. The women in the crowd went mad, disappointed they hadn't been picked.

Brett handed the guitar to his bass player and started to sing "Rescue Me." Picking up her hand, he stared into her eyes when he got to the chorus.

*Rescue me,*
*I need someone to rescue me*
*Take me home, and rescue me*
*I need you to rescue me*

His heart accelerated, not due to exertion, but to the touch of her skin. Her hand, smooth as silk, fit perfectly inside of his. His fingers, having a mind of their own, laced themselves through hers. Her eyes went big and her lips parted, reflecting mild surprise as he squeezed her hand in silent dialogue.

Mesmerized, he studied her face as he sang to her, just as studiously as she avoided his gaze. Only the barest hint of makeup was visible on her face. Her eyes reflected hazel in the lights, her lips full and tempting in a face so fresh and wholesome he could cry. Tall and willowy, she wore a simple sundress that was less New York and more somewhere else. He said a silent prayer that he'd see her later at the after-party.

When the song finished, he put his arm around her waist and his lips to her ear. "What's your name?"

"Jessa," she said into his free ear, her lips brushing his hair. His scalp tingled on contact.

Brett turned to the crowd. "Give it up for Jessa!"

Rousing applause followed as he led her back to the edge of the stage. Usually, he simply took his surprised guest by the hand, led her away for a few steps, and then a roadie would come to escort her away. This time his hand never left her waist. If he could have stopped the concert and kept his arm around her all night, he would have. Her eyes widened when he leaned in to graze her cheek with his lips. Velvet. That's what her skin felt like to kiss.

"Thanks," he said before Paco lifted her back over the barrier. She looked back at him, her fingers still touching her cheek where his lips had been.

*Shit.* His stomach did a somersault. The second he let go of her, he was lost. If she didn't show up later, he would personally sponsor a search party to find her. Maybe Cara was right. Maybe there was someone else out there for him.

# Chapter 30



CARA SAT IN THE FRONT row of the Beacon with the rest of their entourage, glad to be securely ensconced in her seat after an estrogen-fueled day and a short stint as social director.

Mission accomplished on selecting one of the three designs for the bridesmaids' dresses, and Sienna's getting everyone's measurements. But it hadn't been easy. Sienna had done such a good job creating the designs, the girls had trouble choosing which one they liked best. They ended up picking their selection out of a hat. Lunch was fabulous, and they all had a gorgeous pedicure to show off as a result of their spa visit.

When she got back to the penthouse with the girls, she realized that she held all twenty-five concert tickets. Between the wedding party and all of the Guardians Angel had invited, they had a taker for every ticket. Too bad herding cats would've been easier than getting everyone organized for this event.

By eight o'clock, Cara had finished playing mother hen and left the remaining tickets at Will Call for anyone who arrived late. One quick text on where they could find them and her job was done. They were all smart, functioning adults, human or Nephilim. They'd figure it out.

Cara glanced down their row and frowned. Everyone had arrived except Michael. *He'd better not bail*, she thought, knowing how excited Sienna pretended not to be to see him.

Besides the Guardians interspersed among her girlfriends, she felt the Nephilim energy blanketing the building, locking it down tighter than Fort Knox.

Sinking back into her seat, Cara was mesmerized by Brett. She recognized many of the songs once she'd heard them, and felt like a dunce for not making the connection. Brett's talent was beyond impressive; he truly was a sensational performer. From the moment he came out onto the stage, he owned it. On top of being a skilled musician and vocalist, he knew how to work the crowd. Not to mention he looked like a schoolgirl's dream in black leather with his tawny hair loose at his shoulders. Her chest swelled with pride as she watched him.

Michael slipped in next to her and Simon at the end of the first set, wearing a sheepish grin. Cara eyed him suspiciously, wondering if his delay had anything to do with Sienna, who was conveniently seated at the opposite end of the row. Deciding not to pry, she let it go.

Still stewing over Brett's *American Idol* comment, she sat up straighter in her chair when he picked Jessa out of the audience to come up on stage with him. For a split second, Cara thought that he might choose her, and breathed a sigh of relief when he didn't.

And then it hit her… Jessa. Why hadn't she thought of it before? Constantina mentioned he was meant for another…

*Jessa is perfect for Brett, completely perfect! Oh, my Lord!* Cara was elated, watching him sing to Jessa, holding her hand delicately in his and lacing his fingers through hers. His energy told her what she wanted to know… he was intrigued. But her elation turned to puzzlement when Jessa's bitter lemon fear hit her tongue. Why would Jessa be afraid of Brett? Why would anyone be afraid of Brett?

"Is everything okay?" Simon asked with his lips close to her ear.

She leaned in to his ear. "Does Jessa seem afraid to you?"

Simon stared at Jessa for a few seconds and then leaned back down to Cara. "Strange. I sense more than mild apprehension. She does seem afraid."

Cara's brow bunched in thought. How could she find out without getting all up in Jessa's business? But if there was a chance Jessa could make Brett happy, Cara was all in.

As Brett finished off the acoustic set, his eyes traveled frequently to where Jessa sat.

Simon tapped Cara on the shoulder. Wearing a wide smile, he said in her ear, "I think he likes her."

Cara nodded. She couldn't agree more. Things could get interesting as the night unfolded… barring any demon attacks, that was.

# Chapter 31

*BRETT*
*New York City. Beacon Theatre. Saturday, May 25, 11:30 PM ET*

AFTER THE SHOW, Brett couldn't have showered faster if someone had told him the place was on fire. If nothing else, he didn't want to waste a minute of his time getting downtown to the after-party.

He threw on a pair of underwear. *Thank you very much*, he thought, glad that he didn't have to go commando for the rest of the night, before slipping into a clean pair of jeans and a black T-shirt. Glancing in the mirror, he decided to duck into his room at Simon's to change before he went up to the roof party.

Like a man possessed, he needed to find Jessa before she disappeared into thin air. He couldn't explain what had come over him when he'd taken her up on stage. Yesterday, he'd been pining away for Cara, and tonight a whole new world of possibilities opened up for him. Although he could be impulsive, he wasn't normally fickle when it came to his choice of women; he abhorred one-night stands and avoided groupies like the plague. His feelings for Cara hadn't disappeared, but had faded into proper perspective—she was engaged and in love with someone else. On the other hand, he was drawn to Jessa like a magnet.

*Fuck.* He took a deep breath. *I need a drink to calm my nerves.* He glanced at his watch—eleven-thirty. The party was just getting started, and he didn't want to miss a minute more than necessary.

"Amigo, you ready to go?" Paco asked, as Brett emerged from the dressing room with his hair still damp. He left everything behind for Roxy to handle, as usual.

*You have no idea.* He nodded.

"Angel's waiting out front."

Brett let go a sigh of relief. "Lead the way."

"I'll cloak you and we'll slip out the front door," Paco said, putting his arm around Brett and leading him through the empty theater, past the crowd of fans into the waiting car. A fully visible Guardian entered behind them, leaving the crowd none the wiser that three people, rather than one, had gotten into the vehicle. Angel took off the moment the door of the SUV closed. Paco released Brett, and they became visible in the backseat.

Angel peered into the rearview mirror. "Great show, m'ijo. You looked like a piece of *beef*cake up there," he said with a chuckle. As always, Angel laid down the opening salvo with the creative use of a meat-related term.

Brett let out a small laugh. "Thanks, amigo. Glad you enjoyed the show."

"I thought I might need to protect your ass from Simon. Now, maybe not," Angel said. "Pretty lady you chose from the audience tonight. The face of an angel on that one."

Brett found that ironic coming from Angel. "You should know, my friend," he teased and then blushed. "She was pretty, wasn't she?" His voice took on a dreamy quality, thinking again of those beautiful curls of hers and how much he wanted to run his fingers through them.

Angel's dark eyes glanced back at him from the rearview mirror. "You have it bad, I can tell."

"Come on." Brett rolled his eyes. "I just met her for like thirty seconds. How can you say I have it bad for her?"

Angel chuckled again in his annoying fashion and said, "You're a walking hormone. I can smell it on you."

"You can smell me?" Brett squeaked, turning beet red. His heart beat faster.

"I'm Nephilim. I can do a lot of things. But don't worry. The pretty lady won't know unless you tell her."

Relief washed over Brett. The whole Nephilim thing had really freaked him out at first, but the more he understood, the less it bothered him. Their cloaking ability was a Godsend, and he'd be using that one whenever he could.

Brett froze. "Hey, what did you mean about protecting my ass from Simon?"

Angel gazed back at him. "Are you kidding me? After what I just said? Simon can smell you a mile away from Cara. You're like a regular 'Eau de Brett' perfume factory!"

Brett's cheeks grew hotter, and he threw his head back onto the headrest. "Shit, I had no idea." Mortification wrapped around him like a straightjacket. Angel's comment in Connecticut about the "hormone meltdown" finally made sense.

Brett furrowed his brow and shoved Paco into the silent Guardian sitting on the other side of him. "Why didn't you warn me, man? You've been up my ass since I got here and you couldn't have given me a heads-up?"

Paco looked stoically at Brett. "It wouldn't have helped, amigo."

"Just be lucky he can't read your mind." Angel snickered.

"Are you shitting me? Don't tell me you can read my mother-fucking mind!" Brett said.

"Only a Telepath could. I think you're safe on that one. Don't get *sus calzones* in a wad."

Brett's shoulders slumped with relief. "And I thought I needed a fucking drink *before* I got in the car." First order of business when he got back: slamming back a shot so he didn't make a jackass out of himself in front of this girl.

"Get ready for that drink, li'l bro, we're here."

An adrenaline rush ignited the nerves in Brett's stomach. He took another deep breath and reached for the door handle. "Thanks for the ride. You comin' up?" he asked Angel, opening the door of the SUV.

"After I park. In the meantime, these two will continue to cover you for the foreseeable future."

"Oh, come on, give me a break!"

Angel gave Brett a hard stare. "We're not doing this for fun, m'ijo. If you want to spend time alone with the señorita, stay on the deck or take her inside. Don't get cute and disappear outside of the safe house. Otherwise, I will hunt you down and kick your ass in front of her. We clear?"

Brett put his head in his hands and rubbed his face. "Fine," he spat. "You're starting to make me feel like a goddamn prisoner."

"Beats the alternative. Remember that."

Frustration furrowed Brett's brow, making him feel like a temperamental two-year-old. "See you inside," Brett grumbled and slammed the car door. He needed an attitude adjustment, stat.

He could see the glow of the lights on the roof, but the building was blanketed in silence.

"Shouldn't we be able to hear the party from the street? What's up?" he asked Paco.

"Veil of Silence. We figured it wouldn't be too cool for the cops to shut down our party for violating a noise ordinance."

Brett shook his head, impressed. "I should take you guys on tour with me." No sooner had he said it than he realized with annoyance that it was exactly what he'd be doing when they went back on tour in September.

Pulling out the keys Simon gave him, he took the elevator up to the apartment with the Guardians silently in tow.

Everyone was already on the roof. Brett stopped at Simon's bar and poured a scotch—neat—slamming it back before bee-lining his way back to the guest room to change.

Still fuming over his conversation with Angel, he ditched his T-shirt and pulled on a fitted black button down, leaving it open at the neck and untucked from his jeans. He took the elastic band out of his hair and combed his fingers through it, giving it a shot with the blow dryer before he was satisfied enough to be seen in public. The drink had given his cheeks a healthy glow. After dousing himself with cologne in an attempt to mask any hormones, pheromones, testosterone, or any other random, telltale signs of his interest in anyone, he was officially ready to make an entrance.

# Chapter 32

***BRETT***

***New York City. Roof Party. Sunday, May 26, 12:15 AM ET***

BRETT TOOK A DEEP BREATH when he got to the top of the stairs and surveyed the crowd. Even though the place was packed, he spotted Cara, Simon, and a few other familiar faces almost immediately. Then he spotted Jessa, talking to a petite redhead with cool glasses in the corner near the bar. Formulating the best approach, he made his way over to Cara first.

Cara caught sight of him and turned as he approached, beaming at him. He pushed down any emotional reaction beyond a smile.

She ran up to him and grabbed his hand. "Brett, you were fantastic! It was an amazing show." It pleased him to hear that she'd had such a good time. She stepped back and wrinkled her nose. "A little heavy on the cologne, my friend."

His shoulders slumped, suddenly worried. "Long story. Is it terrible?"

She laughed. "No, it's not terrible. My sense of smell has been a little sharper lately." She narrowed her eyes and socked him in the arm—hard. The force of her punch made him wince. "That's for telling the world about my *American Idol* comment."

*Uh-oh. Guess I had that one coming,* he thought, and gave her a sheepish grin as he rubbed his arm. "Sorry. It came out of my mouth before I'd really thought about it. By the way, Ow! You punch like a guy. That really hurt."

186

She gave him an overly cheerful smile. "You can't say you didn't deserve it."

"No, but did you have to leave a bruise?"

"Don't be a baby. You want me to kiss it and make it better?"

He let out a nervous laugh, thinking about the conversation in the car. "Will you stop? Are you purposely trying to get your fiancé to kick my ass or what?"

Her eyes softened and she touched his arm lightly. "I'm sorry, really. I think I've already had one too many."

He winked. "I think you'd better cut yourself off. Otherwise there might be bloodshed… mine."

"I think we're past that, don't you? It's all good. So…" She batted her eyelashes at him and looked over in Jessa's direction. "Want an introduction?"

He blushed and nodded, relieved that Cara didn't seem upset or act weird about it, given their discussion yesterday. *Not that she would, would she?* he reasoned.

She looked him straight in the eye. "This is my rule. I'll introduce you, and then it's all you, kid."

He nodded, smiling.

She took him by the hand and led him over to Jessa and the other girl.

"Jessa, Irene," she said, "I'd like to officially introduce you to my friend, Brett King."

Both women looked up. Jessa gave him a small smile and then looked down, avoiding his gaze, while Irene reached out for a full handshake. "Brett, it was a great show. Thank you so much for the ticket." Her warm and bubbly demeanor made him smile as she pumped his hand.

"It's nice to meet you both. I'm really glad you had a good time. It was a lot of fun."

Cara tapped Irene on the shoulder and gave her a wink. "Eye, would you mind coming with me? I'd like to introduce you to someone who's been dying to meet you."

Irene's eyes lit up. "Lead on, MacDuff. Nice to meet you Brett," she called over her shoulder.

Brett was left alone with Jessa who looked like she was contemplating a jump over the side of the roof deck. Not exactly what he'd hoped for. He hadn't expected her to fall all over him—that would have been a turn-off—but something bordering on friendly would've been nice.

He looked at her warmly, trying to gauge her strange reaction. "Hey, thanks for being such a sport and coming up on stage tonight."

She crossed her arms over her chest, looking uncomfortable. She glanced at him only briefly before she looked back at the ground. "You're welcome," she mumbled.

"Did I do something to offend you?" he asked slowly.

She looked at him with a nervous smile and a sparkle in her eye. "No, not at all. I'm sorry, I should go."

She made a move to squeeze past him, and without thinking, he reached out and gently grabbed her arm. The feel of her skin under his fingers sent a tingling sensation up his arm, stirring him and leaving him short of breath.

"Please don't leave," he whispered.

Her breath caught with a small gasp. She turned her head to meet his gaze with wide, hazel eyes. Her lips parted exactly like they had when he'd touched her on stage during his song.

Panic hit the center of his chest when he realized that he didn't want to let her go.

She looked at his hand on her arm and tried to keep walking. "This isn't a good idea," she said more to herself than to him.

Brett frowned and held her in place. "What's not a good idea? I've barely said two words to you. All I'd like is a chance to fetch you a drink and talk to you for five minutes. Unless, of course, you find me totally repulsive and are honestly considering taking a leap over the side of deck—which is basically the look I saw in your eyes the second I got you alone."

He dropped his hand from her arm and waited for an answer. Again she looked up to meet his eyes. A genuine smile dappled with sadness graced her lips. "I find you far from repulsive, Brett," she said softly. The sound of his name from her lips startled him; the effect so intimate that it gave him chills. His eyes widened in surprise.

"Then why are you leaving?" he asked gently.

"You wouldn't believe me if I told you," she whispered. Before he knew what had happened, she rose up on tiptoe and touched her lips gently to his, kissing him tenderly before running away as fast as her legs could carry her.

Brett stood in stunned silence, touching his lips where she'd kissed him. They tingled with the memory of her velvet touch. He turned and tore after her.

The numbers above the elevator showed its descent. She would be in the lobby before he could even push the recall button. Instead, he took the emergency stairs two at a time. But by the time he reached the front steps, she was gone.


*JESSA*

Jessa had jumped into one of the black SUVs waiting outside of Simon's loft. All were manned by Simon's security company. As soon as she'd asked to be taken back to the penthouse, the driver took off like a shot. She caught sight of Brett out of the back window as he reached the front steps. By then, she was already halfway down the block.

Leaning back into the seat, she let out a deep sigh of relief. She'd been tempted to ditch the party all together, but she didn't want to disappoint Cara and Irene.

Ever since she was a kid growing up in California, she loved rock 'n' roll. Her mom had been a professional musician with the rock band Miscreant Passage, and Jessa had been raised on music. Concerts had been a staple in her life since she was a toddler, complete with a custom-fitted set of tiny ear plugs. Most of her early memories were of rock concerts and being in the company of her mom and other musicians.

When Cara had told her about Brett's concert yesterday night, she'd been both shocked and excited. A fan of King Metaljam, she couldn't deny that Brett was a breathtaking performer. The fact that Cara even knew him was the most shocking part.

The moment he'd caught her eye from the stage, he'd taken her breath away. Joining him on stage had terrified her for reasons having nothing to do with him. But when he'd looked at her with those eyes, she couldn't refuse. And then when he'd touched her, it was like wildfire spreading thought her veins.

The same thing happened when he'd taken her arm on the roof deck—there was an undeniable chemistry between them that threatened to knock her socks off. Having seen all sides of a musician's life, the last thing she wanted was to be a notch in some rock star's headboard.

*Get real, Jessa.* If that was all that troubled her, she wouldn't have run. It's what could've happened if she'd stayed that troubled her. The vision slammed her right between the eyes as he sang to her on stage, winding his fingers around hers. Two images assaulted her at once. One of his beautiful face as he sang to her, and another of him bloody, broken, and writhing in pain because of her.

Jessa rubbed her temples, trying to clear the image out of her mind. If she just stayed away from him, she'd be able to keep him safe.

At least she had the memory of her lips on his to keep her warm.

As if she needed a reminder, the text message on her phone when she'd left the concert had said it all.


IF HE TOUCHES YOU AGAIN, I'LL KILL HIM… ESCHER

# Chapter 33



CARA STOOD WAITING for her drink when she was spun around to see a wild-eyed Brett hanging on her arm. Words tumbled out of his mouth between gasps.

"She left. She's gone. Where'd she go?"

His alarm hit Cara squarely in the chest. Jessa must've run. *Oh boy. Not again,* Cara thought. In their long history, this wouldn't be the first time Jessa had done something bizarre in front of a guy.

"Calm down," she said, touching his arm and pushing soothing energy straight to his core. "If we're going to figure this out, you need to chill." He relaxed instantly under her touch. She looked him in the eye. "You better?"

He nodded and straightened up.

"Come with me. We'll sort this out."

She spotted Isaac talking to Simon. As they wove through the crowd, she wondered with evil glee if she could get away with not-so-accidentally spilling a drink on Isaac as she passed by. Too bad Brett pulled her away from the bar before hers was delivered. Instead, she swung by Simon and pinched his butt. He looked up and she winked at him, before silently telling him she was assisting with a "Jessa Emergency" and disappeared with Brett down the stairs.

They went into Simon's bedroom to retrieve her cell phone. She texted Jessa.

Jessa texted back a couple minutes later to say she had a migraine and had returned to the penthouse to go to sleep. Her socially acceptable shorthand for: "I'm fine. I just need some space." At least Cara knew she was safe. She handed her phone to Brett so he could read her message.

A mixture of panic and longing filled his eyes. "Let's go." He moved to leave.

Cara gently grabbed his forearm. "Can we back up a moment? Tell me what happened."

Brett took a deep breath, his eyes filled with confusion as he told her the story. It didn't make sense; none of it made sense. The fear she'd sensed in Jessa at the concert, her kissing Brett, and then bailing on him.

Knowing Jessa as well as Cara did, the best thing to do was to not push her and let this sit until morning.

She blew out a breath and looked into his eyes. "I know I said I wouldn't interfere, but something's not right. I'll help you find out what it is. But going there? Not tonight. It's not a good idea."

Frustrated, Brett looked like he might jump out of his skin. He pleaded. "Cara—"

"Do you trust me?"

He closed his eyes and nodded.

"I promise—you'll see her again before she leaves, even if I have to steal her plane ticket."

His eyes popped open. "Plane ticket?"

Cara smiled wide. "Sorry, I forgot to tell you. She's a California girl. She lives in Marin County right outside of San Francisco."

Brett's face lit up with delight. "You're kidding me, right?"

"I kid you not, my very handsome and irresistible friend." Then Cara's face clouded over, wondering how much she should say. "Brett, Jessa's one of my closest friends..."

Brett narrowed his eyes at her. "What aren't you sharing? Is she with someone?"

"No, it's not that," she said, knowing Jessa wasn't currently involved. As a matter of fact, she'd had a really rough breakup about a year ago that she refused to talk about. "I think you guys would be fantastic together, but she's *different*."

"What do you mean, different?" he asked cautiously.

"You'll need to get to know her and find out for yourself. Her secrets aren't mine to tell."

Brett sat wrapped in frustration and thwarted desire. "So, you're just going to leave me hanging and confused?"

"Look at me," she said, pulling his gaze to hers. "Be patient for tonight. I have your back, okay?" She smiled. "Come on. Let me go get that drink I ordered."

He let out a deep breath and threw up his arms. "Fine."

# Chapter 34

*MICHAEL*
*New York City. Sunday, May 26, 12:45 AM ET*

AFTER THE CONCERT, Michael bypassed the waiting SUVs and slipped into a cab for his ride downtown. He had the driver drop him off on Houston. Wandering around SoHo and enjoying the warmth of the evening gave him the extra time he needed to prepare himself to face Sienna.

On his way to Simon's Greene Street loft, he took a detour to the liquor store. Michael bought Simon an expensive bottle of Côte du Rhone as a gift for hosting. He also bought a second bottle—an amazing bottle of Sancerre from his dreams—on the hope that he might need it later. Then again, maybe that one he should hand straight to Sienna so she could club him over the head with it for being such an idiot.

After hiking up the five flights of stairs to Simon's, he stashed the white and left his gift on the island with a card.

*Here goes nothing*, Michael thought. Taking a deep breath, he walked out onto the roof deck into the buzz of people. Directly ahead, Cara and Simon stood talking to Brett. To his right, Isaac, his ceremonial Trinity Guardian, was in deep conversation with another linebacker-sized Nephil.

*There she is.* He spotted Sienna on a lounge chair to his left, sipping a glass of wine and flirting with baby-faced Zeke. His pulse quickened and a pang of jealousy hit him straight in the heart, not that he had any right to feel it.

Surreptitiously, he drank her in before she could catch him staring. She looked amazing, wearing a short, clingy dress that caressed every curve, and high-heeled sandals. Sexy and hot. Had he expected anything less?

Filling his lungs a second time, he approached Cara and willed himself to banish thoughts of Sienna. The tingle in his groin signaled an unwelcome filling and tightening. He'd be sporting an erection soon if he didn't do something to distract himself.

Cara spotted him first and waved him over. He went to greet her while still watching Sienna in his peripheral vision. Her eyes would occasionally flit over and scorch him from where she sat.

No way she'd let him off easy.

As Michael approached, Simon gave Cara a little kiss and waved to him before moving off to join Angel and another guest, leaving Michael with Brett and Cara.

He shook Brett's hand. "Great concert, man. I loved it."

Brett grinned. "Thanks, it was a lot of fun. I don't get a chance to play smaller venues or go unplugged very often."

Cara cleared her throat and shot a sideways glance toward where Sienna sat with Zeke. "Our mutual friend asked about you earlier."

Butterflies fluttered in his stomach. Breaking down, he openly stared in her direction. Engaged in conversation, she avoided his gaze.

He nodded. "Duly noted."

*"Well? Haste makes waste,"* she silently teased.

*"I can take a hint,"* he replied. "Would anyone like a drink?"

With no takers on a refill, Michael excused himself and headed to the bar, hoping a glass of wine would calm his nerves.

The bartender handed him his drink. His first instinct was to drain the glass. Instead, he took only a sip. His shoulders relaxed the moment the crisp notes hit his tongue. Taking his drink, he turned to find Sienna with her feet planted and arms crossed over her chest.

"What? You're not talking to me now?" she asked, her sky-blue eyes hard and accusing.

Caught off guard, he stepped back. *And here we go...* "Of course I'm talking to you. Why would you say that?"

She arched her brow. "I'm not sure, let me count the reasons," she said, wiggling her fingers at him. Even pissed, she was... exhilarating.

Time to man up and dig into his arsenal for a little fire power. Maybe what worked with the women he didn't care about would work with one that he did. It was worth a shot.

"Can we go over there and talk?" he whispered, turning on his sexy voice, hoping to diffuse the situation. He motioned to a darker, more secluded corner of the deck by some fruit trees in huge planters.

"Sure," she replied, startled.

He took her arm gently and led her to the privacy wall surrounding the garden.

"Listen, I'm sorry I've been so elusive," he began, realizing as he spoke the words he truly meant them. The comfort he'd found with her in the dreams reached out and engulfed him.

Her eyebrows drew together. "Then where have you been? It's been two months," she asked. It was a fair question and he wished he could provide a suitable answer. The best he could do was to give her this moment.

"I don't know, but I'm not avoiding you now," his voice carried sincerity from his heart. She looked so beautiful. Her eyes searched his and he let them. Her full lips were wet, reminding him of their kiss.

She reached up to touch his shirt collar and swallowed. "I've been dreaming about you," she said and looked away as a blush spread across her cheeks.

Her words surprised him and his face grew warm. "What kind of dreams?" He suspected he already knew the answer.

She met his gaze boldly. "Hot ones... of us in the recording studio."

"Really?" His heart rate jumped.

"Yes, really." Her eyes softened.

He couldn't have felt more naked standing there fully clothed if he tried. *A psychic connection?* He'd never shared dreams before. That warranted some research.

He found it difficult not to reach out and take her into his arms. Despite their intimate relationship while asleep, awake they'd only shared one kiss. Before that, they would've gladly thrown sharp objects at one another. No one had ever come close to unwinding him like Sienna did... then and now.

His eyes slipped down to her hard nipples straining against the clingy fabric of her dress. That's all he needed to see. The erection he'd been afraid of sprang to life with an uncomfortable throbbing in his pants. Any remaining fear drained out of him with the shift in his decision making to below his belt. If he'd had any reservations about making his dreams a reality, he'd subconsciously abandoned them, too. Second thoughts could wait until morning.

For better or worse, he was ready for something he could experience while awake.

"Come with me," he whispered, abandoning his drink on the closest table.

Taking Sienna by the hand, he guided her to the stairs and down into the temporarily unoccupied loft below. He steered Sienna through the apartment and into the privacy of Simon's art studio, far away from the party and any unwelcome interruptions. Closing the door behind them, he pulled her toward the antique daybed with the intention of picking up where they'd left off in the recording studio.

Unable to wait a moment longer, he drew her into his arms and kissed her. His tongue explored her mouth, deepening the kiss as desire poured through him. She returned his kiss with abandon. The feel of her body was welcome and satisfying against him. His fingertips ran over her silken black hair, the smell of jasmine imprinting on his senses.

"I've been dreaming about you, too," he confessed in between kisses.

Pulling away, she met his gaze. "We were so good in my dreams," she said. Trying hard to hide the insecurity in her eyes, she asked softly, "How were we in yours?"

"Incredible… the best. You were amazing," he said, kissing her again for reassurance. She relaxed in his arms, melting into him. He tucked her head against his neck, enjoying the feel of her body against his… finally. "It took all my willpower the night in the recording studio not to rip every shred of clothing off you. That's why I had to leave." His voice was hoarse and deep. He inhaled the scent that clung to her, her hair warm against his cheek as he held her close.

She pulled away again and looked at him with longing. "That makes me feel better. But after all those dreams, if I can't be with you tonight I might scream." Her admission stirred him on a level he had trouble grasping while his lower half gave him a throbbing high five.

His resistance over these last months now seemed ridiculous. He had the strength, at least for tonight, to keep up the façade he showed the world.

Looking around, he made a snap decision and let go of her. "I have an idea. Let's get out of here. But I need to stop by the kitchen first."

"Sounds good to me," she said with bright and eager eyes.

Pulling her to a stop on the way out of the studio, he wrapped her in his arms. "I thought you were going to beat me senseless for being such a jerk."

She leaned back, narrowing her sexy blue eyes at him. "The night's still young. And to be crystal clear, I'm still pissed at you. Just not as much as I want you naked."

He chuckled, enjoying her playful fire. Cara had been right, though. Underneath Sienna's hard exterior really was someone softer, more vulnerable… the woman in his dreams.

Taking her hand in his, they went to the kitchen to retrieve his bottle of Sancerre. After leaving a note for Cara on the kitchen island, they slipped outside and hailed a cab.

He planned to spoil Sienna as if tonight was the one and only night they'd ever have together. A possibility given his track record.

# Chapter 35



*MICHAEL*

*New York City. Mercer Hotel. Sunday, May 26, 1:12 AM ET*

MICHAEL INSTRUCTED THE DRIVER to take them to The Mercer, a boutique hotel, not far from Simon's loft. Sparing no expense, he checked them into the best room available. He wanted to live his fantasy with Sienna in style.

"Wow," Sienna said when they entered the suite.

Michael smiled. They stood in the middle of the living room, a bedroom with a king-size bed to the right. French doors overlooked the bamboo terrace. Not that they needed it, but the suite also contained a kitchenette and two full, oversized bathrooms.

He set the Sancerre down on the table in front of the love seat.

She wrapped her arms around his neck, her jet black hair flowing down her back. "I'm impressed."

"Then I guess my work here is done," he teased and gave her a dazzling smile.

"I'd say it's just beginning." She winked and let him go.

"Glass of wine?" he asked, eyeing the Sancerre.

She nodded, giving him a knowing smile. "Nice choice in wine."

A blush spread across Michael's cheeks as the memory of how he'd used the wine in their dream came rushing back. He cleared his throat and rose. "Music?" he asked, finding the sound system and turning it to something soft and romantic.

After grabbing a corkscrew from the bar, he settled back onto the loveseat and poured them each a glass.

Michael lifted his for a toast. "To making dreams come true?"

"I'll drink to that." She took a sip then set her glass down. "I'll be right back," she said before retreating to the bathroom.

While she was gone, Michael sat sipping his wine, his mind drifting back again to the last dream. A bout of anxiety gripped him and he wondered if his performance would live up to his own expectations. He sighed. No turning back now. Guess he'd find out.

Back from the bathroom, Sienna snuggled next to him. "I have something for you." Eyeing him innocently, she handed him her underwear.

A thrill shot straight to his crotch. "You're going to be my undoing," he teased and placed his wine glass on the coffee table. He tossed the underwear over his shoulder, stood, and pulled her into his arms.

Gazing into her eyes, he turned his lips up in a smile as he wrapped an arm around her and pressed her into his chest.

He glanced at the wine glass. Taking two fingers, he dipped them into the cool liquid, and then slid them under her dress and slowly up along her inner thigh.

Her eyes locked on his and she drew her lower lip between her teeth, moaning as his fingers gently explored her hot, delicate folds under the dress. So wet, all for him.

"You feel incredible," he said softly and kissed her neck, his body aching for her. But first he wanted to give her as much as he could before taking anything for himself.

He gently pushed her back onto the sofa and lifted her dress. Like the dream, she was almost fully bare, her delicious folds exposed, wet and glistening. Parting her legs, he knelt on the floor positioned in between them and sought her out with his mouth, teasing her with his tongue. She moaned and twisted her fingers in his hair, drawing his head closer. He found the feminine smell of her intoxicating.

He pulled back slowly. "You taste as delicious as you feel," he said.

"My turn," she said with a wicked grin. "Stand up."

*Huh?* Not part of his plan. Michael's lips parted, surprised at her commanding tone. He was far from finished, yet he reluctantly did as she asked.

As adept in reality as in his dreams, she made quick work of his belt, and then slid his clothes down to his mid-thigh, springing him free, rock hard and ready.

She looked up at him, pleased. "Remind me later that I owe you an apology," she said and took a sip of her wine.

*Only one?* he thought, amused. There were at least half a dozen apologies he could think of that she owed him.

Grabbing his hips, her mouth engulfed him.

"*Umm... Sienna...*" he moaned, all conscious thought forgotten as he clutched her delicate shoulders in his hands. His nerve endings exploded with sensation. The wine felt cold and tingly in contrast to her hot tongue as she worked him. When her hand moved down to massage his balls, he threw his head back and groaned deep in his throat.

*It'll be a short night if she keeps this up*, he thought.

"Stop. It feels too good," he whispered, gently removing himself from her mouth and away from her grasp.

"My turn again," he said, mimicking her wicked grin. He kicked off his pants the rest of the way, leaving him in just his shirt. Pushing her back onto the couch, he stretched the fabric of her dress back to free her naked breasts underneath.

His eyes widened in surprise, not expecting to see a gold ring threaded through each of her tawny nipples. They hadn't been there in his dreams. How could he have missed them earlier underneath the clingy dress?

The piercings fascinated him, sending a bolt of heat straight down to his already overengorged cock. He licked his lips, needing to touch the rings with his tongue and feel the metal in his mouth.

"Very sexy," he whispered.

He took a sip of the wine. Taking her nipple into his mouth, he bathed it in the cool liquid, sticking the tip of his tongue through the ring and tugging it gently. Sienna rocked back and let out a moan of pleasure.

She grasped his face between her hands and pulled him up to meet her eyes. "Michael, I want you inside of me. Right now." Her throaty voice was deep with desire.

"That can be arranged..." he growled and reached under the seat cushion to retrieve the condom he'd stashed there earlier.

"Give me that," she said, adding "please" as almost an afterthought. She sat up and snatched the condom from his hand.

*She was much more passive in my dreams*, he thought with a shiver. Sharing control wasn't one of his strong suits.

"Wait," he said and drew her dress over her head, removing it completely. "I want to look at you." He caressed her with his eyes. She was so beautiful to him.

She blushed and glanced down. "As good as your dreams?"

He tipped her chin up. "Even better."

She broke into a seductive smile and tugged on his shirttail. "Lose this."

Removing his remaining clothes, he stood naked before her. She reached around to cup his behind and pulled him closer. Taking him firmly in her grip, she swallowed him whole, bathing him in wet heat. He clutched the back of the loveseat in a death grip and fought back the urge to plunge in deeper.

*Does she realize what she's doing to me?*

Then she ripped open the foil and unrolled the condom onto him. Now packaged and ready to go, she reclined back onto the loveseat.

Standing, Michael wrapped her legs around his hips. His heart rate accelerated as he looked at her opened up to him, glistening and ready. He eased himself inside, and she cried out as he entered her. Drawing in a sharp breath, he shuddered from the sensation of her tight warmth around him.

"You feel fantastic," she moaned, breathless.

"*Mmm...* so do you." His fingers held her thighs firmly apart as he stood rocking inside of her, filling her with every inch he had to give. Slowly building his rhythm, he rotated his hips seeking out her special spot to give her as much pleasure as possible.

Dreams aside, nothing compared to his need to make love to her and prove his worth. On a primal level, he craved this down to his soul. Burying himself inside her, he stroked her again and again.

Her body tensed. "Oh, Michael!" she cried, her orgasm rhythmically pulsing around him. To hear her scream his name filled him with deep satisfaction.

Increasing his pace, all he needed to do was look down at her beautiful body connected to his and he found his release.

He quivered in unison with her, his knees going weak from the intensity. Standing paralyzed while the sensation held him enraptured, he shuddered one last time before it subsided. He gazed down at Sienna, disbelieving she was really here with him after all those months. Months wasted because of his stupidity.

With a satisfied smile on her lips and a seductive look in her half-closed eyes, she ran her fingers along his arm. "Can we do that again?"

He whispered, "You can count on it." He was by no means done for the evening. His plan was to keep making love to her until either he couldn't get it up or his dick fell off.

Still inside her, he dipped down and picked her up. Her legs still wrapped around his waist, she threw her arms around his neck. He kissed her deeply, carrying her into the bedroom.

Laying her on the bed, he pulled out and stepped away to dispose of the condom before settling down next to her. Drawing her over onto his chest, he stroked her long, smooth hair.

"That was amazing," he said and kissed the top of her head.

"As good as the dreams?" she asked, looking up at him.

"Better." He tensed then asked, "Did I live up to your expectations?"

She squeezed him. "Absolutely... you were fantastic," she said, lifting her head to meet his eyes. "Don't ever doubt yourself, Michael, especially with me."

Her words were unexpected and they warmed him; a strange tingling sensation traveled along his spine. He pulled her closer and gave her a soft kiss on the lips.

"You inspire me, you know that?" Contentment settled over Michael, all his weeks of worry… gone. The feel of Sienna next to him was as natural to him as breathing, like she belonged there.

And they hadn't traded a single insult.

They rested for a moment in each other's arms.

"Can I talk you into a shower?" he asked softly.

"Sure," she said and then burst out into laughter.

"What's so funny?" he asked, wrinkling his eyebrows.

She rolled over and propped herself up on her elbows. A look of mischief danced in her sky-blue eyes. "I'm just thinking about the look on your face the day I found out you were an underwear model."

"Ugh," he groaned and covered his face with his hands. "Yeah, thanks for one of life's most mortifying moments."

She tugged his hand gently away from his face. "Hey, why were you so mortified? It's not like you were a porn star. I work with models all day long. They're good people and it's a respectable career."

He shook his head, refusing to answer or meet her eyes. The modeling campaign wasn't the part that had upset him. It was the way she'd belittled him and the "pretty boy" comment that had gotten under his skin. She'd played right into his deepest insecurities. Same thing when she'd accused him of being gay. In his former line of work, he'd had plenty of gay friends, but the accusation made him feel like his inadequacies were visible when it came to women. That he had no chance of living up to his father's image…

"Well, here's where I apologize," she said, glancing down at his crotch. "I'm sorry I attacked your 'manhood' that day. There's more than enough of you to make any woman happy."

He groaned again, his face flaming as he rolled over and gave her his back.

Sienna rolled him back over and batted her thick black lashes at him. "What did I say?"

Blushing, he lowered his eyes and the side of his mouth pulled up in a shy smile. "I'm embarrassed."

She *tsked* and gave him a look that said, "I'm so not buying what you're selling." "Oh, please. You're hot, so stop trying to pretend you're above it all. You seem ashamed. Why?"

*Leave it to Sienna to call things exactly as she sees them*, he thought and sighed. "Would you believe me if I told you it bothers me when people judge me based only on my looks? I worked hard at Yale, and I think of myself as a scholar… like my father. Modeling was always a means to an end for me. It's just how I made money from the time I turned sixteen. I've wanted to open a dojo since I was a kid. That's always been my dream… to teach."

She searched his eyes. "It would be hard for anyone who knew you to think less of you for choosing to model for a living." Reaching up, she traced his lips with her fingertip. "The pictures were fantastic, Michael. I saw them. You owned that camera."

He froze. "You saw the campaign pictures?" Conflicting emotions rolled through him. He didn't know if he should be angry or ecstatic. Her admission made him feel vulnerable and exposed.

She touched his cheek and smiled warmly. "Yeah. I have them. You did a phenomenal job with that campaign."

His mouth hung slightly open until the realization hit him that she truly appreciated his work. A smile slowly crept onto his lips and an overwhelming feeling of pride tugged at him.

His hand reached up to capture hers. He closed his eyes and kissed each of her fingertips. "Thank you," he whispered and meant it.

"While I'm apologizing and whatnot, I never thanked you for making me eggs that morning in Connecticut," she said softly.

He opened his eyes and smiled. "Two apologies? I think I'll quit while I'm ahead. Ready to take that shower now?"

The bathroom had a walk-in shower large enough to host an orgy. Tempted to go for round two under the hot spray, they settled for some heavy foreplay and giving each other a full body lather and rinse before Michael shut off the water. Grabbing towels from the rack, they dried themselves and each took a robe off the back of the bathroom door.

Sienna wrapped her hair up in a towel and slipped into a robe. Sneaking up behind her, Michael gave her a kiss on the base of her neck before he swept her up into his arms. She giggled as he carried her back into the bedroom and placed her on the bed.

A tweeting sound came from Sienna's purse signaling a new text. She looked at him. "Let me see who that is." Crawling across the bed, she retrieved the cell phone from her purse on the nightstand as Michael flopped down next to her on the bed.

She looked at the message, laughed, and then handed it to Michael. It was a text from Cara: FOUND THE NOTE. LET ME GUESS. YOU'RE OFF SOMEWHERE HAVING HOT SEX WITH MICHAEL, AREN'T YOU? YOU LITTLE MINX! BE GENTLE WITH HIM AND MAKE SURE YOU DON'T MISS BRUNCH TOMORROW AND THAT HE SHOWS UP TOMORROW NIGHT LIKE HE'S SUPPOSED TO! C

"Going somewhere?" she asked him.

A smile played on his lips as he read Cara's text. He looked up and answered, "Yeah, we're all meeting over dinner to prepare for our business trip on

Wednesday." Cara had told Sienna he moonlighted at Simon's private security company.

Sienna arched a brow. "I'll be right back." She trotted out to the living room and came back with a deck of cards. Holding them up, she asked, "Are you tired?"

"Not particularly," he said, glancing at the cards, curious about her intentions. She must have gotten them from the game table by the television.

"I have an idea."

"It's a little late for strip poker," he teased.

"No kidding. I've already seen the show. And what a show it was, but if you want any more, you'll have to play for it."

He propped himself up on his elbow, curious. "Okay, I'll bite. What do you mean?"

She gave him a sly smile. "We play for points. Each hand is worth a point, and each point is worth two minutes. You can redeem your points in two ways. Ten points for foreplay and twenty for sex, or you can use each point in minutes for anything else. Points can be used for something you want me to do to you, or something you want to do to me."

He looked at her sideways, wondering about the catch and sensing there had to be one. "Sounds like a win-win."

"Could be, but you don't get to choose what I do with my points—I do. That means I'm in control," she said, giving him a wicked look.

*Oh.* His mouth went bone dry, feeling exposed and psychologically naked. Never great at poker, his expression gave him away. The thought of having her do what she wanted was both hot and frightening. Unconsciously, he tightened the tie on his robe.

"You don't like to give up control, do you?" she asked with a mischievous grin.

"Why do you say that?"

"Because if I looked up the word *uptight* in the dictionary, I might find your picture." There was no malice in her tone, just brutal honesty.

"That's a little harsh." He frowned, slightly offended.

She sat Indian-style on the bed and started to deal the cards. Once a full hand was dealt, she looked up and smiled innocently. "Is it?" Picking up her hand, she arranged her cards. "We're playing Twenty-One. You'd better get cracking, or I'm going to have more points to do with you what I will." She removed the pad of paper and pencil on the nightstand and placed them next to her to keep score.

His mouth hung slightly open, he didn't know what to say. He couldn't figure out if he was pissed, annoyed, or just plain turned on. A competitor at heart, he wasn't about to let her win.

Snatching up his cards, he arranged them in his hand. Michael had a feeling he'd just met his match, in more ways than one.

# Chapter 36

*IRENE*
*New York City. Roof Party. Sunday, May 26, 1:45 AM ET*

IRENE WAS ON HER third glass of champagne when she turned away from the bar and lost her footing, slamming hard into a solid wall of muscled man. Her champagne flew up and out of her glass in a spectacular bubbly spray, splashing them both. Assessing the damage, she wished for a black hole to come swallow her up.

"I'm so sorry," she mumbled, mindlessly rubbing her cocktail napkin over her chest. "*¡Hijo de puta!*" she said, cursing under her breath. She needed to slow down on the drinks.

"*¿Siempre usas groserias en español?*" he asked her.

"No, I don't always swear in Spanish. It just depends on my mood. Sometimes I pick Farsi," she replied as heat rose up her neck. Swearing in other languages somehow seemed less rude. Unless, of course, the person you swore in front of happened to speak the same language.

Her gaze slowly traveled up the tall tree of a man standing inches in front of her, over the wet patch of champagne on his shirt, up to the amused face of the caramel-colored god she'd seen at the concert sitting a few seats down from her. She'd overheard Cara call him Paco earlier. The same height and build as Simon, he was massive and gorgeous with short, dark hair and molten brown eyes the color of dark chocolate.

"*Ay Dios mío*," she mumbled and shook her head, continuing to wipe away the wetness from her chest. Of all the people she could have spilled her drink on, did it have to be the hottest man at the party? And that was saying something, considering the amount of hard muscle per square foot jamming up the roof deck.

He laughed. "Can I get you another drink, *niña bonita*?"

Irene blushed at the warmth in his voice and at being called a pretty girl. "Sure, why not?" She smiled at him shyly, hoping he didn't notice her rosy cheeks.

Placing his large hand on the small of her back, he gently turned her back around to face the bar. Resting his body up against hers, he put one arm on her shoulder while he waved the other over her head to get the bartender's attention.

Leaning down, he asked, "Another champagne?"

She nodded. The warmth of him behind her and his lips close to her ear nearly sent her into apoplectic shock; her body quivered at his closeness. Typically, she kept company with the DC milquetoast variety of male. This guy was definitely on the other end of the spectrum. Built like a WWC wrestler, he oozed enough sex appeal to combust her panties.

"Champagne for the señorita, and a Dos Equis." His voice had a silky, smooth quality.

*Maybe I'm drunker than I thought,* she mused, *because this guy is making me swoon.*

With the two drinks in his hands, Paco directed her over to a pair of chairs at the side of the deck and waited for her to be seated before handing her the glass of champagne.

Sitting down next to her, he tapped his beer bottle to her glass. "To a pretty girl with a sharp tongue," he said with a twisted smile.

After taking a swig of beer, he put down the bottle and reached his hand out to introduce himself. "I'm Paco."

She smiled as her hand disappeared inside of his. "Irene."

"You speak Spanish… and Farsi." It was a statement rather than a question.

"Those are two of the ten languages I speak."

He tipped his head in admiration. "That's a lot of languages."

"I'm a linguist for the State Department. You could say it's what I do for a living." She took a sip from her glass. "Do you work for Simon?"

Paco stifled a laugh, and shook his head no. "I'm retired, but freelance through Angel Benitez. I'm currently working on Brett King's security team."

"You look a little young to be retired…"

He just shrugged.

"But you know Simon?"

He shrugged again. "Of course. But I've only had the pleasure of meeting him recently."

*Hmm*, she thought. *Sounds like he hasn't known Simon any longer than Cara.* She filed that tidbit away.

"So, you live in California with Brett?" she asked.

Attempting a little more intelligence couldn't hurt, could it? Maybe she could find out something that would help Simon and Cara. As for Creep and Creepier, Caswell had called this morning to let her know neither of the tracking devices seemed to be working, suggesting the penthouse could be protected by a sophisticated signal jammer. Beyond what she'd planted in the library, she hadn't had the desire to plant anything else—that was tomorrow's task. Since Cara didn't seem to be in imminent danger, Irene left all of her spy equipment back at the penthouse. Alcohol definitely helped her to relax as she pushed off the execution of her plan. Giving herself a small pat on the back for waiting, she gained an added benefit: chances were low that a satellite was trained on her right now from space, capturing the scene of her mooning over someone who the NSA might consider associated with terrorists.

He gave her an intense look. "You sure ask a lot of questions."

She blushed again and looked away. "Sorry, I'm just making conversation."

It surprised her when he reached out and gently touched her cheek sending a flood of heat through her body. "It's okay. I haven't had the pleasure of spending time with such a pretty lady in a long time. I'm forgetting my manners. Forgive me?"

*It should be illegal to look that edible*, she thought. Suddenly shy, she said, "I don't want to keep you if you're working tonight."

"I'm off-duty until tomorrow morning unless Brett decides to leave the building." He cocked his head and gave her a rakish smile. "Are you trying to get rid of me?"

"Absolutely not," she said and took a long drink of her champagne to drown some of her schoolgirl butterflies.

His eyes softened as he looked at her. "Can we start again? I think you were wondering what I do in my retirement when I'm not working in private security."

She found the warm lilt in his voice soothing. She smiled back. "I didn't mean to make you feel uncomfortable."

He gently shook his head. "No, really, it's okay. I've just been spending too much time with a bunch of *hombres groseros*." Paco lifted his beer bottle to a large biker with his same caramel-colored skin. "Like my friend, Angel, here." Angel looked down at them and chuckled as he shuffled past. *Impolite men, indeed*, she thought.

No doubt Paco was charming, and getting more irresistible by the minute as she got drunker and bolder. She batted her eyelashes back at him. "You have my undivided attention."

"Angel and I, we own a few dance clubs in southern California. It allows me to spend my time however I like, so I consider myself retired."

"No family?"

Paco's jaw tightened and he looked away.

Her heart jumped to her throat. "Oh, God. I'm so sorry. I keep sticking my foot in my mouth, don't I?"

He reached for her arm and shook his head. "No, you're asking normal questions. To answer your question, there is no one, no señorita in my life right now."

She didn't press further. It was bad enough that she'd been this nosy.

"So what other languages do you speak?" he asked, steering the discussion away from him.

Plunging in with both feet, she recounted to him how she'd grown up traveling the world and living in different countries as the daughter of a diplomat. They spoke about his childhood in Spain, and then his relocation to France and finally to California. He was pretty vague in his descriptions, but she got the sense that he'd lived a lot in what looked like maybe thirty-five years. He couldn't be more than that… Regardless of the fact that he was probably eight years her senior, he was downright sexy, and who was she to stand on ceremony? Her father was older than her mother and it never mattered to them. Funny, the fact that Paco could be under suspicion based on his association with Simon didn't bother her in the least.

### PACO

Angel sidled up to Paco at the bar. "Amigo, you smell worse than Brett. You got it bad for that little redheaded señorita?"

Paco all but growled in response.

"I mean no disrespect, my friend." Angel threw up his hands in surrender. "You deserve some happiness. It's just been a long time, that's all I'm saying to you."

Paco rubbed his face, glad his back was turned to Irene. "She's a very good woman. That's all I'm saying back."

Angel touched his friend's arm. "We've known each a long time and I love you like a brother. Enjoy yourself, you deserve it. Isabella… she's been gone for a—"

Paco snapped his head around to look at Angel. "Benedictine, don't say her name!" His jaw was set in a hard line. True, he and Angel had known each other for over four centuries, but some topics were unwelcome, even among friends. To be reminded of his Isabella was like a stab in the heart. He'd lost her to cancer in 1976 at the age of fifty-five after an agonizing eighteen-month battle. Every drop of life sucked from her bones as he watched... helpless to do anything but outlive her and drag the pain like an albatross around his neck.

Angel's eyes grew hard and the line of his mouth nearly disappeared. He dug his fingers into Paco's biceps and whispered harshly into his ear, "You listen to me right now. Isabella wanted you to move on, and she made me promise that I would make you. You've had almost forty years to grieve for her. End it. Even if she had lived, you would've eventually watched her die. She loved you too much to see you suffer this long."

He grabbed Paco's head and physically turned it toward Irene who sat with her back to them. "That woman over there, she's the first woman you've reacted to since Isabella. If you have a chance to live out your life with a human then don't fuck it up! You hear me? Do you know how lucky you'd be to have that?"

Paco looked into Benedictine's eyes and saw the naked pain he wore like a battle scar across his heart. He understood. He knew the source of Benedictine's pain, and it exceeded even his own. It was also the reason behind his friend's exile.

Paco closed his eyes and spoke softly. "I only just met her. I don't even know her."

Angel glared at him. "But I know you, and I'm telling you if you could see the life in your own eyes tonight like I've seen, you would do anything..." Angel turned away and wiped his hand across his face. "Do what you want," he said and walked away.

Irene was an outsider and didn't even know he was Nephilim. How could he go any further? Was Angel crazy? It was true that Paco was attracted to her. She was smart, bubbly like his Isabella, and pretty like a little pixie. The thought of Irene warming his bed excited him.

He wanted to throw his hands up and scream in frustration. The last thing he needed was to be reminded of his steamer trunk full of personal luggage just as he was having a good and carefree time.

He rested his head in his hands, the drinks on the bar in front of him. A light tap on his shoulder caused him to turn around. Irene stood there with her hands on her hips.

"A girl could die of thirst over here," Irene said in a sweet and playful voice.

He chuckled. She really was the cutest thing he'd laid eyes on in quite some time. He rewarded her with his biggest, broadest smile.

"Here you go, pretty one," he said and handed her another glass of champagne.

She looked at him with concern and reached up to tenderly touch his cheek. "Are you okay, Paco? You look sad. That smile didn't quite reach your eyes."

The smile faded from his lips and he covered her hand on his cheek with his own as he closed his eyes. A sad smile turned up the corners of his lips. "You are way too observant, señorita. It's late. Can I walk you down to the car?" He opened his eyes and kissed the palm of her hand.

"No, not if you keep doing that," she said, amused and breathless. Grabbing the drink off the bar, she drank it down in two gulps.

"What are you doing?" Paco chuckled, "Are you *loca, Pelirroja*?" He surprised himself when the word passed through his lips. He'd spontaneously come up with an affectionate nickname for her: "Red," because of her hair.

"No. If I didn't just do that, I wouldn't have been able to do this." She stood on her tiptoes and threw her arms around his neck, pressing her lips to his. It took him only a second for the shock to wash off before he wrapped his arms around her back and fully met her kiss with his own. Melting her small body into his, he hungrily searched her mouth with his tongue, exploring her with a more than gentle insistence. His body reacted immediately. He swept her up into his strong arms and carried her through the thinning crowd, down the stairs, and into the guest room where he was staying.

He kicked the door shut behind him. When he reached the bed, she went limp in his arms becoming one hundred pounds of dead weight.

She had passed out.

He laughed deep in his throat and shook his head. Laying her down, he thought, *Saved by the bell*. In truth, he preferred making love with her when he could be sure she wouldn't have any drunken regrets.

It was three in the morning and the party was breaking up. He had a decision to make. Either he could load her into the waiting SUV headed back to the penthouse, or he could let her sleep it off with him in the guest room.

No contest. She would stay with him.

Angel was right, although he hated to admit it. He thought long and hard about whether he should change her into one of his T-shirts, but decided to keep her in the dress she wore. That way, when she woke up, she couldn't accuse him of taking advantage of her. He expected her to have a crippling headache in the morning.

He stripped down to his boxers and threw on a clean T-shirt. Gently removing her glasses, he put them on the nightstand, and then folded her into the covers and lay down next to her. Usually, he slept naked, surrounded by his wings, but that was out of the question. Since temperature wasn't a factor for him, he didn't need a blanket.

Propping himself up on his elbow, he watched her sleep. Staring down at her, he took his finger and pushed back a short lock of red hair from her face. He smiled and dipped down to give her a gentle kiss on the lips before he pulled her back, spooning her into his huge body.

"Good night, *Pelirroja*," he whispered and turned out the light.

# Chapter 37



*MICHAEL*
*New York City. Mercer Hotel. Sunday, May 26, 4:00 AM ET*

IT WAS 4:00 AM by the time they finished their game. They were tied at fifteen points apiece.

Michael had enjoyed playing cards with Sienna. They'd had fun making each other laugh with their poker faces and their reactions to losing a hand or two. He looked over at her as she put away the cards. His desire returned, coursing through him in a wild rush.

*What is it about this woman?* He had never met someone before that could keep him in a constant state of arousal like she could.

While she was looking down, he slipped his hand into her robe and fondled her breast, playing with a nipple ring.

"That's one point, right there," she said with a wicked glint in her eye.

"Oh, I forgot. I can't help it, you're like a magnet. I can't keep my hands off you." He gave her a look of mock innocence.

"I now have more points, so I get to go first."

"Huh? Not fair," he whined.

"Way fair; now sit back while I have my way with you." She planted her hand on his chest and pushed him back onto the pillow.

"So, what are you going to do for your fifteen points?" He asked with mild trepidation.

She smiled. "Oh, you'll find out. In the meantime, here are the ground rules. You can't touch me unless I ask. Since I'm using all my points tonight on what I'm going to do to you, I won't be asking. That's the only rule," she said.

"Okay," he whispered. Discomfort gripped him, catching him somewhere between fear and desire. The fact that he couldn't participate as she touched him raised goose bumps on his skin.

She crawled up his body. "Don't be afraid," she whispered and kissed him on the lips. Retreating, she gently opened his robe, fully exposing him. She started at his collarbone, and worked her way down his body with her tongue, stopping to tease each of his nipples until they hardened under her touch, before journeying lower.

He moaned, his groin growing hotter in response.

Her hot trail led to his navel, down over his rippled abs, and then she disappeared between his legs. Her warm tongue drew each of his balls into her mouth one at a time, tightening them. Desire overcame his fear and he let out another moan. Then she engulfed his shaft in wet bliss, working him until he was rock hard and ready before slipping on another condom.

Parting her robe, she straddled him and guided his length in up to the hilt. He let out a hiss of pleasure as her tight heat welcomed him. After a few strokes on his shaft, she stopped.

He opened his eyes. "Why did you stop?"

She gazed down at him, all wide-eyed innocence. "I ran out of points."

He sighed. Relieved to be back in the driver's seat, he grabbed her hips and flipped her over.

She let out a delighted squeal. Wearing a seductive smile, he rocked inside of her, faster and deeper. Converting his points to minutes, he gave her a good five or six points worth before he pulled out to take a short break to taste her again, his tongue relentless.

She screamed out, "Michael…" grasping the covers in her hands, and arching her hips off the bed. As she recovered, he positioned her in his lap facing him. He wanted to look into her eyes and kiss her as they made love this time.

His gaze caught hers as he gently reentered her, moving slowly inside of her, savoring each stroke as he deliberately brought them both to orgasm. "Sienna," he screamed as he exploded inside her, connecting with her in a way that both frightened and exhilarated him. Exhausted, they collapsed in each other's arms.

Her head rested on his chest. "This has been an unbelievable night."

Smiling, he kissed her hair. "I think so, too."

"I'm exhausted…" She yawned and crawled under the covers while he disposed of the condom. He crawled in next to her and drew her to his body, spooning behind her. His heart beat in a contented rhythm with her warmth next to him.

"Sweet dreams, my beauty," he said and turned off the lights. Sated, Michael dropped off to sleep with Sienna in his arms. But not before recognizing the feeling of happiness from his last dream.


### SIENNA

Sienna lay awake as Michael drifted off to sleep next to her, his breathing even. Fulfillment enveloped her from the feel of his warm body snuggled around her. She reflected on the night they'd just spent together and couldn't imagine how it could've been more perfect… and it terrified her.

For the first time in her life, she'd found someone she could really be herself with. What terrified her was that it could all disappear in an instant. One great night didn't guarantee a future. Yet, she couldn't deny something about him satisfied a deep, unexplainable need within her. Like a moth to a flame, she was drawn to Michael—as much as he seemed to be drawn to her.

Behind his wanton desire, she sensed a strong core of integrity and kindness. He was the only man who had ever cared if she came to orgasm, much less held back his own until she'd experienced hers. He'd done it both times they made love, and in her eyes, that alone made him a keeper. Not to mention, he was smart, funny, and incredibly sexy.

In hindsight, she felt terrible having ever teased him about being an underwear model. Not only did he have the goods, he was more than another pretty face… much more. But her sixth sense told her there was something else, something dark hiding under the surface and holding him captive.

She recognized the subtle shame he carried, similar to her own. Her heart unexpectedly ached. She, herself, was no stranger to darkness.

Gently, she kissed the arm he'd wrapped around her as he slept and drifted off into her own satisfied sleep.


### MICHAEL

The phone rang at 10:00 AM, startling Michael and Sienna awake. He fumbled to pick it up, listening for a second before returning it to the cradle.

Sienna groaned. "Who was that at this hour?"

"Wake-up call," he mumbled, and pulled her back over to him to snuggle, dragging the covers up higher.

"When did you… ?"

"I wrote it on the hotel slip when we checked in. I wanted to make sure we had time before we had to check out," he whispered, kissing the back of her neck.

"Don't get any ideas. I'm still recovering from last night."

He suddenly panicked. "I didn't hurt you, did I?" *Was I too rough?*

She turned to him with a smile and said softly, "You didn't hurt me. But I'll be thinking of you all day, and only in the best way."

He smiled, relieved. "I'll be thinking about you, too." He brushed a piece of hair away from her face. "Call me optimistic, but I figured we'd need the wake-up call. I have an appointment at the dojo with Deva, the instructor who's covering for me while I'm away." He arched a brow at her. "And don't you have a brunch appointment with Cara's parents and the wedding party later?"

She let out a groan. "Shit, I almost forgot."

He pulled her closer, enjoying the warmth of her delicate frame, neither of them making any move to get out of bed. Although disappointed they had to leave shortly, he knew it was unavoidable. His schedule was packed for today. Kai was due to arrive later and join them at Simon's for the meeting this evening. Michael had to brief Isaac on Trinity business. Plus, the situation was heating up. They'd be lucky to make it another day without an attack.

He kissed her on the forehead. "Hey, let's take a quick shower, okay?"

"If we must," she replied, sounding not really happy about it.

Remembering her hypoglycemia from their trip to Connecticut, he rolled over and picked up the phone to dial room service.

"What are you doing?" she asked, puzzled.

"Ordering breakfast to avoid accidentally experiencing your dark side," he said.

She poked him. "Thanks."

An hour later, they were in a cab heading for Sienna's West Village apartment.

"Can we go on a real date next time?" she teased before they arrived.

"Absolutely," he said and kissed her hand.

The cab stopped to let her out. Michael gave Sienna a kiss. "I'll call you later."

She eyed him warily. "Later, later? Or later, three months from now?"

He chuckled. "Later, in a couple of hours."

"Okay." She turned and waved as the cab pulled away before disappearing through the glass doors of her building.

As the cab sped away, he thought of his meeting with Deva and groaned, hoping he wouldn't show any unconscious signs of his hot night with Sienna. Given their history, Deva knew him too well. Even though she agreed to his nonfraternization policy, he knew she'd break the rule if given the chance.

He let out a breath. If he hadn't needed her help and she hadn't needed the job so badly, he wouldn't have been foolish enough to put either of them in this situation.

# Chapter 38



*CARA*

*New York City. Greene Street Loft. Sunday, May 26, 10:00 AM ET*

CARA GLANCED AT THE clock on the nightstand, it was almost ten o'clock. Simon was still asleep, spooned behind her. She relaxed back into him, feeling his skin on hers. Before she met Simon, she'd never slept naked. Now she couldn't imagine sleeping any other way with him next to her.

The party was a raving success. It was close to four in the morning before everyone who wasn't staying the night left. Cara cringed when she thought about the state of the roof deck and the kitchen. They'd have their work cut out for them this morning.

She listened for her guests. Silence. *Guess I'm the first one up*, she thought. Even Chloe was still asleep in her pink toile dog bed on the floor next to them, a lump under a pink fleece blanket embroidered with the word *Princess*.

Brett and Paco were in the guest rooms, and she wouldn't be surprised if Angel was still asleep in a lounge chair on the roof deck where he'd passed out last night. The rest of the Guardians were either stationed at local safe houses or on patrol.

A wicked smile played on her lips. When she texted Sienna last night, it was more than a happy coincidence. Unknown to Michael, he'd been "projecting" during their *sexcapade*. Still new in his role, he probably didn't realize how strong his psychic link was within their Trinity.

Cara giggled, even though it hadn't been so funny last night.

She'd been in the middle of polite conversation with Zeke when it happened. Not only did an image of Michael and Sienna *in flagrante delicto* flash before her eyes, but she was rocked by an intense orgasm. She almost fell out of her chair and could only imagine what Zeke must've thought at her reaction. Politely excusing herself by feigning temporary illness, she searched for Simon. She found his hulking figure standing alone in the stairwell, leaning up against the wall in closed-eyed ecstasy.

They slipped away to his bedroom for a quickie before returning to the party.

They were hit a second time after they were already in bed.

As tempted as they'd been to let Michael know what was happening, they didn't want to spoil his night. *The things you do for your Trinity*, she thought. Cara had been elected by Simon to tell Michael.

Michael, private and very proper, would be mortified when he found out. Thankfully, the phenomenon wasn't bidirectional, since neither she nor Simon had the same type of psychic abilities as Michael.

What put the smug smile on her face was the knowledge that she'd been right all along about Michael and Sienna: they were great together, although she would've preferred skipping the show.

Cara let Simon sleep as she slipped away to the shower. Her head wasn't too bad, only a mild hangover to pay for last night's transgressions. She'd done worse damage.

There were big tasks to tackle this morning, least of which was cleaning the place up and locating all the members of her wedding party for brunch with her parents at one o'clock. The biggest task by far would be strapping on Cupid's bow and quiver to see if she could replicate her success with Michael and Sienna for Brett and Jessa. Even if she couldn't help them blaze a trail to true love, maybe she could at least get them on the same page.

*Speaking of... there seems to be a whole lotta lovin' in the air lately... practically an epidemic,* Cara thought as she flipped off her blow dryer.

Simon continued to sleep soundly after she dressed. Leaning down, she brushed her lips in a sweet kiss over the soft skin of his cheek. He stirred but didn't wake. She snuck out, closing the door behind her.

The apartment was still when she reached the kitchen. She put on a large pot of coffee and started the kitchen clean-up. Discarded cans, bottles, and plates littered the counter even though most of the activities occurred up on the deck. She loaded the dishwasher to capacity and started it. Taking all the recyclables, she placed them into the empty boxes used to cart the alcohol and left them next to the elevator. She'd have the guys take them down to the dumpster in the basement later.

As she wiped down the counter, strong, warm arms encircled her from behind. She leaned back into Simon and inhaled the scent of clean cotton and her favorite cologne. He nibbled her ear, drawing a smile out of her.

"Why didn't you wake me?" he whispered, enfolding her body into the strong muscles of his chest. The warm columns of his arms surrounded her shoulders and his hands rested on her hips.

She turned and put her arms around his neck, peering up into his smiling eyes. "You looked so peaceful." She pulled him down for a kiss, never tiring of feeling his warmth and the touch of his body against hers.

He kissed her on the forehead. "Let me help."

She winked at him. "I think the smell of cooked bacon would draw a crowd; what do you think?"

He headed over to the fridge. "Good idea. Plus, I'm ravenous."

"I'll get us some coffee," she said, pouring them both a cup. The door to Paco's room opened and reclosed. "Make that three cups," she added under her breath.

Paco came into the kitchen with a wide smile on his face. "Make that four," he said.

*Damn that Nephilim hearing*, she thought, raising her eyebrow at the usually stoic Paco and wondering who had kept him company the night before. She glanced over at Simon who was cracking eggs into a bowl. He looked back at her and shrugged, equally clueless.

"You look… happy," she said.

"Do you have any aspirin, Cara?" Paco asked her as he poured milk into his coffee cup, ignoring her comment.

"Yeah, how many do you need?"

"Two and they're not for me," he said.

The guest room door swung open and out staggered Irene. "They're for me," she said. "My head is pounding. For flip's sake, how much did I drink last night?"

Cara and Simon just stared at one another, a look of shock passing between them.

"*Pelirroja*, what do you take in your coffee?" he asked softly.

"Black, *Paquito*," she said affectionately and climbed up onto a barstool, turning to Cara and Simon. "And will you two stop looking at us like that? He was a perfect gentleman. I, on the other hand, passed out like a drunk."

Paco placed the coffee in front of Irene, put his arm briefly around her, and bestowed a kiss to the top of her head. He whispered something in her ear and she smiled.

Cara chuckled and threw her hands up in the air. "We're all adults here. For the record, I think it's cute. Breakfast anyone?"

Simon had the eggs and bacon cooking on the stove top. He was ready to plate the first batch of food when the door to the roof deck slammed open and shut, followed by a groan that echoed down the hallway.

Angel arrived in the kitchen looking like death warmed over. His black hair pasted to one side of his head, he looked at her out of dark bloodshot eyes. "Cara, would you pour a dying man a cup of coffee? Cream and three sugars, please, kind lady."

"Sure, Angel. You don't look so well. Are you all right?" she asked with a sideways glance as she reached for a coffee cup.

"Too much tequila. It came in like a lamb and left like a lion carrying a piece of my skull with it." He slumped on the barstool next to Irene. He looked up, noticing her for the first time. Then he glanced over at Paco who wore his best poker face.

He smiled broadly. "Nice to know sometimes you listen."

Paco turned away to refill his cup, avoiding everyone's eyes. His Nephilim energy curled in wisps around the room, silently telling everyone to back off. The only person unable to feel it was Irene, who walked over to the freezer and pulled out a sixteen-ounce bag of baby peas, placing them on top of her head.

"Eye, are you all right? I've never seen you wear frozen vegetables before," Cara said, stifling a laugh.

"I've never had a hangover quite like this before. I'm enjoying the numbness."

"Just don't accidentally give yourself brain freeze."

Simon set down four plates with eggs, bacon, and toast, keeping his plate by the stove as he made a second batch.

Brett entered the kitchen from the dining room dressed in jeans and a T-shirt. Like the rest of the crowd, he wore dark circles under his eyes like a fashion accessory.

He looked like he hadn't slept at all.

Cara smiled. "Morning, Brett. Breakfast?"

Angel looked over at Brett and smirked. "Bacon for you this morning, m'ijo?"

Brett narrowed his eyes. "Burnt pig flesh? No, thanks."

Cara couldn't figure out if he was cranky because he hadn't slept or because he was wound up over Jessa. She would bet on the latter.

"I'll take his bacon," Irene piped up.

*Obviously the hangover's not interfering with her appetite*, Cara thought.

Simon turned from the stove. "Brett, are eggs okay, or do want some yogurt, fresh fruit, and granola? There's some in the fridge. I can put it together for you."

Cara smiled, appreciating Simon's effort to be hospitable to Brett. Ever since he'd seen the look in Brett's eyes when he looked at Jessa he'd been nicer to him.

Brett poured the remains of the coffee into his cup. "Thanks. Eggs are fine. Fruit would be great, too." Then he reached out and grabbed Cara's arm as she stood leaning on the island. "Can we talk in private?"

She nodded. Taking their coffee, they rounded the corner into the living room.

Brett placed his cup down on the low table next to sofa and Cara followed suit. Keyed up, Brett didn't fully sit but rather balanced on the edge next to her, ready to bounce back up. He raked his hands through his loose blond hair. "I couldn't sleep. I couldn't stop thinking about her. Can we go over to your place? I have to see her."

His eyes held a crazy desperation. She touched his arm. "We'll see her. I texted her this morning and she's feeling better. I know you're anxious, but we don't want to spook her, either. She ran off for a reason, Brett. You need to give me a little time to find out why."

What Cara didn't share with Brett was that Jessa had refused to discuss what had happened. But Cara wasn't about to let it go.

His face crumpled and he held his head in his hands. "What did I do? Why did she run?"

She touched his hair, her heart going out to him, but the pull she'd felt the other day was noticeably missing. "Hey," she said softly, "You didn't do anything wrong; this has nothing to do with you and everything to do with her. I can almost guarantee it."

When he looked up, his eyes held longing, but this time for someone else. "You think so?"

"I know so. After breakfast, we'll get Paco to drive us and Irene back to the penthouse. I'll talk to Jessa first, and then I'll buy you some time with her until we have to leave for brunch with my parents. Deal?"

He gave her a small smile and nodded. "Sounds like a plan."

# Chapter 39

***IRENE***
***New York City. Sunday, May 26, 11:30*** AM ET

IRENE RELUCTANTLY ABANDONED the bag of frozen baby peas at the loft before they left. Neither the throbbing of her head nor the unsavory task of scattering her spy gadgets throughout Cara and Simon's possessions could interfere with the smile on her lips as she looked out the passenger window of the SUV. She wore a dreamy, idiotic look on her face and it had everything to do with the man sitting next to her in the driver's seat.

Cara and Brett talked in heated whispers behind her as Paco drove them back to the penthouse. She tuned them out and thought back to earlier... in Paco's room.

She'd woken up without a single clue of where she was or how she'd ended up there. After a moment her eyes flew open and she gasped... loudly. She lay spooned into a man's warmth, a huge caramel-colored arm draped over her from behind. Closing her eyes, it all came back to her—Paco. Kissing him and wanting him desperately.

"*Pelirroja*," he breathed into her ear. "Are you awake?" His lips gently connected with her neck. Warm jolts of electricity shot through her, awakening every part of her in their path. Too bad her pounding head threatened to ruin the party.

"*Mmm*, that feels so good," she said, baring more of her neck for him to nibble on. He trailed his fingertips down along her arm and then slowly rolled her over to face him. Her eyes still semiclosed, she drew in a breath at the sight of him. His brown eyes warmed when he looked at her.

"Good morning," he said softly and kissed her gently. Irene reached up and wrapped her arms around his neck, deepening the kiss, barely able to believe this handsome god actually wanted to kiss her in the first place.

*Ay Dios mío, he's so delicious*, she thought, surrendering herself to him and ignoring the agonizing pain in her skull.

He responded under her lips, taking over, possessing her with his kiss and leaving her breathless. His hands dug down underneath her back, lifting her off the bed and closer to him until she was pressed up against his body.

"*Pelirroja*, you are a beautiful woman, and if you stay in my bed any longer I may not let you leave," he whispered, his voice silky and seductive.

She cringed as a bolt of pain stabbed her behind the eyes. Her hands cradled the sides of her face. Warmed by her new nickname, she repaid the endearment by using the proper Spanish nickname for Paco's name. "*Paquito*, if my head didn't feel like it was about to explode, you couldn't make me leave this bed."

His face lit up in a smile and he kissed her on the forehead. "May I get you some aspirin, *niña bonita*?"

"You're my hero," she said.

He leaned in for one more kiss before he got out of bed to dress. Ducking into the bathroom, he emerged a few minutes later looking presentable. More than she could say for herself, staring down at her rumpled dress.

"Meet me outside when you're ready," he said, closing the door behind him.

"Irene?" Cara's voice snapped her back.

"Huh? What?" Irene asked, twisting around to look at her friend.

"I asked you what train you're taking later," Cara said.

The thought of leaving suddenly made her heartsick and she saw Paco tense out of the corner of her eye. How crazy was this? She met him last night, and the thought of leaving him made her physically ill. "Um, I planned on taking the five o'clock train from Penn Station," she said quietly. "Why?"

"With you and Jessa leaving, I'm trying to coordinate transportation for later," she said.

"I'll take her, Cara," said Paco quietly, reaching over to take Irene's hand inside of his and giving it a squeeze. "Is that okay with you, *Pelirroja*?"

Irene smiled brightly, trying to cover her anguish. She felt like a lovesick puppy. "More than okay." She kept her hand nestled in his and stared out the window, as Paco drove them into the underground garage.

It took ages to weave their way through the maze of twists and turns before Paco let them out at the elevator leading to the penthouse and went to park.

Cara twisted the key in the special elevator keypad and whisked them up to the top floor. Brett looked like he was ready to jump out of his skin; small beads of sweat formed on his upper lip.

"Brett, hang out while I speak with Jessa. Try to relax," Cara said before the elevator door opened. She looked at her watch. "We'll have about thirty minutes before Sienna and my parents arrive."

He licked his lips and nodded. "Okay."

Irene shook her head, thinking back to last night when Cara filled her in on what had happened. *What the heck was the matter with Jessa?* A famous, hot rock star sings to you in front of almost three thousand people and wants to get you a drink afterward… and you run? The girl needed her head examined.

The penthouse was silent when they entered the marble foyer. Cara turned to Irene. "Can you take Brett into the living room?"

"Sure," she said and led the way into the large open space as Cara cut down the hall toward the guest rooms.

Brett paced, lost in thought. His actions struck a chord with Irene as she struggled with her own unexpected dilemma. "Hey," she said softly. Brett looked up as if noticing her for the first time. "Can you tell Paco I'll be back? I just need to jump in the shower and change quickly before Cara's parents get here."

He gave her a wan smile. "Yeah, sure. No problem," he said and resumed pacing.

Assuming Cara had the "Jessa situation" well in hand, Irene raced back to her room. Not only did she need to get herself ready, but she needed to execute her plan before they left for brunch, reminding herself she was doing this for the greater good of saving her friend. Her head pounded with every step she took, but she'd suffer the discomfort just to get through the next few hours.


### CARA

"Jessa," Cara said, her knuckles softly tapping on Jessa's door before she entered. Jessa sat unmoving on the bed, looking no better than Brett. Her eyes held signs of exhaustion and her shoulders slumped. She looked like a frail, angelic doll in her sundress, enfolded inside of the long curls that draped around her shoulders.

Jessa looked at her as she entered, but made no effort to move. "I'm sorry I'm being so weird."

Jessa's despair hit Cara squarely in the stomach. She sat next to Jessa and wrapped her arm around Jessa's thin shoulders and said softly, "Sweetie, what's the matter? You look awful."

A tear escaped her eye as she glanced at Cara. "I didn't want to put anything in a text or say anything over the phone. But I had to go. If I stayed, something bad could've happened… to Brett."

A chill tickled Cara's spine. "What do you mean? Did you have a vision?"

Jessa nodded. "Not just one."

"What did you see?"

"I can't tell you," she whispered with pleading eyes.

Cara frowned. "Why? You've always been able to tell me before."

"Not this time."

Cara's heart dropped. "Jessa, he's drawn to you… to the point of desperation. Will you at least talk to him?"

"It's not a good idea," Jessa said as she got up from the bed and paced.

"Would it make a difference if I told you he's here?" Cara asked, hoping Jessa would change her mind. Cara weighed her concern over Jessa's visions against Brett's heart and his desperation to see Jessa again. If love was even a remote possibility for them, her choice was clear—she and the others would body block any danger that came Brett's way, if necessary.

Jessa stopped in her tracks, her eyes wide. "Here?" A wave of heat smacked Cara, telling her Jessa felt something akin to what Brett felt.

Cara nodded. "In the living room, and he's not leaving until he sees you."

Jessa cursed softly under her breath.

"Just give him five minutes. Please. I beg you. Nothing can happen to either of you here." Cara held her breath as Jessa silently paced.

"Okay. Five minutes," she finally conceded.

Cara let out a silent sigh of relief. "Stay here. I'll bring him down so you guys can have some privacy."

Then Jessa did the oddest thing on Cara's way out—she closed the curtains.

Cara shook her head and headed back to the living room. Brett stopped pacing and gave her a hopeful look as she approached.

Giving him an encouraging smile, she reached out to him. "Come on, I'll take you back to see her."

Life reentered his eyes as he took her hand.


***BRETT***

"Jessa?" Brett said softly, closing the door behind him. Her shoulders twitched at the sound of his voice. She stood by the closed curtains with her back to him, and then slowly turned to face him.

His breath caught in his throat at the sight of her in the dim room.

"Hi," she said with a small smile. "I'm sorry I had to leave last night."

Wanting to be as close to her as possible, he crossed the room until they were only inches apart. Suddenly aware he might be too close, he took a step back and folded his arms in front of him. "Uh, listen. Cara told me you live right outside of San Francisco. I'm traveling for another week or so, but would you consider getting together when I'm back?" He looked away, trying to hide his desperation to see her again.

When she didn't answer, he shifted his gaze back to her.

Rooted in place, she silently stared at him with a look of pain and longing. He couldn't fathom why she didn't just say yes. Her mouth opened to say something and then shut without a word.

"You're killing me here, Jessa. Please just tell me what I did wrong." He couldn't keep the anguish from his voice. His eyes searched her face. He didn't understand how anyone could affect him the way she did. He didn't even know her, and yet he felt like his whole existence depended on seeing her again. It made no sense whatsoever. But then again, what had made any sense this week? *Nada, nichts*, nothing.

She took a deep breath and reached out to touch his arm. A surge of hope and electricity coursed through his veins, her touch burning his skin. He stood frozen, afraid if he moved she would run again. Instead, she slowly drew him into her arms and rested her head under his neck. His arms instinctively closed around her and he almost whimpered with happiness.

"Jessa, please say you'll see me again," he whispered, feeling like an awkward teenager laying his soul out bare and steeling himself for rejection.

He heard her swallow. "Yes," she whispered—her answer barely audible.

His eyes closed in relief and he held her closer, aching to kiss her.

"Are you sure I didn't do anything wrong?" he asked.

She leaned her head back to look at him. "No. You haven't done anything wrong, Brett." His name rolled off her tongue, caressing his ears. Unable to stop himself, his hand traveled down the length of her curls, letting their softness caress his palm.

"When do you leave for the airport?" he asked.

"Right after brunch. I have a car meeting me there," she said, pointing to her packed suitcase in the corner. His heart dropped. He didn't want to let her go.

He nodded. If he didn't need to leave for France on Wednesday, he'd follow her back. But Cara was right—he didn't want to seem so desperate. Ironic, he could walk outside and get mauled by a thousand women who would jump at the chance to date him. Yet, here he was, standing in front of the one he wanted, and he had to beg.

"So, do you want to give me your number?" he asked.

"Sure," she said, releasing him to get her purse. Her withdrawal left him bereft.

She pulled a business card from inside and walked back to hand it to him. He read it:

SERENITY SPA | JESSAMINE DRAKE | LEAD PRACTITIONER | 415-555-3422

"I'll call you as soon as I get back, okay?" he said, placing the card in the pocket of his jeans.

She nodded and smiled shyly at him, her hazel eyes bright. Hardly able to draw in his next breath or to take his eyes from her, he slowly pulled her into his arms and kissed her, his lips meeting the velvet softness of hers. Holding her close, he melted into her, his tongue gently parting her lips as he deepened the kiss.

With a surge of energy, she kissed him back with a passion that left him light-headed. Jessa's hands around his waist seared his flesh, igniting a sudden need inside of him to feel her naked skin on his. He gently pushed away from her, not wanting her to feel his groin springing to life. The last thing he needed her to think was that he only wanted her for sex.

"I should go," he said, unable to speak above a whisper.

"I know. Thanks for coming here," she said, trailing her fingers down his cheek and setting him on fire all over again.

He gave her a dimpled smile and tried to control the pounding of his heart. "Have a good time at brunch, and travel safe. I'll see you soon."

She smiled sweetly. "Bye."

He backed out of the room and closed the door behind him. He passed Paco in the hallway and gave him a wave on the way back to see Cara.

His spirits soared, still tasting their kiss on his lips, already looking forward to returning home in ten days. He touched his pocket, feeling her card through the thick denim. Mission accomplished. He'd be seeing Jessa again.

Cara sat patiently waiting on the couch. Her eyes lit up when she saw him. He beamed, giving her a silent thumbs-up on his way over to see her.

A smile spread across her face.

He sat down next to her on the couch. "It's all good."

"Good," she said. "Paco went to see Irene. When they're done, he'll take you back to the loft."

Brett yawned, stretching his arms up and over his head. "Fantastic. I'm beat. I plan to sleep for the rest of the afternoon." He could rest now that things were finally settled with Jessa. His heart was afloat with thoughts of their kiss, and his mind was already at work planning their first date.

# Chapter 40


*IRENE*

*New York City. Fifth Avenue Penthouse. Sunday, May 26, 12:15 PM ET*

"WHO IS IT?" Irene asked at the gentle knock on her door.

"It's me, *Pelirroja*." Paco's muffled reply came through the door.

Her heart did a little flip, the sound of his voice warming her. "One sec," she said before flying into a tizzy to remove the towel swathed around her head and to run a brush through her hair. Still in a robe, she kicked off her slippers in an effort to look less geeky before answering the door.

His large frame filled the doorway, making no move to enter. "I need to take Brett back to Simon's, but I'll be back later to pick you up downstairs," he said, averting his eyes. Beneath the silky quality of his voice, she heard an underlying sadness. Something in his energy had changed; he'd made an emotional retreat and thrown up a wall. She almost gasped out loud from the sudden pain that assaulted her chest. Had something happened since he parked the car?

"Is everything all right? You don't seem like yourself all of a sudden."

His eyes flashed coldly. "How would you know what I'm like? We've just met," he snapped.

Stunned by his sharp words, she felt tears spring to her eyes. "I'm sorry," she said softly, barely able to speak. "I can take a cab later."

She turned and ran to the bathroom, closing the door behind her and sinking down onto the floor. Her lungs burned for oxygen and her heart shattered painfully. Unable to stop them, tears cascaded down her cheeks as she muffled her sobs with the sleeve of her robe. How could he have been so wonderful to her and then so incredibly callous? It made no sense. They had shared a wonderful night, and waking up in his bed had been nothing short of a dream. Despite her hangover, he'd given her a couple of minutes of happiness in her lonely, dateless existence. And it hurt to think he might have regretted it.

What was she thinking? Men like him never looked at her. Maybe he'd come to his senses and decided she wasn't pretty enough for him. Maybe they both drank too much last night. It wouldn't have been the first time she'd met someone, thought they connected, and then never heard from them again.

Grabbing a tissue, she blew her nose. Someone softly knocked on the door. "What?" she growled, expecting it to be Paco.

"Eye, it's me, Cara."

Her shoulder slumped in a mix of disappointment and relief. "Come in."

Cara's eyes filled with concern. "What happened? Paco raced out of here like his pants were on fire. Did you guys have a fight?"

Irene took another tissue and dabbed at her eyes. "No, it was the strangest thing. I asked him if he was all right, and he just snapped. I knew it was too good to be true. Men like him don't date women like me," she said, crying again.

Cara joined her on the bathroom floor and squeezed her into a hug. "Stop talking crap. Women like you? You mean smart, funny, pretty women?"

Irene squeezed her back, filled with love for her friend. "No, I was thinking more about the kind of woman who swears like a sailor in your native tongue, drinks enough to pass out in your bed, and leaves you with a monster case of blue balls."

Cara giggled. "Will you please stop? I don't know Paco well, but what I do know is that he's typically a gentleman."

Guilt overcame Irene as she thought about how she was about to betray Cara in an effort to save her. Maybe this was her punishment… losing the only man who ever looked at her like she was special.

The doorbell chimed, echoing through the penthouse.

Cara popped up and headed in the direction of the door. "Crap, that's either Sienna or my parents. My money's on Mom and Dad."

Irene let out a deep breath. "I'll be out in five minutes."

Cara looked back and smiled. "Your hair smells fantastic."

"Thanks," she said with a small smile. Paco had even managed to take her joy out of using Cara's honeysuckle shampoo.

That was that. She would take a cab. No need to for an uncomfortable ride later.

*It was nice knowing you, Paquito.*

Besides, she had a plan to execute and a friend to save.


## *PACO*

As Brett snored softly in the backseat, Paco gripped the steering wheel until his knuckles were white and silently cursed, using language far stronger than Irene had used the night before. If he could beat himself for his own stupidity, he'd do it. Today's date had been poking at him for a week, sitting right outside his threshold of recall.

When he'd taken the key out of the ignition after he'd parked, it had clicked. Today was his wedding anniversary. Remembering Isabella's birthday or the day she died had never been a problem for him. But remembering their anniversary had always been a challenge, even when she was alive.

Realization and guilt had torn through him. He felt like he'd dishonored her memory by taking an interest in Irene. That had never happened before, because he'd never been interested in another woman since Isabella had died. He usually followed Angel's philosophy when it came to women. Scratch your itch and move on; never the same woman twice.

But Irene was different. She moved him the way Isabella had when they'd first met. That instant connection they'd had. He'd felt at ease, instantly at home, and protective of her. Not to mention her kiss. *Ay Dios mío.* Her kiss ignited passion that he'd buried deep in his soul, making him want to weep from longing.

He cringed at the sharp words he used with her. He'd be lucky if she ever wanted to speak to him again, much less forgive him. The tears in her eyes sliced his heart in half. He was a brute for making her cry. Although… he'd spoken the truth. She really didn't know him. She didn't know about Isabella or his pain. Even more importantly, she didn't know he wasn't fully human. But that wasn't her fault.

Paco released a heavy sigh. Maybe Angel was right, maybe this was the time to let go and come back to the living. If he let her leave tonight without seeing her, he'd spend eternity kicking his own ass when what he really wanted to do was to make tender love to her for a solid week.

*Pelirroja, what have you done to me?*

# Chapter 41

*CARA*
*New York City. Fifth Avenue Penthouse. Sunday, May 26, 12:45 PM ET*

CARA RAN DOWN THE HALLWAY to answer the door. On her way past the living room, her cell phone chimed from the coffee table. She darted over and plucked it out of her backpack before continuing on to the front door.

Through the peep hole she spotted a head of jet black hair and let Sienna in. Prada handbag dangling from her arm, she strolled across the threshold wearing sunglasses. "Are Richard and Corrine here yet?" she asked, referring to Cara's parents.

Holding up her phone, Cara leaned in and gave Sienna a quick peck on the cheek. "Mom just sent a text. They're stuck in traffic and will meet us at Sarabeth's."

"Where are the girls?" Sienna asked, looking around.

"They'll be out in a minute." Cara suppressed a grin at the telltale rasp in Sienna's voice and the sunglasses. "Hard night?"

Taking off her shades and giving Cara a devilish smile, she said, "*Hard* is one way of putting it, and it more than made up for the five hours of sleep that I traded." Sienna's hair was pulled back in a sleek ponytail. With her skinny jeans and high-heeled sandals, she looked her usual picture of chic... The dark circles under her eyes were the only visible evidence of her late night.

"Dare I ask?"

"You may dare, but I'm not talking, other than to say I was right," Sienna said, self-satisfied.

Cara tilted her head, amused. "Oh? About what?"

"He's got the goods," Sienna replied with a wink and headed in the direction of the living room, her heels clacking across the marble tile.

Cara followed behind her, shaking her head. *Been there, seen them,* she thought. Michael's unintentional live picture show was one discussion she didn't look forward to having with him later.

"You had a good time?"

Sienna's face softened and she lowered herself onto the sofa. "Yeah. Really good."

Cara sat down next to her and touched her arm. "I'm so glad, Senny. I think you guys will be good together."

Blushing, Sienna averted her eyes and pulled Cara into a hug. "Thanks for being such a good friend."

Cara squeezed her. "I just want you to be happy. You deserve it, and so does Michael."

Jessa emerged into the living room, hauling her suitcase behind her. Her face lit up when she saw them. "Hi, Sienna. Cara, should I put this next to the door?"

Jessa had an ethereal glow about her that had been missing earlier. No longer stressed or consumed with worry, Jessa reflected a smooth serenity in her features.

*Brett's visit had been a good idea after all,* Cara thought.

Cara popped up to help her. "Catch up with Sienna. I'll get that." Taking the suitcase from Jessa, she headed back to the foyer. The wheels echoed across the marble as she rolled it to a stop next to front door. Her cell phone chimed again from the living room, where she'd left it.

"Can someone get that?" Cara yelled, and headed back to the living room.

"Got it," Sienna replied. A moment later she yelled back, "The driver is downstairs."

Cara had arranged for a limo large enough for everyone. Since they no longer needed to wait for her parents, they could go whenever Irene was ready. Cara was already looking forward to her next cup of coffee.

On cue, Irene came down the hall. "What gives? You both disappeared last night."

Cara could feel Irene's sadness behind her brave face. Only Cara knew the reason for the slight redness hidden behind her glasses. Now, if she could get Irene and Paco back on track, she'd be three for three.

Suspicion grew stronger in Cara's mind as she reflected on the sudden epidemic of insta-love popping up among her friends. True, the density of choice

Grade-A males surrounding her lately was exponentially larger than normal. Add a great concert, after-party, and some alcohol and you have a fine recipe. No doubt. But come on. Irene, Jessa, and Sienna all hooking up in one weekend? Constantina's words echoes in Cara's head, *"The Twelve are magnetically drawn together and surrounded by powerful emotions. Sometimes those feelings and emotions will manifest when you physically meet one of the others…"*

*Could it be possible… ?* Cara wondered.

Sienna shook Cara's arm, knocking her out of her reverie. "What are you thinking about? You've got this deep, serious look on your face."

"Uh… nothing," Cara said, faking a smile.

Jessa glanced at Irene suspiciously. "Um, I don't recall you sleeping here last night. Anything you care to share?"

Irene paled.

Cara jumped to her rescue. "Hey Ladies, let's continue the inquisition in the car."

"Can I meet you guys downstairs in five minutes? I have a call I need to make before we go," Irene asked, pointing toward the guest room.

"No problem. Take the elevator down to the garage when you're done," Cara replied, maneuvering everyone out the door to give Irene a way to sidestep Jessa's comment.

*Ugh,* Cara thought. *The only downside to all this romance is the heartbreak that sometimes follows.*

# Chapter 42



*ACHANELECH*

*France. Château du Feu. Sunday, May 26, 7:00 PM GMT +1*

"EM!" ACHANELECH SCREAMED over the pounding din of hammers—and who knows what other tools—at work above his head. Plaster dust rained down onto his laptop in a sudden stream. "For the love of Lucifer," he mumbled through gritted teeth. "Emanelech!"

He blew the dust off the keyboard and slammed his fist on the desk, tempted to hit more than the polished wood. "*Em-an-el-eck!*"

*Where in Hell was that infernal woman?*

Emanelech came tottering through the doorway at top speed in four-inch high-heeled shoes, out of breath and waving her tablet. "Acchie, what's the matter? Did you set the drapes on fire again?"

He rolled his eyes. "What are they doing up there, rebuilding Rome?" he snarled, pointing at the ceiling.

She shot a glance upward and consulted her tablet, passing her finger over the surface. "No… that would be the renovation of Luc's room," she said, chewing her lip.

"Luc's—we're hosting a Convocation not restoring a hotel!" Achanelech said as heat crept up his neck. Another stream of plaster pebbles showered the top of his head. He growled and swept his hand over his hair, coming away with a chalky white film covering his palm.

"Will you relax already?" she snapped, planting her hand on her hip. "This is to restore ourselves back into Luc's good graces, remember?" Her expression turned to a pout. "I want to make sure he's comfortable."

Achanelech ground his teeth as his head pounded in time with the hammers, and changed the subject. "Any more RSVPs?"

Her finger returned to the surface of her device. "As a matter of fact, yes, one of the troublemakers from Africa, Wormwood, responded. I told him to keep his diseases at home this time. Last thing we need is an outbreak of Bubonic plague this go 'round."

He let out a breath. "How many does that make?" Achanelech asked in a weary voice.

"Um…" Emanelech's lips moved as she counted the responses. "Ten."

"Who are we missing?" he asked, walking around and leaning back against the edge of the desk.

"Xaphan in Africa and the South American contingent," she replied.

This meant they still hadn't heard from Abaddon and Astraroth, either. Of the three, Xaphan, the keeper of the fires of Hell, was his least favorite. Then again, he hated them all. Now, if he could only keep the flaming "pissing matches" between him and Xaphan to a minimum.

After a quick knuckle rap to the open wooden door, a short lean man, wearing a gray suit and black-framed glasses with small round lenses, walked briskly inside.

"Excuse me," Heinrich said in a clipped tone and clicked his heels together. "*Fraulein*, 'zere is a problem."

Emanelech narrowed her eyes. "What kind of problem?"

Heinrich's frown deepened. "Labor issue."

"What kind of labor issue?" she asked.

"Strike."

"Strike? What in Hell does that mean?" Achanelech snapped, suddenly seeing a monetary request in his future. Over the pounding above his head, he made out a faint chanting coming from the grounds.

Emanelech glared and waved him off. "I'll handle this, Acchie."

"I'm afraid *ve vill* need to hire some outside resources for *ze* food," Heinrich said.

"For the food or for the 'food'?" she asked with a raised brow.

"'Ze… kind you *zerve* on a plate, *Fraulein*," he sputtered.

That would be easier than the other kind of sustenance they required. The capture of human souls was exceedingly more difficult than roasting a pig.

Achanelech shook his head and headed for the door with his laptop and cane. "I'll leave you to sort out the details, *Chérie*, while I find a quieter place to work."

Given the vast number of workman buzzing around the château and the entertainment Emanelech had been collecting in the dungeon, his best course of action was to head straight to the stable before she nagged him about any more party planning details.

He had more important things to do like executing the plan to capture Eae's Nephil son, and hiding his dealings from Escher before that English dandy ruined him. The question was how to do it all before the Convocation started in a little over a week…

# Chapter 43

*IRENE*
*New York City. Sarabeth's. Sunday, May 26, 2:00* PM ET

IRENE PASTED ON A SMILE, pretending to listen to the conversation going on around her as she sat in Sarabeth's with her friends and Cara's parents. On Fifty-Ninth Street at Central Park South directly across from the Park, Sarabeth's was located in the heart of upscale midtown real estate and reflected the opulence of its neighborhood.

Irene nibbled on her goat cheese omelet, which would've been amazing if she could've actually tasted it. Her eyes darted to the lush trees across the street, wishing she could escape into the greenery.

She hadn't lied to Cara about the phone call. After she'd planted the bugs and trackers in Simon and Cara's belongings, she'd called Ellerton to inform him the deed was done.

Having the penthouse to herself eased her anxiety and gave her the freedom to carefully examine the contents of the walk-in closet Cara shared with Simon. Irene had enough shoe devices to plant one in every pair of lug-soled boots Simon had in the closet. Once that was done, she planted one in his shaving kit, the coin pockets of two pairs of his jeans, his belt, and the only suitcase she could find. Cara had left her backpack behind on the coffee table, snagging only her wallet on her way out, making that part simple. Before she left the apartment, Irene checked the library. The laptop was gone.

The whole operation had taken her five minutes to the second. If the NSA couldn't track and monitor Simon among all of those devices, there was something seriously wrong with them.

On her way out, she'd left her suitcase by the door and looked around with a heavy heart, thinking of the bittersweet time she'd spent there. But her mission was clear: find out what was going on and protect Cara. If Simon was innocent, she'd protect him, too. If he wasn't, she had a wedding to stop.

"How are your folks doing, Irene?"

Irene's attention snapped over to Cara's dad, Richard, a big bear of a man with a cap of white hair and intense blue eyes. She'd known him since her freshman year at Georgetown.

Her pasted-on smile still in place, she said, "They're doing fine. Dad's looking for an overseas assignment. But mom's laid down the gauntlet and said this is her last move outside of the country unless he can get her back home to Ireland." Her mom had been born in Galway, immigrating to the United States in the early '80s. Hopefully, Irene's double-agent role would also ensure her father's aspirations wouldn't be thwarted.

Cara's mom, Corrine, smiled at her. "Has your mom been home lately?"

"Yeah, she went back to visit six months ago."

Corrine leaned over and whispered in Irene's ear. "You've been quiet today, sweetheart. Is everything all right?" Cara was a younger version of Corrine, with the same auburn hair and kind green eyes. Thinking of Paco, disappointment gripped Irene followed by the displeasure over her coerced NSA assignment, and a lump grew in her throat over Corrine's concern.

Irene gave her a small smile and mustered up every shred of sincerity within her. "I had a really late night. I'm just tired."

She squeezed Irene's hand. "Okay, let me know if you need anything."

Irene lapsed back into her state of "present but not accounted for" while Sienna recounted something amusing that had happened to her during work this week involving a shirt in the shape of an igloo.

Out of the corner of her eye, Irene caught Paco's hulking frame as he entered the restaurant. Her heart leaped, and then filled with trepidation. Was he here to compound her humiliation? She couldn't find it within herself to look at him.

He walked up to the table and stopped next to Cara. "Excuse me for interrupting, but would you mind if I asked Irene to come outside for a minute?"

Irene glanced up to find his pleading, chocolate eyes focused directly on her. He'd changed into a blue button-down shirt and tan slacks, his dark hair styled to perfection. She sighed. He looked good enough to eat, and he was definitely her flavor.

Cara cocked an eyebrow at her from across the table. "Eye?"

Irene stared back at him blankly, masking the anger, hurt, and humiliation swimming around inside of her. She'd opened herself up to him and he'd made her cry for no apparent reason. Her heart hammered, wanting to run far away, yet wanting to know why he'd done it.

"*Por favor?*" he pleaded softly, this time to her, in the silky melodic tone she found so sexy.

Everyone at the table stared at her, holding their collective breath.

Slowly, Irene pushed out her chair and walked past him to the door without saying a word.

"Thank you," she heard Paco say to Cara before he followed her outside.

She waited with her arms crossed over her chest as if to protect her heart. His hulking figure approached, not stopping until only a few inches separated them.

"*Perdóname. No quise hacerte daño, Pelirroja,*" he whispered, placing his huge hands on her shoulders.

She pouted. "Then why did you hurt me and why should I forgive you?"

He gently tipped her chin up to look at him. Pain filled his eyes. "There are things you don't know about me, that you must," he replied and swallowed.

Her heart softened, but she needed more than that in order to forgive him. "When you snapped at me…" She looked away. "I thought…"

"What did you think?" he asked softly.

"That you regretted kissing…" The lump in her throat prevented her from finishing. A tear slipped down her cheek and she brushed it away.

"No, no, no, *Pelirroja*," he said with anguish and pulled her into his broad chest, wrapping her in his warmth. "It's just the opposite." He held her tight to his body for a moment and then stepped away, grabbing her hand. "Come with me." He led her across the street toward Central Park.

They walked into the nearest entrance and found a bench. Birds tittered overhead, and sunlight filtered through the trees above, projecting the gentle movement of the leaves all around them. Sitting down, he pulled her closer and took a deep breath. Pain entered his eyes again. "Today … is my wedding anniversary."

Her heart dropped. "Your what?"

Shaking his head, he took her hands in each of his. "My wife died of cancer years ago. I haven't …"

Relief, mixing with sadness for Paco, washed over Irene. "Oh, I'm sorry. I didn't know." She gently squeezed his hands.

He furrowed his brow and his eyes sought hers with liquid warmth. "That is my point. How could you? We've just met. This is the first time our anniversary..." He paused and brought her hands up to kiss them. Closing his eyes, he held them to his lips.

Her breath caught in her throat at his gentle touch, her desire for him reigniting inside of her. "Paco—"

"Let me finish," he breathed. Opening his eyes, he looked at her with longing. "This is the first wedding anniversary since her death that I'm with someone who makes my heart beat again."

Unable to stop herself, she cupped his cheek and leaned in to touch her lips to his. In one movement, he pulled her onto his lap and into an embrace. The heat of his kiss overwhelmed her senses as his mouth hungrily sought hers. His lips soft yet insistent, the taste of his kiss was pure heaven. He held her close, his hand gently massaging her back.

Breaking away, he tucked her head under his chin, and whispered, "I want to see you again, *Pelirroja*. I don't want to say good-bye to you."

She breathed in the warm scent of his neck. The pleasant spiciness and pure male smell of him sent a rush of heat through her entire body. "I don't want to leave, *Pacquito*. I wish I could stay."

"Let me take you to the train. Next time, I will come to you wherever that may be."

Bliss filled Irene and she smiled into his neck. The world looked brighter again. But Irene's smiled faded when she realized there was a lot he didn't know about her, either. In the world of secrets, hers might be worse. Given his affiliation with Simon and Cara, would she be called to lie to him, too?

Then again, hadn't she already?

# Chapter 44

*CARA*

*New York City. Greene Street Loft. Sunday, May 26, 5:30 PM ET*

CARA RELAXED IN A CHAISE lounge, basking in the fading sun as she listened to Brett strum on his guitar. He experimented with different chords, composing a new song inspired by Jessa.

*He's so gone.* She glanced around the roof deck, relieved it was back in its usual state of order after last night's festivities. With Irene and Jessa on their way home, she could finally relax. All the emotions of the weekend had sapped her energy, dulling her senses.

"Hey, what does a guy have to do to get a hug around here?"

Cara's head snapped around and Brett stopped strumming.

"Kai!" she said and jumped up to greet him. "I must be off my game. I can't believe you were able to sneak up on me like that." Even at thirty-one years old, dressed in a T-shirt, long shorts, and sandals, Kai looked more like a college kid than an esteemed scientist.

Flanked by Simon, he walked toward her with a smile and a welcoming twinkle in his blue eyes. His conservatively cut blond hair was tousled, probably from the fingers he'd recently run through it. Although she and Kai talked several times a week, this was the first time she'd seen him in person since his visit to the Sanctuary eight weeks ago.

She couldn't stop the rush of heat that consumed her, and cringed the moment she caught a whiff of her wildflower scent. She swore silently, *Damn Nephilim hormones.*

Ignoring her inappropriate physical response, happiness bubbled up inside of her. She threw her arms around his neck and kissed him on the cheek. His arms encircled her waist and he squeezed her into an embrace. The familiar warm, masculine scent of him filled her nostrils.

"Good to see you finally," he said softly.

Relief filled her having Kai here, safe in her arms. She couldn't help feeling protective of him. Old habits die hard. "Ditto," she whispered before she let him go.

Brett grinned at Kai and gave a nod in Simon's direction. "Better be careful or the big guy over there might kick your ass."

*Nothing like saying exactly what's on your mind,* Cara thought and glanced back at Simon.

Simon's arms were crossed over his chest as his eyes traveled between her and Kai, scowling. "I doubt that will be necessary," he gritted through his teeth.

Her annoyance flared, and she turned back to Kai.

Kai's eyebrow twitched at Cara. *"Huh?"*

*"I'll explain later,"* she replied, glad that she and Kai shared a special telepathic frequency separate from her Trinity. One of Kai's gifts as a Messenger, from what she could tell, was his unfettered ability to speak to her telepathically. They'd discovered it when they were held captive by Le Feu. Kai was able to answer her call when no one else could.

Cara eyed Simon who stood stewing behind Kai. She'd get the intros done and then see what was bugging him. Clasping her hands, she turned to Brett. "Kai, I'd like you to meet to my friend, Brett King."

They gave each other a smile and extended their hands.

"Nice to meet you," Kai said. "I'm sorry I had to miss your concert," When his hand touched Brett's, a ripple of energy tickled Cara's spine. *Interesting,* she thought.

"No problem. There'll be others," Brett said. "By the way, Cara's been talking you up."

"Cara, I'll be downstairs. Michael called, he's on his way," Simon glared at her, his mouth set in a hard line. The cloud of energy swirling around him reached her from where he stood.

*What the heck?* Simon's emotions turned her stomach… literally. She released a heavy sigh and left Kai with Brett.

*"Can I speak with you privately?"* she asked silently. Without stopping, she looped her arm through his and spun him around, dragging him to the door by

the stairs. Not an easy feat, but her newfound Nephilim strength made it doable. She almost smiled at his shock. When the door clicked shut behind him, she let him go.

He paced like a caged animal, not meeting her eyes. "You sure you're not in love with Kai? You reacted to him out there the way you react to me." He stopped to look at her, the anger in his eyes and the chill in his voice cut through her. "Do you know what it feels like to see the woman you love look at someone else like she wants to make love to him?"

"What's gotten into you?" Her temper ignited, fueled by a liberal dose of Nephilim PMS from the hormone release, and her eyes hardened. "And, yes, actually I do. Before I met you, I watched it for years every time Kai looked at Melanie. So, yeah, I do know how it feels. But that's not what you saw. The only man I want to make love to is standing right in front of me," she said, jabbing him in the arm with her finger.

He glowered back at her, locking his arms over his broad chest. "Then what did I see?"

She met his gaze. "You saw me greeting a dear friend."

His jaw tightened. "It seemed like a little more than that to me… from what I could *smell*."

Never had she wanted to hit someone like she wanted to hit Simon that moment. Then again, he'd never been such an irrational idiot. She dug into her pocket and threw her cell phone at him. He caught it with ease.

She glared at him. "I thought we discussed this the other night. Maybe you're too old to remember what Nephilim adolescence feels like and how out-of-control your hormones get. Call Constantina, she'll remind you. But, I'm telling you right now—you're letting your guilt over not being able to save me cloud your judgment. Get a grip!"

Simon growled behind her as she turned on her heel and went back out onto the roof deck to join Brett and Kai. She'd predicted her raging hormones would eventually get her into trouble, but really? Later, she'd use some of them to screw some sense back into Simon. In the meantime, if he came within her sight before she cooled down, projectiles would fly.

"Everything all right?" Kai asked as she approached.

Cara let out a breath and nodded.

"Hey, I hope you guys don't mind, but I'm going to jet back down to my room," Brett said, scooping up his guitar. "See you later."

Cara gave him a crooked smile. "Thanks. Good luck with the song."

Brett winked and headed for the stairs.

Cara crossed her arms over her chest, simmering over her exchange with Simon.

"Hey, look at me." Kai clamped his hand on her shoulder. She met his gaze. "Everything okay?" he asked softly, his eyes searching hers. She was accustomed to sharing almost everything with him as one of her closest friends. But she didn't trust herself to speak for fear she would say something about Simon that she'd later regret.

Instead, she blew out a breath. "Yeah, just give me a minute. Simon's being irrational. I'm so angry I could spit. Let's talk about something else until I cool down."

He didn't press.

"How did everything go with Sara in Virginia?" Cara asked.

"Well. Mom and Jerry were thrilled to take her for a couple of weeks. Ishmael is staying to guard her, so I'm feeling only half as crazy leaving her there." Kai's mom had married Jerry, a plastic surgeon, when Kai was young. He'd never met his father, but his mom insisted he was a good man. All Kai had to remind him of his real father was the silver ring he wore. It was the only jewelry he owned besides the plain gold wedding band he wore on his opposite hand.

Taking his hand, she pulled him toward the roof bar. "Try to relax. She's in good hands. Now fill me in on Melanie while I get us a drink." She let him go and slipped behind the bar. He pulled up a stool. She couldn't help but relax and fall back into her comfortable pattern with Kai, finding his presence both soothing and satisfying.

He tented his hands on the bar. "We're hopeful. Her treatment is progressing well, but I have to admit it's more like exorcism than therapy. If they weren't affiliated with the Angelorum, I'd be suspicious."

Cara ducked down to look in the refrigerator. "Wine, beer, soda, or water?"

"What kind of beer do you have?"

She poked her head up and smiled. "Your favorite." Taking the bottle opener, she flipped off the caps on two Heinekens and handed him one of the green bottles.

"Thanks." He tapped his bottle to hers.

"What kind of treatment are they giving her?" Cara asked and took a swallow.

"They're teaching her some coping mechanisms to prevent future attacks. Believe it or not, there are similarities between curing multiple personality disorder and her form of demon possession. She opened herself up to be a conduit, and they're trying to shut her back down. The portal on the back of her neck is going to take more work. They're still trying to figure out how to remove it."

"How's she feeling?"

"They won't let me talk to her until I get home, but they tell me she's pretty positive. Much better than when I called you." He took a long draught from his beer.

"Heavy stuff. How are you holding up?" Cara asked.

"As well as can be expected, I guess." He put down the bottle and sadness filled his eyes. "Cara... it's hard. I... I don't know..." He shook his head and looked away. His emotions stirred and she was hit with the pungent taste of his distress. Cara suppressed a look, clearing the taste of dirty gym socks from her tongue.

She came around the bar and gently placed her hand on his shoulder. "What's the matter? Tell me," she asked gently.

Before she could push any calming energy into him, he hopped off the barstool and let out a breath. "Everything. Everything is the matter."

"Um, could you be more specific?"

"This *life*, Cara." He frowned and raked his hands through his hair, his wedding ring flashing in the sun. "I want my ignorance back. Ever since I recovered the missing notes on the Nephilim vaccine, my life's been a frigging mess. Between Melanie becoming a head case, my career being blown sky-high, and having my family stalked by demons... I don't know. Is that specific enough for you?"

"I'm sorry, Kai."

He turned away from her. "No, I'm sorry. Sorry for all the fucking mistakes I've made..." He swung around to look at her, his pain and anguish gripping her.

"What mistakes? What are you talking about?" He wasn't making any sense.

"You, Cara. You," he whispered and looked away.

Her mouth dried out. "What do you mean? What about me?"

"Remember the last time we were together before I told you I was getting married?"

She closed her eyes. How could she forget? It had been the last time they'd ever made love. He'd been on the outs with Melanie and came down from MIT to visit her for the weekend.

He turned to her and took her hand, staring at her with an intensity she hadn't seen in a long time. Goosebumps rose on her arms. "Cara, I didn't marry Melanie because I loved her more than you. I married her because she was carrying my child," he said.

Cara froze and the air evacuated from her lungs. "What?" she choked unable to catch her breath. Shock rooted her in place. All this time she'd thought he didn't love her. Even when he came to see her and apologize before the Tribunal, he'd never told her.

His eyes sought hers. "She ended up losing the baby after the wedding. I hadn't wanted you to know… The only thing I've ever done right since is Sara. She's one of the only reasons I'm able to hold it together right now."

Cara stayed rigid, tasting another truth lying right underneath the surface. "Why?" she whispered, her heart hurting for them all.

He looked away, but not before she saw his eyes glistening with unshed tears. "Look at me, Kai."

Turning to face her, his soft fingers glided over her cheek and the pain in his eyes touched her core. "You're going to make me say it, aren't you?"

She nodded, too afraid to speak without bursting into tears.

"I wanted you back, Cara. I planned on leaving Melanie and coming back to you," he said, a tear slipping down his cheek. She reached up and brushed it away. "Now you know the truth," he whispered.

Her eyes watered and spilled over. Through her connection to Kai, she felt the burden he'd been carrying lift and fall away. He had needed to tell her more than she'd needed to know. Even so, the truth didn't change anything.

She squeezed him tight to her body, wanting to absorb his pain. "I'm so sorry, Kai, for you, Melanie, everything. You made the best decision that you could at the time. I'll always love you, Kai. I know how hard that must've been. Thank you for sharing it."

She still believed what she'd told Kai at the Sanctuary. Everything had worked out exactly as it should have. The intensity of their love had given them the strength to save the other, repaying their soul's debt to prove their loyalty to one another. But their chance for a romantic relationship had already passed.

He spoke into her hair. "I feel better now that you know the truth. What I would've done if fate hadn't intervened. I'm sorry. I'm just feeling like a crap husband. I know it's irrational, but I'm angry at Melanie."

"Do you love her?" Cara asked.

"Yes."

"Then please try to forgive her and make it work," she pleaded. "You deserve to be happy. Forgive yourself for the past and whatever else is leaving the taste of guilt on my tongue," Cara said and released him.

"Easier said than done but I'll try," he said, wiping his face, and then rolling his shoulders to release the tension. "Listen, I'm sorry I unloaded this on you. Really. It's all in the past anyway."

"No. I'm glad you told me."

He shook his head. "Simon's lucky to have you. I'm happy if you're happy. Speaking of…" He eyed her. "What was up with Brett's comment and your little stairway discussion with Simon before?"

"Let's just say this is the first time Simon has seen this Nephilim puberty thing in action near another man."

He frowned. "I don't follow."

She blushed. "Nephilim can smell pheromones, which we appear to release when we're aroused. Unfortunately, almost anyone and everyone triggers my arousal these days. I need your medical advice to get this under control like yesterday."

A smile spread across his face. "You still find me arousing?"

She rolled her eyes and smirked. "Don't let it go to your head."

His smile faded and he arched a brow at her. "Simon isn't jealous, is he?"

Her shoulders slumped and her heart softened when she thought back to her discussion with Simon about Kai. "He's not so much jealous as he is insecure about his ability to protect me like you've been able to. He admires you and feels indebted to you for saving my life. But between his own personal baggage and his Victorian sensibilities, he thinks that he should've been the one who saved me. Honestly, it probably doesn't help that you and I have had a romantic relationship."

Giving her a playful smile, he said, "Lucky for you, Tyler's long gone."

Her mouth hung open. She wanted to slug him. "I can't believe you said his name out loud to me." Tyler was the only name she loathed to hear, especially from Kai. If Cara hadn't been on the rebound after Kai married Melanie, she wouldn't have had a second heartbreak on top of her first after a surreal whirlwind weekend with a certain Irishman.

"Well, he's the only other guy you'd slept with before Simon, right?"

"Thanks for the short review of my sexual history." She grimaced. "And since he never saved my life, he doesn't count. You're such a creep sometimes." She shoved him and he went sailing halfway across the deck, landing on his butt with a hard *thump*.

"Shit, woman! Watch it with your newfound strength, will you?"

She reddened and dashed over to him. "Oops. Sorry about that… kind of. You okay?" She chuckled and offered him a hand up. "For the record, Simon broke my post-Tyler celibacy."

Kai scowled and took her proffered hand. "What you mentioned on the phone last week about your body changing? You were right. Obviously, you've gotten a lot stronger. And you've grown. I sized up the difference the minute I saw you," he said as she pulled him to his feet. He dropped her hand and brushed himself off. "By the way, you feel like a linebacker when I hug you. Frankly, I find that a little disconcerting."

Given Kai's photographic memory, she believed him. Knowing him, he could provide the difference in her measurements down to the millimeter.

Lifting her shirt, she exposed her midsection and well-carved six-pack. "Check out these puppies."

His eyebrows shot up. "Nice. Now, hold up your hand to mine."

Dropping her shirt, she placed her palm vertically against his and watched his eyes widen. Her hand was the same size as his, which said something. He had good-sized hands for a man. A runner, he had a lean build with good muscle tone, and at six foot, he was on the tall side of average for a man. As a matter of fact, there was *nothing* small about Kai.

"That explains why you're wearing your engagement ring around your neck next to your diamond pendant." Unconsciously, she reached up and fingered the ring.

He gave her an appraising stare. "I have my portable lab in a suitcase downstairs. I'll draw some blood and get it couriered over to the Sanctuary so they can start working on it before we arrive. And I'll see what I can find out about your overactive hormone problem."

Cara's insides warmed. When Kai worked, he was in his element. "Thanks for being here."

His mouth quirked up into a smile. "You're the only other reason I'm able to stay sane, you know. Listen, I'll do what I can to make Simon feel more comfortable." He let out a breath and swiftly changed the topic. "By the way, I'm selling the house."

"Really? Why? Too many bad memories?"

"That and I feel like we're sitting ducks there. Luke's been racking up the body count to protect us. We've had at least one demon or soulless attack a week since the rescue. At least we know how the demons are getting into the house now."

"Holy crap! Why didn't you tell me?"

"And you would've done what, exactly? Jump on a plane?"

Planting her hands on her hips, she smirked. "Uh, yeah."

"That's exactly why I didn't tell you," he said smugly.

"Uh-huh. Last time you didn't tell me something, you ended up getting kidnapped. When are you going to learn your lesson and just tell me everything?" she teased.

He laughed. "I always do, Mother Hen… eventually."

*"Michael's here,"* Simon said in a sulking tone, his voice echoing in her head. She wondered if he'd spoken to Constantina yet.

"Simon just called. Michael's here. Ready to go join the others?" Cara asked.

"Can I ask you a question first?" The intensity in his blue eyes stopped her. "Do you ever just ache for 'normal'?"

*He had no idea*, she thought, and met his gaze with equal intensity. "Every day, Kai. Every day."

# Chapter 45

*CARA*

*New York City. Greene Street Loft. Sunday, May 26, 6:15* PM ET

"HEY, MICHAEL," Cara said, entering the kitchen with Kai.

Michael broke out into a wide smile when he saw them and came to greet Kai. "Hey, good to see you. How was your trip in?"

Their hands touched in greeting, and Cara left them to it.

Her attention was magnetically drawn to Simon.

Apparently, he'd been busy while she was upstairs with Kai. He stood purposefully ignoring her while he worked at the stove, his broad back to her. His emotions churned around him. Self-doubt, hurt, anger… she tasted them all in a jumble of sour grapes and crushed aspirin.

She softened when she looked at him. She loved him more than words could express. Why didn't he understand that?

One thing she'd learned about her fiancé is that he either cooked or painted when stressed, making the kitchen and his art studio his two safe places. The only other place she'd seen him utterly in his comfort zone was leading a mission.

His shoulders tensed as she sidled up behind him. "Are you still mad?"

The heady aroma of melting chocolate filled her senses before she peeked around his arm and spotted eight individual ramekins. Chocolate soufflés.

His silence and the tense set to his jaw answered her question. As she suspected, he wasn't cooking just to feed them. A major dose of stress relief was woven into this culinary exercise.

"Did you call Constantina?"

"Yes," he said flatly. Still refusing to look at her, he continued to stir the batter.

"And you're still mad."

He stopped stirring and turned his head, his blue eyes flashing. "Yes."

Her Irish temper bubbled up inside of her, twisting her mouth into a frown. "For what, exactly? Didn't she explain the hormone thing to you?"

*"Keep your voice down,"* he commanded telepathically.

Cara's face warmed as her blood pressure rose. *"Then let's take this somewhere else. I refuse to feel like I've done something wrong… because I haven't."*

Dropping the spoon, he strode out of the kitchen, down the hallway, and into the master bedroom. She raced to keep up. Closing the door behind her, she let loose.

"What's the matter with you?" She wanted to stomp her foot in frustration. "You're acting like I cheated on you or something."

He clenched his hands and paced without speaking, wrapped in a blanket of anger. She wanted to scream. Instead, she took a deep cleansing breath and walked over to him.

He stopped to glare at her, his mouth a tight line. "I heard what you said to Kai."

She froze in place and asked cautiously, "What do mean, you heard what I said to Kai?"

His anger transformed to hurt. "I heard you…" He folded his muscled arms over his chest and swallowed, then looked away. "I was coming up to apologize after I called Constantina. I heard you talking through the door."

Cara withered inside. There were some conversations that should never be overhead or repeated. Her discussion with Kai on the roof happened to be one of them.

She sat down on the bed. "What part did you hear?" she asked, softly.

He looked up at her with hard eyes. "The part where he told you he was coming back for you, and then you both cried." He strode to the door. "Don't let me stand in your way."

She leaped up and grabbed his arm. "Did you stay to hear the rest of it? Or are you just going to judge me on the piece you heard out of context?"

"Does it really matter?"

"Yes, it matters! Simon, how many times do I have to tell you? I chose you— you alone. I love you. But I can't help that I once loved other men, including one who happened to have saved my life. That's just the way it is."

His features twisted into a mask of anger and hurt which was reflected in the swirl of energy surrounding him. Seeping into her physical space, it filled her with discomfort. "Maybe it is. But right now, I want to be alone." He opened the door. "I'm going to stay here tonight."

Unable to contain her anger, a vein pulsed in her neck. "Fine! I'll go back to the penthouse with Kai. Enjoy your cold bed tonight… soul mates or not… maybe the Trinity Stones were wrong!" She regretted the words almost the instant they passed through her lips.

He slammed the door behind him so hard it rattled on the frame, followed by the sound of his size fifteens stomping back to the kitchen.

Tears of frustration sprang to Cara's eyes and she threw herself back onto the bed. Could Simon be right? Could her friendship with Kai be wrong? Kai was married and her heart had moved on to Simon. She valued their friendship dearly and although she would always love him, she was no longer in love with him. Would she have to give him up to avoid hurting Simon? Could she? The thought of losing either of them tore at her heart.

A soft knock sounded at the door. *"Cara, may I come in?"* Michael. His caring voice elicited more tears and made her ache for Simon.

*"Sure."* She sat up and wiped the mascara stains from under her eyes with her fingertips.

He slipped inside. The door latched closed with a soft click.

Settling down beside her, he wrapped his arm around her shoulders. "Hey, I could feel your distress from the kitchen. Is there anything I can do?"

Cara loved Michael for his compassionate nature. He'd been a comfort to her many times since she'd entered this crazy life.

"Beside beat some sense into Simon? No," she said, sniffling. Leaning her head on his shoulder, she breathed in his cologne and relaxed. "I don't know what to do. Simon overheard something he shouldn't have. I can't deny I've loved Kai. But, it's not like that now. I'm crazy in love with Simon. I wouldn't cheat… ever. And neither would Kai."

"Just give Simon some time to cool down." Michael kissed her forehead, and paused. "But you need to know that Kai's not over you no matter what he's told you… even if you're over him."

She jerked her head back and crinkled her nose. "Michael, he's never led me to believe he's wanted more than friendship." That wasn't a surprise given his situation. Then it hit her. "Wait… how would you know that?"

Michael looked away.

"Michael?"

He gave her a sheepish look. "I think it's easier for guys to see it in other guys, but married or not, Kai is still in love with you."

She shook her head. "I'm sorry, what?" Michael had no idea how much she would have begged to hear those words two months ago before she'd met Simon. How was that even possible? Could she have been too blinded by all those years of thinking he never loved her to see it? Even though Kai's confession on the roof had been a complete shocker, he'd spoken about his feelings in the past, not the present.

Michael squeezed her shoulder. "If it helps, he's fighting those feelings. He loves you too much to interfere with your relationship. And please, don't ask how I know."

He spoke with an authority that meant Kai had told him... or he'd read his mind. Cara couldn't count the number of times that Michael knew things about her that she'd never told him. On more than one occasion, Constantina had hinted that Michael had hidden abilities.

*Oh. My. God.* He could read thoughts... her personal thoughts, Kai's personal thoughts.

Cara stiffened, wrenching herself from Michael's embrace. Her eyes bore into him. "You're a Telepath, aren't you? That's one of your gifts."

Michael reared back as a surge of bitter lemon fear rippled through him. No use denying it. She could taste the truth.


### MICHAEL

Panic coursed through him, his body ready for flight. "Cara... I..." He popped up onto his feet ready to bolt. He'd gone too far this time and accidentally exposed his secret.

*Does no good deed go unpunished?* he wondered, feeling like a coward and wanting to avoid the brunt of her rejection.

She grabbed his arm. "Wait." Her green eyes held his, questioning as if wanting to understand.

He had to look away. "Please don't tell Sienna," he whispered. If she found out, she'd push him away too like his closest friends had done when he was a child. He'd stopped sharing his gift after that. The few times he'd tried as an adult, friendships had cooled when those he thought cared for him turned away in fear.

He wasn't ready to abandon the glimmer of happiness he shared with Sienna the night before. He planned to see her again later, hoping for a second night. Miraculously, his old nightmares had not returned to ruin his world but Sienna finding out about his telepathy might just do it.

Wrapping his arms around himself in a hug, he shifted uncomfortably on his feet, taking Cara off guard, who stared at him with her mouth ajar. Not able to control his movements, a tremor of anxiety shook him from head to foot.

*What will they think of me now? Will Cara and Simon shun me?*

Without warning, Cara drew him into a tight hug. "It's okay, I've been there myself. Breathe with me," she whispered, referring to her history of panic attacks. She expanded and contracted her chest against him. His breathing steadied and he relaxed in her arms, resting his head next to hers. "Why didn't you tell me?"

"Couldn't. No one knows. Please don't tell," he pleaded, fighting the paralysis of his vocal cords.

Cara's warm hands rubbed his back, comforting him. "*Shh*, I won't say anything. It's your secret. But you should at least tell Simon."

The thought of telling Simon curdled his stomach, but not as much as Sienna finding out.

"Still friends?" he asked, sounding pathetic and confused, loathing his weakness. Their role reversal unnerved him.

"Of course. What kind of silly question is that?" Her breath felt warm on his hair, and her strong arms stayed firm around him. He found her Nephilim strength eerily soothing. The taste of her sincerity resonated on his tongue with a hint of maple and he knew she spoke the truth. His eyes watered with relief and the loneliness he carried all these years disappeared a little with her acceptance. Of all his secrets, this one was the least damning.

"I think you have an amazing gift," she said. "I'm sorry it's caused you pain."

"Thank you," he whispered.

"I love you like a brother, you know. You don't have to hide from me." She kissed his forehead and let him go.

They sat back down on the bed. He let out a deep breath, wanting to explain. "My father was the only person who knew. Not even my mother knows… But I can control it." He searched her eyes, wringing his fingers together. "I'm not a voyeur. I don't spy on people's thoughts."

*Well, not unless it's something really important,* he admitted to himself.

"I trust you." She reached over and squeezed his hand. Calming energy entered his hand where she touched him.

"Changing topics, how was your night with Si—"

Simon's stern voice interrupted inside of their heads. *"Cara, Michael, come out to the kitchen. Isaac's been attacked."*

# Chapter 46

*CARA*

*New York City. Greene Street Loft. Sunday, May 26, 7:00* PM ET

SIMON BRUSHED PAST CARA and Michael as they reached the kitchen, apparently on his way back to the bedroom.

"Is Isaac all right?" Cara asked with a frown as he passed. Isaac may have been her least favorite person, but she definitely didn't want anything bad to happen to him.

"He's been taken to Beth Israel," Simon replied without stopping. Cara breathed a sigh of relief knowing that Simon wouldn't be walking straight into a battle and that Isaac was in good hands. Given Cara's obsessive knowledge of hospital locations, she'd been stunned to learn that an Angelorum clinic was hidden in a wing of Beth Israel Hospital.

Angel was armed and ready when she and Michael arrived in the kitchen. His dark features clouded with concern as he paced, his boots clomping on the kitchen floor. Angelic weapon hilts jangled from his belt, the blades only manifesting when summoned.

For all the times she'd seen Angel, she'd never seen him wearing a traditional Guardianship uniform. Today, he wore the black pants and matching T-shirt. The short sleeves revealed intricate tattoos, more detailed than Zeke's and Noah's, covering his dark skin and adding to his tough image. His duster lay over one of the chairs next to the counter.

Paco entered from the living room, still in the button-down and slacks he'd been wearing at Sarabeth's. Brett and Kai filed in behind him.

"I'll get my weapons," Paco told Angel.

"No. You stay here with Brett," Angel ordered. "Take the next patrol when Luke comes back," he added, referring to Kai's Guardian. "I can't take any chances."

Paco's body language clearly stated he wasn't happy about staying behind. Cara sensed something unsaid between him and Angel. Paco's jaw flexed and his eyes flashed before he replied, "Call me if you need me."

"I'll come," Michael said.

"You're not coming, either," Simon's firm voice said from behind them. "I need you here, too." He entered the kitchen dressed identically to Angel. His blond hair was pulled back in a tight ponytail at the nape of his neck, ready for work.

"Why not?" Michael asked, frowning.

Simon ignored Cara as he stomped by. His masculine scent mixed with his displeasure. He exchanged a long glance with Angel most likely paired with a few silent words on their telepathic frequency.

"I appreciate the offer, Michael, but we're taking this one by air," he said, walking over to the stove. He grabbed the timer and thrust it into Michael's hand. "Here. You're the only one I trust not to set the kitchen on fire. Take the soufflés out when it rings." Turning on his heel, he strode down the narrow hallway with Angel. A rattling chorus of angelic weapons accompanied their heavy footfalls.

Cara watched Simon's retreating figure and let out a slow breath. Simon's anger wasn't something she'd experienced in a while. The distance it created between them gutted her. She remembered something else Constantina had told her about the Twelve: "At times love will be the Twelve's greatest strength, and at others, their greatest weakness."

She tore off after them down the hall, catching them on the roof.

"Simon!" she yelled.

He faced her, his expression hard and intimidating. She barely recognized him. A sliver of fear rippled through her.

Her lip quivered. *"I love you. Please be careful... I'd die if anything happened to you."* She pleaded telepathically, gripping the doorjamb to hold her steady.

*Okay, maybe that was a tad over the top,* she thought. But she meant it.

His expression softened and he gave her a small nod. "Stay inside while I'm gone," he said, his tone less biting. Giving her his back, he faced east with Angel. Their wings slipped out through the hidden slits in their shirts and rapidly unfurled, filling the space between them. The white, downy brilliance blinded her, making her squint. She ached for their silky-feathered embrace against her bare skin.

His wings arching high above him poised for flight, Simon gave them a good shake before he crouched and leaped into the air in tandem with Angel, vanishing before her eyes as they cloaked.

Cara returned downstairs to find everyone clustered around the island. One thing Simon was right about: Michael was the only one of them who knew his way around a kitchen. He was hunkered down in front of the industrial Viking stove, eyeing the baking desserts while Paco, Kai, and Brett sat around trading glances.

"What's going on?" Kai asked her, his eyebrows knit in a frown.

Cara shook her head. "Damned if I know. Paco? Anything you can tell us other than Isaac was attacked?" The Angelorum's method of parsing out information on a need-to-know basis had long since gotten on her last nerve.

Michael stood up and gave Paco a warning look.

Cara huffed and turned to Michael, planting her hands on her hips. "You have exactly thirty seconds to spill what you know or I'm leaving."

"Cara—" Michael started.

"Stop protecting me! It's pissing me off. Between you and Simon, I feel like a damned prisoner."

Brett choked out a snide laugh and tucked a stray blond hair behind his ear. "Welcome to the club."

"Look," Paco said calmly. "Wait until they get back and we'll discuss it… all of it. Isaac was on his way here to brief us, so I can't tell you anything even if I wanted to. One thing I can't do is let you leave."

The timer rang. "Hold your breath and nobody move for the next minute. If these fall, Simon will have my head," Michael said, grabbing the potholder off the counter.

"How can you think about food right now? Who cares about the goddamn soufflés!" Cara snapped.

Michael raised his dark brows. "I care. I'm starving." The strong smell of chocolate filled the kitchen. Cara refused to be dissuaded.

"Listen," Brett said, "sounds like there's nothing we can do. If we're going to be prisoners, I'm with Michael. Let's eat."

Cara ground her teeth. "Fine. Enjoy them. I'll be in the living room." She rounded the corner and threw herself down on the leather sectional. A soccer game blared on TV.

*No possible way that's staying on*, she thought, and reached for the remote and lost herself in a home decorating show on HGTV.

"Hey." Kai settled down next to her, close enough so their thighs almost touched. She scooted away to create some distance. The last thing she needed was to compound her problems. Michael's words resonated in her head. Kai couldn't be in love with her. It just wasn't possible.

"I'm sorry. Simon's angry and it's because of me. I can talk to him…" Kai offered.

She let out a sigh and patted his leg. "It'll be fine. He's struggling with his own issues, and I'm not helping the situation. You haven't done anything. Your biggest offense is that you're male." Giving him a small smile, she said, "And I like you just the way you are."

The elevator dinged open followed by a thunderous crash.

"Cara!" Michael yelled from the kitchen.

A jolt of fear ran through her as she bolted for the door.

# Chapter 47



*CARA*

*New York City. Greene Street Loft. Sunday, May 26, 7:20 PM ET*

"ZEKE!" CARA SCREAMED as she caught sight of the Guardian's tattooed arms. He lay semiconscious in a bloody heap. Red speckled his pale baby face, but the damage was elsewhere. His dark hair and black clothing were soaked through. Crimson slashes covered his white plumage, reminding her of a large, injured bird. The hilt of his sword was still clutched tightly to his palm, signaling he hadn't surrendered to his enemies.

Kai stepped in front of Cara, reaching for Zeke's wrist to check his vitals.

Placing her hand on his shoulder, she gently pushed him aside. "I have this one. Stand back," she said, dropping to her knees next to Zeke.

"How so?" he asked, wearing a skeptical look.

"You'll see." His energy was weak, but she hoped it was strong enough to avoid a tug-of-war with Jonas over his soul. Lucky for her, there was no sign of the purple-eyed Transporter.

Michael guided Kai and Brett back farther, knowing what would come next. She'd never tried healing a Nephil, but there wasn't any reason to believe it would be any different than healing a human.

Whispering her opening prayer, she called her pillar of power by shooting up her imaginary hand into the Flow and pulling down the healing energy into the top of her head. Moments later, a column of bright, white energy slammed down into her, filling her chest and circling around her heart. The energy expanded, creating a Ring of Power and ejecting Michael and the others deeper into the kitchen while engulfing her and Zeke in its blazing glow. Eyes closed, Cara mixed her love with the swirling energy, feeling it gain momentum and warm her insides. Opening her eyes, she extended her hands to Zeke. Rather than hovering like she had with the stranger on the street, she placed them directly on him to create the circuit. It may not have added much in the way of healing but it made her feel like she was giving even more than she had. If anything happened to him on her watch, she couldn't imagine having to face Simon.

"Keep breathing for me, Zeke," she whispered. Healing energy flew from her left palm into Zeke, pushing out his injuries. As his weaker energy funneled into her, she spun it through her chest and reenergized it before sending it back into him, kick-starting his cells into healing at a superhuman rate.

The blood slowly evaporated on his brilliant plumage and color returned to his face; a peaceful expression replaced his pained grimace. His blood-soaked body dried rapidly like time-lapse photography. After a while, the energy returning into Cara was equal to the energy she pushed back into him, signaling the healing process was complete.

Cara pictured herself releasing the tendrils of energy she held in her imaginary hand, returning them upward into the Flow. And then she gave thanks.

The white light surrounding her and Zeke disappeared. She turned to Paco, "Can you carry him into our bedroom? He should sleep for a while. I'm not sure how long, since he's Nephilim and already predisposed to rapid healing."

Paco nodded and picked him up. She turned and braced herself for the reactions of her "uninitiated" witnesses. She hadn't bothered to cover the blazing light show this time like she had on the street.

Michael smiled at her. *"Nice job."*

Brett stared at her open-jawed. "Holy shit, that was way cool. Can I do that?"

Blushing, she said, "No, your gifts are different."

"Cara, that was amazing. I had no idea..." Kai said, looking at her with admiration.

Down the hall, a low groan rumbled in Zeke's throat followed by violent flapping and an ear-splitting squawk. The powerful breeze blew Cara back. Turning her head away to protect her eyes from the gust caused by Zeke's wings, she battled forward into the gale force winds. She jumped out of the way as one of Simon's oil paintings rattled off of its hook and crashed to the floor next to her.

Paco called out in the angelic language, his voice resonating over the noise. Zeke ceased his wing beats and the wind tunnel in the hallway calmed as Cara reached them.

Zeke was ass-up in a fireman's carry over Paco's shoulder and none too happy about it.

"Put me down," he barked, trying to dismount as he retracted his wings into his body.

"Stop moving before I drop you on the ground," Paco growled and set Zeke on his feet. He glanced down at his shredded shirt and the scratches covering his muscled forearms. "You ruined a perfectly good shirt, my friend."

"Sorry, I thought it was them when I came to." Zeke ran his hands down over his body, feeling for injuries. Then he glanced at Cara and gave her a small smile. "You fixed me up, didn't you, doll?"

She nodded and then it hit her. "Were Simon and Angel with you?" she asked with a pounding heart.

"No, they're at the clinic with Isaac. They sent me back here. I was attacked on the way from the hospital."

With a sigh of relief, she motioned him toward the bedroom. "Let me get you a change of clothes. Then you can tell us what happened."

"He's not the only who needs to change." Paco looked at his tattered sleeves and headed for the guest room. "I'll meet you in the kitchen."

"Do I smell chocolate?" Zeke asked, licking his lips.

She smirked, eyeing her handiwork. "Obviously, your injuries didn't affect your appetite." On cue, the smell of chocolate triggered a rumble in her stomach, her resistance to Simon's dessert forgotten.

"I'm good as new, thanks to you," Zeke said, turning back toward the kitchen. "Can we eat first?"

Cara looked at his bloodstained uniform and wrinkled her nose. It would be going straight into the incinerator in the basement. "Um, I can't eat and look at you in those clothes, sorry. How about I go and grab you one of those soufflés while you change. Just help yourself to another uniform. They're in Simon's closet."

He looked down at himself. "I see your point."

Cara left him to change and headed back into the kitchen. The soufflés sat forgotten on top of the stove, cooling. Eight. Enough for everyone including Simon and Angel when they returned.

Michael gave her a mischievous wink. "I heard. Let's meet in the dining room. I'll bring them out."

In the open floor plan of the loft, the "dining room" was merely the space the kitchen melted into facing the front of the building.

"Never a dull moment," Brett said, following her and Kai to the table. "What kind of cool shit will I be able to do?"

She wished she knew. "Honestly, I don't know. I'm hoping we find out this week." Sliding out a chair, she sat down, suddenly overcome with exhaustion. Healing sapped her energy, similar to when Michael had visions or when Simon spent too much time flying. All of their gifts exacted a price.

"When I draw your blood later, do you think Zeke would mind if I take a vial of his?" Kai asked pensively over his tented hands.

"Depends on how big the needle is," Zeke replied as he strode into the room, freshly dressed in one of Simon's Guardianship uniforms. He pulled up a chair. "Why?"

Kai shrugged. "I need some fresh comparison DNA for my tests on Cara."

Zeke winked at Cara. "It's the least I can do. She saved my bacon."

Brett sniffed in disgust. "Please tell me Angel didn't put you up to that."

"Put me up to what?" Zeke asked with a look of sincere innocence.

"Ugh. Never mind," Brett said.

Cara snickered, remembering the ongoing "meat" game Angel played with Brett and knowing Zeke wasn't in on the joke.

Michael walked in with an overfilled tray and set it the table. Paco followed behind him, now wearing a black T-shirt—the scratches on his arms already half-healed.

Taking a seat, Paco folded his arms across his wide chest and addressed Zeke. "Okay, brother. What happened to Isaac and how did you almost get yourself killed? If Cara wasn't here, I'm not sure you would've made it to the clinic."

Zeke picked up a spoon. "Isaac and I were almost here when we caught a whiff of Simon's—I mean, the rogue's—energy a few blocks away. We engaged and he led us straight into a hornet's nest of Dark Ones in a warehouse on the Lower East Side."

"Wait, who?" Cara asked mid-nibble. "What does this have to do with Simon?"

Zeke traded a look with Paco, who just shrugged.

"A rogue Nephil has been following Simon on and off since the day the Sentinel tagged you on the street. We think he works for Le Feu. He was impossible to track until Michael figured out he mimics Simon's energy. That's why we never picked him up. He's been hiding in Simon's shadow."

"How often does something like that happen?" Cara asked. "The same energy thing?"

"About as often as we find a Nephil working for the Dark Ones who's not a genetic experiment," Zeke said. "Never."

"Should I be worried?" Cara tensed.

"Not sure, doll," Zeke squeezed her hand and gave her a look of reassurance. "We're trying to capture him. Don't worry, 'kay?"

She returned the squeeze, appreciating his concern.

Paco frowned. "So just the two of you? Did you see his face?"

"We called in reinforcements the moment we took off after him." His mouth set in a hard line. "And, no, we never saw his face. He stayed cloaked."

Paco's frown deepened. "Why didn't you call us?"

"We're under strict orders not to take any unnecessary risks with Simon, you, or your charges," Zeke said, evenly.

"Whose orders?"

"Constantina's."

Michael shook his head. "This doesn't make any sense. The rogue was the one who warned me the Dark Ones were coming. Why would he lure you into a trap?"

Zeke brushed his hand across his face and tensed. He glanced briefly at Michael and then at Cara. "Here's what's crazy… I don't think that's what he did."

"What do you mean?" Paco asked.

Zeke flipped his chin nervously toward Brett and Kai and asked Paco, "Can I speak freely in front of them?"

Paco turned to Cara. "How much do they already know?"

Cara opened her mouth to answer when Brett piped up, his face pinched in annoyance. "I can speak for myself, and the answer is enough weird shit to give me nightmares for a year. A few more fun facts aren't going to make much of a difference. And in case you're wondering, I've already given my word to Constantina that nothing I've learned is for public consumption. Cool?"

*All right-y then*, Cara thought, proud of Brett for speaking up. She found playing Mother Hen draining, especially since the list of people she worried about had grown exponentially just over the weekend.

Kai nodded. "Same here."

Zeke took a deep breath. "The Dark Ones had something new with them."

"Something new?" Paco asked.

"Yeah, beings like Cara—genetically engineered Nephilim."

"What makes you think they're like Cara?" Kai asked.

"Not like Cara exactly, and not born Nephilim, either. They were soulless… their wings were black as coal and stunted, but they were strong and powerful, like us." Zeke scooped a spoonful of soufflé into his mouth and added, "They're not quite as good as us, but that doesn't matter when you're outnumbered ten to one."

"Le Feu mentioned Forrester wasn't the only lab working on the vaccine," Kai said, hands folded in front of him. "It's possible another one could've succeeded. Interesting, they managed to develop a version with wing development."

In between mouthfuls, Zeke said, "What's really crazy? I think the rogue wanted us to discover them."

"Why?" Paco asked.

"He helped us escape after Isaac was stabbed."

# Chapter 48

*KAI*
*New York City. Penthouse. Monday, May 27, 1:00 AM ET*

HIGH-PITCHED SCREAMS pierced the air, tearing Kai out of a solid slumber. Disoriented, he bolted upright and fumbled to turn on the lamp, not understanding why he was sleeping on the wrong side of the bed. Then he remembered where he was… Cara's penthouse. He and Cara had come here after Angel had returned to the loft alone to brief the group. Simon had stayed behind with Isaac.

His heart pounded as he lunged out of bed and ran into the hallway toward the agonizing sound. He flung Cara's bedroom door open with such force it rebounded off the doorstop.

"Cara!" Kai yelled, his hand slapping the wall until he found the switch.

Light bathed the room.

"Make it stop!" Cara screamed. She sat in the middle of the king-size bed, shaking in a sweat-soaked T-shirt. Movement underneath her T-shirt accompanied by crunching and popping sounds sent a shiver barreling down his spine.

He ran to her side. "Talk to me," he demanded. No time for modesty, Kai lifted her T-shirt to expose her bare back.

"My spine," Cara said, looking back at him as tears rolled down her cheeks in tiny rivers. He choked back a gasp as he watched her bones shift under her skin like something out of a sci-fi flick. A ripple of movement traveled along her spine as the vertebra popped up and back in a continuous path. Her shoulder blades morphed and reshaped until they had moved farther apart. Intellectually, he grasped the Nephilim changes she had spoken to him about, but nothing had prepared him for this.

Out of breath with his chest heaving, Simon filled the doorway. There was no mistaking the wild look of panic in his eyes. "What's going on?"

Cara didn't seem to notice him as her screams escalated in pitch to ear-splitting screeches.

"Growth spurt. Get the medical bag in my room. Silver case," Kai barked. His only choice was to put her under and then make an emergency call to Celine, his assigned Nephilim counterpart, at the Sanctuary. But not before he drew some blood. He'd extract a sample of spinal fluid once she was unconscious.

Simon disappeared from sight, returning less than a minute later with the heavy silver suitcase.

Kai selected a powerful sedative. He looked at Simon. "Help me."

Simon pressed his lips together and nodded. "What do you want me to do?"

"Hold her arm so I can draw some blood. Then I'll inject her." He snapped an empty vial onto a syringe.

Cara wailed as Simon pulled her onto his lap, cradling her as she screamed and thrashed. Using his free hand, he steadied her arm, pain etching a deep line across his brow. Kai recognized the look; he wore the same one the night he tried to comfort Melanie before her trip to Sequoia. His heart ached for Simon, understanding better than anyone what he was going through.

Cara's arm quivered and her body tensed as Kai sank the needle into her skin and depressed the plunger. Once the vial was full, he swapped it out for the sedative.

Less than three minutes later, Cara's howling stopped and she went limp in Simon's arms.

Kai ran his hands through his hair and dropped his head in his hands. "Shit."

"What's wrong?" Simon asked anxiously, cradling Cara's unconscious body next to his heart. The movement under her T-shirt had ceased.

Tipping his chin at Cara, Kai said, "Why don't you make her comfortable, and then we'll talk in the living room. She'll be out for the rest of the night." Kai glanced down at his boxers, suddenly feeling underdressed. "Let me put on some clothes. I'll meet you out there in five minutes."

Simon nodded and his Adam's apple bobbed as he swallowed.

Kai headed back to his room. How could he admit to Simon that he was out of his depth on this one? He may have learned a great deal about Nephilim physiology in the last several months, retaining it in his photographic memory, but he still didn't know what he didn't know. After they talked, he'd ring Celine. She'd be in the lab by then.

He slipped on jeans and a golf shirt and met Simon in the living room. Still in uniform, Simon sat leaning forward, resting his elbows on his thighs and sipping something from a glass. He cleared his throat and pointed to a second glass. "I hope you like brandy."

Not really his thing, but Kai welcomed the burn as he took a sip.

"I'm going to need to your help, Simon."

His head snapped up. "What kind of help?"

"With Cara. I'm not with her every minute. You're the only person who comes close. Can I teach you a few things tomorrow? To do in case of an emergency?"

"Sure," Simon replied. Kai figured it might help Simon regain some self-confidence. Make him feel more useful in times of medical crisis. In reality, Simon already made a formidable assistant.

"Good. In the meantime, do you remember your adolescence? Do you remember anything like this happening to you? Painful growth spurts, bones shifting? Hormone rushes?"

Simon released a breath and gripped his glass. "Mine was a milder version of what Cara's been going through. And I never experienced anything as painful as tonight, even when my wings emerged for the first time. My adolescence was gradual."

"Is this how all her growth spurts have been?" Kai asked.

Simon shook his head. "Nothing like this until tonight. Complaints about aches and pains, but nothing a few aspirin couldn't solve. She's never mentioned anything beyond that."

Kai nodded. "Have you ever seen or heard of anything like this before?"

Simon's jaw tightened. "It's rare, but yes."

The hairs rose on Kai's arms. "And?"

His eyes filled with anguish, and he whispered, "The two I know of died. Flaws within the human cells of the mothers caused massive cell rejection right before their adolescence ended. It's called Nephilim Adolescent Collapse Syndrome."

Kai heart went into free fall and hit his stomach. He stared at Simon, speechless.

"But Cara's not really going through true adolescence. Something similar but not the same, right?" Simon growled, his eyes pleading. "An adjustment to the DNA?"

He wished he knew. "I'll get the samples I took today flown to the Sanctuary tomorrow. We'll get a handle on this quickly. If she has another episode, we should take her to Beth Israel for some interim tests." Given Cara's unique situation, the Sanctuary was still their best option. It housed their most advanced genetics and physiology labs and all their specialists.

"Don't let anything happen to her, Kai," he gritted, his eyes shining. "And promise me you won't tell her anything until we know for certain."

"I promise," Kai said. "But I need you to promise me something in return."

"What's that?" His eyes connected with Simon's.

"Stay cool. Don't panic or she'll know," Kai said.

"Agreed."

Guilt stabbed Kai in the chest. Simon and Cara deserved happiness. He hoped that he hadn't made a mistake in the formula he'd used to save Cara; that he hadn't accidentally handed her a death sentence.

Simon looked at the drink he held in his hands. "I'm sorry, Kai. For my behavior earlier. I meant no disrespect."

Kai's admiration for Simon grew. Without a doubt, Cara had chosen the better man. Now, he'd do what he could to make sure they had a future together.

Kai rose and clasped Simon's shoulder. "None taken. You're a good man, Simon. She loves you… only you."

With that, Kai drained his glass, turned on his heel, and headed to the guest room to call Celine.

He prayed she'd have some answers.

# Chapter 49



SHE AWOKE WITH SIMON'S warmth spooned behind her, his arms securely embracing her as if trying to prevent her escape. Still asleep, she listened to his rhythmic breathing. Her anger from last night faded and she inhaled his familiar scent.

She kissed the arm closest to her lips. "I thought you were sleeping at the loft?"

He squeezed her closer. "I couldn't sleep without you next to me. I'm sorry I doubted you," he whispered in a sleepy voice from behind her. "Will you forgive me?"

"Maybe," she said softly. "What happened last night? I remember seeing you…"

"Kai drugged you. How are you feeling?"

Whatever pain she'd had last night was gone. "Fine."

He kissed her hair. "Tell me what to do for complete forgiveness. I'll do whatever it takes."

She relaxed back into his naked body. Her hormones awakened from the touch of his skin against hers, and a small smile formed on her lips. "Whatever it takes?"

Shifting her hair out of the way, he touched his lips tenderly to her neck. "Whatever it takes…" She could feel him harden behind her, his naked arousal pressing against the small of her back.

Desire hit her in a deluge. Reaching behind her, she lifted her nightshirt and wrapped her hand around his thick girth. Guiding his silky tip underneath her, she slid back onto him.

Enveloping him in her slickness, her nerve endings exploded with need.

He let out a sharp groan. His hands found her hips, and he rocked his full length into her, cradling her body. His movements were focused, slow, and loving.

He nibbled her ear and whispered, "Don't ever leave me, Cara. I can't breathe without you."

She found his hand and brought his large, perfect fingers to her lips, kissing each fingertip. The feel of him was exquisite inside of her, her love for him bubbling up and overwhelming her. "How could I? My soul is inside you."

Snuggling her close, his arms flexed around her as he plunged deep, yet gently. Sounds of pleasure vibrated from his lips. Another wash of heat spread through Cara as his penetrating thrusts found their mark. Without warning, Cara caught the wave of her orgasm and stifled her cries as she clutched him tightly with her warmth.

His hips pumped harder and he rocked himself in as far as he could go, widening and filling her before he quietly exploded with a powerful shudder. His body went slack behind her. He pulled her closer, wrapping her inside of the muscled columns of his arms.

Purring in her ear, his heart beat rapidly against her back. "Was that a good start?"

She smiled. "I'd say so… You've never been so quiet, though."

"I said I'd do whatever it takes to show you. Alerting your former lover we're making love would be very bad form. And I understand how that might make him feel."

"Thank you. That was kind and very thoughtful."

"I want to be the man you deserve…" His voice trailed off.

She twisted her head around to look up at him. Anger no longer burned in his eyes. Instead, they reflected a fierce love that shone brighter than anything she was accustomed to seeing. Any residual doubts she had melted away.

"I didn't mean to hurt you," she said.

"Enough said." His lips came down on hers in a kiss before the couple settled back with their limbs tangled into a satisfied heap.

"Tell me about Isaac," she whispered, enjoying his warmth around her. "How is he?"

"He'll be out today. The knife wound was deep. It pierced his heart, so they wanted to keep him overnight." He let out a breath. "Something odd is going on. The Dark Ones put on a good show for us, but my gut's telling me something isn't right."

Her brow knit. "How so?"

His fingertips stroked her hair. "A rogue Nephil who we think works for the Dark Ones lured Isaac and Zeke to a warehouse and then helped them to escape. Why not just kill them?"

"Zeke mentioned that the rogue's been shadowing you since the Sentinel found me," Cara said.

"Yes, and it's been one of the most puzzling issues plaguing us since then. He's been spying for certain, and out of nowhere feeds us information on Saturday. Odd. Very odd."

"What about the Nephilim with the black wings? You think maybe they wanted us to know they've succeeded in making the vaccine?"

He sighed. "I've thought about that. It's possible but to what advantage?"

"Maybe this was an act of intimidation. To let us know they plan a full attack on the Guardianship during the battle," Cara said, moving her feet against the soft skin of his under the covers as she thought.

"But we already anticipated that. Though, to your point, the entire exercise reeks of a peacock preening. The only plausible explanation is that they're trying to throw us off track, confuse us as to their true objective."

"Did Isaac say anything about the Nephilim? Zeke seemed to think their enhanced strength wasn't quite up to par. It's not like they can use the angelic weapons…"

"The Dark Ones have an arsenal of their own. As we have our weapons, they have theirs. Had Kai not injected you with the Nephilim DNA, you would've died from Achanelech's demon blade. Make no mistake, angel essence is what saved you."

A chill rippled through Cara. "I didn't know that." In her opinion, there was way too much she still didn't know. Definitely her fault. She avoided asking the questions for fear of the answers. But ignorance could cost them their lives. It's about time she took her head out of the sand and got educated. She chose one of the questions that had been niggling at her. "Lucifer was cast out of heaven with one third of the Heavenly host. Where are they hiding? Between soulless, possessions like Melanie, and demons, I can't keep it straight. Explain it to me so it sticks."

Simon nibbled the back of her neck. "You sure you don't want breakfast first?"

She sighed. "Not this time."

He tightened his arms around her. "I'll give you the abridged version. For every one of the three hundred Angelorum, there is a Dark One manifest on Earth… like Achanelech and his consort. They live among humans. The others live in the corridors between Hell and Earth, accessible by one of thirteen portals across the seven continents. North America has only one; it's located close to San

Francisco. Some places have two, such as South America and Europe, and then there are the places with three—Asia, since it contains the Middle East, and Africa."

Cara sniffed. "Let me guess. There's a correlation between the number of portals per continent and the human atrocities that happen there?"

Simon gave her a squeeze. "We believe so. As such, the Angelorum chose to reside in France near one of the European portals."

"They have only one compound?" Cara asked.

"Yes, but that's recent. Around the time I was born, the Angelorum decided to settle together in the current compound."

"Why did it change?"

Simon's chest rose and fell behind her. "I don't know, love. That's a better question for Constantina. But to answer your original question, if summoned, a disembodied fallen angel—now considered a demon—can temporarily inhabit a soulless or possess a human conduit like Melanie Solomon. In their native form, they look like what attacked you in your apartment. That's the simplified version."

"Thanks... I think." Somehow, that didn't make her feel much better. If there were only three hundred fallen manifested like Achanelech that explained a few things. Like why the entire world wasn't teaming with Dark Ones.

At the mention of Melanie's name, Cara heard Kai open the guest room door.

"Our company is awake. How about that breakfast?" she asked, giving his arm a kiss.

He nuzzled her hair with his nose. "One more thing. To stay in human form and heal from injuries, the Dark Ones need a steady diet of human souls."

# Chapter 50

*ESCHER*
*New York City. W Hotel. Tuesday, May 28, 5:50 PM ET*

"YOU LITTLE WHORE," Escher sneered as he brought the cane down on the girl's backside for the fifth time. She lay naked at the foot of the bed, bound, and on full display for his viewing pleasure. Her whimpering and soft cries aroused him under his clothes.

He tangled his hand in her long, curly hair, strawberry blonde like that of his lovely step-daughter, Jessamine, and pulled her head back until she screamed.

"Quiet or I'll really give you something to scream about," he gritted next to her ear. She bit her lip to squelch the sound of her crying.

If only Jessamine would bend to him like the paid prostitute in front of him. His minions had followed his lovely girl to New York, losing track of her until she arrived at the Beacon Theatre. He still hadn't recovered from the shock of seeing her surrounded by the Angelorum. Even more insulting, she let that rock star touch her on stage for all to see. The humiliation of her choosing someone like that blond surfer child over someone refined such as him… it was unfathomable.

Why was she so compelled to look beyond him? With her mother gone, what possible reason could she have? She had no way of knowing he'd been responsible for her untimely death.

Between lavishing her with gifts and using his considerable charms, he couldn't understand why she didn't fancy him.

*The little bitch.*

He scowled. He would make good on his promise if she so much as looked at that rock star again. Or as close to it as Lucifer would allow, given that the little wanker was one of the Twelve and potentially worth much more alive.

He brought the cane down with a satisfying crack. The girl did nothing to hide her scream this time. "Please stop," she whimpered. Red welts crisscrossed her behind.

The hotel room door clicked open followed by the sound of a clearing throat. He froze mid swing.

"Master, my apologies for the interruption." Samuel's deep, melodic voice came from behind him. "Luc is on his way up. He asked that you... um, finish up, before he arrives."

"He's early," he pressed his eyes shut and growled. Then he grabbed the girl with one hand and threw her at Samuel with superhuman strength. "Pay her and slip her out of here unseen."

"Yes, Master," he replied, as she flew into Samuel's waiting arms, whimpering. He snatched her clothes from the chair, lifted her over his black leather-clad shoulder, and promptly disappeared from view before letting himself out.

Escher had to admit, Achanelech's Nephil was a much better minion than some of the demon and soulless underclass he had working for him. Smart, too. Instead of torturing the poor bloke and drowning in his own distaste, Acchie should've leveraged his considerable talents. Samuel was quite a rare bird indeed.

Escher sneered. Maybe he could procure him permanently. *Hmm. Something to consider.*

A knock sounded at the door.

Catching a glimpse in the mirror, Escher straightened his ascot and smoothed his suit jacket. Other than his aching balls, he was absolutely smashing and ready for old Luc.

"Do come in, Master," Escher said, and bowed.

Luc entered, dressed impeccably as usual in a finely tailored suit, no staff or cane in sight. "Escher," he said with a tip of his chin.

"Unarmed today?"

Luc smirked and parked himself on the nearest settee. "Never. How did the show-and-tell with the Nephilim alpha batch go with the Angelorum?"

Escher clasped his hands and paced. "Better than expected. We attacked just short of killing them as you requested."

"Good. Very good. They will surely underestimate us based on those second-rate experiments. Does the lab in Connecticut have the final formulation ready for me?" Luc asked, rubbing his hands together.

In answer, Escher pulled the attaché case from under the bed. He entered the digital password on the keypad, and the locks popped open. A dart was held inside the foam interior. "Here it is—one injection—complete with nanotrackers."

"Excellent. She is the key to this battle. But without her transformation into a full-blooded Nephil and the location of the Angelorum Sanctuary, we have no way to gain our prize. While the Angelorum is clutching at straws, we'll take them from an angle they'll never expect. Those fools think this will be another antiquated battle by air… imbeciles." Luc's eyes glowed red as he wore a self-satisfied smile. "Not to say we won't give them what they expect."

"Everything is in place," Escher said, snapping the briefcase shut. "In the meantime, batches are being shipped overseas. You'll have your army right on time."

"Brilliant." Luc popped up off the settee, invigorated. "Now make my day and tell me you've taken care of the NSA."

Escher's stomach soured. On that front, he'd made no progress. He placed his hands on his hips and paced. "Still working on that one. The best I could figure from Achanelech's business records, he's been selling illegal arms in Afghanistan to al-Qaeda. Stupid bollocks. No wonder he's on the terrorist watch list. According to our U.S. contacts, the file on Achanelech has been sealed. The investigation has gone underground. Since the wanker is back in France, I checked my international sources at both Interpol and MI5. Nothing's come up. For all I know this is a Black Ops assignment now."

Luc ground his teeth and let out a deep, impatient breath. "If he had half of Emanelech's brain cells, he'd be a force to be reckoned with. I've made it clear to her that she'd better not let him screw up again. If he didn't hold power over Semyaza's spawn, I would've destroyed him eons ago."

Escher looked at him askew. "Why's that so important?"

"You'll find out with the others," Luc said. "It's all part of this cosmic chess game we've chosen to play. We have one chance to better our fate and escape Judgment Day, or to screw it up for eternity."

Luc headed for the door. "Call me when you're ready to take the girl. And try not to kill any of the Twelve. The girl is my key but the others play a part in our success." He twisted the knob and stopped, giving him a hard, red stare. "Unlike Achanelech… you can be replaced. Just remember that."

Escher involuntarily swallowed, powerless to respond to Luc's threat.

Like Achanelech and his consort, Escher had been a guest in Hell and didn't relish a return visit.

# Chapter 51

***IRENE***
***Paris. Wednesday, May 29, 1:00*** *AM GMT +1*

"*Mademoiselle Hickey, bienvenue à Paris,*" said the fine-looking, young Frenchman who stood waiting to greet her as she exited Customs at Charles de Gaulle airport. "*Je m'appelle, Gerard.*"

Welcome, indeed. And didn't he look chipper at one in the morning. She smiled. "*Merci. Enchanté, Monsieur Gerard.*"

"Let me take those for you. There is a car waiting outside for us." He grabbed her bag and headed for the passenger pickup area.

Irene was still riding the high of her weekend despite her unofficial assignment with the NSA. The Knuckleheads at Fort Meade had promised a full setup at an apartment across the Seine from the U.S. Embassy in the Seventh arrondissement, near Les Invalides and Rue de l'Université. A comfortable bed and all the spy equipment she could possibly handle.

Just peachy.

Her assignment was to monitor Simon's activity once he arrived in Paris. As long as the bugs stayed operational, it should be simple. Easy peasy.

Other than Cara mentioning their Paris office was within walking distance of the Louvre, Irene didn't have a clue as to the location of Simon's security company. So far, the NSA hadn't done any better. No businesses were found registered under his name.

This could turn out to be a dull assignment. If she wasn't so worried about Cara's safety, she'd take dull all day long.

Irene stared out the window as the chauffeured car raced toward Paris and the thousands of dots of light poking holes in the night sky. Nicknamed the "city of light" due to its position as a vast educational center during the Age of Enlightenment, Paris is mistakenly thought of as the "city of lights" by many. Tonight, she would go with the misnomer.

Gerard hit a button, raising the smoky privacy screen between them and the driver and turning on the interior light. "Mademoiselle, Monsieur Caswell asked me to give you this."

He pulled an aluminum attaché case from the floor next to him.

She eyed it warily and tensed. There was only one thing that traveled in that type of attaché case. He clicked open the locks.

*Sometimes I hate when I'm right*, she thought. Two guns and a silencer were held firmly in the stiff gray foam interior.

"For fuck's sake, is he serious?" she said looking at the weapons, her pulse quickening. On the other hand, she threw an appreciative glance at the sub-compact .380 Ruger LCP. It made a nice concealed carry… if she needed one.

"Here. This is for you, too." Gerald held out a drawstring bag.

She looked inside: A cell phone, ammo, and a variety of holsters, including a thigh holster for the Ruger.

"Why all the fire power? This is a surveillance job," she asked with a sinking feeling, suspecting the NSA hadn't told her everything.

He shrugged and gave her an apologetic look. "It's not my job to ask questions, but this might help." He pulled out a large envelope with an NSA seal and handed it to her.

Taking a deep breath, she broke the seal and pulled out a manila envelope without a logo. All it contained was a phone number on a slip of plain white paper.

*Bastards.* She recognized the protocol; it explained the weapons. She'd just been taken off the grid.

Irene fished the cell phone out of the bag. She gritted her teeth and dialed. "*Bonjour*, Miss Hickey." Caswell sounded almost gleeful. She stayed silent. "An operative will be in touch shortly for your next assignment."

"Wait, what? Next assignment?"

"It's not Simon Young or Cara Collins we're ultimately interested in, but who they can lead us to. Monitor them as agreed until you're contacted. Based on what you've told us so far, we managed to find a small surveillance clip of Simon Young in Paris taken less than a week after the warehouse explosion. He walked into a building a couple of blocks from the Opéra. We'll courier the address to your apartment. Start there." He hung up before she could respond.

Counting to three, she gripped the phone until it cut into her palm, and then blew out a breath. They wanted her to lead them to the French terrorist, Le Feu. She wished she could speak to her dad. But she'd have to save that chit for when she really needed it and only if things were guaranteed to go pear-shaped again. Make that watermelon-shaped, because this time he'd truly disown her.

At least they didn't expect her to use the weapons on her friends. They were for the "next" assignment.

Her purse vibrated with a text on her personal phone. "*Excusez moi,*" she said to Gerard.

She fumbled around until she found it. The message put an immediate smile on her face, sweeping away the sour taste of her discussion with Caswell.

I MISS YOU, PELIRROJA. WHEN CAN I SEE YOU AGAIN?

Her insides warmed. What she'd give…

I MISS YOU TOO, PAQUITO. I'M IN PARIS ON BUSINESS FOR THE NEXT COUPLE OF WEEKS. Her lips turned into a pout as she typed. This totally sucked.

REALLY?

REALLY.

WOULD YOU LIKE TO HAVE DINNER ON SATURDAY?

Huh? Irene stared at his message in confusion. IN PARIS?

YES, PELIRROJA, IN PARIS.

Her heart skipped a beat. He'd told her he'd come to her the next time… She never expected that to mean all the way to Paris. To accept would be totally against protocol. Then again, what was the worst the NSA could do? Fire her from her nonjob? She hesitated only a second before responding: YES!

I'LL HOLD YOU IN MY DREAMS UNTIL THEN, NIÑA BONITA.

She released a dreamy breath. So what if he was a terrorist? He could blow up Paris for all she cared. At least she'd die with a smile on her face…

# Chapter 52



*SIENNA*

*New York City. Tuesday, May 28, 7:00 PM ET*

SIENNA LEFT HER WEST VILLAGE apartment on foot dressed in a clingy knit dress and flats, her high heels stuffed inside of her oversized Prada handbag. She had one stop to make before jumping into a cab for Brooklyn.

She had seen Michael every night since Saturday, and tonight would be no exception. The thought drew a knowing smile to her lips and gave her a twinge down below. Intent on surprising him, she'd left her underwear at home and planned on bringing a little "present" with her.

Knowing what a big step it had been for Michael to invite her to his brownstone, Sienna couldn't contain her excitement. Sadly, tonight was her last chance to see him before his week-long business trip with Simon's private security company. She missed him already. The thought of being without him made her physically ill.

*Pathetic?* Probably.

She ducked into the infamous Pink Pussycat Boutique on Fourth Street, five minutes later emerging with the brown paper bag tucked safely next to her heels. Putting her creativity on overdrive, Sienna had an idea to soften Michael up.

Boy did he have issues giving up control. Whenever she wrestled away the reins, his eyes held an unmistakable look of panic. Although he put on a brave face, she wasn't fooled and couldn't fully enjoy herself while sensing his discomfort.

To top it off, he hadn't spent the night with her since the Mercer. Rather than sleep comfortably next her, he would leave after she drifted off to sleep. His sparring sessions with Simon didn't start until 8:30 AM, and the subway commute from the West Village to Brooklyn wasn't that long. Classic fear of commitment. It had to be. Yet, when it came to birth control, he'd been willing to trade their latest test results so they could ditch the condoms since she was on the Pill and neither of them had been with anyone else in over a year. Go figure. Either way, she had her work cut out for her.

She savored the challenge.

Despite his issues, Michael had more than lived up to her dreams. She couldn't believe how good they were together, and how much fun they had. Between the physical activities and card games, they spent hours into the night sharing stories. He even reviewed some of her designs and gave constructive comments.

They no longer snipped at each other, having finally found the right outlet for their passionate exchanges. But her attraction to him went beyond him being heart-stopping gorgeous, smart, and sexy. He was really good to her.

Being with him made her feel like she'd come home.

Sienna hailed a cab and crawled into the backseat. After giving the driver Michael's address, she picked up her cell and dialed him.

"Hello?" a woman answered, a provocative tone deliberately applied to the simple one-word greeting.

Maybe she had the wrong number? Sienna paused and looked at her phone. Nope, it was Michael's name on the display.

"Is Michael there?" Sienna asked tentatively, trying not to think the worst.

"We just finished our… workout. He's in the shower. Who's this?" she purred.

"Who's this?" Sienna snapped.

"His… partner," she replied.

Ice water rolled through Sienna's veins. Partner, as in sex partner? So much for all the happy thoughts she'd been having. In a split second, her world had flipped from light into darkness.

Stunned, Sienna pressed END, her devastation transforming into unbridled rage. The heat of anger started in her belly and traveled throughout her body until it radiated from every pore in her skin. She shook. They hadn't been together even a week, and he'd already cheated on her!

Two could play at this game. *Hell hath no fury and all that bullshit. Boy was he ever going to regret this…*

By the time Sienna reached Brooklyn, she had hatched a plan.

## *MICHAEL*

*Where the hell is my cell phone?* Michael wondered as he waited for Sienna to arrive. It wasn't in his bedroom. He couldn't find it anywhere. It must be at the dojo.

*Oh, well.* He'd get it later.

After finishing an early evening sparring with Deva, he'd raced home to shower before Sienna arrived. Shopping for food earlier, he planned on making her a nice dinner. Since they'd spent the last two nights in Manhattan at her place, he'd taken the plunge and invited her over. Still nightmare-free with no unwanted hints of cinnamon, he prayed it was a sign his past was losing its grip. If so, his secret would be safe forever, and maybe he'd have a shot at a normal life after all.

He glanced around his living room to admire his quick clean-up job. Not that there'd been much to pick up, but he made a special effort to make the place perfect. Between his eye for design, his mom's help, and a little bit of money, he was proud that his place had a mature, grown-up feel rather than the garage sale look of a bachelor pad. Sleek modern furniture, some black and white photography surrounding the flat screen mounted on the wall, and a neutral color pallet with a splash of aqua did the trick.

Sienna was the first woman he had invited for dinner since he bought the place last year. At first, he felt uncomfortable extending the offer, wondering if they were moving too fast. But in the end, he decided "to hell with it" and gave himself a pat on the back for consciously working on his self-esteem and control issues.

She might even stay overnight. The thought made him a little queasy and sent a small shudder through him. But he'd take it one step at a time.

Their night at the Mercer, and every night after that, had been amazing. The jury was still out on anything long-term but this was definitely more than "friends with benefits." Surprisingly, he was okay with that.

He opened a bottle of wine while he waited, deciding to see how hungry she was before making dinner. If the last couple of nights were any indication, food would be the intermezzo between courses of bedroom-related activity.

He said a little prayer that they wouldn't be interrupted by Angelorum business tonight. Anything could happen with the looming attack. The Guardians had investigated the warehouse on the Lower East Side yesterday, finding it empty with no trace of their enemies. Had it not been for Cara's encouragement, Michael might've thought twice before extending tonight's invitation to Sienna.

The bell rang as he uncorked the bottle of red in the living room. Setting it down next to the glasses on the coffee table, he went to answer the door.

He ran his fingers through his hair, still damp from the shower. His heart beat a little faster as he opened the door and let Sienna in.

# Chapter 53



*CARA*

*New York City. Penthouse. Tuesday, May 28, 7:30 PM ET*

THE DELICIOUS SMELL of béarnaise sauce wafted up from the stove. Cara wrapped her arms around Simon's waist from behind and rested her head in the hollow of his back, inhaling the fresh scent of cotton mixed with citrus.

"*Mmm.* Smells good," she said.

He dipped the wooden spoon into the saucepan. "Want a taste?"

"Definitely," she said, playfully nipping his back and sliding her hand down along the front of his jeans across the relaxed budge underneath the fabric.

"I meant the béarnaise," he said followed by a deep chuckle.

"I know, but I keep thinking about what Irene said," she said in a deep throaty growl. "I'm picturing you cooking in just an apron."

He laughed. "Let's save that for when we don't have a house guest." He twisted in her arms and offered her the spoon.

"Deal." She closed her eyes and savored the sauce. "*Mmm.* This is the only way to eat asparagus in my book." Simon had prepared one of her healthy favorites for dinner: salmon served with asparagus and a crisp green salad with vinaigrette.

Simon rested the spoon on the stove and swept her into his arms. "And what would you like me to cook for you while wearing just this apron?" He asked, and then buried his face into the soft skin at the base of her neck, nuzzling it.

"I'll get back to you on that one." She giggled from the tickle of his feather-light touch as his groin hardened against her.

"Would you consider returning the favor?" he asked in a low, sexy voice.

"As long as you don't really expect a meal out of it," she said. Her cooking skills were worse than awful.

"Um … am I interrupting?" Kai asked, throwing up his hand as he walked into the kitchen with a smirk.

Simon winked at her, dropped his arms, and turned toward the stove. "Dinner's ready. Why don't you both take a seat at the island?"

"Sorry to make you wait." He put down his cell phone and pulled up a stool.

"No need for an apology. Cara mentioned you liked salmon," Simon said. "I hope this meets your expectations."

"I've no doubt if last night was any indication," Kai replied and patted his stomach. "I wish I had even half of your culinary talent."

Cara couldn't have been more pleased at the friendship she felt forming between them. After she and Simon had returned from meeting with the wedding planner in Connecticut, Kai had spent the afternoon with Simon teaching him some basic medical tasks—like how to check her vitals, draw blood samples, and take basic measurements, among other things.

"Did you talk to the Sanctuary?" Cara asked, eager to hear his news as she took a sip of her Sauvignon Blanc.

Kai's smile faded. "Yeah. They're still running tests. I won't have full results until we're at the Sanctuary. Your basic labs were fine, but Celine wants to do some genetic testing when we're back. In the meantime, I found out something interesting."

"What's that?" Simon asked, his shoulders stiffening.

"Nephilim pheromones can act as an aphrodisiac. But it's usually strongest in males."

"Really? Why's that?" Cara asked, between mouthfuls of salmon.

"Even though Nephilim can't procreate, they have a strong mating instinct. With so few females born compared to the number of males, it's the male who releases the most powerful scent in order to get a female to choose him over the others. It's subtle when it's between two Nephilim but between a Nephil and a human—it's ten times worse for both parties."

*Finally. Some justification.* "Thank you," she said, giving Simon a wide smile.

He let out a breath. "Point taken," he said, and stabbed a couple spears of asparagus.

"Did you talk to Sara? How's she doing?" Cara asked, quitting while she was ahead to bask in her hard-won validation.

Kai's eyes softened. "She's doing well. My mom's doing a spectacular job of spoiling her."

"That's what grandparents are for, aren't they?"

He pushed his food around on the plate, distracted. "Yeah. She's growing up so fast sometimes I forget she's only four. She's been saying the craziest stuff lately."

"What do you mean?"

"She said not to worry about her, that Isa—her name for Ishmael—will keep her safe while I focus on what's important to keep the world safe."

"You're right. Seems like a very grown-up perspective for a four-year-old," Cara said, finishing her last bite of salmon.

Kai sighed. "Yeah. She's been saying things like that since before the rescue. "Kinda weird, huh?"

"Define *weird*," Cara said. Her whole life was weird.

"Do you think it's possible she could be gifted in some way?" Kai asked.

Cara thought about it. Kai could have passed something down to Sara, since the Messenger traits pass through the father. "It's possible…"

Out of the corner of her eye, Simon's fork stopped on the way to his mouth.

"Speaking of weird, Simon how's Isaac—"

Simon held up a finger signaling for her to give him a moment.

She gave him a quizzical look, and turned to Kai who just shrugged. Simon grabbed the pad of paper and pen from a basket in the center of island. He wrote a word and pushed the pad over to Cara and Kai.

Michael.

Cara frowned. "Why isn't Michael talking to both of us?"

Instead of answering, Simon winced and reached up to rub his temple. A moment later, a chuckle boiled up in his chest. Simon bit his lip, struggling to suppress his laughter.

Cara frowned at him. "What's going on?"

Simon burst out laughing until tears cascaded down his cheeks. He wiped them away as he gripped his side.

Cara glanced at Kai. No help there. Was Simon losing it? "What's going on? I've never seen you laugh so hard. Are you still talking to Michael?"

Simon shook his head.

"What's going on? Why didn't he call me, too?" That was their usual protocol. At least once a day they shared a three-way conversation.

Kai sat back and tried to hide a grin.

Still clutching his side, he held up a palm. "It's a guy thing," he managed to say, gasping for air.

"A guy thing? What's that supposed to mean?" she asked.

Kai sat back and glanced at Simon… like he knew what was going on.

*Is testosterone the price of entry on this joke?* Cara wondered in a huff.

"I've got to go, love." He rose and leaned across the granite to give her a quick kiss before heading down the hallway, his laughter waning to a steady chuckle.

Cara yelled after him, "Wait, where are you going?"

"Brooklyn," he said from the living room followed by the sound of the terrace door sliding open. "Can you wrap my dinner for me? I'll finish it when I get home."

"Wait, is it safe? You shouldn't go alone."

"I'll fly down and pick up Paco on the way. See you later," he said, the sliding door closing behind him.

"What the hell? What couldn't Michael tell me?" Cara said to Kai.

Kai grinned at her.

Cara narrowed her eyes at him. "You heard the conversation, didn't you?" Before she could grill him, her cell phone rang.

Cara looked at the display and then back at Kai. "It's Sienna."

"Better pick it up." He chuckled, and returned to eating his dinner.

"Hey, Senny. What's up?"

All she heard was the sound of Sienna crying. Cara stiffened and went on high alert. "Sweetie, what's the matter?"

Sienna sniffled, blew her nose, then said meekly, "I handcuffed Michael to his bed and left him there… naked."

"You did what? Why?" Well that explained a lot. She didn't want to know how they'd ended up with a pair of handcuffs in the first place.

"He cheated on me," she whispered through her tears.

"Senny, what are you talking about? There's no way that's true. Not even a small chance. I promise. What happened?"

"I called him before I went over for dinner, and a woman picked up his phone. She said they had just had a—'workout'—and that he was in the shower."

Cara spun through her earlier discussions with Michael. He'd mentioned a packed schedule, including a special late afternoon training match with Deva. Michael had once mentioned that he suspected she still hoped to rekindle their old romance. But Cara was sure Michael would never go there. He'd been happier this week than she'd ever remembered, and it had everything to do with Sienna.

"Senny," Cara said in her best schoolmarm voice, "he had a sparring match with Deva at the end of the day. She probably just answered his phone. He has zero interest in her. The only person he has any interest in, at all, is you!"

There was silence on Sienna's end of the phone. "Do you think she tried to make me think something was going on when there wasn't?" she asked timidly, followed by the sound of more nose blowing.

"In a word, yes! They dated back in high school. She's probably been jealous ever since she found out about that sex-fest you had at the Mercer on Saturday night. Senny, he hasn't had a steady girlfriend in a long time. He's not a man-whore. I promise."

"Really?" she asked in a small voice that contained the first hint of regret. "Can you send Simon over to set him free?"

Cara fibbed, not able to reveal that the telepathic SOS had already been received. "Of course."

"Shit, so you don't think he cheated on me?"

Cara shook her head even though Sienna couldn't see her. "Um,'fraid not. You just ruined what could have been a perfectly good night."

"Oh shit. He's never going to forgive me. I would've never been this angry if I didn't care about him so much," she wailed.

In all the years Cara had known her, Sienna had pulled many spectacular stunts. This one just nudged into the number one spot.

"Well, I'll give you points for both creativity and execution," Cara said. "I think this even beats the time you released all those baby pigs from the 4-H fair into the high school library. They were cleaning up pig poop for a week."

She sniffled. "I wasn't doing this to be funny. I was so angry. Cara, I don't want to lose him. I… Can you help?"

Cara released a breath. "I think you're going to need to beg for mercy, but I'll see what I can do. Hang in there." Why did the road to romance need to be this rocky?

# Chapter 54

*MICHAEL*
*Brooklyn, New York. Tuesday, May 28, 8:15 PM ET*

MICHAEL LAY STEWING as he waited for Simon to come and release him. Thanks to Sienna, she had single-handedly supplied him with two of the most mortifying moments of his life. The first time was back at end of March when she made a mockery of his manhood in front of Cara over the Calvin Klein campaign, and then this. If he added the foursome disaster—that would make three. She had played a part in them all.

God help him, but he wanted to bury himself inside her and pound some sense into that beautiful head of hers.

While he'd been lying there, Michael thought about what Sienna had said. The only logical explanation was that he'd left his phone at the dojo and Deva must've answered it. That alone was enough to piss him off. She clearly violated his privacy.

Sienna had spewed something about a workout and a shower as she left, and given how he'd spent his afternoon, technically nothing Deva had told Sienna had been a lie. But he could imagine that, depending on how it was said, it could've been construed in exactly the way Sienna had understood it.

*Fucking Deva!* He had every intention of blowing back over to the dojo to confront her once he was free and dressed. He would pick it out of her head if he had to.

Michael heard the front door open and Simon's heavy footsteps enter the house.

"Back here, Simon," he said.

"Be there in a minute."

Michael kept his eyes on the doorway, his face hot with embarrassment. Simon's low chuckle echoed in the hallway as he stopped in the bathroom.

Michael rolled his eyes and yelled to Simon. "You wouldn't be laughing if our positions were reversed."

"True, but it's improbable that I'd ever end up in your position," Simon called from the hall. Knowing Cara, Michael had to agree, making him feel even more foolish.

Simon's smiling face filled the doorway as he tossed a towel with uncanny precision. It landed on Michael's midsection. "I thought you might appreciate a little modesty. Now, where are the keys?"

Michael lay back, relieved. "On the dresser, next to you."

Simon plucked them off the wood surface and strode over. Standing over Michael, he unlocked the handcuffs one wrist at a time and stepped back.

Michael slowly sat up and shook his arms to get the feeling back into them after having had them suspended above his head for an hour. Then he rubbed his wrists.

Simon, chuckling, twirled the handcuffs around his finger, and settled in the chair next to the bed. "Pink and fuzzy. Sienna's?"

"Well, they're not mine," Michael said, giving him a dirty look.

Simon tried to wipe the amusement from his face. "This situation is too ironic. Don't you have a black belt in karate?"

Michael narrowed his eyes. "What's your point? Subduing her wasn't exactly on my mind."

"It was obviously on hers." Simon grinned.

He shook his head. "You didn't tell Cara did you?"

"Didn't need to. Sienna called her the minute I left."

Lying back on the bed, Michael groaned. "Fucking hell. That's one good reason not to date the best friend of my Soul Seeker."

Simon's deep voice filled with concern. "You promised to tell me the whole sordid tale for my troubles. What happened?"

Michael glanced at the towel on his lap then back at Simon. "Give me a minute while I put on my clothes and try to regain some dignity."

Simon smirked and motioned for him to take his leave.

Michael secured the towel around his hips and got up. Leaning over to the chair where Simon sat, he tugged his polo shirt out from behind Simon's back and grabbed his jeans off the floor on his way out.

When Michael returned he relayed the sanitized version of the story and his theory about Deva.

"After you confront Deva, what are you going to do about Sienna?" Simon asked.

It was a fair question.

Michael hung his head and sighed. "I can't leave it like this while I'm gone. I need to go see her. I'm pissed that she didn't even give me a chance to explain. She just jumped to the worst possible conclusion and left me here. I trusted her…" Michael was torn inside. He definitely didn't want to end it with her, but he didn't want to let her off the hook, either.

Simon clasped Michael's shoulder. "Her passion runs deep for you, Michael. If it didn't, she wouldn't have tried to hurt and humiliate you like this. She punished you with the same intensity as her feelings for you. That's a woman's way."

The corner of Michael's mouth turned up. "Let me guess, Sensual Pleasure training."

Simon smiled and relaxed back in the chair. "It's in the female psychology section of the coursework. I've been brushing up since I met Cara."

During his Messenger training at the Sanctuary, Michael had completed a class in Sensual Pleasures. He'd been putting his learning to good use lately.

Michael smirked. "Is there a section on jealousy? I'd like to give it to Sienna."

Simon took a deep breath. "Let me tell you exactly what I think. Get to the bottom of this and work it out, because the two of you are good for each other. You both just need to get out of your own way."

In his heart, Michael knew Simon was right. He gave him a wry smile and stood up. "Thanks, I appreciate you coming to help me. And thanks for the advice."

Simon rose with a chuckle. "Anytime. Good luck with Deva and Sienna. I'm sure Cara will fill me in on the rest of the story. Let me know if you need anything else. Otherwise, I'll see you tomorrow."

Michael walked Simon out to where Paco stood waiting next to the door. They went their separate ways. Simon and Paco back to Manhattan, and Michael, at a near run, back to the dojo.

# Chapter 55

*MICHAEL*
*Brooklyn, New York. Rising Sun Dojo. Tuesday, May 28, 8:50 PM ET*

MICHAEL PUT HIS KEY in the lock and entered the back door of the dojo at quarter to nine. While Deva was finishing up her class in the main room, he snuck into his office unnoticed.

He snatched his cell phone from his desk where he'd left it and looked at the recent calls. A call had come in from Sienna at seven-ten and lasted for less than a minute. Luckily, his phone was password protected, so there wasn't much else Deva could do except answer it.

Tossing his phone back on the desk, he sat down to wait. Leaning back in his chair, he crossed his feet and put them up on the desk. Deva kept her purse in the file cabinet drawer, and she wouldn't be leaving without it.

Ten minutes later, Deva walked in wearing her *gi*, her light-brown hair up in a ponytail. She stopped dead in her tracks, and gasped. "Michael, what are you doing here?"

He gave her a menacing look and pointed to his cell. "I came to pick up my phone."

Deva shifted uncomfortably. "Oh, you could've just called. I would've dropped it off for you."

Without preamble, Michael asked, "What did you tell Sienna when she called?"

Deva wore a look of guilt as she stood open-mouthed. It saved Michael the trouble of dipping into her head.

"I, um, told her you had gone home to shower, and I, um, asked her if she had a message." Deva stumbled while trying to fake doe-eyed innocence.

*Bullshit*, he thought.

This time, Michael dropped his shields and dove into her head.

*Damn it, I knew he'd figure it out. But it was worth it if she never speaks to him again.*

Michael scowled and took his feet off the desk. "Deva, we both know that's not what you told her. Why don't we confront the elephant in the room."

Deva's discomfort turned to defiance. She crossed her arms in front of her. "Fine."

Michael stood up and prepared for a fight. "You need to decide if you can continue to work for me, knowing that we won't be together again… romantically. I don't love you that way, Deva. We're friends. We have a business relationship—that's all. Nothing else. Not ever. Is that clear?" Michael's voice rose as his anger escalated.

Deva's head tipped back as if he'd struck her, tears welling in her eyes. "I thought…" her voice trailed off.

"You thought what, exactly?" he snapped.

"Never mind, it doesn't matter," she replied, a tear slipping down her cheek.

Michael gave her a piercing look. "It does matter. I want this out in the open. We need to decide if we can move forward. I'm leaving tomorrow. I need to know if I have to make alternate plans with Rodney or possibly shut down the dojo next week."

She nodded, tears now freely spilling over. "Fine! What about the night we spent together before you opened the dojo, what was that? Just a booty call? You didn't feel anything for me then? You asked me to work for you a month later. Why?" she said, doing a little indignant screaming of her own.

Michael cringed. He should've known based on their history that Deva wouldn't be a good candidate for his "friends with benefits" policy.

He softened and he told her the truth. "I'm sorry. I've never been good at this. I hired you because we were friends, and you needed a job. You're highly qualified and I trusted you. I slept with you for the same reason… we were friends and I trusted you. It was a good night, Deva. I assumed we were both adults, no commitment required."

Deva crumbled into the chair in front of his desk and gave him an anguished look. "I figured once you got this place going and finished grieving for your father, you would slow down enough to see me again. To see I was right here in front of you."

The mention of his father gave Michael a twinge. It was true, he hadn't finished grieving for his father, but that hadn't held him back from Sienna.

His anger diffused and he let out sigh. "I'm sorry if I left you with that impression. It wasn't my intent. Can I still trust you after tonight? Can we move forward or do you want to leave? I need to know where we stand." Her answer would determine how he'd spend the rest of his night.

She wiped away her tears and took a deep breath. "I'll stay for now. I'm sorry, Michael. It won't happen again," she said and met his gaze. "You can still trust me. I promise."

He gave her a small smile. "Thanks. You're a good manager. The staff and the clients all like you. I'm lucky to have you here." As much as he wanted to fire her, in reality, it was a mess of his own making.

She rose from the chair, and he walked around the desk to join her. He touched her arm. "Listen, Dee, you're a woman with a lot to give. Trust me, I'm no picnic. You deserve someone who'll go the distance for you. Don't settle for anything less."

Her mouth quirked up in a half-smile. "You giving relationship advice—pretty ironic, don't you think?"

"Even old dogs can learn new tricks."

"You really like her, don't you?" Deva said, shaking her head.

He gave her a warning look and leaned back against the desk with his arms crossed in front of him. "No thanks to you, I have to go and convince her that I didn't cheat on her."

"Sorry. Can I write her note or call her or something?" Deva said, sheepishly.

Michael wiped his hand over his face and sighed. "No. I got this one." Although he didn't look forward to confronting Sienna.

Deva nodded and extracted her purse from inside the file cabinet. "Anything else, Sensei, or can I head out?"

Michael headed to the office door. "Let's head out together."

They locked up the dojo for the night. Deva confirmed that she would be there bright and early to do paperwork. She'd run the dojo in his absence as planned.

Michael hopped into a cab to Manhattan, not exactly sure what he was going to do when he got there.

# Chapter 56

*SIENNA*

*New York City. West Village. Tuesday, May 28, 10:10 PM ET*

SIENNA HAD CRAWLED INTO a pair of night shorts and a matching tank when she'd gotten home. Her dress lay discarded in a crumpled heap on her bedroom floor, along with her hopes for the evening. After downing a protein shake to replace the dinner she'd missed, she took out a corkscrew and opened a bottle of wine.

She was on her second box of tissues as she sat on the sofa in the living room, listening to music, and drinking the wine from the bottle. *Fuck the glass.*

After she'd hung up from her call with Cara, she'd been doing a stellar job of wallowing in self-pity over her own stupidity. Thoughts of how good it felt to seduce Michael in the hallway kept looping through her head. Her mouth was at home on his body. She'd almost abandoned her plan the moment she'd touched him. Then again in the bedroom when she sat on top of him and secured his hands; it would've been so easy to slip him inside of her.

Her entire motivation for buying the handcuffs had been to do just that—have her way with him until she had him screaming in ecstasy. That was the plan until the fucking phone call.

Okay, maybe she should've listened a little longer before she left him there deliciously naked for Simon to find. She winced, thinking about what a big step it had been for him to invite her to his home. He'd planned on cooking dinner for her. And she'd ruined it. How could she have been such an idiot?

The tears wouldn't stop. Grabbing another tissue, she gave her nose a good blow.

The doorbell buzzed and she froze. *Michael.* Her tears instantly dried. *Shit.*

Taking measure of her surroundings, she didn't like what she saw. She dashed to the bathroom to retrieve the waste basket and shoveled in her used tissues before returning it and the tissue box to the bathroom. She hit PAUSE on the iPod remote and ran to put the wine on the kitchen counter.

She glanced into the nearest mirror. Ugh. She looked like hell, but there was nothing she could do in thirty seconds to make it any better. Maybe being caught on the back foot could work to her advantage.

The doorbell buzzed again. Taking a deep breath, she cracked open the door with the chain still intact.

Michael scowled with his hands crossed over his chest, tapping his foot.

"Are you planning on doing me harm?" she asked through the chained crack. Seeing him filled her with a combination of fear and elation.

"As well deserved as it might be, no. I'm not planning on harming you. May I come in?" he asked.

*Crap, he's really mad.*

Sienna removed the chain and opened the door wide enough for him to enter. He walked briskly into her apartment, and she closed the door behind him.

She might as well start with a good offense. "I'm sorry, Michael. I—"

"You're *sorry*?" he interrupted as he paced with his hands clenched at his sides. "Do you realize how humiliating that was for me? To have Simon come and release me? The only thing that would've been worse is if were Cara or my mother!"

Sienna couldn't help it. The thought made her smirk.

"It's not fucking funny!" he yelled, his neck a bright pink.

She bit her bottom lip to prevent the nervous laugh threatening to escape. "I think it would've been funny if it were your mother." He must've thought so too for about a second because a ghost of a smile passed over his lips.

"Admit it, you just smiled."

He held onto his scowl. "Sienna, I'm fucking pissed at you."

She smiled sweetly. "I know, because you've said 'fucking' twice since you got here." Michael didn't swear as a general rule, so she found it both shocking and amusing when he did. Maybe she was rubbing off on him.

"Sienna! Knock it off," he snapped and stamped his foot. "Why is it that you can drive me to the brink of insanity?"

"Just special I guess?" she said in a small voice.

He threw his hands up the air. "Woman, you drive me bat shit crazy! You know that?"

"Who answered your phone? Deva? Cara told me you worked out with her this afternoon."

Glaring at her with daggers in his eyes, he snapped, "Yeah. If you'd stuck around for another five seconds, maybe we could've figured that out instead of you leaving me tied to the bed with my dick hanging out."

*You look very sexy tied to the bed with your dick hanging out,* she thought, a smile escaping this time. "So, you didn't cheat on me?"

"No, Sienna. I didn't cheat on you. Do you want it in blood?" he said with anger etched deep in his brow.

Maybe she had half a chance of fixing this—as long as she didn't make any more stupid moves. She probably wouldn't need Cara's help after all.

"I'm sorry. What can I do to make it up to you?" Sienna took a step toward him, and his body went rigid, stopping her in her tracks. "I don't want to lose what we have, Michael."

His face softened. "I don't either," he replied and lowered himself onto the sofa. Afraid to get any closer, she sat on the club chair next to it.

Clasping his hands, he leaned on his thighs and flashed a cool smile. "I've thought about acceptable restitution. I think I've come up with something satisfactory."

*Uh-oh, I'm in trouble.* "Restitution, huh? Give me your thoughts."

He leaned back and rested his arm along the back of the couch. "First, I want one hundred points credited to my bank."

Sienna gasped. That was a lot of card games. "*Okayyyyy,*" she said slowly, recovering.

He smiled wickedly. "I'm withdrawing seventy-five points right now." He slipped the pink furry handcuffs from his back pocket and threw them on the coffee table.

Sienna panicked. "Are you serious?"

He got up and lifted her up off the chair into an embrace. His hot and smoldering gaze caught hers, reminding her of the Calvin Klein ad. "Dead serious. Haven't you heard that make-up sex is the best? Especially if it's creative?"

His lips met hers, tenderly at first, and then with increasing insistence until he conquered her mouth. Being back inside the warmth of his embrace and pressed up against the hard muscles of his chest set her on fire.

Her hands snuck underneath the back of his shirt to touch the smooth hollow along his spine. Her nails traveled down into the top of jeans until they found his bare ass.

He grasped her arms and gently pulled them out. "This is my party, remember?"

She gave him an innocent look. "What? I'm not allowed to touch you?"

"Only until I get you into the bedroom, then its handcuffs for you, cupcake."

She narrowed her eyes. "You promise you won't return the favor and leave me handcuffed and naked for Cara?"

He chuckled, wrapping his arms securely around her. "As tempting as that would be. No. But you'll just have to trust me." He kissed her on the top of her head, and then spun her around. Giving her a tap on the butt, he gently nudged her toward the kitchen. "Go get some ice and meet me in the bedroom."

She eyed him suspiciously. "Are we talking a bucket or a glass?" she asked on her way.

He laughed. "You deserve a bucket but a glass will do."

She stumbled to a stop on her way into the bedroom and her breath caught. He'd already taken his shirt off and placed it neatly on a chair. Standing half-naked next the bed, he was sexy and beautiful. Her eyes swept top to bottom, from his high cheekbones down along the curve of his neck to the smooth muscles of his torso and lower to his rippled abs; the red family crest tattoo on his chest an added turn-on.

He clasped the dress she'd discarded on the floor and held it out to her. The corners of his mouth turned up. "I think you owe it to me."

Suppressing a smile, she handed him the glass of ice and snatched the dress from his hand. "I'll be back."

Her heart leaped on the way to the bathroom, she wouldn't dream of denying him the full package. She took the opportunity to repair her face with some strategically placed make-up, and then shimmied into her dress, sans underwear, and headed back.

"Your wish is my command," she said, stepping into the heels lying inside her bedroom door.

Michael sat on the bottom edge of her bed. The glass of ice and handcuffs lay on the nightstand.

"You look beautiful." He stood up, encircling her in his arms. She felt at home again wrapped in his warmth. She stared into his royal-blue eyes and nearly melted. She wanted him now more than ever, in any way that she could have him.

He slowly lowered his lips onto hers and closed his eyes as he kissed her, pressing her body closer to his. His lips were soft and gentle—loving. Breaking the kiss, he hugged her hard. "Baby, you make me crazy in so many ways," he whispered into her hair.

She smiled into his shoulder, his tenderness almost bringing a tear to her eye. The familiar scent of his cologne mixed with the heady smell at the base of neck. "The feeling's mutual."

He chuckled and then kissed her hard and deep as his hands started their journey over her body. Slipping his hand underneath her dress, his fingers slowly traveled up her inner thighs. She was already wet, her body reacting from the moment he'd asked her to put the dress on naked underneath.

His fingertips lightly brushed the wetness between her legs, while he edged down the top of her dress. His mouth found her breast, delighting in the gold ring through her hard peak.

Two of his fingers slipped inside her, exploring her deeply, as the tip of his tongue tugged on her nipple ring. She let out a loud moan of pleasure as he had his way with her, shivering with anticipatory wonder as to what he had in store for her.

One thing was sure. It would be a long night.

Pulling his fingers out and giving her breast one last nip, he lifted her up and positioned her on the bed. Her legs dangled over the edge. Slowly, he slid her dress up to her waist.

He knelt down between her legs and whispered, "I'm going to taste you, before I lose myself inside of you." Her legs over his shoulders, he plunged his tongue inside of her, probing and exploring before he moved up to lick between her folds. Heat and need filled her core.

He slid his tongue up further to caress and suck on her swollen spot, setting her on fire. She cried out, on the edge of orgasm.

Michael pulled away. "I don't want you to come until I'm inside of you," he growled, lowering his jeans without taking them off. His erection sprang free, anxious and throbbing. Sienna never failed to marvel at him. Thick, long, and beautiful, like the rest of him. He wrapped her legs around his waist and pressed past her opening. Thrusting all the way in until his body was flush with hers, he filled her to capacity. The slick friction of his skin on hers set her nerve endings alight with pleasure as he settled into a rocking rhythm.

"Oh, Michael," she moaned. Absorbed in the awareness of him, she wrapped her legs more tightly around him, digging her heels into his buttocks.

His long fingers grasped her hips. He threw his head back and closed his eyes, letting out a satisfied moan from his throat. Moving inside of her, he thrust in deep and rotated his hips, heightening the sensation.

Opening his eyes halfway, he looked down at her. "Does this feel like a man who's cheating on you?" he asked breathlessly on an inward thrust.

Barely able to think, she replied with equal breathlessness, "No."

If you could tell someone was cheating on you by the way they made love to you, this wouldn't be it. Mark had cheated on her, and he never put this much effort or skill into it. She knew down to her core that Michael gave her everything he had when they were together. He may have loved to call the shots, but he never held out on her. Ever.

He increased his rhythm, messaging her from the inside. His movements were fluid and deliberate. "Does this feel like someone who doesn't care about you?"

"No," she moaned. Of course he cared about her; she could feel it in everything they did together. She cared a great deal about him, too. If anything, she cared too much.

Pounding hard, he sought her G-spot with every delicious stroke. "Does this feel like someone who doesn't want to please you?" He struggled to speak. She could feel him getting close as he swelled inside of her.

"No!" Sienna screamed as the volcano of her orgasm built. He always pleased her—every time. He seemed to get more enjoyment out of pleasing her then reaching his own climax. Although he always accepted the pleasure she gave him graciously and fully enjoyed it, even when he had to abandon control.

This time, when he slammed into her, her orgasm erupted and she felt herself shatter around him.

A final scream escaped his lips as he joined her. His pulsing matching hers, yet he kept moving for a few more thrusts until he couldn't go on. Rather than collapsing down next to her, he scooped her up, keeping himself buried deep and kissed her.

He kicked off his jeans, and then carried her to the bathroom and turned on the shower, one-handed. Looking into her eyes, he asked, "We back on the same page?"

"One hundred percent."

"Good, I'm going to put you down now." He pulled out of her. Slipping her dress off over her head, she jumped into the shower with him following behind.

"Commando, huh? That was a surprise." She wet her hair and flashed a quick glance at his crotch.

He wiggled his eyebrows at her. "You gave me the idea."

Michael grabbed the shower pouf and soaped it up. Joining her under the water from behind, he tucked his body around hers and drew the soapy ball in slow circles on her front.

"We have a lot more points to spend. If we stay in here too long, it'll be tomorrow morning before we know it," she said.

He nibbled on her ear and teased, "I believe the phrase was 'my points, my rules'?"

"Just sayin'," she said, turning around to rinse. As much as they loved the shower, if he expected to do anything with that glass of ice cubes and those handcuffs, they'd better get to it. She had to work tomorrow.

"Good point," he conceded and quickly washed the rest of her, before washing himself.

They slipped into fluffy white robes she'd just bought and kept on hooks behind the door.

Sienna towel dried her hair and twisted it into a bun on her head. Michael stood behind her, his chin on her shoulder and his arms around her waist as she secured her hair. Looking at him look at her in the mirror made her smile. He nuzzled her neck, taking a deep inhale. There was a sameness and harmony in the way they looked with him tucked behind her… and the way he made her heart beat. Everything felt right in her world again.

"Ready?" he asked.

She nodded with a smile.

He carried her into the bedroom, and placed her in the middle of the bed. Straddling her, he grabbed the handcuffs from the nightstand.

"Wait!" she screamed. "Show me the keys first."

Rolling his eyes, he retrieved them from his jeans. He dangled them from his pinky before placing them on the nightstand next to the now melting glass of ice.

"Satisfied?"

She nodded.

He resumed his position astride her. Taking her wrist, he clasped the handcuff around it with a snap and secured it on one of the rungs of her antique iron bed. He strung the handcuffs around one of the vertical iron bars and captured her other wrist.

He looked her in the eye, and then peeled back the flaps of her robe, the cool air hitting her skin. Her nipples immediately hardened. Reaching over, he fished out an ice cube from the glass.

"Half-melted ice is the best." He put it into his mouth and then removed it. "Just getting off any excess water," he explained with a crooked smile.

Lying down next to her, he started the cube's journey at her lips. Caressing them with the ice and then kissing her with his warm mouth. The cube journeyed down her neck, followed by his tongue, eliciting a gasp. He worked his way down to her breasts, circling the cube around her left nipple. The metal of the nipple ring grew cold quickly, sending a shiver down her spine. Lifting the ice cube, he took her into his hot mouth warming her while using the ice cube on her other breast, giving her the most exquisite sensation between hot and cold. He alternated from side to side until the cube was gone, and then picked up another.

Sienna panted. Her body pulsed between her legs, wet and ready for him.

Slowly, he trailed the ice down her belly to her navel and around each of her pelvic bones, while exploring her skin with his mouth until the cube was gone. This time, he popped a cube into his mouth and went down on her. He licked and teased her, alternating between using the cube and his tongue to explore her.

The sensation made her scream out, the feeling almost painful in its pleasure. He tugged gently at her nipple rings as he licked her, sending shock waves through her in a serious case of sensory overload. Without warning, an orgasm crashed over her, shaking her core as she lay helpless with her hands restrained above her head.

"Michael!" she screamed, not caring if the neighbors heard her.

Slowly, he worked his way back up her body, opening his robe and touching her skin-on-skin. He was hard and ready.

He released her from the handcuffs and lay down next to her. Positioning one of his long legs between hers, he rolled her onto her side. Moving her up just a little higher on his hip, he glided right into her slick wetness. Pressing her into the hard ridges of his chest, he locked his arms around her and looked into her eyes as they lay face-to-face. He kissed her forehead and gently rocked inside her, the motion lulling her into a state of quiet ecstasy.

"You feel like Heaven," she whispered, her eyes half-open.

He kissed her softly on the lips before resting his face next to hers on the pillow. "I'm going to miss you while I'm gone."

A smile tugged at her lips. "I'm going to miss you too, baby." She tucked her head onto his chest and closed her eyes, lost in the sensation of his gentle thrusting caresses.

"I could last all night like this," he whispered into her hair.

"I'd pay anything for this to last all night." Her mouth found his and she kissed him with every ounce of emotion she had left in her. Placing his hand on the back of her head, he kissed her back, pouring into it seemingly all he had to give. She could feel his kiss down to her toes. Being with him left her breathless.

When his lips left hers, Sienna gazed deeply into his royal-blue eyes. "Michael, I promise I'll never doubt you again."

He smiled and continued to gently rock inside of her. "I want you to remember this night in case the temptation ever comes up again."

Sienna flashed him a distraught look. "I—"

He put his fingers to her lips. "*Shh*, let me finish," he said, stoking her hair. "I want you to feel how much I care about you, how much I desire you, and how much I want to be with you. Do you feel it?"

He increased his pace slightly, sending an electric shock wave of sensation through her.

"Yes," she said softly. He hugged her tightly, his cheek touching hers.

For almost an hour they lay wrapped in each other's arms while they rode the gentle sea of Michael's thrusting, her nerve endings alive with exquisite pleasure.

Kissing the top of her head, he whispered, "Why don't I take us home?"

Without waiting for a response, he shifted into position on top of her and did exactly that. He drove them home.

Her orgasm gripped her hard, carrying her away in a volcanic explosion of ecstasy so powerful that the contraction of her internal muscles was almost painful. Michael followed with a forceful shudder, releasing inside of her as he pulsed in the aftermath.

He collapsed down next to her, breathing hard. She threw her leg over him while they recovered, her heart pounding as she lay spineless in his embrace.

He laughed. "I guess we can call it a seventy-five point night."

She pulled him close, and asked, "Will you stay?"

A look of mild panic flashed through his eyes, and then he gave her a wan smile. "I'm sorry, I have to go. Maybe next time?"

Disappointment washed over her. She didn't want to push it. So she let it go. "Okay."

Closing her robe, she lay on the bed and watched him get up and prepare to leave. He placed his robe neatly on the chair. Standing naked and gorgeous in front of her, he collected his clothes. "I'm going to clean up. I'll be right back."

Loneliness washed over Sienna. She didn't want him to leave tonight much less for a week. How would she survive a whole week without him? God, she hated being such a girl.

He poked his head back in. "Walk me out?"

She followed him to the front door. He turned and pulled her into a tight embrace. She relaxed into his now familiar warmth. "Despite everything, I had a fantastic evening. I'll give you a call while I'm gone.

Sadness prevented her smile from reaching her eyes.

"I'll miss you," he whispered.

"Me, too." After one last quick kiss, he was gone.

Sienna didn't know why a tear slipped down her cheek.

# Chapter 57

*CARA*
*New York City. Green Street Loft. Wednesday, May 29, 6:30 AM ET*

"YOU LOOK LIKE HELL." Cara gave Michael a peck on the cheek as he walked into Simon's loft through the stairwell door dressed in black and carrying a duffel bag. Dark crescents lay under his eyes again this morning. Sienna was having a detrimental effect on his sleep.

"At least I have a smile on my face." He winked and bent down to pet Chloe who was sniffing his pants leg. Even she was ready for battle in her pink Kevlar dog coat.

"Things better in paradise?" Cara smiled and gave him a playful squeeze on the arm.

He nodded. "Any coffee left?"

She pointed him toward the unruly crowd in the kitchen. "Better get there fast."

He dropped his bag down by everyone else's next to the elevator and waded into the sea of black in the kitchen. Everyone was suited up and armed to the teeth. Well almost everyone. Brett was the only one unarmed due to his lack of weapons training. Even Kai knew his way around knives thanks to Luke.

As for her, blessed blades were sheathed all over her body: waistband, thighs, wrists, ankles. Hopefully, she wouldn't accidentally stab herself.

Kai got more than a few surprised stares when he'd produced Achanelech's jewel-topped knife—the one that had almost killed her—as they walked into the kitchen. Her side ached just looking it at. Unable to heal the jagged scar left behind with her Nephilim DNA alone, she had needed her healing powers to fully erase it.

"Be careful with that, Kai," said Simon, eyeing it warily, "It's a powerful weapon."

Kai's mouth pinched into a thin line. "Will it work on the Dark Ones?"

Simon nodded.

"Like cutting through butter. It'll send 'em straight to hell. But—"

Angel interrupted. "It's lethal to a human without angelic blood... after it makes you *loco*. At least put a sheath on it. I'll check for a spare with my civilian weapons." He headed off toward the mound of luggage.

A spark of fear flashed in Kai's eyes. "Good to know."

Isaac whistled, calling for everyone's attention.

"I'll drive Simon's Escalade. Zeke will drive mine," said Isaac, giving orders with military precision. He seemed to have something to prove after the attack on Sunday. This would be the Dark Ones' last chance to make a move before they left and he'd be damned if they succeeded on his watch. At least that's what Cara had gleaned through her eavesdropping earlier.

He pointed to her, Michael, and Simon. "You three and Chloe come with me. Angel, Paco, and Luke will accompany Kai and Brett. We'll park next to the plane; and stay in tight formation until you're all aboard. If all goes according to plan, Zeke will take Angel to Newark for his commercial flight home to California after the rest of us leave Teterboro for the Sanctuary. If not... we're under strict orders to get Cara, Simon, Brett, Kai, and Michael on that plane—whatever it takes."

Butterflies rumbled in her stomach. Fun.

"Noah is going to take the baggage in advance and have it preloaded on the plane so we can take off fast. Any questions?" Isaac asked with an ice-blue stare as he passed a hand over his blond spiky hair. "Oh, before I forget. Just in case." He slammed a bottle of pills on the counter. "You guys, Kai, Michael, and Brett. Take one." Then he glanced at her. "You too, Cara. You still haven't built full Nephilim resistance."

"To what?"

"Demon energy as they manifest. These will prevent the headaches."

"Damn. I would've killed for a bottle of these babies just last week," Brett said, snatching it off the counter and removing the twist-off lid.

Cara had been pleasantly surprised to learn Brett was adequately proficient at mixed martial arts. Too bad he wasn't trained in weapons. Even so, he looked badass in black with his hair back in a tight blond ponytail.

"Why do we get the headaches?" Cara asked.

He glared. "So you know to run."

Wish she'd known that the first time around. She wouldn't have hesitated and nearly gotten herself killed.

"There's another downside for you," Isaac said to Cara.

"What's that?" Kai interjected as Brett handed him the bottle.

"It'll block her ability to detect soulless energy," Isaac replied, then glanced at the troops and slapped the granite island. "Let's roll."

Cara's knee nervously bobbed up and down all the way to Teterboro Airport as she stared out at the gray overcast sky. Michael sat up front with Isaac while Simon sat next to her in the middle row seats with Chloe. The pill may block Dark Ones' energy but it did nothing to dull her ability to read emotions. Everyone's nervous energy turned her stomach. "You guys are making me feel sick."

"Sorry, love, not much we can do about that." Simon squeezed her hand.

"Noah finished loading the bags," said Isaac, receiving the silent message on their Guardian frequency.

They pulled through the gates of the airport first while the second SUV followed close behind. The Angelorum hangar was at the far end of the airport in the northeast corner.

In the distance, the luxury Gulfstream G650 private jet sat on the tarmac and appeared ready to go. Nice to know the Angelorum probably had about as much money as the Catholic Church.

That good news was negated when Chloe popped up between her and Simon with her hackles raised and a low growl in her throat. Noah's SUV was nowhere in sight.

"Not good," Cara said, her pulse quickening while her sense of perception stayed dead from the pill. She glanced at Michael, "You don't feel anything, either, do you?"

He shook his head with his lips pressed in a tight, worried line.

Simon leaned forward in the seat and plucked a hilt from his belt. "There's something out there, near the hangar."

"Yup. Feel it," said Isaac. "Angel, Paco, and Luke got it, too."

"What's Noah say?"

Isaac flashed an icy stare in the rearview mirror. "He's not answering."

*Great, another trip straight into the hornet's nest,* Cara thought.

The growl from Chloe's throat rose to a crescendo. Simon said a few words to her in the angelic language and she quieted.

Isaac stopped the truck two hangars away, the second SUV coming to a halt behind them. He turned in his seat to face them. "Engaging the Dark Ones while trying to protect all the humans with us will be tricky. If we cloak them, we handicap ourselves, leaving only three of us to fight unencumbered. The quicker we can get Cara, Michael, Brett, and Kai onto the plane, the better chance we have of getting out of here without casualties."

"Agreed," Simon said. "But order of priority should be…" then Simon went silent.

Isaac nodded. "Wise."

"Hey! Fill us in. Why did you cut out on the last part?" Cara asked, annoyed.

"Sorry, I wanted to brief the others on our channel," Simon replied then turned his attention back to Isaac. "Let's call in reinforcements once we figure out how big a battle we have on our hands."

"*Ahem.* Order of priority?" Cara asked.

Simon eyed her sternly. "You going to fight me on this?"

"Depends."

"There's no room for 'depends,' love," he snapped. "If you defy me, you put us all at risk. Understand? I need your trust and, this time, to do what I say. Agreed?"

She released a breath. "Fine."

"You first, Brett second," he said. "The others in whatever order is most convenient."

"But—"

"No buts," Simon said. "You're the only one who can heal us in case of injury and Brett is unskilled with weapons, not to mention you've both been named. So listen and do what you're told when the time is right."

"All right," she conceded though not thrilled about it. But she had to agree with Simon's logic. The thought of losing anyone terrified her.

He kissed the top of her head. "Thank you."

"Here goes," Isaac said and continued on toward the plane.

# Chapter 58



***BRETT***

***Teterboro Airport. New Jersey. Wednesday, May 29, 7:50*** AM ET

"BRETT, STAY WITH PACO when we get out of the truck. Hear me?" Angel growled from the front seat where he sat next to Zeke. Luke and Paco had the second row while he and Kai had been relegated to the third.

Brett was in no position to argue. Angel, Paco, Luke, and Zeke had been yammering on for the last few minutes in a language that almost didn't sound human. He leaned over to Kai. "Do you have any clue what they're saying?"

Kai shook his head with his arms crossed in front of him. "No more than you do. I don't speak the angelic language."

Powwow over, Zeke put the SUV in drive.

Luke leaned over the seat in front of them, his eyes flashing between Brett and Kai. "There's trouble brewing up ahead, so prepare for a fight. We're going to try to get you both onto the plane as fast we can but it'll depend on what's waiting for us. If you see any black-winged Nephilim, assume their powers are like ours. They were uncloaked when Zeke and Isaac encountered them on Sunday, but don't assume they can't cloak. Got it?"

Brett nodded in unison with Kai.

"Kai, you and I fight back-to-back. Brett, Paco will cloak you and move you toward the plane after they load Cara."

"Is there any reason we don't just turn around and fly out of here on a commercial flight?" Brett whined.

"That would be a sign of weakness," Luke said with a crooked grin.

"A Nephil backing down against Dark Ones? Never happen," Angel shouted from the front seat. "M'ijo, you wound me. Where are your *cojones*?"

*In my pants where they belong*, Brett thought with a deep frown.

The SUV rolled to a stop behind Isaac.

"Lock and load," said Zeke from the front seat, gripping a sword hilt in his hand.

Brett filed out with others, sticking close to Paco. Swords drawn in full blaze surrounded him and Kai. In front of them, Simon and Isaac held their blades alight with Chloe between them, hackles raised, and Cara and Michael at their backs with their weapons drawn.

Energy crackled uncomfortably over his skin on the empty tarmac. His heart hammered in response to the adrenaline coursing through his body. Not unlike taking the stage for the first time in front of one hundred thousand people.

Whatever was here with them was invisible to the eye. A growl rose from deep in Chloe's throat ahead of him, her tail up and curled. Lasers shot from her eyes— like the day he met Cara—as she scanned the perimeter, the blue light hitting what looked like an invisible shield surrounding them.

Brett swallowed hard and tensed. Nope. They definitely weren't alone.

Paco whispered in his ear. "Get ready…"

The shield dropped, exposing an army of black-winged thugs with menacing stares. Men of all shapes and sizes surrounded them. Nothing like the Angelorum Guardians, these guys looked like they'd been plucked off the street and had wings grafted to their bodies.

A battle cry sounded and they charged.

Paco grabbed Brett, turning them both invisible and dragged him away from the impending fray. Their team fell into formation, back-to-back, and went full force at their enemy.

Angelic swords met their mark, taking out a quarter of the motley crowd within the first few minutes. Brett couldn't believe his eyes as the angelic swords turned the black-winged Nephilim into columns of black sand with each death blow before collapsing into piles and blending into the tarmac.

Paco slowly circled them around to get closer to the plane while Simon and Cara fought in a coordinated dance nearby. Without seeing one another, they lunged and parried in tandem, slashing and spearing the less skilled demonic Nephilim.

Meanwhile, Chloe prevented the ones caught in her laser from advancing while Michael and Isaac held off another couple to his left. As someone who knew what it took to be proficient in martial arts, Brett was awestruck by Michael's prowess. Using his knives two-handed, between the aerial moves and leveraging one opponent against another, he was taking on five at a time and winning. Michael was a sight to behold. Brett let out an appreciative whistle, glad he couldn't be heard behind their veil.

Meanwhile, Angel and Zeke took on the demon Nephilim by air. White and black feathers flew in a jumbled blur as high-pitched squawks filled the air and the layer of black sand accumulated on the asphalt tarmac.

Brett's jaw hung slightly open, feeling like he was watching a three-dimensional video game. Only it was real. He couldn't forget that.

Luke and Kai were holding their own with a bunch of the others farther away from the plane.

Out of the corner of his eye, Simon and Cara disappeared from sight and the stairs surreptitiously touched the ground on the other side of the plane.

"When Simon returns, you're next," Paco said. "For now, we stay here out of sight and out of the way."

Fine with him; he enjoyed watching their team kick some ass.

No sooner did he have that thought than a crimson slash appeared across Luke's wing followed by an inhuman squawk when Kai ducked. Luke spun around. Pushing Kai out of the way, he blocked a stab to the heart and knocked the other Nephil to the ground. With a wide slash of his blazing sword, he cut the black-winged Nephil's head from his shoulders. The sound of sand pouring onto the pavement signaled the black-wing's defeat.

Simon reappeared without Cara, sword drawn and ready to fight. He jumped back in to assist with the quickly dwindling number of black-winged misfits.

Brett glanced under the plane; the stairs were gone.

"Let's go." Paco led him by the shoulder. "I'll call the captain when we're closer," he said, touching the Bluetooth in his ear.

Brett swelled with pride for their team, staying glued to the action as he and Paco drew closer to the plane. The team was much better skilled than these evil dudes.

A woman's scream ripped through the air from inside the hanger, freezing them in place.

"Fall back," shouted a high-class English accent. A man wearing an expensive suit emerged dragging a woman in a black dress and high studded heels, her head covered in a burlap bag. Next to him, two beefy black-winged Nephilim dragged out an unconscious Noah.

The remaining ragtag black-winged Nephilim leaped into the air on the English guy's command and flew into formation behind him.

Zeke and Angel touched down next to Simon, breathing heavy. Their wings furled and disappeared.

"Escher, you're such a piece of shit, you know that?" Angel said and spat on the ground.

"*Tsk-tsk.* That truly is a matter of opinion, Benedictine. So nice to see you again, Old Chap," Escher smiled politely.

This guy was a fucking demon? He looked like he shopped on Bond Street.

The woman struggled in his arms, getting nowhere. "You fucking prick," she gritted.

Brett's heart dropped. He knew that voice… Wait a second, those shoes.

Escher's fingers tightened on her biceps, and then he ripped off the hood.

"Roxy!" Brett screamed and broke free from Paco, escaping the veil.

He ran full tilt at the guy named Escher.

# Chapter 59



*CARA*

CARA BIT HER NAILS as she watched the fight from the plane window, her heart thumping wildly behind her ribcage. At least their blessed weapons were as effective against these new Nephilim as they were against the plain vanilla soulless, giving Kai and Michael equal chances to defend themselves. Kai had yet to use Achanelech's blade.

*"Duck!"* she screamed to Kai through their telepathic link as one of the Dark Ones' Nephilim swung his weapon straight at Kai's head.

He ducked but the sword bit into Luke's wing.

*Shit.*

She raised her hand to send out some distance healing.

"Cara Collins… at last we meet."

Cara jumped and spun toward the voice behind her.

The first thing she noticed was his eyes. Dark red. Impeccably dressed, he carried a staff. His black hair was pulled back into a ponytail, revealing an otherwise handsome face.

A shiver shot straight to her toes. She recognized him from the portrait on the Meeting Room's painted ceiling.

"Lucifer," she said and tried to swallow past the dry lump in her throat.

He tilted his head. "My friends call me Luc Morningstar this side of Hell."

"You have friends?" she asked before she could stop herself.

His smile bordered on charming. "As unbelievable as it may be, yes, I do have a friend or two."

Cara's internal alarms sounded, reminding her of what Constantina had said during her training about Lucifer's guise when she'd asked why he was painted as a beautiful angel rather than as a demon. *"To remind us all he was once loved and that sometimes evil comes in beautiful packages."*

Clever, she thought. *What better way to vanquish your enemy than to put them at ease and appear unassuming?*

"Are you here to kill me?" she asked, surreptitiously reaching for one of her knives.

"Not today, Miss Collins. You're worth nothing to me dead." Then he eyed her hand and pointed his staff. "Your weapons won't be of much use." He slipped a knife from her wrist sheath before she even detected his movement. "Here, allow me."

Her mouth dropped open as he plunged the knife into his own chest, wearing a wide grin. Without flinching, he stabbed himself repeatedly. "See? Pointless. To destroy me, you'll have to be much more creative."

He returned the knife to her sheath as quickly as he'd taken it.

"Then why are you here?" she asked tentatively, afraid to breath or move.

"To ensure you are in a position to help me when the time is right," he replied.

"To help you? Why would I help you?"

He planted his staff in front of him, and chortled. "Because you'll have no choice."

Despair reached up and grabbed her by the throat. A moment later, melodic music resounded in her head and the voice from her Calling whispered sweet sounding words only she could hear, dissipating her doubt. She couldn't understand the language spoken yet the message was clear: she wasn't alone.

Straightening her spine and looking him straight in the eye, she smiled serenely. "Don't be so sure about that… Luc."

"May you be a worthy adversary, Miss Collins." He glanced out the plane window. "I see my diversion is working nicely."

Cara looked to see what he meant. She gasped when she saw Roxy and Noah being held outside, and Brett running as fast as he could toward them.

"I leave you with this," Luc said, followed by a prick on her neck.

Her hand flew up. She pulled her finger away to find a small red stain from a drop of her blood. "Damn you!" She wanted to give herself a swift kick for being stupid enough to turn her back on him.

"Already been done," he whispered, his voice fading.

She whirled around, not surprised to find he was gone. He was good, she'd give him that. Then again, he'd had an eternity of practice. Whatever it was, he'd gotten what he'd come for.

Easily.

One thing was certain: if she planned on winning the battle, she needed to up her game. Rubbing the stinging skin on her neck, she wondered what he'd just done to her.

# Chapter 60



*MICHAEL*

BRETT RAN BY HIM screaming at the top of his lungs, straight toward Escher Grant and his demon horde.

"King!" Roxy yelled, her eyes wide with fear as she struggled in Escher's arms.

*Is he out of his mind?* Michael wondered and moved to go after him.

Simon grabbed his arm. "Stay put. Paco has this."

A strong breeze blew after Brett. Then he disappeared and all was silent.

"King!" Roxy yelled again, her tears trailing black eye make-up down her face.

"You are an annoying woman," Escher said, and shook her hard, snapping her head to the side.

*We need to do something,* Michael pleaded silently to Simon, his hands twitching at his sides. At least Cara was safe in the plane.

*Be patient.*

"Jus' let her go," Angel growled.

Escher narrowed his eyes. "And why should I do that?" He gazed down at her; she dangled like an angry ragdoll from his hand. "I'm a little peckish. Maybe she'll taste good."

"Fuck off, asshole," she gritted.

He clamped his hand on her jaw and pulled her face toward his. "What do you say, chippie? Give your tasty soul to Escher, won't you?" His upper-class accent slipped to reveal less polished roots.

"Never," she ground out, unable to move her mouth.

"We'll see about that," he lowered his lips to hers.

Out of nowhere, an angel wearing a white tunic and pants with high-arching white wings appeared next to them. He clasped his hands in front of him and slowly shook his head. "I wouldn't do that if I were you, Amon," he said, his voice even and calm.

Escher's head snapped up. "Mind your own business."

Michael held his breath. *Could it be… ?*

"You know the rules. Consumption requires consent. She refused you. I'm sure the Angelorum would happily accept your forfeiture."

Escher snarled at him.

"I refuse, you son of a bitch," Roxy spit at him, and then glanced at the angel. "Thanks, whoever you are."

*"Who are they talking to?"* Simon asked.

Michael kept his eyes glued to the three. *"You can't see him?"*

*"See who?"* Simon asked slowly.

*"Jonas."* Michael and Cara answered in unison. Michael glanced up at the plane to see Cara's distraught face pressed to the window.

At the mention of his name, Jonas looked directly at him. Now Michael knew what Cara meant when she described his intense purple eyes. *"Messenger Swift."*

*"Why can I see you?"* Michael asked telepathically, his heart pounding uncontrollably.

A smile came to Jonas's expressionless face, making him look almost human. *"Worry not, Messenger. I'm not here for you today. You've seen the dead, hence you can see me."*

*Huh?* He didn't stumble through his day tripping over dead people. Jonas had to mean his father's visit six months after his death. The night at the dojo his father appeared to tell Michael he'd been chosen to be Called as an Angelorum Messenger.

Escher shook Roxy. "I wouldn't thank him if I were you, ducky."

"Why's that?" she sneered.

In a blur of motion, Escher swiped a knife he had hidden in his jacket across her throat with surgical precision. Her eyes bulged and her lips flapped open and closed as a sea of red spilled down over her dress.

*"No!"* A shrill scream from Cara inside the Gulfstream ripped through Michael's head. He pressed the heels of his hands to his temples as the sound jostled his brain.

"Because he's here to collect your soul," Escher said and dropped her to the ground in a lifeless heap.

Jonas glared at him and growled. Escher looked away, unable to meet Jonas's gaze.

Michael gasped and shrunk back as Jonas morphed from his angelic form into a ten-foot towering reaper complete with black robe and scythe. "I look forward to the day that I can release the souls inside you, and deliver you to the one prison you'll never escape." The demonic timbre of his voice raised every hair on Michael's body.

"Promises, promises," Escher said.

"I never make promises I can't keep, demon," replied Jonas before melting back into his serene angelic guise. "Your pride just sealed your fate," Jonas added with a tip of his head, and then engulfed himself and Roxy in a circle of light.

Michael watched Jonas tenderly separate Roxy's soul from her bloody body inside the light and tuck her glowing form under his wing. Instead of taking her up and away, he flew over to where Michael stood.

*"Will you take Miss Collins a message for me?"* Jonas asked telepathically and glanced at the plane.

"Yes," he whispered, enthralled by Jonas's purple gaze. His breath hitched as his brain failed to fully process what his eyes had seen. Michael tipped his chin toward where Jonas had stood with Escher. *"Why did you change forms a minute ago?"*

Jonas tilted his head. *"Not every soul is taken to Heaven, Messenger Swift. Some are dragged to Hell. My attire varies accordingly."*

Michael chewed his lip and nodded. *"What's your message?"*

*"Tell Miss Collins that she must return to the meadow to find the answers she seeks."*

*"I'll tell her,"* Michael responded. Unsure of what the message meant, he committed it to memory.

Then Roxy whispered in Jonas's ear and he nodded. She smiled peacefully at Michael. *"Tell King I'm okay, and that I love him. Don't let him feel guilty, promise?"*

"Promise," he whispered as a single tear trailed down his cheek.

*"Have faith, Messenger Swift,"* Jonas said. *"That message is for you."*

And they were gone.

A strong gale filled the air in their wake, and the sky filled with white wings as the reinforcements arrived and uncloaked.

If only they'd come a few minutes earlier…

# Chapter 61

*BRETT*

BRETT LOOKED ON IN HORROR as Roxy's body crumpled to the ground, covered in blood. He struggled with every ounce of strength he had against Paco and Angel who had him locked in an iron embrace under a veil of invisibility.

"*No!* Oh no," he cried. His legs buckled and he dragged the Guardians to the ground with him. "He killed her!" His eyes blurred and hot tears flooded his cheeks.

"I'm so sorry, m'ijo," Angel said, his voice thick with emotion.

"Why didn't you save her?"

"Not everyone is meant to be saved," he said gently, his eyes as wet his Brett's. "She was a good girl, that Roxy."

"He dies. He needs to die," Brett gritted out, hate burning a hole in his chest. "I'm going to destroy him, whatever it takes."

Angel and Paco lifted him to his feet. "Don't talk foolish. If anyone deserves that honor, it's me," Angel said, pain blazing in his eyes. He wrapped his arm around Brett's shoulder, squeezing him hard to his side. "I've been after this bastard for the better part of one hundred and fifty years. He's not easy to catch."

"Why are you after him?" Brett roughly brushed away the wetness on his cheeks with the back of his arm, caught off guard by Angel's admission. It was deeply personal, whatever it was.

Angel pressed his lips together and looked away. For a second Brett thought he wasn't going to answer. Instead, he turned back and shook his head, not able to meet Brett's eyes. "He stole someone from me, too," Angel whispered. "And he'll pay if it's with my last dying breath."

"Tell me what to do. I want in," Brett said vehemently.

"You start by getting on that damn plane," Angel said and pointed to the private jet.

"Done. What else?" Brett said and ground his teeth.

"You accept your Calling as a Messenger when it's offered. Then you discover your gifts and focus on your mission. When the big party is over, we'll save Escher for ourselves. We'll send him to Hell together," Angel said.

"It's a deal," Brett shook Angel's hand, but the bargain didn't lighten the weight of Roxy's death.

A moment later, white wings dive-bombed the demons from the sky. The team left on the ground joined the fray with weapons blazing.

Angel's brown eyes warmed as he clasped Brett's shoulder. "I'll take care of Roxy, m'ijo. You go to the Sanctuary." Then he traded a look with Paco. "Take him to the plane, and I'll have Isaac get the others."

Brett's shoulders slumped. "I'll pay for the funeral," he said over the lump in his throat.

"Don't worry. I'll take care of everything. Now go," Angel said, letting go of them and heading off into the melee.

"Brett," Cara said as Paco escorted him into the plane. The pilot secured the door behind them, and then retreated to the cockpit.

Cara's green eyes were filled with tears. She threw her arms around him. "I'm so sorry about Roxy," she whispered.

"I couldn't save her," he choked out, pressing her close. He'd watched Roxy die, unable to do anything to prevent it. Nothing. *Nada.*

"I know," Cara whispered and kissed his hair. "It happened so fast... even I couldn't save her."

Brett buried his face deep next to Cara's neck and tightened his grip around her, wanting to find relief. The sweet smell of her skin and hint of her shampoo provided comfort as he let his grief overtake him. He wept on her shoulder, clutching her as if his life depended on it, trying to purge the pain gutting his insides—afraid that if he let go, he would shatter at her feet.

Her arms wrapped around him like iron bands, followed by a wave of loving energy that washed over him gently, caressing him down to his soul.

"She was my best friend," he managed to say, only able to breathe through his mouth with his overstuffed sinuses. His head ached and all he wanted to do was curl up on the leather bench seating behind them in a fetal position and disappear.

He squeezed his eyes shut. What would Angel tell her family? What would *he* tell her family?

The Rexton clan had practically adopted him when he met Roxy in college. She was the youngest child, the only girl, and the apple of her four bruiser brothers' eyes. It was because of the Rexton brothers that Brett took up mixed martial arts. Her brother, Skylar, had been Brett's trainer and close friend since he turned twenty. It wasn't unusual for Brett to fly him in to join legs of King Metaljam tours. The thought of telling Sky about Roxy turned his stomach.

Outside of Roxy, her brother, and the AABC guys, he couldn't claim a long list of real friends. Business associates and acquaintances, yes. Friends, no. Losing Roxy cut him deep. He couldn't imagine life without her there to keep him in line and to manage his professional life. Hell, to manage his whole life.

"Let's sit down," Cara whispered and dropped her arms. Taking his hand she led him to a nearby seat. "I'll be right back."

She returned with a wad of tissues which he gladly accepted, and then sat down beside him.

"Sorry. I didn't mean to unload like that," he said as he wiped his eyes and blew his nose, his head still feeling like it might explode from the pressure behind his eyes. "Thanks…"

"She was your best friend. Enough said." Leaning over, she kissed the side of his head.

Brett flipped back to the anger stage of his grief and frowned. "Escher Grant will pay, if it's the last thing I do, Cara," he said, gritting his teeth.

Cara's eyes bore into him and she squeezed his hand. "They all will, Brett. And we'll do it together. I promise."

He nodded and decided to keep his and Angel's plan to himself.

"They're here," Paco said quietly from behind them, and dropped the stairs for the others to board.

He and Cara popped up out of their seats to greet them. Chloe trotted in first looking like she was ready for the Westminster dog show in her pink coat. Kai and Michael spilled into the plane next, followed by Luke with his bloody wing askew.

Simon and Isaac boarded after Luke, struggling with Noah's dead weight between them. "Paco, get the pilot. We need to make tracks," Isaac barked as he and Simon laid Noah down in a large carpeted opening between two one-seat rows. Lucky for them, the custom interior had plenty of space to maneuver.

Zeke popped in last as Cara ran over to Noah. Simon and Isaac backed away to give her room.

"Luke, I'll get you next. Stand over by Simon and Isaac while I work on Noah." Cara swept her gaze over the rest of them. "I'll look at everyone one by one after I get these two fixed up."

Other than some cuts and scrapes, everyone else looked fine.

Brett glanced out the nearest window. The tarmac was empty with the exception of mounds of black sand lying in random patterns and covering a wide swathe around the plane. By his estimation, the remains of more than one hundred demon Nephilim littered the asphalt.

"Where's Angel?" Brett asked, expecting to see his friend before they left.

"Taking care of Roxy," Zeke said with a sympathetic look.

Isaac spoke up. "Change in plans. I'll be staying behind in place of Noah. We'll handle everything on this side with Angel, including a cover story for Roxy's death that doesn't include Brett."

"But—"

Isaac met his eyes with an ice-blue stare. "I'm sorry, brother, it's the only way. Trust us. We'll do right by her."

A lump rose up in the back of Brett's throat. All he could do was nod.

The pilot parted the curtain, looking shaken, and emerged with Paco. "Are you ready for takeoff?"

"Yes, Captain," Isaac said. "Si, you got this from here?"

Simon clenched his jaw and nodded. "Yeah."

"Zeke, let's go," Isaac said and disappeared through the cabin door. Zeke followed, and glanced back at Cara. "Take care of my boy, doll."

"I have it," she said with a tight smile.

The door slammed shut with a *thunk*. Simon secured it from the inside and took a seat near Paco and Kai as Cara's light show descended in full force. The light expanded, pushing out a forceful breeze that flew over Brett's skin. He stumbled back and caught the edge of one of the seats next to Michael who'd had the foresight to get the farthest away before Cara did her thing.

Unable to look away, Brett prayed his gifts would be as cool and as useful. Something that could bring down Escher, but good.

Michael grasped his forearm. "Hey, let's go back there a second." He tilted his chin toward the back of the cabin. With Cara's breeze at their backs, they left the others and made their way to the farthest row, slipping into two of the four seats flanking a sleek wood table.

"You were great out there," Brett said. "I saw you from where Paco had us cloaked."

"Thanks." Michael smiled sadly and took a deep breath. "I have a message for you… from Roxy."

Brett's shoulders tensed. "What do you mean?"

"I see dead people sometimes." He shrugged. "I guess it's one of my gifts."

Goosebumps rose on Brett's arms. "Did you see her after she died?"

Michael nodded. "She wanted you to know she was okay, and not to feel guilty over what happened. And that she loves you."

Brett swallowed and his vision blurred again. "She said that?"

"Yeah. The guilt part? She made me promise not to let you feel guilty." Michael rested his hand on Brett's shoulder. "Can you help me keep that promise?"

At least he didn't have to promise not to avenge her death. That would've been a promise he couldn't have kept. "Yeah," he choked out, trying to get his shit back together. Cara was one thing, but he couldn't handle more waterworks in front of anyone else.

Kai approached them a few minutes later. "Hey. Cara wants to check Michael over."

"I'll head up with you," Brett said, the lump in his throat finally back under control.

"Brett, I'm so sorry about Roxy," Kai said clapping him on the back and pulling him into a brief man-hug before they joined the others.

He had to admit, the outpouring of support from the group warmed him. He felt better. Not so alone. Maybe this whole cluster fuck would lead to something good. New friendships even.

By the time they reached the front, Luke was seated and looked good as new, his wings no longer visible outside his black uniform. Noah had been moved to one of the seats that flattened into a bed. He still looked the same… unconscious.

"He all right?" Brett pointed to Noah.

Cara wore a worried look, her hands planted on her hips. "His energy's good. His breathing and heart rate are fine. But he's unresponsive. I don't get it."

"Demon magic," Paco chimed in, arms crossed over his broad chest. "Good that we're taking him to the Sanctuary. They'll be able to pull him out of it. It's not the first time Escher has woven a spell." Then he added under his breath, "*Pendejo.*"

*"Asshole" wasn't nearly a strong enough insult,* Brett thought.

The engines rumbled to life. Except for Chloe who was curled up in a pink ball asleep on one of the leather seats, they all looked a little rough and in need of a stiff drink.

"Buckle up," Simon said and took his seat.

Brett sat next to Michael while Kai took the seat across the aisle.

Kneeling down next Noah, Cara touched his wrist, and then placed her hand on his heart one more time. Rising, Cara swayed on her feet.

"Come sit down, love," Simon said, patting the seat next to him.

She spun a slow circle suddenly looking disoriented and stumbled. "I forgot to tell you…"

A look of worry etched across Simon's forehead. "Are you all right?"

"Lucifer was here," she said, ignoring his question.

*Lucifer? That Lucifer?* Brett thought.

Cara held her cheeks and giggled like she was high. "His friends call him Luc Morningstar."

Simon, Michael, and Kai all unbuckled and jack-in-the-boxed out of their seats, looks of worry turning to panic.

Simon bolted over to her, and gently captured her arm. "When? When was Lucifer here?"

No response.

"Cara?" Simon asked as she stared into space.

No longer hearing him, she pulled out of his grasp and spun in a slow circle. "He'd said I'd help him. But I won't. I just wish I knew what he injected into my neck," she mused.

Then her head fell back and she collapsed onto the carpet.

The plane took off and all hell broke loose.

# Chapter 62



*KAI*

"LUKE, GET MY MEDICAL BAG!" Kai barked as he dropped to his knees next to Cara and fought the strong sense of déjà vu. This would be the second time in as many months he'd been charged with saving Cara at the hand of a demon.

Simon was poised on the floor next to him with a look of controlled panic behind his eyes, ready to assist. This, too, was becoming a habit.

Kai touched his shoulder. "Hang tight with me?"

Simon nodded, his jaw twitching.

Luke handed him the metal case from where he'd left it next to Noah. Kai removed the stethoscope and took her vitals.

"Her heart rate is slightly elevated and her skin seems hotter to the touch than normal," Kai said, his eyes fixing on Simon's. "She's running a fever. I'll draw some blood and use the mini-lab. Noah should've left it near the cockpit for me when he loaded the bags earlier. Roll up her sleeve for me."

Simon blew out a breath and did as he was told, easing the black garment up her arm and removing her wrist sheath.

*Damn it, Cara. Why didn't you say something sooner? The fucking King of Darkness injects you with something and you don't think to bring that up? And you think I keep shit from you?*

Kai fished a syringe from his kit, maintaining his calm exterior while blood pulsed through his ears in an out-of-control conga beat. The plane's climate control blew cool air over him, drying the moisture beading over his lip.

*Don't do this to us again, Cara. Hear me?*

Michael and Brett hovered nearby looking equally as distraught.

Kai sank the syringe into her vein and drew a vial of blood. Enough to keep him busy for the six-and-a-half-hour plane ride to the Sanctuary.

He looked up into Simon's expectant eyes. "Make her comfortable in one of the reclining chairs. I'm going to be at this for a while." He handed Simon the ear thermometer, stethoscope, and blood pressure cuff. "Check her every thirty minutes, write down the results, and bring them to me. I'll be working in the galley." Kai gave himself a mental pat on the back for teaching Simon some basics, even if only to boost his confidence. Given Cara's evolving condition, Kai was thankful for the extra help.

"Got it," Simon said, wearing a brave face. But he couldn't hide the haunted stare that Kai knew so well.

*"The prophecy? Could this… ?"* Michael's voice hitched, echoing in Kai's head.

Simon's shaky reply followed. *"Too soon. I'm almost sure of it."*

Kai's pulse quickened as he eavesdropped on their private conversation.

*"What are you talking about?"* Kai asked. He'd never had the heart to tell them that he could tune into any conversation on any frequency if he tried. Though he seemed to default to the one used by Simon, Michael, and Cara. Even as the Center Stone of their original Trinity, he shouldn't be able share that link. His private channel with Cara was even more unusual.

Simon's eyes flashed up and filled with surprise. *"You can hear us?"*

*"Yeah, and then some."*

Simon swept a hand over his face and traded a glance with Michael. "Let me move Cara, and then Michael and I will follow you to the galley."

At Michael's request, Brett stationed himself at Cara's side, and then Simon and Michael followed him back to the kitchen area.

Simon closed the curtain behind them, while Kai hauled the minilab up onto the galley table and cracked it open. He removed the laptop first, and then powered up all the equipment.

"I'm listening," said Kai as he worked while Michael and Simon shifted uncomfortably on their feet. "And start at the beginning." He glanced at Simon. "We have plenty of time until your next check on Cara."

After Michael and Simon finished recounting Cara's run-in with Jonas, her destined date with Lucifer, and the meetings he'd missed, every hair on his body stood on end.

"Sorry. Everything had been on a need-to-know basis up until now," Simon said.

Kai snapped and pounded the table. "I'm Cara's physician and the Center Stone of your Trinity. You didn't think I deserved to know?" he said, feeling his face pinch with annoyance but knowing his anger had more to do with his frustration over his own screwed up life and the place Cara held in his heart than her medical needs. He momentarily wondered how much Simon had to do with keeping him ignorant. Regardless of how he still felt for Cara, he'd never do anything to hurt them or their relationship.

"It's not personal, Kai," Michael said evenly as if reading his mind.

Kai sighed and shook his head. "Sorry I snapped. I appreciate the heads-up. Simon, let me see what's happening with our girl here in the lab while you go out and take care of her. 'Kay?"

Simon's lips tightened. He nodded and said, "Just don't let anything happen to her, Kai. If anyone can save her, it's you." There was no mistaking the anguish written on his face as he turned and disappeared through the curtain back into the cabin.

Simon's words hit Kai in the chest. He hoped more than anything that their hypothesis was correct—that Lucifer didn't inject her with something lethal—and that he wouldn't be needed to pull any miracles out of a hat.

Because this time, he was fresh out.

# Chapter 63

*CARA*

Cara awoke on the plane with Kai, Brett, Simon, and Michael all hovering over her. She watched four pairs of wide eyes in varying shades of blue fill with relief.

"Why are you looking at me like that?" she asked.

"You mentioned Lucifer had injected you with something and then promptly collapsed as we took off," Kai said, sounding as annoyed as he was relieved.

"I remember," she said, reaching for her aching head. "Everything started to spin and then went black."

"I ran some tests. Your white cell count is off the charts, so you're fighting whatever it is. Your temperature broke, but I'm still waiting on the next set of labs," Kai said and checked his watch. "Another ten minutes."

Simon squeezed her hand, followed by a taste of his lemony fear. "How are you feeling?"

"I'll be fine," she said and managed to sit up. She clasped her forehead as a wave of dizziness hit her. "Lucifer wasn't trying to kill me. At least not yet. In his words, I'm worth nothing to him dead. He needs me… for something. I just don't know what."

"Something requiring a change to your body chemistry I'd guess, and probably only a means to an end. I'll figure it out, but I need the Angelorum lab to do it," Kai said with a look of determination.

"You scared the shit out me." Brett stood frowning with his arms locked across his chest, his eyes glistening. After Roxy, she totally understood. Losing two friends in one day would've been… unspeakable.

"Ditto," Michael smiled warmly.

"Sorry," she said and reached for them. Michael gave her his hand freely while Brett gave his begrudgingly, and she squeezed them both. "I'll try not to do it again."

They nodded and went to sit down.

Kai kissed her forehead. "Glad you're back," he said and went to fetch her labs, leaving her with Simon who gathered her into his arms and crushed her into his chest. "You scared me, too," he whispered so the others couldn't hear.

Untucking her head, she gazed up into his haunted eyes. "Don't worry. I'm fine." Her lips met his in a warm kiss. He gave her a final squeeze, and then led her by the hand back into the one private sleeping berth, shutting them inside. Sitting down, he reclined the sleeper seat into the flat position and pulled her on top of him.

"I just want to hold you," he whispered, his eyes carrying a quiet desperation.

She kissed him again and melted down into his arms. "I love you," she said and slept the rest of the flight on Simon's chest.

# Chapter 64

*CARA*

***France. Angelorum Sanctuary. Wednesday, May 29, 10:45 PM GMT +1***

PANIC GRIPS CARA HARD as she lies blindfolded and immobile on the cold concrete floor, struggling to breathe. A searing pain in her upper back forces her to take shallow breaths, while the rest of her bones ache with dull pain. Lying partially on a downy blanket, soft and warm through her thin clothing, she tries to roll on top of it and away from the cold, hard floor.

A muffled moan escapes her lips through the gag covering her mouth as she comes into full consciousness. She fights against the ties binding her hands and feet, wondering how she's gotten there. She doesn't remember. All she remembers is that Simon is in danger.

"*Shh*, don't fight. I won't hurt you," whispers a voice with a deep, familiar richness. Warm hands gently lift her, until she lies in what feels like the crook of a large muscular arm. Her pain lessens with her shift in position. "I'll remove the gag, and then the blindfold. Please stay quiet. I promise no harm will come to you."

She tastes the sweetness of truth in his words. A moment later, his energy hits her foggy brain with a burst of recognition. But how can that be? And then she knows…

He removes the gag. She runs her tongue along her teeth, trying to get rid of the overly dry sensation that fills her mouth.

"Where am I? And how did I get here?" she asks with caution, still blindfolded.

"There's been an accident. I brought you to safety." His hand gently tucks a strand of hair behind her ear with the touch of a lover.

She freezes.

His voice grows gruff to stifle the embarrassment she tastes. "Please accept my apology. I know you're betrothed. You have nothing to fear from me."

His next declaration comes through as a thought on her telepathic link, his voice shifting to a tone of reverence. *"I understand why he loves you so."*

Electricity snaps over her skin, the kind that kick-starts her heart. Confusion grips her, followed by a surge of apprehension as she thinks of Simon. "Why have you been following us? Who are you?" she asks, trying to clear the cobwebs from her head.

"A friend."

"Will you remove the blindfold?" she asks.

"Again, I apologize. Give me a moment," he says, and slowly edges up the fabric as she lies in the crook of his arm. She squeezes her eyes shut until it slips up and over her head.

Opening her eyes in tiny slits, she lets them adjust to the dim light. Then she glances up to look into the face of the rogue…

A knock at the door interrupted Cara's dream, reluctantly rousing her from an exhausted sleep. Her eyes fluttered open with the second soft knock.

*If I'd just been able to see his face,* she thought as the dream slipped away.

"Just a minute," Cara yelled and glanced at the clock. Between the jetlag, fighting, healing, and Lucifer's mystery injection, she was wiped. Some quick math told her they had landed less than an hour ago. So much for feeling refreshed after a quick nap. According to Kai, her body was still fighting Lucifer's injection. In the meantime, Kai would be in the lab finding out whatever he could.

After the third soft knock, Chloe's warm body deserted her and headed for the door.

Cara groaned and pressed the heel of her hand into her eye socket to dull the throbbing. Her head felt like it was swaddled in cotton. A wave of dizziness seized her when she stood. Steadying herself on the chair next to the bed, she waited until it passed and then padded over to open the door.

Constantina stood waiting demurely on the other side of the threshold wearing her white High Council robes. Her delicate Grace Kelly–like features were peaceful and glowing.

"Come in." Cara stifled a yawn with the back of her hand and stepped aside to let Constantina pass.

"I'm sorry to wake you, dear one." Concern touched Constantina's delicate brow. "You're not yet restored from your ordeal. Give me your hands."

Eyes at half-mast, Cara closed the door and complied without question. Constantina pushed energy like the lapping of ocean waves through Cara's hands, chasing away the exhaustion. The fog lifted, leaving her mind clear and refreshed.

*Better than a pot of coffee*, Cara thought, and gave Constantina a hug, hanging on for an extra second. "Thanks for the energy push."

Constantina squeezed her back and released her. "Kai, Michael, and Simon have fully briefed me on what transpired with Lucifer. We have our best scientists available to help Kai with his diagnosis. Are you feeling well enough to still meet with the Council before our meeting with the others later?"

"I should be fine after a shower," Cara said after a quick glance at her signature black yoga pants and T-shirt. She raked her hand through her bed head. "Give me fifteen minutes?"

Cara slipped a white guest robe over her clothing in the antechamber leading into the Angelorum Sanctuary. Pastel colored candles burned along a line of wall sconces, filling the room with the fragrance of summer lavender and sage.

"Are you ready?" Constantina's gaze was warm, her hand poised on the knob of the plain wooden door.

*As ready as I'll ever be.* Cara nodded. No longer able to avoid why she was here, tightness gripped her stomach.

Cara entered through the door behind Constantina, their footsteps echoing across the second floor catwalk into the cavernous, high-domed Sanctuary.

High-tech fixtures on the ceiling gave the illusion of natural light shining in from above. In front of them, five levels of bench seating circled the round room—enough to accommodate all three hundred of the Angelorum Watchers.

The seats designated for the High Council were one level down on the opposite wall. Eleven of which were currently occupied. Dressed in glowing white robes, the Council members rose in unison as she and Constantina reached the stairs.

Silently, they led the way to the ground floor.

Cara glanced down at the sand-filled elliptical enclosure, almost four hundred square meters with raised edges. The sight of the Trinity Stones filling the Trinity Pool stole her breath. She'd only seen them once before, with Constantina, after the Tribunal verdict two months ago. Flat, smooth, and triangular, the stones were held together by a gem in the center with a different rune inscribed at each point.

Small in size, several of them could fit in the palm of her hand. Each one represented a single Trinity of three souls who, now, or in the future, would play a part in an event that could tip the balance between good and evil.

A kaleidoscope of colors coursed through them as their unintelligible cries rang out to her telepathically, sharing secrets in a language she didn't understand. Something Constantina had told her came to mind: destroying the Trinity Stones destroys the souls and their destinies.

When Cara reached the ground floor, her eyes were hypnotically drawn to the center of the pool and the usual cluster with her Trinity Stone. Magnetically held together, the cluster contained the secrets of the Twelve.

Hopefully, she'd learn some of their secrets today.

The High Council filed in around the horseshoe-shaped table next to the Trinity Pool and sat with the exception of Angelis and Constantina.

"Welcome, Cara." Angelis reached out his arms in greeting, pulling her from her thoughts. He smiled and the skin around his warm brown eyes crinkled. An attractive middle-aged man, he looked more like a businessman, with his short brown hair peppered with grey, than the leader of an angelic protectorate. When she'd first met him at the Tribunal, she had expected a wizened old man with a white beard.

Cara smiled as he grasped her shoulders. "Thank you. It's an honor to be invited into your private Sanctuary."

Her eyes gravitated to his rounded upper lip, the only anomaly on his face. Like Constantina, as one of the three hundred Angelorum Watchers, Angelis was missing the philtrum over the top of his lip.

Dropping his hands, he pointed to the two empty chairs facing the Council. "Please. Be seated."

Cara's gaze swept over the Council. Although she'd seen them during the Tribunal, she'd be in trouble if she had to pick them out of a line-up. They looked only vaguely familiar.

Rather than joining the rest of the High Council, Constantina sat in the seat next to Cara, facing them.

Constantina said a few words in the angelic language to Angelis who nodded and said to Cara, "We'll speak only in English for your complete understanding."

"Before we begin, I'd like to introduce to you to the members of the High Council." He eyed Constantina. "I assume you have knowledge of basic Angelology. Is that a fair assumption?"

Cara blushed, recalling her confession to Constantina that she wasn't very religious. She swallowed. "I know the basics, but I'd appreciate some additional detail."

"Ah," Angelis nodded. "I shall do that." He paced in front of the others as they sat quietly, waiting for their introductions.

Locking his hands behind his back, he reminded her of a college professor about to teach to a class. "Each Council member belongs to one of the four Choirs of angels, and represents one of the twelve Orders of angels. For the sake of ease, I've asked each Council member to sit in hierarchical order." He smiled, adding, "No pun intended."

Cara couldn't help but smile back at his attempt at humor.

Angelis pointed behind him to Cara's left. "Starting with the First Choir, and the first three Orders. We call them the "invisible ones," because they embody divine light and wisdom. To the far left sits Sara, representing the Supernels; Christos, representing the Celestials; and Isiah, representing the Illuminations."

Each nodded a greeting to Cara as their names were called. Although they had different hair color, ranging from light to dark brown, and varied in age, they all had the same eyes: a glowing vivid blue not found in nature.

"Next, we have the Second Choir, and the three angelic Orders of pure contemplation. Seraphina represents the Seraphim. Her role is to keep divinity in order. As much as we encourage her to take another human name, she prefers this one," Angelis said, turning and softly chiding her.

Seraphina smiled at Cara. "When you've lived as long as I have, there's comfort in the familiar." She traded a glance with Angelis which led Cara to believe they might be more than friends.

Angelis pointed to the fifth seat. "Judah is our resident Cherubim, his order represents happiness." Judah, the youngest and most attractive of the Council members, gave Cara a friendly wave. He looked nothing like the iconic chubby child typically seen representing his Order.

Angelis pointed to his empty seat. "I represent the Thrones. We control energies and are responsible for the Flow and all the healing powers you tap into with your gift. On your right, we have the Third Choir. Ciara represents the Dominions. They are responsible for order and connectedness, balancing the spiritual and material worlds for mankind. Next to her we have Ezekiel, representing the Virtues responsible for interconnectedness. I'm sure you've heard Constantina mention to you once or twice, 'there are no coincidences'?"

Cara glanced at Constantina and nodded. How could she forget? Up until now, she hadn't really thought about how the various angelic Orders influenced their human lives. But it only made sense, didn't it? She'd never asked Constantina which Order she belonged to, and after that explanation, she was surprised it wasn't the Virtues.

Pointing further to his left, Angelis continued. "Virgil represents the Powers, our sponsoring Order and the fathers of our Nephilim. Their job is to stop demons from overthrowing the world. They are the angels of birth and death, and also provide our sixth sense as the angels of warning."

Virgil bowed his head to Cara. She tipped hers back.

Without thinking, Cara's hand shot up, waiting to be called on.

Angelis stepped aside and motioned for her to speak.

She looked at Virgil. "May I ask a question about the Transporters?"

Gray hair shorn close to his head, Virgil was one of the more elderly members of the Council. "You may," he said evenly. His eyes were a piercing cornflower blue bordering on purple.

"Are the Transporters part of your Order?"

"Yes, they are."

She folded her hands nervously in front of her. "Thank you." For what it was worth, she now knew something more about Jonas. A being of birth and death he'd said…

Virgil's gaze intensified. "That cannot be your only question, child."

Cara stared wide-eyed. *Um, yeah. Actually it was.*

His face softened and he nodded slowly, understanding settling into his features. "Ah. It's too soon, I see. Think on this: why is it the Transporters hold a special importance for you?"

Like a deer caught in headlights, her heart sank. She didn't have a clue. To think that she was the one chosen to lead the battle… At times like this, she thought there must surely be someone more capable than she was.

Sensing her discomfort, Virgil replied, "Fret not, young Cara. Always remember: symmetry exists in all things. The answer lies within the combined halves."

She gave him a wan smile, storing his wisdom for later.

"Thank you, Virgil. Let's carry on, shall we?" Angelis clapped his hands and turned to Cara's right. "The fourth and final Choir contains the three Orders considered the angels of the world. Hershel represents the Principalities who oversee global reform, religion, and politics. Next to him is Gabriel, representing the Archangels. They are the ones who govern the affairs of the Messengers and their families, and sometimes take human form to change the tide of human events. They have the ability to funnel energies bidirectionally between Heaven and Earth."

Angelis pointed to Constantina. "Finally, the Angels, the Guardians of humankind. Their job is divine inspiration and protection."

Taking his seat in the center of the horseshoe, Angelis said, "Now that we've dispensed with the formalities, let's address the matter at hand."

The thrum of the Trinity Stones grew louder in the background. Cara scanned their faces again, wondering about the traitor. It saddened her to think one of them had secretly fallen.

"Events have moved slowly over the last two months, but that's about to change. The Trinity Stones have confirmed more of the Twelve. Constantina will brief you later. In the meantime, the time has come for us to share more details regarding the Prophecy."

Cara's heart sped up.

"Since the time of Christ, the Sanctus Angelorum has provided the ballast against the pull of Lucifer and his fallen minions, the Dark Ones. In order to live, the fallen and their demons must prey upon the souls of men. Our job has been to maintain the delicate balance on Earth to ensure their power doesn't tip the scales too far in one direction. Are you familiar with the Book of Revelations, Cara?"

Cara shifted uncomfortably in her seat. "The Second Coming, Judgment Day… is that what you mean?"

"Yes. That's the one." Angelis grinned, a playful twinkle in his eye. "Our predecessors, Semyaza and the Watchers of old, were bound and cast down into the earth under the desert, where they remain, awaiting Judgment Day. I assume you recall the secret text of our existence, the Book of Human Angels? It's no coincidence that the Dead Sea Scrolls, penned during the same time period, contain the Book of Enoch and the story of the original Watchers. Our book contains an alternate plan, a loophole, if you will, for the Dark Ones… to escape Judgment Day."

The skin on Cara's arms tingled and rose in gooseflesh.

Angelis continued. "But they must win the battle you will lead in order to do so."

Cara's mouth went bone dry. She raised her hand again and waited for Angelis to acknowledge her. "I have two questions."

He bobbed his head. "Go on."

"How are twelve people going to wage a war against the Dark Ones?"

He smiled broadly, clapping his hand on a thin box in front of him that she hadn't noticed. "With spirit, ingenuity, and a well-hewn plan."

*As long as it's not "a wing and a prayer,"* thought Cara before she managed to ask her second question. "How does defeating us allow them to escape Judgment Day?"

Tapping the box again, he said, "My dear girl, that's part of the puzzle you and the others must solve. Not only does the Book of Human Angels contain our story, it contains the blueprint of your battle plan. Part of which is in this box."

Cara eyed the box, dreading the answer before she even asked the question. "Where's the other part?"

"Hidden… even from us. Your next mission will be to find it."
She was afraid he'd say that.

# Chapter 65



*KAI*

**France. Angelorum Sanctuary. Wednesday, May 29, 11:00 PM GMT +1**

"ARE ANY OF THE RESULTS back yet?" Kai asked the tall, attractive Nephilim physiologist as he entered the lab with a fresh cup of coffee. A poor substitute for sleep but his only acceptable option.

He planned to pick up where he'd left off with the comparative blood work of Cara's blood next to Zeke's. He figured he'd get a baseline before he dove into the results of the post-Lucifer injection samples.

He had Celine working on those. She was in the process of queuing up the test results based on the hourly samples he'd taken on the plane until Cara had awoken and disappeared with Simon. He drew one last sample when they'd arrived.

As for the growth spurt samples, they had been inconclusive. Celine needed to do a different type of genetic testing panel to see if Cara had the abnormality that caused Nephilim Adolescent Collapse Syndrome or what she called NACS. He'd sneak those tests in with the others during Cara's appointment.

"I may have figured something out," she said, walking over with a report in her hand. "Hold this." The nametag stitched to her lab coat read DR. CELINE, DAUGHTER OF ARIEL. At six foot three, she had the body of a well-built man in drag. But given Cara's ongoing changes, Kai had no doubt there was all woman underneath the white garment. The thought sent a shiver of loneliness through him.

Would he ever be able to make love to his wife again? He released a breath. God, he hoped so.

"Kai?" She rustled the report in front of him.

"Sorry, just thinking," he said, taking the report with his free hand as he drained his coffee cup.

She squeezed his shoulder and her eyes filled with concern. "You need to get some sleep. I can take it from here for a few hours."

He blew out a breath. "I can't. I need to keep going."

Celine nodded. "Something struck me while I was working on the sample from the plane. So I pulled one of the baseline tests you'd started. For your comparisons, did you use a sample from the refrigerator or a live donor?"

"Live donor. Why?" he asked.

Ignoring his question, she asked, "Whose blood did you use?"

"One of the young Guardians on our team," he replied.

Celine nodded. "Wait here." She walked into the refrigerator, closing the mammoth door marked with a biohazard symbol behind her. Inside, they stored samples of anything and everything imaginable—from tissue samples to diseases. They could probably wipe out the entire planet with the contents inside just one of the antechambers within the frozen sixteen hundred square meter room.

Celine emerged a few minutes later. "Bring the report I handed you."

He met her at the sophisticated piece of equipment located in the opposite corner of the lab.

"Let's try this." She placed the sample she retrieved from the freezer inside and punched in a series of sequencing codes. The machine sprang to life.

"What are you thinking?" Kai asked, rife with curiosity.

Arms crossed, tapping her foot, she said, "You'll see… maybe… if I'm right."

He chuckled. "You're very rarely wrong."

"True. It's part of my charm." She smiled warmly.

They'd worked together for the last several months since he started his assignment with the Angelorum. She'd been a brilliant lab partner and truly enjoyable to work with. Plus, she had a surprisingly good sense of humor.

Working had been the perfect distraction to keep his mind off of his family issues, giving him a release and allowing him to maintain his sanity. Over the last couple of months, Celine had supported him, giving him a crash course in Nephilim physiology down to the genetic level. Looking back, he was amazed that he'd actually been able to engineer the vaccine he'd used to save Cara.

The timer rang. Celine pressed the print button and the machine spit out the results.

Celine laid the documents side by side on lab table. "As I suspected… Cara is showing true adolescent markers. Here, see this?" She pointed to the chart.

"That spike?"

"Yes. It's a special protein that will disappear when she matures in Nephilim terms. You can't compare her to samples of post-adolescent Nephilim."

"So she really is going through adolescence? Why haven't we spotted it before?" he asked, wondering how he'd made such a blunder.

"We weren't looking for it." She frowned, and rubbed her chin while she paced next to him. "It never occurred to me until you sent the request from New York. Given her human age and the ages of the Guardians sampled for their DNA, I always assumed the vaccine was post-adolescent. It never occurred to me that the DNA would revert to adolescence once administered. From now on, you need to use test samples from Nephilim who haven't yet made the change."

Kai gave her a sideways glance. "What change?"

"The transition into Nephilim adulthood."

"Why do you look so worried?" Kai asked.

Celine stared at him gravely and shook her head. "We need to do the genetic testing as soon as possible to rule out NACS, but that's only one thing in a long list of worries. There's something else… but I need to do more tests to confirm it. If I'm right, the vaccine is adapting and Cara's human DNA is fusing with her Nephilim DNA in an unexpected way."

"How so?" Kai asked as a chill traversed his spine.

"Part of the DNA is expressing traits found only in the males of our species. She's carrying multiple distinct types of DNA inside her. In simple terms, she's becoming a chimera. This may explain the intensity of her adolescent urges and slightly aggressive behavior. My bigger concern is the impact on her skeletal structure."

Kai paled. "Male as in *man*?"

Celine arched a brow. "I don't expect her to grow male genitals if that's your concern. Come sit down. I'll explain." She led him over to a pair of chairs in the lounge area and spent the next hour explaining in excruciating detail what the "change" and the genetic abnormalities could mean for Cara. The phrase "uncharted territory" came up at least a dozen times.

Cara was afraid of how fast she was growing. In reality, there was a possibility she wasn't growing fast enough.

His reaction at the conclusion: *Shit.*

"At least there's a silver lining… kind of," she said, pointing to the table with the samples she was working on.

"And what's that?" Kai asked.

"Cara's body is fighting, and eliminating, most of what Lucifer injected into her.

Kai eyed Celine warily. "Most?"

She nodded. "All the foreign biomatter is being destroyed and absorbed into her body. Problem is, not everything in the syringe he used was biomaterial. Some of it was… um, mechanical."

Kai's eyebrows popped up. "Nanomaterials?"

"Yes. Microscopic computers."

"For what?"

"Could be anything. But we need to be prepared. They could be transmitting data about anything from her physiology to her location," Celine said over her tented hands.

Kai rubbed his temples and sighed. "That can't be good."

"We need to tell Constantina immediately about all of it. Honestly, I'm more worried about Cara's transformation and ruling out NACS than Lucifer's nanomaterials right now. After we break the news, you need to sleep, and then we need to lock ourselves in this lab until we can determine what's going on. It will take a few days to run all the protocols once we get the right samples," Celine said, and then placed a hand on his shoulder. "Don't worry, Kai. We'll have a team on hand when the time comes, in case we need to do emergency surgery."

A chill passed over Kai. He'd done this to her. "Let me tell Cara first, after the meeting. I owe her that…"

Celine's eyes were kind. "I understand. In the meantime, I'll start working on whatever protocols that I can. But we need to get her in here for those genetics tests. After that's done, we'll tackle the mechanicals."

# Chapter 66

*JESSA*

*Marin County, California. Serenity Spa. Wednesday, May 29, 2:00 PM PT*

"CAN WE HELP YOU with that?" Jessa asked from where she stood. A floral delivery guy maneuvered his way through the front door of the spa. At least she thought it was a guy. The arrangement was so large she couldn't see his face behind the flowers.

"I think I have it. Mind if I put it down on the front desk?" asked the masculine voice behind the bouquet.

"Um… how about over here instead?" Jessa led him away from the front door.

This had to be a personal delivery. The Spa's flowers had arrived yesterday.

Her receptionist, Callie, popped up. "Let me help you."

Among the three of them, they managed to get the flowers onto a table that normally held a hair care display.

"Can one of you please sign?" The delivery guy held out an electronic device with a stylus.

"Jessa, I'll sign. You open the card," Callie said.

"Make that cards," Jessa replied, removing both the small and larger envelope from the plastic cardholder. She opened the smaller one first.

CAN'T STOP THINKING ABOUT YOU. —BRETT

A wide smile spread across Jessa's face. *The feeling's mutual,* she thought, touching her fingertips to her lips. She'd revisited the feel of his kiss and his strong embrace over and over since Sunday morning. Those pleading blue eyes of his made her weak in the knees.

"Lemme guess, that cutie you met in New York?" Callie asked, all smiles as she settled back behind the reception desk, the roar of the delivery truck fading into the distance.

"Yup," Jessa said, aware of the sappy look she had to be wearing. She didn't exactly mention who Brett was when she'd told the girls about him. Much better that way—for everyone's sake.

"Sweet! Can't wait to meet him."

She suppressed a sniff. *If you meet him.*

Why couldn't she have a normal life? No visions, no psychotic stepfather with a pretentious British accent, no goons following her every move.

Escher's creepy henchmen were probably watching her right now. Out of spite, she looked out the front door and stuck her tongue out when Callie wasn't looking.

God, she hated her life. The only upside was her mother had left her enough money to live comfortably and independently. The best move her mother had ever made was insisting on a prenuptial agreement when she married that prig, and putting all her wealth in trust for Jessa.

The phone rang, and Callie picked it up. "Serenity Spa?"

Jessa tipped a rose woven amongst the flowers to her nose and inhaled its sweet smell. A date with Brett. What she'd give for that. The thought made her heart beat faster... if only she could ensure his safety.

Lost in pleasant thoughts, she mindlessly opened the second envelope and slid out a picture. Her breath seized in her chest. A black and white photograph of Brett with his band in New York City dated Monday, May 27th with a note in red marker.

IF HE SO MUCH AS BREATHES IN YOUR DIRECTION, I'LL RUIN HIM IN EVERY WAY THAT COUNTS. ALL MY LOVE, ESCHER

Callie hung up the phone and asked excitedly, "What was in the other envelope?"

Jessa just shook her head, not trusting herself to speak. Rather than bursting into tears like she wanted to, she took a deep breath and then said to Callie, "I'm going to do that thing again. You know the one where I work out my frustrations against my bastard stepfather?"

Callie gasped. "One of the notes was from him?" she asked in a hushed whisper.

Jessa nodded vigorously. "I'm a prisoner in my own life."

A look of pity crossed Callie's face. "Go for it. Your next appointment isn't for another thirty minutes."

Jessa stomped back to her office, slammed the door, and threw the lock. Best investment she'd ever made… soundproofing.

She stood in the center of the room and screamed until her lungs were empty.

# Chapter 67

*CARA*
*France. Angelorum Sanctuary. 11:55 PM GMT +1*

CARA SAT ALONE in the conference room located in the medical wing of the Angelorum compound, mulling over her meeting with the High Council.

Leather seats surrounded the oval wood conference table, easily large enough to seat twenty people. Pin lighting in the ceiling illuminated the room with a warm glow, and what looked like a translucent television screen covered one wall. The clean and modern design, coupled with the skillful use of wood, glass, and leather, gave the room a high-tech feel like the resort in Geneva where she attended an international investment banking summit two years ago.

Sipping a can of Diet Coke to beat back another wave of jetlag, she stared at the table with the weight of her responsibility draped heavily around her shoulders and fingered the diamond next to her engagement ring on her necklace. She wondered about the thin box Angelis kept touching.

Warm lips touched her ear. "Penny for your thoughts, and a dollar if I'm in them," Simon said before nibbling her earlobe.

She leaned back into him, a jolt of electricity traveling through her and coaxing a smile to her lips. "How about ten if you're naked?"

A deep chuckle rose from his throat. "For that, I'd gladly give you twenty." Dressed in black Guardian regalia, he sat down next to her. "You're early. How did your meeting go with the Council?"

She slumped into her chair. "Overwhelming. Kind of a "good news, bad news" scenario. Angelis said there's plan for the battle contained in the Book of Human Angels. That's the good news. The bad news is part of it is missing. Constantina said she'd brief us later."

He laid his hand on her shoulder, and leaned in to kiss her forehead. "We'll figure it out."

"Speaking of meetings, how was yours?"

Rubbing his brow, he sighed and shook his head. "Versailles is teaming with Dark Ones, and people have started to disappear."

"Kidnapped?"

Simon shrugged. "That or murdered."

Hairs raised on Cara's arms.

Jovial voices and footfalls sounded from outside and the door flung open.

Michael's tousled near-black hair popped through first, an amused glint in his eye. "Didn't I tell you there were some interesting options on the curriculum?" he said. Brett followed him in faded jeans and a T-shirt with the collar cut out.

"Yeah, but seriously? Any skin-on-skin contact, or live practice sessions?" Brett wiggled his eyebrows and gave Michael a crooked smile.

Kai walked in behind them looking distracted but the rose-colored blush on his cheeks showed he was listening. Cara could sense his embarrassment. "It's a simulation, actually," he mumbled.

Through the banter, Cara couldn't help but notice a synergy between the three of them. Seeing them together like this, she felt like an intruder in their private moment. At the same time, love for them all coursed through her. She was happy to see the pall of Roxy's death not dangling around Brett's neck. The distraction was probably exactly what he needed.

Simon cleared his throat next to her. Their conversation abruptly stopped.

Kai noticed her first. "Hey, guys." Then he frowned and sent a message over their telepathic link. *"Cara, I don't want to alarm you or Simon. But we need to speak when the meeting's over. I have your labs."*

*"Absolutely. Should I be worried?"*

His eyes tracked Michael and Brett to hide their discussion. *"I don't know."*

She resisted the urge to drag him into the hallway when she registered his bittersweet answer. But there wasn't anything she could do about it right now anyway.

Michael tried to wipe away his grin, slipping into a seat on the opposite side of the conference table. "How's it going?"

"Hi, guys." Brett tucked a clump of blond hair behind his ear and sat beside Michael.

Kai pushed back the chair next to Brett.

She crossed her arms in front of her and smirked. "So. What have you been up to?"

"Kai couldn't join us, but I gave Brett the tour." Michael coughed into his fist and said, "We were discussing some options for the Messenger coursework."

Simon's mouth split into a smug smile next to her. "Hmm. There's only one course of study that would have you all shifting in your seats like that."

"No need to spell it out, Simon." Michael turned red and gave him a warning look, casting a quick glance in her direction.

Cara rolled her eyes. "Oh, please. Like I don't know you're talking about Sensual Pleasures training. If you want my vote, do the woman in your lives a favor and take it."

Simon chuckled deeply next to her.

Kai tried to hide the dirty look he gave her. *"Thanks a lot."* He fired over their personal telepathic channel.

*"I never had any complaints."* She fired back innocently.

Brett laced his fingers behind his head, his dimple denting his cheek. "There's not much to improve on, but I'm willing to give it a shot."

Constantina glided into the room, closing the door behind her. She'd changed out of her robes and into a blue dress the color of her eyes, her blonde hair pulled back in a tight bun.

"Ah, I see you're all here. Good." She took a seat at the end of the table closest to them, and beamed at Brett and Kai. "I'm so pleased you've both officially accepted your Messenger Calling."

*"Congrats,"* Cara said to Kai telepathically. He flashed a look at her, and smiled. Given Kai's agnostic beliefs, this was a big step for him.

"When will I find out more about my real father?" Brett asked, tension filling his shoulders.

"Shortly." Constantina sat at the head of the table and clasped her hands. "Thank you all for your patience. Destiny sometimes takes a circuitous path as we follow our free will and make our choices. It also takes time to unfold, taking us on journeys we may not expect to have, yet delivering us exactly where we need to be. I think that will be true for all of you."

Investment banker to Soul Seeker. *Yeah. Circuitous was one word for it,* Cara thought.

"Up until now, Cara, you and Simon have walked alone in the knowledge of your place. Today, I will officially confirm more of the Twelve."

"How many more?" Cara asked Constantina, already knowing about Brett.

"Patience, dear one," she replied and pressed her lips together, her shoulders tense. "I've already shared some of this with you and Simon the night of our dinner last week. Angel wasn't all together wrong when he mentioned there was something I wasn't willing to reveal. There's a reason we're meeting in this part of the compound, and not in the section designated for the High Council."

"Is this about the traitor?" Simon's jaw clenched.

"Yes. What I didn't fully disclose was that I've suspected an infiltration since the time you were born," she said, glancing at Simon.

Cara frowned. "For almost one hundred and fifty years?"

Constantina nodded, pain reflecting in her sad smile. "That's why I secretly enlisted an old friend to help more than half a century ago outside the auspices of the High Council…before I descended into this lifetime. At my request, he agreed to descend for one lifetime and become the Wanderer."

"Was he murdered like Angel said?" Brett asked intently.

"Not by your definition," she said cryptically with a tight smile. "But that's not what I brought you here today to discuss." Constantina's eyes shifted from Brett to Cara. "Cara guessed rightly in New York that you, Brett, are the Third of the Twelve who will lead our battle against the Dark Ones."

Brett frowned at Cara. "You knew and you didn't tell me?"

Cara shook her head. "I'm sorry. It wasn't my place. But even so, if you hadn't lived through the last several days, would you even have believed me?"

He opened his mouth and then closed it, crossing his arms in front of his chest. "You have a point."

"Let Constantina speak," Simon said firmly.

"Thank you. Four of the Wanderer's children are destined to be part of the Twelve. Brett is but one."

Brett's lips parted in surprise. "There are four of us?"

"More actually. But only four boys—now gifted men—have been chosen. You are his third son."

"Who are the other three?" Brett asked anxiously.

"Two are near. We're still trying to verify the identity of his second son. He was the only child living outside of the United States, and whose surveillance arrangement was unknown to me."

A thousand questions screamed a path through Cara's head. She looked at Constantina. "Wait. I don't get it. Why do you call this man the Wanderer? Who was he?"

Constantina smiled sadly. "I called him that to protect his identity. No one knew his earthly purpose except for him, I and, eventually, Benedictine. He was very special, and so was his bloodline. We needed him to create offspring and to keep his children hidden. How better to hide them than as the children of other men? His sons, together, form an essential function to the Twelve. Without them, we will not succeed."

"I don't understand. Is that why I'm here?" asked Kai, a shimmer of apprehension in his eyes.

Constantina smiled kindly at him. "Dear one, how much do you know about your real father?"

Kai swallowed and his eyes glistened. Unconsciously, he moved back deeper in his chair, distancing himself from the table. The bitter lemonade taste of his fear danced on her tongue.

"Not much," he whispered, shaking his head.

She said gently, "You, dear one, are the Wanderer's first born."

Constantina's words hit Cara right between the eyes. *Kai and Brett are brothers?* Her mouth hung open and her eyes bounced between their faces, searching for the similarities.

She traced the same angle of their high cheekbones and the shape of their eyes. The color was similar yet not the same. The fullness of their lips—yes—the same. The shape of their noses was different, providing the largest disparity. Piece by piece, she plucked out the resemblance. As Cara thought back, she vaguely remembered Brett reminding her of Kai when they'd first met.

Cara watched shock spread across Kai's face, melting into understanding as he sat silent and stunned. Kai always thought his father had abandoned him. Now he knew that was the plan all along. Her heart wretched for him, knowing how much his father's abandonment had scarred him.

"Kai, Brett. Please understand, your father is an amazing soul. I can promise you both, even though he couldn't be with you, he loved you both very much."

A scowl played across Brett's face, his anger flaring. "Then how could he let someone else raise me?"

"He made the ultimate sacrifice in doing so. He did it to keep you safe."

Brett slammed his hand on the table. "What the hell does that mean?"

Constantina looked at both Kai and Brett. "He's never left you. You both still bear his gift."

Looks of confusion passed between them.

"Place your hands on the table," she said quietly.

Slowly, they lifted their hands onto the conference table and Cara spotted their rings. How had it not registered that they wore the *same* silver ring? She'd known Kai for almost ten years, and he never took his off.

She blinked. How had she missed such an obvious connection?

Her eyes were suddenly drawn to Michael who swayed, grabbing the table's edge to steady him. His shift in energy tripped her internal alarms. All color drained from his face, leaving it the color of rice paper—a sharp contrast with his near-black hair. His high cheekbones jutted out from his face, casting a dark shadow. Without warning, he jumped up and out of his chair, sending it crashing to the floor.

"No, no, no!" he shouted, shaking his head. "It can't be true," he mumbled, his eyes wild and unfocused.

*What the hell?* Panic shot through Cara, and she bolted from her chair followed by Simon. "Michael, what's the matter?"

Ignoring her, he ran for the door, shoving chairs roughly out of his path.

Simon strode after him.

Brett sat wide-eyed at the table, staring after Michael, while Kai sat lost in his own thoughts, barely noticing Michael's loud departure.

"Stop! Let him go," said Constantina. Simon froze in mid-stride inside the door.

Cara's head whipped back to Constantina. "Why? What's going on? Why did Michael freak out like that?"

A wan smile touched Constantina's lips. "Because inside Michael's pocket is a ring that looks exactly like Kai and Brett's." She took a pause and a deep breath before continuing. "Cara, Michael's father was the Wanderer. He's his youngest son…the fourth child."

# Chapter 68

*CARA*

PRESSING HER EYES SHUT, Cara absorbed the full force of the news. *Holy Mother in Heaven.* No wonder he freaked out. "We can't just let him go like that," she said softly.

"But we must. There's a journey Michael needs to make before he can move on… before we can move on. He must face his past in order for all of us to have a future."

"Past? What past?"

"Everyone has a past, Cara. It's a question of whether or not it holds you hostage. I'm afraid this is a necessary step for him to take as he becomes the Center Stone of another Trinity," Constantina looked deep into Cara's eyes. "There's only one person who can heal him… if she accepts her Calling."

Like tumblers inside a lock clicking into place, everything suddenly made sense. The smell of cinnamon, the shame, dark secrets that leave a stain on the soul—it all crystalized in Cara's mind. Michael wasn't the only one of her friends who had dark secrets.

There was only one other person Cara knew who held anything close to that buried deep in her past.

Sienna.

"There's one more thing that you all must understand." All eyes shifted to Constantina.

"Knowing that Michael Swift Sr. was the Wanderer in this life, isn't nearly as important as knowing who he is in Heaven. As I mentioned, a dear friend granted me a favor to descend in an *unawakened* state for one lifetime in an effort to repair a misstep he, myself, and one other made long ago."

Cara sifted through Constantina's words. *Unawakened.* That meant while Michael's father was alive he wouldn't have had any more knowledge of his prior existence than someone like her.

"Who was he, Mother?" Simon asked, tension riding over his shoulders.

"So much lies within a name, Chamuel. I wish you hadn't abandoned yours." She smiled serenely. "The Wanderer is the warrior who vanquished the Fallen during the Great War in Heaven..."

Cara's jaw dropped open as she recalled one of her first lessons in the meeting room above the Library with Constantina as they stared up at the ceiling murals.

*"See the other prominent angel in the painting to the right?"*

*"Yup," Cara said as she looked at the very beautiful, yet fierce-looking angel wielding a sword of brilliant light.*

*"That is the Archangel Michael who led the angelic army as they waged war and defeated Lucifer and his minions. In the end, Lucifer and his followers fell from the grace of God and were literally stripped of their wings and cast out of Heaven down to Earth... where they still reside."*

"The Wanderer was the Archangel Michael...." Cara gasped. She couldn't decide which piece of news to react to first: Michael and Kai being the Wanderer's Children, or the Archangel Michael descending into human form to become their father.

"Are you kidding me?" Brett's voice held an edge of sarcasm as he gave Cara an incredulous look. "My father was an *Archangel*?"

Kai sat silently, lost in thought.

"Not just any Archangel, but one who is special among men and angels alike," Constantina said. "It's not uncommon for an Archangel to take human form to change the tide of human events."

"Wait a second, what misstep?" Cara asked.

Before Constantina could answer, Kai interrupted. "Who killed him?" His voice a mere croak as he spoke for the first time since Constantina had announced he was the Wanderer's firstborn son. "Who killed our father?"

Constantina sat up straighter in her chair. "He wasn't murdered, dear ones. He was *released* per the covenant he signed before he descended."

*A covenant he probably never remembered signing,* Cara thought. "Released how?" she asked slowly with a sense of dread.

"He ascended, leaving his physical body behind."

"Just like that, he dropped dead?" Brett said from across the table, frowning.

"In a manner of speaking, yes. In another, no. He had to be awakened in order to be released."

"Why didn't he just live out his life like everyone else?" Kai asked quietly. "Why leave?"

"He was needed elsewhere. Make no mistake. He'll be fighting with us. Just not here on Earth."

The coil of dread tightened in Cara's stomach. "Who released him?"

"The only one who could... *Jonas*."

# Chapter 69



*MICHAEL*

***France. Angelorum Sanctuary. Thursday, May 30, 12:25*** AM GMT *+1*

MICHAEL RAN TOWARD THE EXIT of the medical center. His hand slammed down on the release bar with enough force to send a painful shockwave past his elbow. Nearly losing his balance, he stumbled into the underground city street.

He sucked in heaving breaths of air until his lungs burned, needing to escape. Rage and panic mixed in a volatile cocktail, propelling him forward. He ran along the cobblestone pathways past elaborate buildings and cathedrals underneath the stone sky, not caring that he looked like a man possessed. He didn't care about anything. His world had collapsed. Everything he believed, and believed in, had been ripped away. His father, a man he'd worshipped, had betrayed him.

His control crumbled and his mental shields came crashing down. Cara's voice blazed through—"*Why did Michael freak out like that?*"—competing with the group of inductees he ran by on the street. Their thoughts assaulted him in a deluge.

"*Why is he running?*" wondered a passerby. "*Oh my! He's going to run someone over at that pace,*" thought another. Voices layered one on top of another in a rapid buzzing mosaic.

He clasped his hands to his ears trying to push them away and ran faster.

Michael barreled into his room. Clothes flew in an airborne stream. Toiletries, cologne, shoes, everything he had. Stuffed and shoved haphazardly into his suitcase. Holding the top down with all his strength, he zipped it.

Claustrophobia engulfed him, stealing the air from the room.

*Need to sleep. Need to forget.*

He cursed and reopened the suitcase, removing the bottle of pills he kept in his toiletry bag. They'd been in there since his father's funeral. He took them to sleep that first month. His usual dose was half a pill. He dry-swallowed three.

He zipped his suitcase back up and arranged for transportation, wanting to put as much distance between him and those who had stolen his father. As fate would have it, the next plane was leaving shortly.

Fifteen minutes later, Michael reclined in his seat on the Angelorum jet, feeling numb. The sedatives hit him hard, sweeping him into a deep sleep and straight back to the day his life changed when he was eight years old. The one day he wished he could forget forever.


**Chicago. September 1996**


Michael's finger depressed the door bell, the sound echoing down the vast hallway inside. He shifted nervously on the porch and glanced back across the street at his house a few doors down. A small gust of wind carried the first few leaves of the season onto the porch. Michael pulled his windbreaker tighter around his thin shoulders while he waited.

*Why did Chicago start to get windy before the summer ended?*

He'd been absorbed in a Sponge Bob marathon on Nickelodeon when his mom had tapped him on the shoulder. "Sweetie, Dr. Farris just called. Roger wanted to know if you were available for a play date. He has a new video game."

Only two more days of summer vacation were left before third grade started. Spending time with Roger, the shy kid with the aura of a wounded animal, didn't really appeal to him. Roger was going into fifth grade this year. He was older than Michael by over a year but somehow seemed younger. They'd been playmates when Michael was much younger, when Roger's parents were still married. They'd separated last year, so Roger only stayed at the large house down the road part-time. That was about the time Michael stopped hanging out with him. Roger didn't seem to like himself much. He thought about himself as damaged goods. Michael knew it was wrong to poke around in other people thoughts, but sometimes his curiosity got the best of him. The one thing he'd learned was that people could be mean. They might not say mean things, but they'd think them.

He scrunched his face with a look of distaste, and slid his body down the leather sofa with his legs hanging off. "Do I have to?"

"Michael, you've been watching television since lunch. Just go for a few hours and come back in time for dinner at six o'clock."

Michael made a sour face and pushed himself off the sofa. "Uhh…"

His mother shook her head and chuckled. "You make it sound like I asked you to go clean your room. Would you rather do that?"

Nope. Video games sounded much better than that.

He rolled his head and headed into to the hall closet to get his sneakers.

"Take a jacket, sweetie, there's a chill in the air today. Must be a storm coming."

Michael groaned.

One of the large double doors cracked open. Roger's Dad, Dr. Farris, answered the door in workout clothes. He wiped his face with a towel and smiled at him.

"Hi, Dr. Farris," Michael mumbled. "Is Roger here?" He pulled his Cubs baseball cap lower on his head and nervously looked past him.

"Come in," he said, slightly out of breath. "Roger's mom took him out for school supplies. He'll be back in a few minutes. Hang out in the family room until he gets back."

Michael stepped into the cavernous hallway which led to a two-story living room. Dr. Farris slung the towel around his neck and led the way. The kitchen and family room were off to the left. Michael could hear the TV get louder the deeper they got into the house.

A little younger than his father, Dr. Farris was smallish for a man. Michael, although skinny, was already tall for his age at five-foot-three inches. He didn't have to look up far to see Dr. Farris's face. Dr. Farris was also rounder than his dad, who had all muscles and no fat. Michael hoped to look like his dad rather than Dr. Farris when he grew up.

*Why did he ask me to come over if Roger isn't here?* Michael wondered, tempted to dip into Dr. Farris's mind to find out. But he promised his dad he'd really try not to do that.

Dr. Farris stopped in the kitchen doorway and pointed to the family room. "I'll bring you a can of pop while you wait. Just turn on whatever channel you like."

Michael shrugged and kept going. His mother would be angry if she knew he drank soda. If it wasn't organic or healthy, his mom didn't buy it. He hoped it was cola. He loved cola when he could sneak a can.

Michael grabbed the remote and sank down into the giant sectional. He found the Sponge Bob marathon and smiled.

"Here you go," Dr. Farris said, handing him a cold cola and setting down a basket of potato chips on the coffee table.

*Score,* he thought.

"I'll be back in a few minutes to check on you. Like I said, Roger should be home any minute now."

Michael took a large slog from the can, his fingers chilled from the condensation on the outside. He put it down and grabbed a fistful of chips. Yup, Mom would definitely be mad. The salt hit his tongue in a rush. He grabbed the soda and drank half of it, loving the way it bubbled on his tongue.

Catching that episode midway through, he watched as it ended and another started.

*Tired, so tired all of a sudden,* Michael thought. His vision grew blurry; Sponge Bob turned into a mass of colored blobs, no longer in focus.

*Dreamy, everything feels so dreamy…*

His mouth tasted funny and he slipped into blackness.

Not asleep, but not awake, his body jostled in someone's arms as they climbed the stairs.

*Tired,* he thought, his eyes fluttered open then shut. *Can't keep my eyes open.*

*Bed.* He lay on his stomach, his cheek touching a cool sheet. Cinnamon assaulted his nostrils and he drifted off.

His eyes opened but he couldn't move as someone slid his pants down his legs. Cool air wafted over his bottom. He tried to open his eyes. They kept closing even though the cinnamon smell made him want to throw up.

"*Shh,*" warm breath tickled his ear. "You're such a pretty boy, Michael. Why did you have to be so pretty?"

A scream ripped from Michael's lungs, echoing off the cabin walls inside the plane until the air around him sucked him back into blackness.

# Chapter 70

*MICHAEL*
*New York City. Thursday, May 30, 3:00 AM ET*

DAZED, MICHAEL SWAYED on his feet in front of Sienna's apartment door, preparing to knock. A momentary flash of guilt passed through him for arriving unannounced in the middle of the night. But Michael's thoughts were too muddled from the sleeping pills to give him serious pause. What he'd learned in the conference room had fractured something inside him and threatened to crack him open.

He glanced in the mirror across the hall and flinched at his appearance. Still wearing yesterday's clothes, now slept in and wrinkled, he looked rough and disheveled. For the first time, he didn't care that he was nowhere near his usual state of fashionably pulled together. All he could think of was burying his face in Sienna's long black hair, and losing himself inside of her to find relief. Without a second thought, he'd asked the driver to bring him straight here from Teterboro airport.

He'd never needed anyone like he needed Sienna right now.

His hand froze halfway to the door.

*I've been bad.*

Just like that, the thought poked through. The long-buried memory that had taunted him, hiding at the edge of his consciousness during the plane ride, came crashing down, assaulting his senses. The air rushed from his lungs as it took him back.

He was five years old. His father had punished him for hurting his sister, Susan. Michael had wanted her to go back to where she'd come from. He didn't want to share his father. Transported, the scene played like a movie reel in his head.

Anger bubbled up and burned inside his chest. He wanted to hurt his brothers as much as he had wanted to hurt Susan.

Shock and shame washed over him. Things suddenly made sense. His shoulders slumped. He'd been bad again. He knew what he needed... to be punished.

*It was my fault.* That's why he didn't tell his father what had happened... how he'd been hurt by Roger's father.

Dr. Farris's words rang in his memory: "Your father won't love you anymore after he knows what you did with me. If you tell him, he'll toss you out like garbage."

He'd been bad then too for eating stuff he wasn't supposed to. If he'd refused the soda, he would've been stronger—strong enough to run away from Roger's father.

The cloying scent of cinnamon wrapped around him. Controlled, adult Michael fell away as his mind spiraled down and unlocked the Pandora's Box containing five-year-old Michael's fear and shame until it consumed him.

Standing rooted in place, Michael knocked on Sienna's door.


*SIENNA*

Startled awake at the knocking, Sienna threw off the covers and nearly bolted to the door, wrapping her robe around her as she ran. "Oh, thank God."

All night, she'd practically slept with one eye open, hoping—no praying—that Cara was right. That Michael would come to her.

Sienna was still reeling from her conversation with Cara yesterday afternoon, starting with Michael's meltdown after he'd found out he had secret older siblings—brothers, and ending with his immediate disappearance.

*At least Michael's father had the good taste to have his illegitimate children before he married Michael's mother*, Sienna had thought. From what Michael had told her, he'd had a close relationship with his father and his death had hit him hard. She could only imagine how devastated he must've been when he'd heard the news.

"I'm almost positive he's headed to you, Senny," Cara had said.

After that tidbit, Cara had dropped an even bigger bombshell...

"*What* might happen to me *when*?" Sienna snapped, her heart thundering in her chest.

"This is an open line, so I can't give you a lot of details," Cara had said, distraught. "It's like what happened to me in Connecticut. Remember?"

How could Sienna forget Cara's amazing light show at the Farmhouse? It kicked off their cross-country trek to save Kai and his daughter.

"Tell me again, *what* I am?" Sienna said, nervously rubbing her forehead.

"A Soul Seeker, Senny," Cara replied. "You're like me but your gift may be different. Whatever you do, don't tell anyone—it could put you in jeopardy—and stay away from anyone who looks like a homeless woman."

"What? Why?" Sienna asked, overwhelmed.

"Long story. Zeke will watch over you for now. Think of him as your own private security guard. You won't see him, but he's there. I'd be there too if I could, but Kai's got some, um, medical concerns… they won't let me leave the Sanctuary until they get a handle on them."

"Oh shit, now I'm going to worry about you, too," Sienna wailed.

"I'll be fine. Just call me if Michael shows up or if you're Called."

Sienna sniffed. "Don't worry. You'll be the first to know after me."

"I'm sorry I can't be there for you, Senny. I really am, but please trust me. You're more important than you know."

Cara left her with a few more surreal tidbits of information and hung up.

Sienna looked through the security peephole, and breathed a sigh of relief to see Michael standing on the other side.

Her fingers flew over the locks and chains. She flung open the door. "Michael—"

Her relief evaporated the moment she spotted the dazed look in his bloodshot eyes. She'd expected him to be upset but nothing like this. He looked like he hadn't slept in days. Propped up against the doorframe, he could barely stand.

*Broken.* That's how he looked, and it shook her.

"Come in." Pulling the robe more tightly around herself, she took his limp hand and led him inside. She gave a quick look around the hallway. *No suitcase?* She locked the door with a pounding heart, her internal alarms ringing.

He looked drugged. "Did you take something, baby?" she asked, examining his eyes more closely. His pupils were glassy and dilated.

"Some sleeping pills," he replied in a small voice she barely recognized.

*Oh my God,* she thought. "When? How many did you take?" she asked softly, fighting down panic.

"Three. Before I got on the plane."

Her shoulders relaxed. She needed to do something; at least getting his stomach pumped wasn't one of them.

*Think quick*, she thought. *Shower.* He'd want a shower if he was in his normal state of mind. It would buy her some time. Seeing her sexy, always-in-control Michael like this pierced her heart and sent a tremor straight to her soul.

Then it hit her.

She'd claimed him.

*Mine.* A fierce protectiveness welled up inside her. He was hers, and she wouldn't let anything happen to him. She'd make this better.

Seeing Michael like this, Sienna wondered if there was more to it than the revelation about his siblings. Taking a deep breath, she prayed for strength to deal with whatever he threw at her.

She guided him into the bedroom, and then slowly removed his clothes down to his underwear.

He looked at her as if seeing her for the first time. "Senny, I need you."

Her breath hitched. He'd never called her by her nickname before. Those four words touched her heart, meaning more than he could ever realize.

Putting his hands on either side of her face, he lowered his mouth onto hers, kissing her gently at first, and then with a growing insistence.

Metallic residue from the pills hit her taste buds.

She pulled away and asked softly, "When was the last time you ate?"

He dropped his hands, his desire dampening. "Sometime yesterday, maybe," he said, his voice dull and lifeless.

"Wait here for me." She sat him on the edge of the bed, and he drifted off again, somewhere inside his head.

She rounded the corner and ran straight to her fridge and the stock of protein shakes she kept for her hypoglycemia. She grabbed one.

*Please, Lord, help me through this night*, she thought.

The refrigerator door blew shut, and an unseen force of energy came slamming down from above, shooting outward through her body. She stood frozen in place, wrapped in a blinding white light.

Her Calling, just as Cara had described it, whipped through Sienna's body.

A cyclone of energy propelled her spirit upward. Soft, harmonious voices caressed and surrounded her, lifting her higher with every note. Increasing in velocity as it came down through the crown of her head, the energy traveled through her heart and radiated out of every pore, leaving confidence in its wake. Her arms rose involuntarily from her sides.

Angelic music played inside her head, and a voice spoke, standing out over the melodic song. It addressed her silently but clearly. *"You have been chosen. Do you accept your place as a servant of a Trinity?"*

Sienna answered with the words Cara told her that she should use, "Yes, I accept my place."

The disembodied voice continued. *"Blessed be your journey. Hold holy your Center Stone."* Two threads of energy struck her from above, rattling her teeth as they entered her crown. Her body shook violently as the two separate strands vibrated like dissonant piano wires down the length of her, nearly knocking her off of her feet. The strands entwined and spun, picking up velocity until they reached hurricane force and merged in harmony. As Sienna thought her body would shatter from the pressure, the kinetic frenzy peaked, exploding outward and covering the inside of her skin in a gentle molecular rain. Michael's image danced in her mind. The buzzing inside her skin was Michael's frequency—how he felt at the cellular level. Her essence was connected to his.

The music reached a melodic crescendo, and slowly the light faded, returning Sienna to full consciousness. When the voices and the buzzing were gone, she swayed on her feet with the protein shake still clutched in her hand. The bills that had been on the kitchen counter fluttered to the ground.

*Okay, that was super weird… in a good way*, Sienna thought. Funny, she didn't feel any different. Gathering her wits, she raced back to the bedroom… and Michael.

# Chapter 71



REMOVING THE LID, she handed the shake to Michael. "Drink this."

Without protest, he drank the contents. She discarded the empty can on her nightstand and guided him into the bathroom.

Sienna turned on the hot water.

"Is it all right if I take off your underwear?"

He nodded. That was good. At least he was lucid enough to understand her. She slid his Calvin Klein briefs down his legs. He stepped out of them without being asked, and stood naked and beautiful before her.

Wearing nothing underneath her robe, Sienna dropped it to the floor, then coiled and secured her long jet black hair into a bun on the top of her head. The last thing she needed was a thirty-minute date with her blow dryer. She didn't want to leave Michael alone for even a second.

Stepping behind the shower curtain into the tub, she guided him in behind her.

Michael stood stock still as she washed him, gliding the soapy shower pouf over his body.

*I can do this*, she thought. *I need to be strong.* He'd trusted her by coming here, and that was everything. He was her Center Stone and she somehow had the power to heal him. She wished she knew what that meant. Even after her kitchen experience, it wasn't clear.

"Senny?" he said softly.

She looked up, his blue eyes locking on hers. "What is it, baby?"

"I feel numb inside."

The shattered look in his eyes wrenched her insides. "Can you tell me what happened? Why you feel numb?"

"I've been bad," he replied softly, childlike.

His words sent a chill through her. "Why would you say that? You're very good in every way," she said, feeling like a mother speaking to a child.

"No, Senny, I'm not. I've done bad things." Tears welled in his eyes and his lower lip quivered.

Sienna swallowed past the dry lump in her throat. "Let's dry off, and then you can tell me what you did, okay?"

He nodded.

She toweled herself down and then turned the towel on him. The strength of his body juxtaposed with his fragile state of mind both broke her heart and built her resolve.

Her next move was to get him into bed to sleep this off... unless there was some divine intervention on its way to unlock this mysterious gift she had. She slipped him into the robe she'd bought for him that hung on the back of the door and led him back to the bedroom.

Before he reached the bed, he said, "I'll be right back." For a moment, his voice returned to its normal masculine timbre. A spark of hope ignited inside her. Maybe he'd be all right after all.

She sat on the bed and waited.

He returned carrying her father's old wooden fraternity paddle she kept hanging on her living wall among a montage of college and sporting memorabilia. The clubby décor reminded her of the library in the house she grew up in.

She gasped, her eyes widening in panic. "Why do you have that?"

His slumped shoulders and the look in his eyes—a mixture of sadness, resolve, and shame—stole her breath.

Dropping his robe, he stood naked before her and handed her the paddle. "Senny, I need to feel pain so that I don't feel numb anymore."

Too shocked to speak, Sienna's breath returned in tiny pants.

Her hand moved on autopilot, taking the paddle and placing it on the bed beside her. She bit back the urge to scream, forcing herself to remain calm. That didn't stop the vein in her neck from pulsing wildly.

*Keep it together,* Sienna, she told herself. *Don't break his trust.*

"Why do you want me to hurt you, Michael?"

"Please? Do this for me?" he begged.

Fearing he would break if she refused, she bit her lip and nodded.

"Sit back farther," he whispered, hanging his head. She shifted toward the middle of the bed so her feet no longer touched the ground.

He lay naked on his stomach across her lap, his generous front pressed down on the tops of her legs through her robe. She stared down at his perfectly smooth and muscled backside.

"Please, Now." He looked at her, the side of his face resting on the bed.

Her hand crept slowly toward the paddle. Part of her would've felt better if his request was for sexual pleasure, even though that wasn't really her thing. But his reason was darker and much deeper. She couldn't escape the shame that rolled off him, striking a chord inside her.

Above all else, she cherished Michael's trust.

He was hers. She'd do this for him…

But would he be able to face her afterward? And would she be able to face herself?

Out of nowhere, a sweet melodic voice from her Calling echoed silently in her head. The whispered words, even though spoken in a language she didn't understand, gave her the knowledge that this was the right choice. Strength surged through her.

She gripped the paddle securely in her hand. Taking a deep breath, she brought down the first blow.

"Harder," he whispered.

She raised the paddle and brought it down a second time.

"Again."

After the third, his skin was a light shade of pink.

"Again," he said softly.

She brought down the next blow.

"Harder."

He cried softly, tears leaking from his eyes in a slow trickle. Her heart ripped in two.

She brought the paddle down harder. Her vision blurred. She grimaced. Anger, not at Michael but at what had broken him, churned up in her gut.

This time, the paddle hit his ass with a loud slap.

"One more," he whispered.

After the last blow, she flung the paddle across the room. "How could you want this?" she yelled at him as tears spilled down her cheeks.

He said nothing. But the dead look was gone, replaced by something else— peace and conscious intelligence.

She shifted out from underneath him and lay down next to him. Wiping the wetness from under his eyes with her fingertips, she kissed the top of his head.

"I'm so tired, Senny." His eyes sagged shut.

Her heart melted. He was back.

"Come on, baby, let's go to sleep," she said, wiping her face with the back of her hand.

She peeled back the sheets and they crawled underneath.

"How are you feeling down here?" she asked, touching him gently on the behind.

"A little sore, but fine," he replied. He pulled her arm around him and twined his fingers with hers as she spooned behind him.

"Talk to me, Michael."

"I'm just trying to get myself unstuck, Senny. That's all," he said, and drifted off to sleep in her arms.

She wasn't exactly sure what he'd meant, but they'd made it to the other side. A strange tingle echoed inside her skin, reminding her of the sensation she'd felt in the kitchen. Without a doubt, she believed Michael would heal from here. She could stomach everything that had happened, except for the look of shame in his eyes. That look connected to a dark spot in her soul, to the time her uncle had touched her and made her do bad things.

She pressed her lips to his shoulder and kissed him. Holding him tight, she dropped off to sleep thinking there wasn't anything she wouldn't do to erase that look in his eyes.

"Michael, come here!" his father yells.

Michael shudders under his bed. He did a bad thing. He'd pushed baby Susan's carrier off the sofa. He was mad; he'd been the only child and now she was here. He liked it when Mommy and Daddy only paid attention to him. It made Mommy cry when the carrier fell onto the floor and when baby Susan fell out. Baby Susan cried really loud. Now he's in trouble.

But he still wants her to go away and live with a new Mommy and Daddy.

His father peers underneath the bed. His face is red, and his eyes and mouth are mad. Michael loved Mommy, but he loved Daddy more. He was scared his father wouldn't love him anymore because of what he did… and because she was here.

Michael cries as he father drags him out by his arms and lifts him to his feet.

"Michael," his father says with icy calm, "Come with me. Right now."

Michael's crying stops abruptly and he freezes in fear.

Daddy's never been this mad before.

"Walk to my office," he says.

Michael opens the door of the spare bedroom his father uses at night and on weekends. The sound of his mother and baby Susan crying echoes downstairs, as his father shuts the door.

"Do you know that you could've really hurt your sister?" His voice sends a chill up Michael's small back.

"I don't want her here," he mumbles.

His father sinks his fingers into Michael's thin shoulders and shakes him. "She's a part of this family and I love her as much as I love you. You should be ashamed for what you did," he says. "Pull your pants down. You're getting a spanking you'll never forget. To make sure you never give me a reason to do it again."

Michael's lower lip trembles. "I don't want to pull my pants down. I don't want a spanking," he says in a little voice.

"It's not about what you want. It's about what you deserve. Now do it!"

He cries as he pulls down his shorts and his big-boy underwear.

"Come here," his father says calmly. He lifts Michael up and puts him over his knee, exposing his naked bottom. Then he spanks Michael with the flat of his hand.

Michael continues to cry, now because it hurts. Only bad boys get hit on the bottom. He won't do it again. She can stay, he decides. *I don't want Daddy to make me feel bad and not love me.*

His father stands him up when he's done. Michael wipes away the stray tears on his wet cheeks with the back of his hand.

"Go stand in the corner for a ten minute time-out," he says.

Michael reaches down to pull up his shorts.

"No, keep them down," he commands, "as a reminder. Go."

Michael hangs his head and shuffles over to the corner, shorts and underpants around his thin ankles. He cries softly in the corner.

"I'll come back when the time is up." The anger is gone from his voice. "I'm sorry, Son. I love you very much, but you can never do something like that again. I hope this felt bad enough that you'll never try."

"I won't. I promise," he cries in a small voice. Michael would never do anything again that would make his father angry. Or make him not love him. He would never, ever, be bad again.

Sienna woke from the dream with a start, tears streaming down her face.

Michael was gone but he'd left a note on the pillow next to her. "Thank you and please forgive me. Love, Michael."

She released a wail and wrapped her arms around her knees. Her heart hurt like she'd been punched in the chest.

"Oh, Michael." She wanted to take that young boy into her arms and tell him that she loved him. Even more, she wanted to take the man he is now into her arms and tell him the same.

Now she understood. His mind had been stuck in that terrible moment when he'd been punished as a child. He believed he needed to be punished for his guilt of not wanting to share his father with the others, for feeling betrayed by his father and ashamed for having all those feelings. In his mind, he needed to be punished the only way he ever remembered.

It explained so much.

He'd become so afraid of ever letting go, of losing control. To him that meant punishment and that he wouldn't be loved, while control of his emotions meant safety.

That's why he was afraid to relinquish his control to her.

But he'd trusted her with his secret.

She read the note again. In the subtext, she sensed he thought he may have lost her, too. He signed the note with *Love*. For Michael, that was a lot.

Letting out a heavy sigh, she used the covers to dry her cheeks. She had to call Cara, but didn't her want to know she'd been crying.

Her brain sifted through the events with Michael. There wasn't much she was willing to share. This rarely happened, a situation that she couldn't talk about with Cara. But this time, it was Michael's privacy she protected, not her own.

She cleared her throat and hit Cara's speed dial.

"Zeke said Michael showed up to see you," Cara said breathlessly.

"Yeah. But before we talk about that, it happened—the Calling thing," Sienna said.

Cara gasped. "Are you okay? How did it go?"

"Totally fine. Just confused as hell. I feel Michael like a second skin. It's kind of weird. What now?"

"That's how I feel with Kai. Hang tight on next steps. I'll let you know as soon as I find out. I promise."

Sienna scowled, and then sighed. "Anyway, Michael stayed here last night but he left before I woke up."

"How was he?" Sienna could hear Cara's apprehension.

"He was groggy from some sleeping pills. I got him showered. He was upset but better by the time we fell asleep."

"You sound exhausted. Will you be okay?" Cara asked.

Sienna's lips tugged up in a smile. "Yeah… He called me 'Senny' last night. He's never done that before."

Cara was quiet on the other side for a moment. "Sweetie, in his heart I know he loves you. Please be patient with him. He'll be worth the effort."

"He's already worth it. But I don't know if he knows how to love," Sienna replied softly, thinking back to all she'd learned about him. The question remained: would he be able to face her again after last night?

"I believe in you both. Have some faith," Cara said.

"I'll try."

"I'll stay in touch and let you know when I find out anything else."

"Okay. Me, too. Thanks."

"Love you, Senny," Cara said and hung up.

Sienna called Michael's cell. It went straight to voicemail. She didn't leave a message. Putting down the phone, she braced herself to start the day. It was an effort for her to get out of bed.

*If he comes back, I'll teach him how to love, or die trying,* she thought as she headed to the shower.

# Chapter 72

*MICHAEL*
*United Airlines Flight, UA500, Thursday, May 30, 11:00 AM ET*

MICHAEL STARED OUT the window over the clouds, heading for Chicago. He'd slipped out of Sienna's while she slept, but not before he'd inserted the dream into her subconscious. He'd never be able to tell her out loud what had happened, but he could show her. She deserved to know… at least about that.

Gratitude filled him for what Sienna had done for him last night. He wouldn't recover overnight, but he'd made a personal breakthrough that would allow him to move forward, hopefully with Sienna by his side. Professional help would get him through the rest.

The question was: would Sienna forgive him for what he'd put her through? It wasn't everyday your lover showed up at your door in a drugged daze asking to be beaten with a paddle. She'd handled it incredibly well, considering. Not to mention, she'd done a bang-up job—his ass still hurt.

Then there were all the other things he had yet to tell her. Would she forgive him for those, too? Or was he just destined to lose her?

Looking out over the puffy cloudscape, he played with the silver ring on his finger. He hadn't worn it in years. His father had given it to him on his sixteenth birthday, and told him to always keep it safe. He didn't wear jewelry because of his profession, so he stored it in his safe. When Constantina had requested he bring it with him to the Sanctuary, he'd been surprised it still fit.

After leaving Sienna's, he'd stopped at his apartment to change and to pick up his bag. That's when he realized he'd left his cell phone back at the Sanctuary.

He had to use a landline to call his mom to tell her he was coming. She seemed to be expecting his call, another indication that this was all really happening. He needed to know what she knew.

He took a deep breath, enjoying the soothing view out the plane window. Something about it calmed his troubled soul. The plane was due to touch down at O'Hare at twelve noon central time. Michael had planned on taking a cab to his mother's house in Oak Park, but his sister, Susan, had insisted on picking him up since she didn't have classes today. One summer session away from her undergraduate degree in psychology at Northwestern University, she planned on continuing straight through the Master's program, starting in September.

After his father had died last October, his mother had sold their Brooklyn brownstone in Park Slope almost immediately and moved back to Chicago where his parents had grown up. Michael had been born and raised there up until his father had accepted a senior position at Watson & Haskins in Manhattan the summer before he entered high school. He'd been fourteen years old, and Susan had been nine.

Michael missed his family, but considered Brooklyn his home now. It was where he belonged. He'd worked with single-minded focus to get to where he was ever since he'd won his first competition at nine years old. At twenty-six, he was living his dream.

But, it wasn't until last year that he'd received a cash infusion to help his plan come to fruition.

Although Michael's family was affluent, his parents had insisted he and Susan make their own money from the time they were old enough to work. Michael started modeling at sixteen when his mother's friend, an agent for a prominent Manhattan modeling agency, approached him. By the time he was twenty, he was in high demand during college breaks, scoring the Calvin Klein campaign when he was twenty-one. At twenty-four, he was teaching at a local dojo and still modeling to have enough income to rent an apartment and save for his own business.

Lulled into the soothing pull of blue skies over the wing of the plane, Michael thought back to how everything had changed on his twenty-fifth birthday…

Michael had just finished a modeling job for a men's cologne when he'd arrived at his father's Upper East Side office. Watson & Haskins was posh with polished mahogany paneling, fine art, and Persian rugs up the wazoo.

"Hey, Son. Thanks for coming." Michael's father clapped him on the back warmly. Taller than Michael at six foot three, his father was handsome, slender with a runner's body, and finely clad in a custom-made suit. He reminded Michael of a young Robert Redford with sandy blond hair, intense royal-blue eyes, and just as much charm. Michael had inherited his mother's dark hair, but had his father's eyes and sense of style.

"How could I refuse?" Michael said with a crooked smile.

"I'm sorry that I was so cryptic, but I didn't want to spoil the surprise," his father said.

Michael gave him a puzzled look, thinking his dad was just going to take him to lunch. His father just smiled, and turned on his heel. Michael followed him through the maze of hallways to his office.

"Don't look worried," his father teased, as Michael sank into one of the guest chairs. His father settled behind his desk, and pulled out a leather portfolio with a round silver clasp.

"What's that?" Michael asked.

"It's your *twenty-fifth* birthday present," he replied and clasped his hands. "Michael, your mother and I decided when you and Susan were young that it was important for you both to learn core values, like the value of money, for one."

Michael nodded. He'd spent most of his life surrounded by affluence, yet everything he had he'd provided for himself with the exception of a roof over his head and the core of his college education. Obviously, his parents had given him gifts for holidays and birthdays, but they'd never given him money just for asking or purchased things without a reason.

"I know you've worked hard at everything you've ever done, but your dream is to have your own business. You're mature enough now to make the right choices. With that said, I'll sleep better at night knowing you own the roof over your head, and that you have the opportunity to do what you love. So, I'm giving you a trust fund with enough money to open your business and for a substantial down payment on a modest house or co-op. On top of that, $100,000 will be deposited on your birthday every year into an account to cover the expenses of your home and your business regardless of whatever income you make. This should allow you the flexibility to offer some of your time to your special groups, something I know that's important to you," he said, referring to Michael's volunteer work—teaching martial arts to the mentally challenged and disabled two afternoons a week.

Michael sat speechless, his eyes wide in disbelief.

"Cat got your tongue?" His father teased with a twinkle in his eye.

Michael turned liquid in his chair. "Thank you," he said. A tear of happiness escaped his eye. He quickly brushed it away as his mind raced with possibilities.

His father smiled warmly, "I'm very proud of you, Son. You're a good man. You deserve to have the life you've dreamed of…" For a split second, something passed through his father's eyes… a memory. His father had realized that Michael caught it, and gave him a brief warning look.

"*Don't worry, I won't pry*," he responded telepathically. The truth? He'd been tempted. He and his father were both Telepaths and shared many of the same gifts. But Michael suspected his father had even more gifts he never mentioned.

"Thanks," he said out loud, and slapped the desk. "So, how about some lunch?"

# Chapter 73



*MICHAEL*
*Chicago, Illinois, 12:15 PM CT*

MICHAEL SPOTTED SUSAN standing next to the baggage carousel.

"Hey, Susie-Q," he said with a wide smile.

"Hey, Handsome," she said and threw herself into his arms. Susan was tall for a woman at five ten and had their father's runner's build. An accomplished triathlete, her strength came from more than good genes. She had their mother's dark eyes and wore her dark hair short. Dressed in jeans, a T-shirt, and sneakers, she kept her face devoid of make-up.

"So, how's Penny?" he asked as she released him.

Susan had "come out" right after she'd started Northwestern. She'd met Penny the first week of school slightly less than four years ago, and they'd been together since. His parents had been accepting and supportive. Although Michael had acted surprised, he'd suspected it, having already picked up on a stray thought or two. He was glad she'd never felt the need to hide it. There were already too many secrets in his family.

Her face lit up, hopeful. "She's great. Dinner tonight?"

He gave her a weary smile. "It depends. I may have to leave as quickly as I came."

They walked toward the parking lot.

"What's the big rush?"

"I'm in the middle of an assignment. I'm doing some investigation here in Chicago," he replied, disliking that he had to stretch the truth—a necessity when it came to the Angelorum.

Although Susan had his father's blood, she'd never displayed any special qualities and wasn't throwing off any special vibes like his brothers. *Brothers*, the word stuck in his throat. He still couldn't believe it.

"Yeah, Mom said you've been working a second job. What's the deal?" she asked.

Susan didn't know about his trust fund; his father had made him promise not to tell her. She would still receive hers when she turned twenty-five. Until then, she would need to be self-sufficient just like he had.

"I've been moonlighting for a private security business. Pays well. Deva runs the dojo when I'm on assignment."

Susan gave him a devilish look. "So, how is Deva? Still trying to get in your pants?"

Michael rolled his eyes. "Only in her dreams. I've made it abundantly clear to her that I don't date my employees."

"Pardon the pun, but she's had a hard-on for you since high school," she said.

"Interesting choice of words." He still hadn't forgiven Deva for the stunt she'd pulled with Sienna.

They reached the car and Michael threw his bag into the backseat.

"So, anyone to speak of?" she asked.

He couldn't help the small smile that crept onto his lips. His sister may not have been telepathic, but she was observant.

"Oh, do tell!" she said enthusiastically. "You haven't had a girlfriend in like a hundred years."

He glared. "Gee, thanks."

She shrugged. "It's true, isn't it?"

He gave her a sideways glance. "I met someone." Although he tended to be guarded when it came to his personal life, he usually made an exception for Susan. They had a reasonably close relationship. He'd always watched out and protected her when they were growing up… except, apparently, for the one time he tried to injure her as a newborn.

"Well, don't make me beg. Tell me about her. Is she pretty?"

His insides warmed. "Yeah, she's beautiful. Smart, sexy."

"What's she look like?"

"A little shorter than you, maybe five-seven. Long black hair, blue eyes the color of the sky, and a knockout body," he said.

Susan narrowed her eyes. "I sense a *but*."

He frowned. "She might be pissed at me right now," he said, not willing or able to get into the details.

"Take flowers the next time you see her, and then beg for mercy," Susan advised with a smile. "Oh, and flash those big blue eyes of yours at her. That'll do it, guaranteed."

He grinned. "Do flowers work for you?"

"Usually. What does she do?"

"She's a fashion designer," he replied.

"Nice, right up your alley."

"So, how's Mom?" he asked, trying to find an out.

Susan sighed, her smile gone. "Good. Better these last couple of months. Much better than when you were here at Christmas."

Guilt stabbed Michael in the chest. Had it really been six months since he'd seen his mom? He needed to get out here more often.

"I miss Daddy, too, Michael."

"I know," he replied, and squeezed her arm as they drove. "I'm sorry I've been… absent." He'd gotten so caught up in his own grief that he'd never stopped to think about how much his family needed him. He'd do better…

"So, what have you and Penny been up to?" he asked, navigating to happier thoughts.

She brightened and spent the remainder of the ride getting Michael caught up on her news.

Susan drove through the iron gates up to the 1920s Spanish-style colonial. Michael's mom had been filling him in on her decorating progress during their weekly phone calls. She'd furnished one of the five bedrooms specifically for him. He suspected decorating provided an outlet for her grief.

Susan parked in one of the three garages and they went inside.

"Mom, we're home!" Susan yelled from the front foyer.

"I'm in the kitchen," she shouted.

Michael followed Susan.

"Michael, it's so good to see you, honey," his mother said, coming at him with open arms. He stooped down to hug her, squeezing her small frame tightly. At five three, she was the shortest in the family and looked like a smaller version of Susan with a short brown bob and welcoming brown eyes.

"Hi, Mom," he whispered into her hair and let her go.

"You must be starving. I made a nice lunch," she said.

Michael's stomach rumbled at the mention of food. He hadn't eaten anything solid in over a day. All he'd had was the protein shake at Sienna's and the smoothie he'd made when he'd gotten back to his apartment.

"Lunch sounds great. What'd you make?" he asked.

She smiled, "One of your favorites. Salad greens with avocado, beets, grapefruit, and shrimp dressed in vinaigrette."

His stomach rumbled again. "Nice. I'll go wash my hands," he said, heading for the bathroom in the front hall.

His missed his mother's meals. He'd been raised on whole foods, nothing processed. Growing up, if he and Susan didn't like what was on the table they'd gone to bed hungry. As soon as they turned twelve, they had to make one meal a week. Depending on how difficult the recipe was, his mom would be the sous chef and answer any questions they'd had. On Sunday afternoons, they would pore over her magazines and cookbooks, searching for selections in order to have their list of ingredients ready by Sunday night for her Monday morning shopping trip. He had to thank his mom. As he got older, it had paid dividends. Neither his ex-girlfriend from college, Cathy, nor Sienna could cook to save their hides.

He went back into the kitchen.

"Sweetheart, your plate is on the table. I'll join you in a minute," she said, preparing her plate.

"Thanks," he said and continued into the dining room.

Susan sat waiting for them.

Michael's eyes widened when he saw his salad.

"Mom, this looks great. Any reason for the Paul Bunyan–sized portion?" he asked as she walked in and then dug into his food. His taste buds danced in culinary bliss the moment the salad hit his tongue, his eyes closing as he swallowed the first bite.

"I heard from a good authority that you might be hungry when you arrived," she said cryptically and picked up her fork.

He picked Constantina's name out of his mom's head. So much for sneaking into town. Then again, it wouldn't take a brain surgeon to figure out that he'd end up here. If he had to guess the chain of events: Cara had called Sienna to warn her he might be coming; Sienna had called Cara to tell her he had come and gone; Cara had told Constantina that he had made it to New York; and then Constantina had called his mother, who had told her he was coming. Voilà! Sometimes he wondered how someone of his intelligence could miss something so obvious. Honestly, he really didn't care if anyone knew where he was as long as they didn't interfere.

"I guess she was right," his mother said.

Michael stared down at his empty plate. "I guess she was."

"Who was right?" Susan asked.

"Michael's employer," his mother responded and left it at that.

Susan got up with her empty plate. "Hey, I'm sorry to eat and run, but Penny and I are training this afternoon for a triathlon. We're scheduled for a swim at the Y." She looked between Michael and her mother with anticipation, "Dinner later?"

Her mother gave her a vague smile. "That will depend on your brother's schedule."

"If I don't have to rush off, we'll go to dinner," he said to appease her.

She grinned, satisfied. "Great. See you later."

After Susan left, his mother gave him a melancholy smile. "I know you have a lot of questions, sweetheart. But let's just have some dessert first. I have some fresh berries…"

He nodded. He'd waited this long, he could wait a few minutes longer. She worried he hadn't eaten enough, so he'd comply. His heart tightened, guilt assaulting him again that he hadn't spent enough time with her.

She came back with two bowls filled with berries.

"Thanks, Mom."

They ate in silence.

"Mom?" he asked, "how did you and Dad get together? You were high school sweethearts, right?"

His mother rested her spoon next to her bowl, and folded her hands. "It's true, we dated in high school, but we went to different universities. By the end of our freshman year we decided to see other people. We never stopped caring for one another even though we ended up in other relationships, and then he moved away."

"How did you get back together?" he asked, wondering about the years in between, the years his dad had fathered other children.

Her face took on a dreamy quality. "He'd just gotten home from California after graduating from Stanford with his MBA. He'd lived there for five years after he'd left Chicago. My family had a Memorial Day party and invited his family."

"So you reconnected at the party?"

She nodded, her eyes glistening. "Yes, and that was it. We knew that we wanted to be together. He made a short trip back to California to move the rest of his things, and came back for good. We got married in a small ceremony on Labor Day weekend. By then, I was already several months pregnant with you."

Michael's eyes widened. "You were pregnant when you got married?"

She chuckled. "Don't look so shocked, sweetie. We were both ready, and no one had to bring a shotgun." She took his hand in hers. "Sweetheart, your father loved you very much. He loved all of his children very much," she paused and looked down. When she looked up, tears hovered in her eyes and she whispered, "I know there were others…"

He sensed her pain. "How long have you known?" he asked quietly.

She smiled through her tears. "A while."

Numbness started to creep back into Michael.

"Why didn't you tell me before? Does Susan know?" he asked anxiously.

"Michael, you should understand your father by now. This wasn't to be spoken of. He left me instructions in case he died before you came to him directly. He told me that you'd seek me out, and only then could I reveal his wishes. Constantina called earlier. She knew I knew. She just doesn't know what I have…"

Michael frowned. "What do you have?"

"A diary," she said, glancing at his finger. "You'll need your ring to open it."

"My ring?" Michael asked, confused.

She brushed the tears from her eyes. "Yes, to open the lock."

That raised his eyebrows.

"Your ring is a key made by one of the Angelorum's alchemists. It contains a couple drops of your father's blood, causing it to vibrate at a certain frequency. The vibration releases the lock."

"Alchemy—as in fairy tales?" he asked. Michael didn't know which stunned him more: the matter-of-fact tone his mother used when she spoke about alchemy, or the fact that she'd seriously used the word *alchemy* in a sentence. He started to understand what Cara had meant when she called each new discovery she made about the Angelorum a "through the looking glass" moment.

"Where's the diary?" he asked.

"In the safe upstairs. I'll get it for you."

"Have you read it?" Michael asked, giving his mother a pained look.

"No, Sweetheart. I don't have a key, only you and your brothers do. It'll be up to you to share it with them. Know that's what your father wanted. He wanted each of you to have access to the contents."

He nodded absently, lost in thought.

She collected their plates and went through the kitchen on her way upstairs.

Michael's world had shifted off its axis. The foundation for everything he'd believed was a lie. Emptiness settled into his gut as it became more real. He had nursed a small seed of hope that it was all a mistake. But it wasn't. It was true, and suddenly he felt like a stranger in his own family. How could his father have perpetrated this fraud so thoroughly?

For the first time, he thought about his brothers and how they must feel. At least for him, his father truly was his father. For them, the men they'd thought of as their fathers were simply not. Their fraud had been perpetrated by their mothers. They'd all been betrayed by someone, and they'd never had the opportunity to know his father or to receive his love firsthand. But they'd each gained three brothers… and a sister.

He winced. *What would they tell Susan?* Probably nothing, making both him—and his mother—part of the betrayal.

*Shit.* Michael put his head in his hands. There would be more people hurt before this was over.

His mother returned and placed the book in front of him. "Michael, try not to judge your father too harshly. He punished himself enough over what he'd done while he was alive, that much I know. But I also know how much he loved you and how proud he was of you," she pleaded.

Michael eyed the diary. "I'll try. I'm going to take this upstairs if you don't mind."

"Okay, sweetheart," she said, still looking distraught.

He pulled her into a tight embrace. "Don't worry, Mom. I love you."

Michael grabbed his bag outside the kitchen, carrying it with the book up to the guest room.

# Chapter 74

*MICHAEL*

MICHAEL CLIMBED ONTO the queen-size bed to get comfortable, for what, he wasn't sure. He fluffed the pillows behind him and laid the diary on his lap.

The book, if you could call it that, was actually a beautiful bound portfolio the size of a large photo album or scrapbook. On closer inspection, the deep aqua-blue cover was shagreen, the skin of a shark or stingray. His father used to have a collection of antique eyeglass cases and snuff boxes made from the exotic skin that he kept in his office. The portfolio had silver hinges along the left and right side edges, and a strip of solid silver down the middle which opened in the center. A deep circular indentation bridged both sides of the solid silver strip. The bottom and top sides of the portfolio were protected by silver panels, the packaging acting as a box for the contents inside. There was a sigil on the upper left side of the portfolio. He recognized his family crest—it matched the red Messenger mark tattooed on his chest.

"Here goes nothing," he said, removing the ring from his finger. He placed it into the circular indentation, and pressed down. With a snap, the lock released and the silver strip in the center parted.

He carefully opened the portfolio. The contents were bound to the right-hand side. Like Hebrew or Arabic, the angelic language was read from right to left.

The cover page was written in his father's handwriting. On it, a simple inscription, "The Wanderer's Children" with his father's name, Michael Swift Sr., and his family crest.

Michael took a deep breath and flipped the page. There were four sections. He started with the first.

A picture of a baby boy wrapped in a hospital blanket lying in a bassinet was mounted on the first page. Written underneath the picture was, "Kai Seth Solomon, Born January 23, 1982, 7 lbs., 8 oz." Farther down was a short entry:

*Welcome to the world, my son. The hardest thing I've ever had to do in my life was to walk away from you knowing that you'll never know that I existed or how much I love you. What I can promise you is that I'll always watch over you.*

*Love, Your Father*

Michael's throat tightened as he read the passage.

He flipped to the page of Kai on his first birthday.

*Kai,*

*Happy Birthday, Son. Even as a one-year-old, I can feel your power and sense your gifts. You will be a powerful Messenger someday. My blood runs strong in your veins. I hope that by staying away, you will be safe. Constantina was right to have me hide our bloodline.*

Michael froze when he saw Constantina's name. Not only did she know about the mission—she was the one who'd sent him. The betrayal clenched his gut, reminding him that not one but two people had betrayed him.

He cradled his head in hands.

Taking a deep breath, he flipped through the rest of Kai's section. It was filled with pictures from the time he was an infant until as recently as last year: school pictures, sporting events, journal articles he'd written, pictures of him receiving awards, his wedding picture, pictures of his daughter, Sara.

His father had obviously done, or paid someone to do, some heavy surveillance. There were many more personal journal entries to Kai. As Michael read them, he started to feel like an intruder. He understood why his father had wanted him to share the contents with his brothers. They deserved to see what it contained.

Michael skipped to the second section. It contained a name he didn't recognize. His father's second-born son. Michael swallowed. He briefly leafed through the section. Based on the newspaper clippings, Brett wasn't the only famous sibling of the four.

The third section was as he expected, all about Brett, starting with a picture of a cute chubby newborn with his father's blue eyes. The section included more memorabilia, including the obituary for Brett's brother, Colin, of an overdose, along with pictures, articles, concert ticket stubs, and other items.

His father had written journal passages after almost every picture and piece of history. No wonder the binder was over four inches thick.

Michael hesitated as he turned to the last tab—his tab. With a deep sigh, he flipped it.

It started the same as the others, with a picture of him as a newborn and the inscription "Michael Swift Jr., March 10, 1988, 8 lbs., 2 oz." His father's note underneath:

*My dearest Michael,*

*This is one of the happiest days of my life! The fact that you will grow up knowing that I'm your father, and that I can spend every day with you makes me happier than I thought I could ever be. I've been watching your brothers grow from afar for five years, and it has torn me apart. But to be able to hold you more than once and to be a part of your life is the best gift I could ever hope for in this life. I love you so much, and look forward to savoring every day.*

*Love,*

*Your Father*

Michael could feel his father's joy and pain shoot through him with every written word. It soothed him knowing how difficult this was on him, and that he'd truly loved each of them. He released a breath and paged ahead. He'd come back later and read more. What little he'd read had already drained him emotionally.

He'd already discovered what he'd come here for—the truth, and, by default, the second son… his missing brother.

Michael stopped at an entry made when he was five years old. He froze. A picture of him with a haunted look in his eye holding baby Susan stared back at him. He remembered having it taken the night he'd been punished. The writing on the entry was blurred as if drops of water had fallen onto the page.

Michael read it.

*Today, I raised a hand to my son. Oh, please God, forgive me! He could've hurt Susan badly, and I saw red. I wanted to punish him for jeopardizing a life I fought so hard to bring into this world. Every life is precious. He needed to learn never to do something like that again to Susan. But I'm afraid I may have caused an irreparable break within him. He's just a small boy, too young to understand certain things. I was so angry, I told him he should be ashamed, and he was. I felt his shame. He thought I didn't love him, and that's why I was punishing him. I pray he forgives me, and I will spend my life proving how much I love him. He's a good, sensitive boy. He's so special. I can't believe I raised a hand to my son. There just didn't seem like a better way to teach this lesson…*

Michael's eyes were wet. It hadn't been water but his father's tears that had smeared the ink.

Weariness overtook him, and he closed the portfolio, snapping the lock shut. Setting it aside, Michael pulled the blanket up from the bottom of the bed and crawled underneath. He curled into a fetal position, only vaguely aware of the tears still falling softly from his eyes as he fell asleep.

"Michael." The voice was crystal clear—his father's voice. His eyes fluttered, trying unsuccessfully to open.

"Don't fight me, Son," he said softly.

Michael did as he was told and relaxed, remaining in the state caught under the veil of sleep between dreaming and waking—knowing this wasn't a dream. Michael's eyes opened this time to see his father standing at the foot of the bed, surrounded in light. He looked exactly as Michael remembered him, like a young Robert Redford dressed casually in the clothes he died in—jeans and a button down shirt.

Michael stared, knowing this place was just a facsimile of the room where he lay asleep.

"Dad, is it really you?" he asked, the blanket falling away as he sat up. The pain related to his father's death hit his heart with the speed of a freight train.

"It's really me. I haven't been able to manifest since the night I came to your dojo, the night I told you of your Calling. Even now, I can only come as far as your unconscious mind."

"I have so many questions…" Michael said, over the lump in his throat.

"I know, Son. Time is precious, and there's a lot I need to tell you before the pull becomes too strong and I have to leave," he replied, trying to mask the urgency in his words.

"What pull? Where are you? In Heaven?"

"No. I'm with Hannah in the place where the veil is thin enough to… stay in touch. We're here with… others, waiting to help you," he said.

Michael snapped to attention. His father was with Cara's grandmother. "What do you mean?"

"Michael, we're part of your bridge. You'll need us all for the Final Battle," he said. "But the longer we stay, the stronger the pull to take us over to the other side, into Heaven. Next time, you may need to come to me," he said.

"What bridge? And how will I get to you?" Michael struggled to understand, panicking he wouldn't know what to do.

"The bridge between Heaven and Earth," he said. "The most important thing right now is to find your brother. I'm sorry about how this had to unfold, but it's you and your brothers who play a vital role as part of the Twelve."

"What kind of role?"

"Each of you has special gifts. Combined, the four of you are the most powerful communication device the Angelorum Twelve have at their disposal. You, Michael, are the linchpin to that communication."

Things snapped into perspective for Michael. He was ashamed for putting his petty concerns ahead of something so much greater. A rush of cinnamon surrounded him.

"Don't ever hang your head in shame again, Michael," came his father's stern reaction, and then his voice softened. "Forgive yourself for what happened with Dr. Farris. It wasn't your fault, Son. I wish you had told me while I was alive instead of carrying this painful burden alone. Nothing could ever take away the love I have for you. And please forgive me for what I put you through. For that, I'm deeply sorry."

Tears sprang to Michael's eyes. He could feel the crushing ache he'd been carrying loosening and separating from his soul. His spirit grew lighter, the smell of cinnamon dissipating.

"If there's one last thing left I have to teach you, it's never be afraid to love. Love is life's most precious gift and the only thing you can take with you into Heaven. You have many new people in your life to love. Give them as much love as your heart can give, and receive as much as they are willing to give in return. The heart is infinite in its capacity—may you never find any boundaries in yours. Do you understand?" Light blazed around his father as he spoke.

"Yes, I understand." He needed to embrace the love that surrounded him—from his family, Sienna, Cara, his new brothers, whoever else he met going forward. He needed to loosen his control and let them in.

Most of all, he needed to make peace with his past.

His father looked over his shoulder with sudden agitation. "Michael, I have to go. Find the Book of Four Rings. It holds the final piece of what you seek."

"Where do I look?"

"Search the diary. I love you, Son. Send my love to your mother, brothers, and sister."

His father vanished.

Michael eyes flashed open. He knew what he had to do.

# Chapter 75

*MICHAEL*
***Chicago, Illinois, 4:00*** *PM* *CT*

MICHAEL PARKED HIS MOM'S car at the curb in front of the suburban house where he grew up, north of Chicago. Clutching the steering wheel, he took a few deep breaths.

He glanced over at the modern split-level where Roger used to live and shuddered. Dr. Farris had sold the house not long after he'd attacked Michael, and a new family with older children had moved in that Christmas. Even now, Michael had trouble looking at the house.

Two years after his attack, the story had hit the papers: "Local pediatrician caught molesting young boy during the night in Chicago hospital." As far as Michael knew, Dr. Farris was still behind bars.

*May he rot in Hell after that...* Michael thought bitterly.

Michael's eyes shifted to the woods behind the house. The neighborhood backed up into a strip of undeveloped land that was owned by a trust and keep as preserved land, despite all the attempts builders had made over the years to buy it and change the zoning.

A few kids rode by on bikes and then disappeared around the corner onto the next street.

Michael grabbed the backpack on the front seat, locked the car, and took the public path at the end of the street into the woods. Midway down the path, he veered off into the trees and tracked back to the section of woods behind the Farris house. Michael swept through the brush which cleared as the trees grew taller and their high canopies blocked the light, leaving areas free of undergrowth.

He walked until he found it. The massive oak still stood with its five-foot-wide trunk, hiding his secret buried somewhere at its base.

Sinking down with his back to the tree, he clenched his fists and the memories came flooding back.

*Can't run, hurts,* Michael thought. Limping deeper into the woods behind the Farris house, he wanted to hide. Tears blurred his vision as he stumbled over branches and through the brush until it cleared. He looked behind him and could no longer see the house.

A big oak blocked his path. Its branches fanned out far and wide, creating an umbrella in the sky. The trunk was huge, yet somehow inviting in its immensity. Its lowest branches were like arms, offering a promise of comfort.

Michael sank down along the tree's trunk and sat gently on the ground. He hugged his knees and cried, not knowing what to do or how to hide what had happened.

*Daddy won't love me anymore,* he thought. That's what Dr. Farris had said. *"If you tell him, he'll toss you out like garbage."*

*Am I really garbage now?* Michael wondered, crying harder.

If only he hadn't drunk that pop.

He wished he was like that karate guy, Jet Li, in the movie he watched with his father. The bad guys knocked him out, but when he woke up he broke away and beat them up. Nothing like this would happen to him. Jet Li could defend himself. Beat up anyone who tried to hurt him.

Michael's tears dried as an idea formed in his head. He could do that. He could learn karate and be as good as Jet Li. Then no one could ever hurt him again.

It was getting darker. If he left now, there would be just enough light to make it home.

He winced as he got up. There was one more thing he needed to work out. He couldn't let his father read his mind. Lucky for him, he'd just taught Michael how to shield his thoughts, explaining that they weren't the only two Telepaths in the world.

*If I act perfect, no one will ever know... That's what I'll do.*

Slowly, Michael got up and took the small spade from his backpack. He dug a wide hole at the base of the tree. With uncanny precision, he found what he was looking for under ten inches of packed soil. He extracted his mostly intact Cubs cap. Balled up and protected inside the heavy canvas was a small pair of bloodstained boy's briefs.

Clenching them in his hand, a tear broke free and rolled down his cheek. "It's time to set you free," he said.

He pulled what he needed from the backpack. Following Boy Scout rules, he built a small fire pit. He struck one match and then another until he had a small blaze going. Taking the cap and briefs, he tossed them into the licking flames.

Standing back, his eyes stayed glued to the fire as he watched the evidence of his black day burn until it disappeared forever.

# Chapter 76

*SIENNA*
*New York City. Thursday, May 30, 11:45 PM ET*

SIENNA'S HEART LEAPED when she heard his knock at the door. She'd made up her mind. Her heart wanted more. Sex was no longer enough. That said, she wasn't going to make it easy for Michael. He'd have to work for it. Otherwise, how would he ever appreciate her?

Just to be sure, she looked through the security peephole. Flowers covered the hole. On second thought, maybe she wouldn't be that hard on him.

She cracked open the door.

Lowering the bouquet, he looked at her with big blue puppy dog eyes, wearing an apologetic smile. "Hi," he said.

Arching a brow, she said, "Hi? That's all I get?"

Still holding the flowers, he swept her into his arms and carried her into the apartment.

She wouldn't let him sweep her off to bed to avoid talking about what had happened. "This can't just be about sex anymore, Michael," she said.

His eyes locked on hers. "It's not," he said softly but definitively. He put her down, laid the flowers down on the nearest table, and pulled her into an embrace.

Pushing back a tendril of her hair, he stared into her eyes. Soft and welcoming, his lips met hers in a tender kiss, his arms tightly circling her waist. She melted into his hard body, each line and ripple familiar as it connected with her.

"I'm sorry," he whispered into her ear as he held her.

"How sorry?" she whispered back, enjoying the warmth of his body next to hers.

"More than you'll ever know," he replied.

"I was so worried about you," she said, her veneer cracking. He squeezed her tighter. Tears sprang to her eyes, "That dream. You gave me that dream, didn't you?"

"Yes," he said in the barest whisper.

"Cara told me you could do special things. Since we've shared dreams before… Did that really happen to you?"

"Yes," he repeated, holding her close.

"It hurt me to see it."

"I'm sorry. I thought you deserved to know after what you did for me."

"Thank you for trusting me."

He pulled back and cupped her cheek. "Can you be patient with me? I have some things that I still need to work out, but I want to be with you while I do."

Her heart sped up. "What are you saying, Michael?"

"I'm saying that I don't want to run anymore. That I want to be with you." Tipping up her chin, he searched her eyes with a look she never expected. Her breath caught. "I'm saying that I love you, Senny. That I really want to be with you."

Her heart burst wide open, and tears of happiness slipped down her cheeks. She crushed him against her chest and whispered, "I love you, too, Michael."

He rested his head next to hers. "I thought maybe I'd lost you, pushed you too far."

"When I read your note, I didn't know what to think. You didn't return any of my calls…"

He sighed. "I forgot my phone when I left Cara and the others. I never had it with me. I didn't mean to worry you. I came back as soon as I could."

Shifting out of his embrace, she wiped her eyes and smirked. "You owe me, buddy."

With a mischievous glint in his eye, he asked, "What do you want as reparation?"

"I want fifty points credited to my account, and I reserve the right to use that paddle again," she said with a wicked look.

His crossed his arms. "What? That's a lot of points. Are you going to go all *50 Shades* on me?"

"If you don't answer me, I'm going to up it to seventy-five," she said, narrowing her eyes.

"Lady, you drive a hard bargain. Fifty points it is." He sighed and stuck out his hand. "Shake on it."

They shook and rather than letting go, he drew her into him.

She nuzzled the soft skin of his neck. "Well, don't just stand there, take me to bed."

"With pleasure," he growled, scooping her up and whisking her into the bedroom.

"My points, my rules," Sienna said when he set her down.

Wasting no time, she unbuckled the belt on his jeans in record time. Lifting his shirt over his head, she tossed it to the ground. Trailing kisses over the hard muscles of his abs, she worked to release him from his pants.

She sprang him free, already hard, and pushed his clothes to his ankles. He kicked them aside, and she took him in her mouth. He let out a moan as she drew him in, trying to swallow him whole as she caressed him with her tongue, her fingers kneading his balls. She loved the sweet taste of his skin, wanting to memorize the intoxicating feel and smell of him. Since her Calling, she was suddenly aware of him in a more organic way, his energy merging with hers the closer they got physically.

One thing was clear. Every inch of him was hers.

"Sienna," he gasped, gripping her shoulders.

Pulling himself out of her grasp, he pushed her onto the bed. "I know this is your party, but may I?" he asked, looking lustfully at her thighs.

She nodded. What the hell. If that's what he wanted, who was she to stop him?

He removed her jeans and thong in one fluid motion. Kneeling at the foot of her bed, he pulled her down to meet his mouth. His tongue was her undoing, unlocking a volcanic orgasm.

As she lay panting, he stood and guided himself into her. Letting out a low growl, he drove himself home. His long, smooth strokes lit up every nerve ending in her core as he caressed her from the inside, filling and stretching her to perfection. Their fit was custom made to give her the most intense orgasms she'd ever had.

Quickening his pace, the wave of her ecstasy started to crest with earth-shattering potential. He threw his head back, swelling inside of her until their passion erupted. They cried out in unison, pulsing in and around one another. She could almost feel the blood move through her veins as her climax engulfed her in an unceasing wave.

"Michael!" she cried, as her body and spirit united with him in a way it never had before. The prickle of electric rain under her skin spread through her in a blanket of pure love and happiness.

Collapsing alongside her, he pulled her into his arms as his chest heaved wearing a bliss-filled smile. "That was... beyond amazing." He kissed her hair. "I promise that I won't leave you like that again."

"Good. I might not forgive you next time," she said, gazing into his eyes. She leaned in and kissed him.

His expression softened. "I never thought that I could have someone like you."

She blinked. "Why would you say something like that?"

"I've always been too afraid," he confessed.

"Of what?"

"That someone like you would never love me," he whispered.

Sienna swallowed, sensing another breakthrough. "Was it easier for you to pretend it was just about the sex?"

He nodded. "I'm sorry. I hope I didn't make you feel bad."

She shook her head. "You've always made me feel special, Michael. You've never treated me like you just wanted me for sex," she said, running her fingers through his hair.

"I'm glad."

"You're a good person, Michael. You've been that from the beginning. It's one of the things I love about you."

"Thanks." He kissed her gently.

"... and you rock in bed."

He blushed. "You inspire me. It's never been this good with anyone else. That's the truth."

"Ditto."

He squeezed her tight. "I love you so much," he said, kissing her hard. When he came up for air, he winked. "Want to go again?"

"Can I take the rest of my clothes off first?" she teased, looking down at her shirt.

"Yeah." His forehead scrunched into a frown. "Were you serious about the paddle?"

She gave him a wicked grin. "Don't be bad and you won't find out..."

He chuckled. "Fair enough."

They sat up and he removed her shirt.

"Can I stay tonight?" he asked.

Her heart squeezed. "I've never asked you to leave," she said softly.

"I know. I hate that I have to leave again tomorrow morning, but I need to head back to Cara and the others. I'll stay in touch this time."

"Okay, otherwise… the paddle."

He laughed. "Deal," he said and pulled her closer. "Round two?"

"Uh-huh." She rolled on top of him. "Time for me to use more of my fifty points," she said, pinning his arms above his head.

The look of panic he usually wore when she took control was nowhere to be seen.

"I trust you," he whispered.

His words melted her heart. Trust and love were the two biggest gifts he had to give, and he'd given them both to her.

"I love you, baby. I'm going to make you feel good now," she said softly.

"Okay." He smiled.

She spent the rest of her fifty points giving him all she had and making sure that he enjoyed every second of it.

There would be time tomorrow to update him on her news, and break it to him that he was her Center Stone.

Tonight, it was just them. Nothing else mattered.

They collapsed an hour or so later, spent and happy. For the first time since their night at the Mercer, they slept soundly wrapped in each other's arms… for the entire night.

# Chapter 77



*CONSTANTINA*
**France. Angelorum Sanctuary.**

"ISHMAEL?" Constantina gave her daughter Hope's former Nephilim mate a quizzical look as she entered her chamber, and closed the door securely behind her.

The white-haired albino Guardian bowed his head, hands clasped in front of him. "Eae."

"What are you doing here? I thought you were assigned to guard Dr. Solomon's daughter." Concern gripped her as did a feeling of sudden uncertainty. Had there been a change in the Trinity Stones?

A small blonde-haired child stepped out from behind Ishmael. "He *is* guarding me."

Constantina's brows knit at the mature and serious expression on the four-year-old child's face, and her heart skipped a beat behind her breast. "I don't understand," she whispered.

The child's eyes gazed up to meet hers and a wise smile touched her lips. She pulled a talisman on a silver chain from underneath her pink blouse, and placed it in Constantina's hand. "Hope gave me this before she died, to keep me hidden. I was afraid Achanelech would find it when he kidnapped me. Didn't you wonder why the demon blade had no effect when it scratched my cheek?" Sara said with a precocious look that didn't match the maturity in her tone.

Constantina stumbled backward and crumpled into the chair behind her. Tears welled in her eyes when the child's energy hit her with full force.

The child's eyes glistened as she spoke, her tiny hand reaching for Constantina's. She whispered, "I'm sorry. This was the best that I could do. After the Wanderer gave up his mission before having his last son, I was left with no choice. Michael and his sister's souls had already been chosen. This was the closest I could come..."

Sara reached up and caressed Constantina's cheek. "I couldn't let you do this alone, my love."

Constantina looked into the child's eyes, at the old soul peering out who she'd known her entire existence, and breathed, "Leo..."

# ABOUT THE AUTHOR

By day, L. G. O'Connor is a corporate executive in a Fortune 250 company. By night, she's a writer of adult Urban Fantasy, Paranormal Romance, and Contemporary Romance who lives in Northern New Jersey. She lives a life of adventure, navigating her way through dog toys and soccer balls and loaning herself out for the occasional decorating project. When she's feeling particularly brave—she enters the kitchen.

Visit www.lgoconnor.com to sign up L.G.'s Newsletter to receive special perks or check out her blog.

FIND or FOLLOW her:
Facebook: http://www.Facebook.com/lgoconnor1
Twitter: https://twitter.com/lgoconnor1
Goodreads: http://www.goodreads.com/author/show/7690970.L_G_O_Connor
Book Site: www.WanderersChildren.com
Email: lg@lgoconnor.com

If you enjoyed this book, I would greatly appreciate it if you would spread the word. You can help in any of these ways:
RECOMMEND it to family, friends, online forums, discussion groups, book clubs.
REVIEW it on Amazon, Goodreads, or any other review site.
LEND it to anyone who loves Paranormal Romantic Suspense or who is looking for a change of pace from Literary Fiction.

L.G. O'CONNOR

# ENDNOTES

Character List

## <u>Angelorum</u>

**Angel Benitez.** Leader of the Avenging Angel's Bikers Club (AABC) in Los Angeles; "retired" Four Hundred–Class Guardian. Brett King's guardian since age ten. Also known by Nephilim name, Benedictine.

**Angelis.** Angelorum High Council Leader.

**Brett King.** Rock star and lead singer of King Metaljam. Secretly protected by Angelorum since the age of ten.

**Cara Collins** [*kare* + *a*; with soft *c* sound]. First of Angelorum's Holy Twelve expected to lead the final battle. Soul Seeker in the Collins Trinity.

**Chamuel, Son of Eae** [*sham* + *u* + *el*]. Given Nephilim name of Cara's former Trinity Guardian, now fiancé. With suspension from Guardianship he uses his human identity, Simon Young.

**Chloe** [*clow* + *e*]. Cara's faithful Whippet. An Angelorum Sentinel who can sense Demons.

**Constantina** [*con* + *stan* + *tina*]. Angelorum High Council member. Cara's mentor, and Chamuel's mother in a prior human incarnation.

**Deva Feldman** [*dee* + *va*]. Michael's former high school girlfriend and loyal employee.

**Eae** [*a* + *e*]. Angel who thwarts demons. Constantina's true angelic identity.

**Irene Hickey.** One of Cara's best friends from Georgetown University. Linguist for the State Department in Washington, DC.

**Isaac, Son of Heiglot.** Head of Tri-State Guardians, ceremonial replacement Guardian in Collins Trinity for Chamuel, Chamuel's best friend, and brother of Chamuel's deceased first love, Calliope.

**Ishmael, Son of Derdekea.** Sara's assigned Guardian. Former mate of Constantina's daughter, Hope.

**Jessamine Drake** [*jess + a + mean*]. One of Cara's best friends from Georgetown University. Owner of Serenity Spa in Marin County, California.

**Jonas.** Leads the Powers Suborder of angels, the Transporters.

**Kai Solomon** [*ka + i*; same as the word *kite*, just cut off the *t* sound]. Cara's first love in college, the Center Stone of her Trinity, and currently her personal physician.

**Luke, Son of Ismoli.** Kai's assigned Guardian.

**Melanie Solomon.** Kai's wife. Recovering from demon possession.

**Michael Swift Jr.** Messenger of the Collins Trinity. Owner of Rising Sun Dojo in Brooklyn.

**Paco.** Angel Benitez's second-in-command in the AABC; Four Hundred Class "retired" Guardian.

**Roxy Rexton.** Brett King's publicist and best friend from college at USC.

**Samuel.** Rogue Nephilim controlled by the Dark Ones.

**Sara Solomon.** Kai's four-year-old daughter.

**Sienna Sargent** [*see + n + a*]. Cara's best friend from high school. Designer for Italian designer Nicolas Alda.

**Simon Young.** See Chamuel.

**Zeke (Ezekiel), Son of Itqal.** Young Tri-State Guardian reporting to Isaac. Mentored by Isaac and Chamuel.


## Dark Ones

**Achanelech** [*ack + n + el + ik*]. Archdemon King of Fire. One of Lucifer's thirteen lieutenants. Also known by human identity Le Feu.

**Chaos & Destruction.** Emanelech's twin humanoid ice minions.

**Emanelech** [*em + n + el + ik*]. Archdemoness of Ice. Achanelech's consort.

**Escher Grant** [*s + sher*]. Human identity used by Amon, one of Lucifer's thirteen lieutenants.

**Luc Morningstar** [*luke*]. Human identity used by Lucifer, the Morning Star.

## The Angelorum (Watchers)

**Angelorum High Council: Each member represents one of the twelve Orders of Angels. Twelve is the number of completeness and wholeness.**

- First Choir: "The Invisible Ones," angels of pure energy, they embody divine light and wisdom.
    - **Sara,** representing **Supernels**: Companions to the Source and all existence.
    - **Christos**, representing **Celestials**: Maintain connection between divine thought and wisdom.
    - **Isiah**, representing **Illuminations**: Emulation of divine light and wisdom through the physical realms.
- Second Choir: Angels of pure contemplation concerned with the universe and the divinity within it.
    - **Seraphina**, representing **Seraphim**: Angels of love, light, and healing fire.
    - **Judah**, representing **Cherubim**: Guardians of light, joy, happiness. Trusted with maintaining the records and the divine science of Heaven.
    - **Angelis (High Council Leader),** representing **Thrones**: Control energies. Responsible for the Flow including all its healing powers.
- Third Choir: Angels who govern the cosmos and its interconnectedness.
    - **Ciara,** representing **Dominations**: Responsible for order and connectedness, balancing the spiritual and material worlds for mankind.
    - **Ezekiel,** presenting **Virtues**: Responsible for interconnectedness. "There are no coincidences."
    - **Virgil,** presenting **Powers**: Warrior angels, they are the sponsoring Order of the Angelorum and the fathers of the Nephilim Guardianship. They are the Guardians of order and peace. They are tasked with stopping demons from overthrowing the world.
- Fourth Choir: Angels of the world and friends of man.
    - **Hershel**, representing **Principalities**: Oversees global reform, religion, and politics.
    - **Gabriel,** presenting **Archangels**: Govern the affairs of the Messengers and their families. Order closest to man and Earth, sometimes taking human form to change the tide of human events.

They have the ability to funnel energy bi-directionally between Heaven and Earth.
- o **Constantina**, representing **Angels**: The Guardians of humankind. Their role is divine inspiration and protection.


**THE HOLY TWELVE (as revealed by the end of Book 1):**
- FIRST:         Cara Collins
- SECOND:        Chamuel, Son of Eae (Simon Young)
- THIRD:
- FOURTH:
- FIFTH:
- SIXTH:
- SEVENTH:
- EIGHTH:
- NINETH:
- TENTH:
- ELEVENTH:
- TWELFTH:

## The Dark Ones (Fallen Angels): (Fallen Angel Name / Street Name)

**Leader: Lucifer / Luc Morningstar**

- Thirteen Lieutenants loosely aligned with each of the thirteen portals to Hell:
    - North America:
        - **Achanelech / Le Feu**, Archdemon, Demon King of Fire
            - **Emanelech / Emily**, Archdemon, Demoness of Ice, Consort of Achanelech
            - Achanelech commands Semyaza's disembodied Nephilim spawn
        - **Amon / Escher Grant**, Fallen Angel with strength over 40 legions
            - Commands **Samuel**, formerly Achanelech's male Nephilim
    - Europe:
        - **Belial / Erik Janssen**, Fallen angel of deceptive beauty that is without worth
        - **Lix Tretrax / Le Vent**, Fallen angel of the wind
    - Asia:
        - **Bernael / Tariq Haj**, Fallen angel of darkness and evil
        - **Lahash / Ming Lu**, Fallen angel who interferes with divine will
        - **Pharzuph / Phar Rush**, Fallen angel of fornication and lust
    - Africa:
        - **Wormwood / Zulu**, Fallen angel who brings plagues upon the Earth
        - **Rahab / Josef al-Jazuli**, Fallen angel of pride with name meaning violence
        - **Xaphan / Sonny Fallon**, Fallen angel who fans the fires of Hell
    - Australia:
        - **Leviathon / Mick Farley**, Fallen angel of the deep seas
    - South America:
        - **Abaddon / Raoul Ladona**, Fallen angel of death
        - **Astaroth / Ezra Snipes**, Grand Duke of Hell
    - Antarctica - Unattended
        -

L.G. O'CONNOR

L.G. O'CONNOR

**TRINITY STONES**, Book One in the *Angelorum Twelve Chronicles* series is available now where all fine books are sold and on line.

*"O'Connor tackles important world building, while also kicking off the story with a bang." ~Publisher's Weekly*

On her 27th birthday, Cara Collins, a single New York investment banker with an anxiety disorder receives a stunning inheritance and is taken under the wing of angels. When Dr. Kai Solomon, Cara's longtime friend and first love, is kidnapped by dark force, Cara must choose: accept her place in a 2,000 prophecy foretold in the Trinity Stones as the First of the Holy Twelve who will lead the final battle between good and evil…or risk losing everything she holds dear.

**Genre:** Paranormal: Angels / Urban Fantasy / Paranormal Romance
**Audience:** Ages 18+ / adult language and content
**Publisher:** She Writes Press
ISBN-13: 978-1-938314-84-1 (Trade Paperback)
ISBN-13: 978-1-938314-85-8 (eBook)

L.G. O'CONNOR

www.ingramcontent.com/pod-product-compliance
Lightning Source LLC
Chambersburg PA
CBHW030648120726
47905CB00001B/112